The TOKI-GIRL and the SPARROW-BOY

BOOK 9

The Oni's Shamisen

Claire Youmans

www.tokigirlandsparrowboy.com
http://claireyoumansauthor.blogspot.com

american i
12022 22nd Ave. South
Seattle, WA 98168 USA

american.i.publishing@gmail.com

Woman, Kitten & Shamisen (1847),
Attr. Utagawa

Table of Contents

Prologue

J apan is a real place and the Meiji Era is a real time, running from 1868 to 1912. This was a wonderfully exciting time around the world as new inventions changed how people worked and how people lived. New ideas and ways of thinking changed how people viewed the world around them, their systems of government, and their relationships with each other. Nowhere was this truer than in Japan, which leapt from a crumbling feudalism to a modern first-world power in that incredibly short period of time.

In the World of Make-Believe, however, there exists a Japan that incorporates both the objective reality and Japan's colorful, adventurous folklore. It comes to life with stories that reflect the lives of normal humans and the not-so-normal folkloric beings who shared this space and time with them.

In the northern part of Kyushu at this time there lived a family that straddled the Artisan and Samurai classes, yet owned their own land without being either nobles or peasants. They worked hard, they paid taxes and they acquired, by adoption, their daughter, Azuki, who could become a Japanese Crested Ibis, or toki, and their son, Shota, who could become a sparrow. Greed and a lust for power resulted in the deaths of the parents and the flight of the children who found only war and tumult on their doorstep when they returned.

How they regain their human heritage, how they cope with their changing world while still remaining their individual and unique selves, how they make friends and help others despite the total lack of certainty in and about their lives gives rise to tales and adventures of the Meiji Era. The Toki-Girl and the Sparrow-Boy series combines history and folklore in a unique blend of magical realism and historic fantasy that allows an accurate portrait of Japanese culture and civilization with all its relentless integrity and quirks.

www.tokigirlandsparrowboy.com contains links to reviews of these enchanting books, a way for you to please leave your own and a glossary of Japanese words used—in a form that can be amended as the series progresses. It also has a list of characters, so they are easier to track through the successive books.

All the books are listed and updated there with information about what happens in each, to make the series easier to follow, plus purchase links to all major retailers. There is also information about the art that illustrates the books and more about the history of this fascinating period. It was a time when anything could happen and most likely did.

Join Azuki, Shota and their friends in all their intriguing and captivating adventures as they live their own tales of the Meiji era!

1

Azuki, the girl who became a toki, laughed as she soared in the thermal. In her form as a Japanese Crested Ibis, she rode the wind. Her powerful white wings, touched with stunning peach accents, worked to carry her far above the mountainous northern Kyushu landscape.

Laughing with her, Akira, the boy who became an eagle, matched her stroke for stroke as they circled each other, dancing in the air. They were close in size, for Steller's Sea Eagles are proud of being the largest among eagles—no matter what those Harpy Eagles might think—and the Japanese Crested Ibis isn't much smaller.

Dancing in the air wasn't limited to birds, Akira thought as the wind softened beneath his wings—only to those who could fly. The Western Dragon Prince Irtysh and the Eastern Dragon Princess Otohime, though divergent in form, had learned to dance together, and Otohime had first learned to do it with her younger and smaller half-sister, their friend, Renko.

5

But nobody did it like eagles!

"Let's dive," Akira cried to Azuki. She didn't answer, but slowed to nearly stall before tipping her long black beak downward and tucking in her wings. Akira drove the air with his own muscular wings to catch her, and they spiraled downwards, twisting closely around each other, racing towards the land.

They learned this from the dragons, who rejoiced in flight as much as the birds, and were smart enough and playful enough to take any airborne idea and expand on it. They all learned from each other.

As they approached the treetops, Azuki called, "Crossover!" and they changed their courses to hurtle past each other before starting the upward curve of their next ascent. Careful to keep exact pace with each other, they curved their angles inward so they would meet at the top of their arc. Akira thought they might cross over again and descend in lazy twining circles before landing.

Suddenly, right between them, a dragon appeared.

Akira and Azuki both dodged to avoid this obstacle, who was small for a dragon, though large compared to them. He was bronze, brown and gold, and in the classic European fashion, his hide was studded with jewels. When he was a human, he looked Japanese.

"Nice flight, you two," the dragon said.

"Susu-chan!" Azuki called. "What are you doing here? Don't pop in like that! It's dangerous!"

"I wasn't in your way!" Susu objected. Youngest of the dual-natured dragons, Susu was Renko's full brother. Otohime was his much older half-sister, child of the Eastern Dragon King Ryuujin. Irtysh was his much older half-brother, child of the Western Dragon Queen Rizantona. Susu was a child prodigy who was afraid of nothing except his fierce and royal parents, and sometimes his grown-up siblings, who could be quite fierce themselves. Renko was young like him and would usually not only let him get away with tricks but teach him new ones. She'd been a child prodigy herself.

"That's only because we're good," Akira said with a mental laugh as the two big birds circled around the hovering dragon. They all spoke in mental speech, convenient for times when their physical beings or their circumstances didn't accommodate physical, audible speech.

"You did spoil our descent, though," Azuki added. "Isn't it good manners for dragons to announce themselves to avoid interrupting others?" Susu looked abashed.

"I should have," Susu said. "I'm sorry. I forgot. I guess I did come in right in the middle. Is it convenient?" That was a popular dragon greeting.

Dragons frequently spontaneously appeared in each other's presences without announcing themselves in advance, which few of them could manage all the time.

Mental speech did not always work for any- and every-one or at different distances. Dragons vanished promptly if they were told to come back later. They enjoyed spontaneity and were sometimes impulsive. Susu, formally His Royal Highness Prince Suoh-Sugaar, certainly was.

"No, but as long as you're here," Akira said with a grin that forgave the dragon child too much and too often, "what can we do for you?"

"Not for me, but for Brother." In the Japanese fashion, Susu usually referred to his relatives by relationship rather than name. He did have other brothers–both his parents had other children–but when he said "Brother," as though it were a name, he invariably meant the one he was closest to: Prince Irtysh.

"How can we serve His Royal Highness today?" Azuki asked formally. She'd had just about enough of this childish nonsense. Susu was old enough to use proper manners!

"Did you know Brother has children?" Susu swiveled to try to follow the birds' line of sight. Birds couldn't hover like dragons could. "Come land on me!"

Azuki and Akira glanced at each other, then swooped in to circle before landing on Susu's broad back.

"I didn't," Akira said as he banked, "No."

"I never thought about it," Azuki admitted. "They don't live with him."

"They're kind of old," Susu told them. "Grown-ups. They all have their own caverns and their own mountains. All over the place. Galina's mountain is north of here, really close to Hokkaido! She's a princess, too. She's older than me, but we like to swim together. I think I'm her uncle." Susu frowned at this. That didn't make sense to him emotionally, though if he worked it out, intellectually, it did. His brother's children....

"So Prince Irtysh has children?" Akira decided to move the original conversation back on track. He positioned himself to land near where Azuki would light down. While the prince was, by rank, His Royal Highness, he preferred a lower level of formality from those among the dual-natured and humans he seemed to consider part of his social circle, if not his friends. Akira didn't know if he would ever be able to truly claim friendship with the suave and sophisticated dragon prince, though he admired him enormously.

"Five!" Susu said. "He's talking to them about those machines he's building for your refugees! He wants to know how many you'll need, so I need to get Tsuruko-san. Then she and Kichiro-san can come back with us and we can all talk about going to the Exhibition! It starts in just a few days!"

Susu was a jump ahead of everybody, as he often was, Azuki thought, though he was frequently misdirected. Tsuruko-san, the Crane-Woman, was working closely with Her Royal Highness, the Eastern Dragon Princess Otohime. Both of them joined the fully human Lady Satsuki, her very pregnant daughter, Anko-*sama*, and all the rest of them, in helping to resettle refugees displaced by the Satsuma Rebellion. Azuki didn't want to think about that. The Rebellion was coming to its end, and its end would be, inevitably, tragic.

"That's where we'll find out about the cotton spinning machine." Akira nodded. "I want to go, too."

BOOK 9 | THE ONI'S SHAMISEN

Emperor Opens Exhibition (1877), Hiroshige III

2

"I'd like to go to the capital when everyone goes to the International Industrial Exhibition," Noriko told her husband.

Yuta frowned. He was successfully establishing a place for himself in Japan's rapidly growing national educational system even as he ran the local schools. He'd retired as a Buddhist monk and turned to education when he became guardian of his niece, Azuki, and his nephew, the Sparrow-boy Shota, following the deaths of their parents.

"Who is going?" Yuta asked.

Noriko smiled. "I truly think just about everyone. You know Prince Irtysh said he needed to actually see the new cotton spinning machine so he could determine how to make them. He mentioned Susu-chan going with him, and Susu-chan won't forget that. He'll want Otohime to accompany them, too."

"She'll have to." Yuta nodded with a slight mental grimace. Otohime was truly dual-natured,

13

with a real human nature as well as her dragon one. Prince Irtysh was not but had learned to create a human simulacrum from Ryuujin, the Dragon King, who had figured out how to do it to develop a better understanding of his three dual-natured children: Otohime, Renko and Susu. Otohime's human form was Japanese, as was Susu's. Renko's was European. Of course Otohime would have to go. A European man carrying a Japanese child, even if accompanied by a European girl, would attract too much unwarranted attention.

"Yes," Noriko replied. "If Otohime wears her Western clothing, they will simply look like a family group and nobody will notice them. Some Japanese people are marrying foreigners now that it's legal. Irtysh wants her to go, of course. It's a chance for them to appear together in the human world, in public, and you know he wants to do that."

"I don't like it, though." It was all well and good for Irtysh, Dragon Prince, to court Otohime, Dragon Princess, but Yuta thought they could and should do that in their dragon forms and in dragon venues, especially since Irtysh didn't have a natural human form. Also, Yuta admitted only to himself, he wanted this, if it had to happen, done out of his own sight. He found it unnerving, especially as his dual-natured niece and nephew were growing up. "He's already proven he can successfully mix with humans."

"We can't stop it. You know that. All we can do is help them stay safe. Azuki-san and Renko-san will want to see the machine. There are art exhibits, too. Renko-san will want to see the calligraphy and"—

"I want to go!" A sparrow shot through the vent over the sliding door and landed on the tatami floor as a skinny adolescent boy with a shock of black hair that was unruly despite being neatly cut in a fashionable Western style.

"Shota-san! Don't just barge in like that," Yuta admonished.

"I'm sorry, Uncle." Shota bowed. "I apologize for the rude interruption. But I do want to go. Where?"

Noriko smiled. Shota was irrepressible.

"The Exhibition in Tokyo," she said. She looked at her husband and shook her head, giving him her sidelong smile. "I told you."

"Are you going, Uncle?" Shota plopped ungracefully down on a cushion between them. "Aunt?"

"I don't think I am," Yuta said repressively. "Somebody has to stay home and keep things going here. I can't leave the school, even if half my senior-level students are going."

"I think I might, though," Noriko said. "I was just talking to your Uncle about that."

"We should only be gone a day," Shota pointed out. "All we have to do is go see the exhibits and then we can come right back. Azuki-san, Akira-san and I can ride with Renko-san." Shota spoke with complete assurance. Renko was, for Shota, even better than a sister, because she willing accompanied him in any escapade. His real sister, Azuki, felt a responsibility to keep him out of harm's way. It would never occur to Shota that Renko might not want to go or might not want to take them all. She would always join in an adventure, or start one of her own. Akira was Shota's best friend even though the Eagle-boy was somewhat older. He understood things Renko couldn't, since she was a girl, but Renko was his best friend, too.

"What will you do there?" Shota wanted to know.

"Shota-san!" Yuta found himself criticizing his nephew yet again. It must be the boy's age. He was overstepping. He had no business questioning his aunt.

"I'm sorry, Aunt." Shota thought he was saying that a lot these days. "I mean to say, this trip is about the refugees. Prince Irtysh must see the new technology. Renko-san's got to go for that. You know how good she is with designing things. Azuki-san will want to go so she can see it and talk about maybe modifying it and Akira-san"—

"Yes, of course," Noriko said, with a placating gesture at her husband. "And my role, like your

Uncle's, is largely in the background, finding resources, keeping records, and organizing things. But you will remember I used to live in the capital.

In these late summer days of 1877 the Satsuma Rebellion wound downward to an inevitable, dispiriting conclusion. Otohime's intense desire to benefit the people of Japan, the humans she considered hers, had turned to the refugees displaced by the war. Those were real people Otohime had seen close up, people who clearly and obviously needed help and she had thought of a way to assist them.

Shota, Azuki, Renko and the Crane-Woman Tsuruko had previously pledged to work together to help others in need. Joined by Akira, Irtysh and human friends, family and allies, Otohime had developed a plan to resettle the refugees and give them a new industry. They could raise cotton and make fabric of it for the burgeoning domestic and overseas cotton markets. Cotton was a luxury fabric in Japan. Only recently had it become available to everyone with the invention of the cotton gin. Production could expand greatly and that took workers.

This new spinning machine making its debut at the First International Industrial Exhibition in Ueno, a district of the capital, Tokyo, would make producing cotton fabric easier still. So would having multiples of the mechanical loom Shota and Renko had modified for Azuki's use with a steam engine, though they didn't plan to give the ones the refugees would use engines.

Manufacturing all these machines quickly required skills they had discovered were common to all dragons, not just the dual-natured few. Dragon-power was something Prince Irtysh could and would provide.

The refugees also needed places to live, farms to work and ways to sell their wares. Their human friend Anko-*sama* and her mother, Lady Satsuki, had become involved in that. In fact, nearly the entirety of the dual-natured's circle of human friends had taken to this project with a will. Good intentioned though the Rebellion had been at its start, it had been soundly defeated, causing much sorrow and destruction.

Lady Satsuki, along with Satsuki's husband and Anko's father, Lord Eitaro, and Anko's husband, Lord Toshio, were not openly aware of the dual natures of most of the others involved. From what Noriko had heard about their long relationship with the family that had become her own when she married Maeda Yuta-*sensei*, and what she had learned from Lady Satsuki herself, though, she was convinced the Yamada family knew most of the complicated story. At least Lady Satsuki was so well bred she'd never let on unless others brought it up first, and her almost imperceptible but total control over the rest of her family was assured.

"You should go," Yuta said abruptly. "You haven't been to see your masters since you started your school."

Noriko had been able to start her own martial arts *dojo* when she received her *Menkyo Kaidan*. This certificate was awarded by her Shaolin martial arts masters in Tokyo. It established her as a *soke*, a master who could teach and award ranks on her own, not under the supervision of another master. Her particular combination of the Chinese Shaolin and the *ninjutsu* she learned during her training as a *kunoichi*—a woman *ninja* or *shinobi* of the Mochizuki School—made her sought after, and she was developing a following among serious students of martial arts.

"When will we go?" Shota wanted to know.

"You know when the Exhibition starts," Yuta said. "The sooner the better, I suppose. You'd better talk to Renko-san and your sister, so you can all find out when it's convenient for Otohime and Prince Irtysh."

"Akira-san should be around!" Shota stood. "I'll go find him!" He jumped in the air even as he changed to his sparrow form and took off through the carved vent over the door.

"Akira-san?" Yuta looked at his wife.

She laughed. "I told you they'd all go. You are right that I should visit Master Peng and Mistress

Feng since it is easy for me to do so, thanks to our friends, but I also had a letter from Sachiko-san."

3

S hota had to fly high into the air to join his sister, Azuki, and his friends, Akira and Susu, where Susu hovered with the toki and the eagle perched on his back.

"Wait for me," he called mentally. "Where are you going?"

Because he, a sparrow, was so small compared to the others, Shota had to devise ways to keep up with them physically. Mentally, he often fancied he took the lead.

"Shota-san!" Susu was happy to see his friend. His parents suspected that Shota talking to Susu while he was still in the egg, before he was even born, contributed to the dragon-child's preciosity. While Yuta-*sensei*, as the first person of any species Susu had seen when he emerged from the egg was Susu's First Friend and a very important figure in Susu's life, Shota and Susu shared a deep bond, too.

"I need to talk to you about the Exhibition," Shota explained as he circled to land on Susu's head. For someone Shota's size, nestling among the skull features described as the dragons' crowns kept him front, center and safe.

Susu was a Western dragon, like his mother and brother, with a long, distinct, neck and similarly distinct barbed tail. He had four legs, with the forelegs somewhat smaller than the hinds, and huge bat-like wings with which he pumped the air. The joints and the tips of his wings were topped with small claws that he could maneuver with great delicacy. Unlike his sinuous Asian father and sisters, who were wingless except for vestigial and largely useless features near their barely visible shoulders, Susu did not have tendrils extending from his muzzle or his head, so the tiny claws came in useful. They were all dragons, though. Prince Irtysh had described them as a single dimorphic species when talking to their mutual mother, the Western Dragon Queen Rizantona. Susu had no idea what that meant, though he was careful to remember it.

"We're going to go get Tsuruko-san," Susu replied. "Brother wants to talk to her about how many machines she's going to need. Is everybody ready?"

Suddenly, the little dragon with his three avian passengers appeared in the air over a small house set on a headland overlooking the sea. It had porches and galleries, a compact fenced yard, and a large garden and orchard following the sloped top of the promontory until it ran into woods, where a steep path led down to a small harbor situated in a broad estuary. There, fishing boats crowded the docks, and, across the river, on flatter ground beyond a cargo dock, a large building straddled the area between sea and shore. This was the community's fish canning operation, started by Tsuruko's human husband, Hamasaki Kojiro. Their family name, acquired only recently, reflected the spectacular location of their home.

Beyond the cannery, a track led into the trees to wind away towards the distant city. It used to be a trail; it had now become a real road. Upstream, beyond the bridge, a village clung to the banks of the river, houses jostling with each other as the land rose up into a woodland dotted with fields and gardens. Tsuruko and Kojiro's house was alone on its perch above the sea, exposed to winds and storms in a way most humans eschewed.

It suited them, though, both for its magnificent view and its privacy. Tsuruko was the Crane-Woman of legend. Their small son, Kichiro, Susu's age, was also dual-natured. They needed to be able to fly.

Azuki reached through her Wishing Rock to call out to Tsuruko. The Wishing Rocks were dragon-made tools that allowed communication among those in their network. Dragons who were close relatives could usually communicate mentally. That seemed to apply to others of the dual-natured who were close by, and even to some who weren't.

Some full humans could use mental speech, as could some other animals, like their horses. The rules were unclear, but were becoming clearer with use.

Dragon King Ryuujin initially had the Wishing Rocks made to keep in touch with Renko when she was small and lacked the power to reach him at distances. Renko herself had made them first for Shota and then Azuki, and the network now included all of the Maeda—Shota and Azuki's—family, as well as Tsuruko, Akira, and Renko's sister, Otohime. It also encompassed Rizantona who had found a way around the rocks, and Irtysh, who had figured out how she did it. Otohime and Irtysh, though technically not related, could communicate without rocks. Nobody was quite sure how they managed that.

This applied to far too many things in their lives, Akira thought, as he heard Azuki call out for Tsuruko. He wasn't the only one who learned something new nearly every day, though that was little comfort.

He'd lived almost all his life with his Steller's Sea Eagle family in far-off Hokkaido. He'd known few humans except those of the indigenous Ainu people his eagle parents insisted he get acquainted with once they learned of his dual nature. Then, all of a sudden, he'd not only learned of the Toki-girl but met her, met the Maeda family, met the dragons, been injured and come to live here in Kyushu with the Maeda family.

Lady Noriko had helped him heal and started him in martial arts. Yuta-*sensei* had enrolled him in school. Finally, wonderfully, he'd acquired a human family of his own in the person of Kaito Minoru-*sencho*, the sea captain who had bought Shota's boat, was teaching them the ways of the sea, and had given Akira a home, a family and a profession by formally adopting him. Sometimes things just moved too fast and the information was overwhelming, but so far, everything had mostly turned out pretty good.

"Azuki-san?" Akira heard this through his own Wishing Rock, which had been made for him by Prince Irtysh. Naturally, Irtysh had made it to coordinate impeccably with Akira's eagle feathers in a gold-flecked brown ringed with yellow and white.

"Yes, Tsuruko-san. May we call on you? We have a request from Prince Irtysh."

"Where are you?" Tsuruko sounded confused.

"We're at your house," Azuki replied.

"Is Prince Irtysh with you?"

"No. Susu-chan brought us. Akira-san, Shota-san and me." Azuki shook her head. "Tsuruko-san, it sounds like this is not convenient. We can come back later. You can call us."

"Wait." There was static and what sounded like whispering in the back ground.

"Come down here," a voice called. Renko, in her form as a blonde European girl, stood on Tsuruko's porch, waving.

"We'll land as humans," Azuki said as she took off. Shota followed. Akira looked at Susu. For all his size, Susu was, in human terms, a very small child.

"Can you land as a human?" Akira said.

"I'm not sure," Susu told him. "I can land and change. I can land as a human if I take off as a human. You know, if I go someplace like we did when you went to get adopted."

"This might work." The others had landed, Akira saw, and were staring up at the two of them. "I'll change into human," Akira said, doing so, straddling Susu's neck. "Now we can go down and you change as close to the ground as you can. If I'm right, you'll be human and I'll be holding you." If not, he thought but did not say, we're both going to get thumped.

"How about if I jump?" Susu decided that changing forms and moving from place to place instantaneously were kind of close, so he tried it.

Then, there they were, on the ground, the tall teen-ager landing awkwardly and stumbling with the weight of the little boy dangling from his arms.

"That worked," Susu said, greatly pleased with himself. "Did you all see what I did?"

Renko rolled her eyes. Her little brother was just too much sometimes.

"We saw it, Susu-chan," she said, "but settle down. This is important." She looked at the others. "Anko-*sama* is having her baby but it looks like it is 'babies'! The midwife thinks she is having twins!"

"Is that bad?" Shota was very sensitive to Renko's expressions.

"Is that two?" Susu wanted to know. His human voice was getting clearer, but was still a little garbled. He looked up at Akira. "Do dragons have twins?" Susu switched to mental speech.

"I don't know," Akira replied. "Eagles usually don't. I've never seen it. Maybe it has to do with eggs. Everybody might need their own egg, I think, but I'm not sure."

"What can we do?" Azuki asked.

"Azuki-san, please come with me. You're Anko-*sama*'s friend, and she might need one." Renko gestured at her small brother, Shota and Akira. "Stay here. We'll call you." She amended that. "You don't have to stay here, exactly, but stay where we can call you, please."

Azuki slipped her hand through Renko's arm and the girls vanished.

"Why can't we go?" Susu said.

Akira looked at Shota and nodded slightly. They were Anko's friends, too. Why couldn't they go? Couldn't they help somehow?

"You weren't there, Akira-san," Shota said. "Neither was I, and you were hardly there at all, Susu-chan, but when you were born, Otohime was upset that your father was there because men aren't allowed to be around babies being born. His Majesty had to be close by so he could accept you once you were born, but he's not supposed to actually watch. Not here in Japan, anyway. That's why none of us should be too close. Even Toshio-*sama* won't be too near."

"But *Sensei's* my First Friend," Susu objected.

"Yes." Shota grinned. "His Majesty and Otohime were fighting about it. Your mother wanted your father to stay, but Otohime said it could be bad for you. His Majesty went to get Uncle to tell Otohime it was all right. And they were all fighting over who should be there and who shouldn't be when you came out of your egg, and they didn't even see you, but Uncle did."

"I saw him," Susu said, nodding his satisfaction at the result. "And that's how *Sensei* became my First Friend!"

4

"Which one will you want to save, my lady?" the elderly midwife peered up at Lady Satsuki. Satsuki was petite, but the old woman was bent from malnutrition and arthritis, and missing several teeth. Still, she was reputed to be the best midwife in Hakata.

Satsuki suppressed a shiver. She stood by the sliding door of the birthing hut built in the garden of her daughter's huge residence. Since birth was as much of a contamination as death, in Shinto terms, it was customary to isolate the laboring mother as much as feasible. If the people could afford it, a separate structure such as this one might be constructed and then removed. What the woman was talking about would make any contamination much, much worse as far as Satsuki was concerned.

"We will save them both," Satsuki said in her most authoritative tones.

"That's bad luck, my lady." The old woman hissed through her broken teeth and made signs warding off evil. "It can only bring ill-fortune. If there are two, and they both survive the birthing, we need to send one back."

"We do not. We are not old-fashioned or superstitious. The Western people keep both babies when there are twins. So will we."

"Usually, people send back the weaker one, but if it's a boy and a girl, they send back the girl, especially in a first birth. Unless the boy's going to die anyway. Boys don't fare as well. Weaker, usually. That's why there are more of them to start."

It sounded like the woman was ignoring her, looking away from Satsuki as though her opinions didn't matter, and that was unacceptable.

Otohime glanced at Tsuruko and shook her head. Renko and Azuki would arrive any second. Neither of them needed to confront this particular harsh reality of human life just yet. They were both still so young!

Tsuruko wasn't sure even she understood. Were they talking of the human equivalent of shoving a malformed chick out of the nest? They couldn't mean killing a child that wasn't even suffering on its way to an early death! Could they?

"You don't want that daughter of yours to have to make the decision, do you, my lady?" there was a warning, wheedling note in the midwife's voice. "It's always hard to do it, but if you send one back, it can come again. Easier for you to decide it than for her."

"We will be sending neither back." Satsuki didn't care if the soul of the baby sent back could return as Anko's next child or any other time that suited it. She would do everything she could to keep both these children here and now. Satsuki had only one living child, her precious, priceless, Anko, but that was not for lack of trying and not for lack of loss. She winced as her daughter screamed and heard the soft murmurs of her daughter's maid, Hira, and her own maid, Kiyo, who were assisting.

"Of course, my lady." The old midwife bowed as much as she could. "You just leave it to me. I'll just see to everything."

She turned to enter the room.

Otohime rushed across the yard to Satsuki. "Go with her. Don't leave her. You know what she means to do."

Satsuki's face twisted in grief. She gripped Otohime's wrist with a terrible force.

"I know what to do here," Otohime reassured her. "Go to your daughter. My child died, though not at birth. If you need help, I can help your daughter, too."

Satsuki whirled, stepped through the door and turned to close it.

"What? What are they talking about?" Renko and Azuki appeared just in time to catch the last.

"Anko-*sama* is having twins, they think," Tsuruko whispered. "That horrid old midwife seem to think it's unlucky and they have to send one back."

"Oh, no," Azuki breathed.

"Poor, poor Anko-*sama*!" Renko whispered almost without sound.

"Tsuruko-san?" Otohime spoke to the Crane-Woman. "Will you please find Lord Toshio and Lord Eitaro? Tell them! They're around somewhere." Otohime glanced around vaguely as though they might suddenly appear.

"Lord Toshio's study," Tsuruko said. "No, Lord Eitaro's so they won't hear too much until they're called." She started towards the path leading to Anko's parents' house.

"Wait, wait just a minute," Azuki said. "Hanako-san told Aunt about something like this happening in the village. They didn't want me to hear, but you know how thin the walls are. Aunt told Uncle and he got angry. He said...just a second. Don't let anybody do anything!"

Otohime nodded as Renko added her own pleading gaze to Azuki's as Azuki turned away. Azuki fumbled in her *inryo* for her Wishing Rock.

"Uncle, Uncle, please, this is important!"

"Niece? What is it? I'm alone."

"Anko-*sama* is having her baby!"

"Well, that's wonderful!"

"No, it's not! Uncle, it's not! They say she's having twins and the midwife wants to kill one of them! She says it's 'sending it back'!"

"NO!" Azuki thought she could hear her Uncle's roar all the way across the island. She was so very grateful her uncle was himself again, at least as far as his relationship with her was concerned.

"That's not necessary at all–unless–is one of the babies deformed? So badly that it's suffering and cannot survive?"

"They're not even born yet. But Uncle, isn't there something else they can do? Even if twins are unlucky?"

"Twins are not inherently unlucky," Yuta snapped. "Sometimes one is deformed or very much weaker and dies. Among the very poor, it's possible that there might not be enough resources to provide for two. I know they say the baby's soul will return quickly and in better circumstances but there has always been another option."

"Lady Satsuki thinks they'll just keep them both."

"It's Lord Toshio's decision, ultimately, not Lady Satsuki's, or even Lady Anko's, but they live in a city. There are Temples that will accept waifs and foundlings. That's what the Imperial Family and the nobility have always done with children they could not let live but did not want to kill. They have even established Temples so a princess could become abbess when she came of age."

"I know they're rich, Uncle, but that's"—

"Temples take in stray animals whenever possible. No Temple will turn away a child. Especially if the child comes with a substantial donation. Tell Otohime."

Azuki spun back to face the others. "Otohime!"

"Shhh." Renko waved at her to be silent.

"This is important. Uncle says Temples take in children nobody wants. We might have to give them money, but"—

"Money's no difficulty," Renko said harshly. She could fabricate money as well as either of her parents or her older siblings!

"Please, please, come this way." Tsuruko ushered in Lord Toshio and behind him, Lord Eitaro.

"My wife?"

"Doing well, I think," Otohime said. "That is not the concern."

"Then what is?" Lord Eitaro growled. Formerly a military commander, known for his quick, incisive and forceful decisions, if not intellectual subtlety, he would not require a long explanation. Otohime wouldn't know this, but Azuki did.

"Twins," Azuki said.

"But that's good," Toshio said. "As long as my wife is all right, and the children are alive and well."

"It's considered bad luck," Tsuruko said gently. "Lady Satsuki is in there with Anko-*sama* and the maids, but the midwife is insisting on sending one back."

"No," Lord Toshio nearly wailed. "No. Not my child. Not either of them. If I am fortunate enough to have two children at once and have my wife survive the ordeal, I will keep them both."

"Until they are presented to you and you accept them, it's not your decision, Toshio-kun." Lord Eitaro, loser of many a birthing battle though not like this, knew the customs well.

"Where does my wife stand on this?" Eitaro asked Otohime.

"She wants to keep both babies," Otohime assured them both. "That is why she is not here. She is with your daughter, your wife, doing her best to make sure of that"

Suddenly there was a cry, then silence, then a baby's cry, then a slap.

"I will take this child," Lady Satsuki's diamond-hard voice pierced the thin walls of the tiny pavilion.

"I'll take care of the next one, then."

"That's the midwife," Otohime said.

"Shall I go?" Tsuruko asked.

The door slid open and Kiyo emerged, holding a wrapped bundle.

"Your Royal Highness," she said to Otohime. "It's a girl." She passed the bundle to Otohime and whirled to rush back into the hut.

"You have a daughter, Lord Toshio," Tsuruko said formally. "Do you acknowledge her?"

"Of course I acknowledge this child. Let me see her." He reached to take the baby from Otohime.

A scuffle sounded from inside the hut.

"Give me that child," Lady Satsuki commanded.

"Not ready for you yet," the midwife said. "Still all bloody"—

"And still breathing. Give it to me."

The baby cried out. Anko screamed, "Mother!" Simultaneously, there was a crash.

"Absolutely not," Tsuruko cried, and dove into the room. Kiyo dashed to help Lady Satsuki, who had been struck to the floor by the midwife, who might be old and bent but was ferociously strong.

"You will give me that baby!"

Azuki had never heard Tsuruko sound so fierce.

"I'll"—Toshio cried. Eitaro laid a restraining hand on his arm.

"We can't," Eitaro said. "We can't contaminate the hut. Not until it's officially over."

"I accept the child," Toshio shouted, gripping tightly to the baby he held.

Suddenly, Tsuruko stood at the entrance to the hut.

"Good," she said. "Here is your son." She held out a second bundle. "Your wife is not ready for you yet."

"Let me take my granddaughter," Eitaro said roughly, reaching for the older child.

Hurriedly, Tsuruko stepped aside as the midwife stumbled out, hauled and shoved all at once in the vise-like grip of Kiyo.

"How dare you strike my lady! I'll have the law on you!"

"I'll have the law on all of you!" The midwife spat at Kiyo. "This is an outrage! They'll curse the whole town! People in their position not doing what's right! Bringing bad luck on all of us!"

Toshio snarled and lunged, trying to hand the second baby off as he did so. Eitaro wrapped his son-in-law in his burly arms, his grandchildren between them.

"Not now!" he said.

Kiyo's shouting summoned a guard and between them, they dragged the midwife to the front gate and pushed her out into the street.

"You haven't paid me!" the woman screeched.

"You deserve nothing!" Kiyo said. "Hitting my mistress! Don't come back!"

"I'll get what I'm owed, you old harpy!"

Kiyo jerked her head and the guard slammed and locked the gate.

Otohime hurried up the stairs to check on Lady Satsuki and, of course, on Anko. Anko's own maid, Hira, had proved competent and resourceful. Lady Satsuki wasn't about to let her own injuries stop her from attending to her daughter. Otohime nodded, returned to the door and held up a reassuring hand.

"Can she cause trouble?" Tsuruko asked Otohime.

"Possibly," Lady Satsuki said from behind the dragon princess. Satsuki had come to join her, gathering all her strength to defend her family. Otohime turned to listen to the woman who was, in her heart, now firmly her friend. She did not know enough about these human customs.

"She has not been paid," Satsuki explained. "We did forcefully eject her."

"I'm not going to pay her," Toshio said, gripping the baby he held. "She was going to harm my child!" Toshio reached to take his daughter, too, needing to hold and protect both his children.

"We can pay her, but I am not sure that's the issue." Eitaro tilted his head and looked at his wife as he passed the bundle of baby he embraced to her father. Satsuki saw things he didn't. After all their years together, when she spoke he paid attention.

"It's public opinion," Satsuki said to him and the rest. "We are violating community norms. We're the ones who are causing trouble by going against superstition."

"Like me" Tsuruko said, remembering. "It's not that what we do is wrong of itself, it's the effects it might bring."

"We could be held responsible for every bit of misfortune to befall this community for years if that hag has her way! And the children themselves could be held to be cursed. But I would do nothing differently," Satsuki smiled at her daughter's husband, now anxiously cradling both his babies, one in each arm.

"Come see your wife, Toshio-san," she said.

"We can take the babies for a moment," Otohime told him.

"There is another way," Azuki said. Everyone looked at her. She told them what her uncle said about Temples taking in unwanted children.

"That might please everyone," Satsuki allowed, her quick mind seeing a potential solution to a difficult problem. "And still keep our grandchildren safe."

"It won't please me, however," Toshio spoke up forcefully. "I will not accommodate dated superstition just to keep some old *majo* satisfied. We will not bow to sorceresses, not at the expense of my children." He climbed the stairs and turned at the entrance to the single-room hut and spoke to everyone. "Since we're trampling on convention, why don't you all come here so we can talk."

Renko scurried over to stand beside her sister. This was all too human for her, and too far outside her experience for her comfort or understanding. Dragons were difficult enough! Imagine even thinking of killing a child! That would never occur to a dragon! Yet she knew it was necessary for her to understand humans, even if they could be evil. She was, at least in part, one of them.

Azuki rushed to Anko and knelt beside her.

"Are you all right?" she asked her friend.

"I think so," Anko told her. "It was amazing. It hurt—quite a lot. But I have my babies out of it. Two beautiful, perfect babies. Who must be hungry." She lifted a hand to Hira, and she and

Kiyo hurried to retrieve the two infants from Lord Toshio.

Toshio knelt at Anko's head, stroking his wife's damp hair as the maids prepared the babies to settle in for a feed.

"We want to keep our babies." Toshio said, not even feeling the need to consult Anko to be sure of her agreement. Anyway, it was his decision, and he had made it. He gently pressed Anko's shoulder. "We want to keep our children with us. We want to raise them. Together. It may not be traditional. It may not even be Japanese, but we want to do this. I am sure we can consult priests and have whatever rituals might be necessary performed to remove any hint of contamination or ill-fortune."

"With enough money." Eitaro was a realist. "That woman could cause trouble, though," he said. "The kind of trouble we don't need. There's too much riding on our success with the mines. That's for the future of the Empire"—

"And with the Rebellion still going on," Satsuki said, "I agree we have problems. But I cannot see how we can fully counteract any trouble that woman might make. Paying her will not be enough, not even if we overpay her and apologize. All the Shinto and Buddhist services in the world might not overcome the whispered evil of folk beliefs. I am not sure how we can stop her."

"I might have a way," Otohime said. The others looked at her. Even in her modern everyday kimono, even frazzled by the day's events, Otohime couldn't help but look like a princess. "If you will trust me, I think we can make the whole thing disappear."

Renko's eyes widened. "Sister, do you really think we can?"

"Yes." Otohime said to Renko, but then she addressed all of them. "You have a house in what was your fief, near the Maeda compound," she said with a glance at Satsuki, who nodded. "Suppose that Anko-*sama* had her babies there? Suppose we could produce witnesses, many reputable witnesses, who would set a time for their birth there earlier than the time that midwife was last seen here? You can trust your staff, can't you?" She looked at Toshio and Anko, and smiled at Renko and Azuki.

Kiyo nodded to Satsuki, whispered to Hira and then said, "Just tell us what you want from us. Nobody attacks my mistress! And in my presence!"

"Now," Otohime said, "You will have to trust me."

Anko gasped. She was exhausted and she hurt, but she was thrilled beyond belief. She smiled at Azuki, her eyes widening with wonder. If what she suspected was true....

"If you will allow Anko-*sama* and the babies to travel with me and Azuki-san, without questioning how I do it, I will make sure they are at your house on the other side of the island when they were supposed to be here and when that woman will remember the babies being born. If you, Lord Toshio, and Lord Eitaro, Lady Satsuki and your staff will follow, you will find them there quite safely when you arrive. Hanako-san, the Maeda housekeeper, can rouse your local staff. Everything will be ready on our arrival. That part won't be any problem at all."

"You would do this, Your Royal Highness?" Lord Toshio sounded like he didn't know what to believe, and Azuki hardly blamed him. "You can do this?"

"My sister," Renko informed him, "is very gifted. She can do it. And I will help."

While Toshio seemed willing to be convinced and Satsuki looked like someone had tossed her a life-life, Azuki wasn't so sure about Eitaro, and, as patriarch, his word would be final.

"Lord Eitaro," she said, "Please trust Otohime. Do you remember when you first met me? I trust her the way I trusted you. You can, too."

Eitaro looked at the young woman standing before him and remembered the shy and gawky girl who stood before him in his audience chamber, the girl—he'd almost forgotten this part—who was supposed to have another side to her, a bird side, that she would show him if she had to, but was painfully reluctant to reveal. It was that reluctance that made him decide that human was what he saw, so human she would be, and her brother, too, with no awkward questions asked.

There would be no need for questions now. She had trusted him. He would trust her.

"How would we do this?" Eitaro asked Otohime.

5

"*Deti!*" Irtysh roared. "Children!" He was not happy. His five children milled around his audience chamber, trying to build and assemble looms like the one he had produced as an example. They weren't doing nearly as well as he expected them to. It wasn't like this was *hard!*

"Look here, *Bratan*," his daughter Valeria said to her twin brother, Vassilli, showing him how she had fused a join between a wooden part and a metal one.

"I can't manage that, *Sestruka*." Vassilli tried again, but the parts refused to join.

"Let me try," Adrik, their elder brother and Irtysh's oldest child, said.

"No, me." Zhenya, Irtysh's second child and eldest daughter, shoved her way in. "I can do it better."

"*Bratya*, please," Irtysh's youngest, Galina, pleaded with their father. "It's too hard. Will you show me how to do it again?"

"You're just slow," Zhenya complained to Adrik. "Do it like this!"

"Enough!" Irtysh roared again, louder this time, and now he underlined it by shooting flames to the roof of the chamber. Vassilli fell into the Lake of Jewels—clumsy oaf—and Galina giggled.

The flames had the intended effect and Irtysh's children immediately quieted, pulled themselves together and lined up in a tidy row, except for Vassilli, who lagged behind since he had to clamber out of the Lake of Jewels before he could get in position next to his twin sister. He and Valeria weren't twins of the kind that shared an egg. That happened but was extremely rare. Irtysh had never seen it or heard of it firsthand, but supposedly it was an occasional occurrence.

Instead, Valeria and Vassilli were an even less common kind of twin. They had arrived in separate eggs produced in rapid order by their mother, Varvara. The physical cost of producing two infants nearly simultaneously had weakened Varvara immeasurably. She remained only long enough to turn the care of the two eggs and her older children, Adrik and Zhenya, over to their father before she vanished. Clutched together, the twins hatched at almost the same time.

Irtysh treasured his children, when they weren't behaving like idiots, and like all dragons was a caring and careful parent who, moreover, truly enjoyed the company of children, which not all of them did. But the loss of Varvara pained him. Had she simply gone to another place to recover and then perhaps become distracted or had she left for another time, as dragons who had tired of life in the present were supposed to do, or, somehow, managed both? Perhaps, like Otohime's human husband, she had died. He never mentioned any of this to Otohime, since he could see it hurt her to think of it. Actual dying happened so seldom among dragons that dragons collectively weren't sure what it entailed. Irtysh preferred not to consider it. At the very least, it implied a permanent absence, which neither of the other alternatives did.

Although he had gone on to have another child, his youngest daughter, Galina, with a new consort, Agniya, and was now considering his future options with Otohime, he always assumed Varvara was somewhere in the universe as he knew it, just not interested in him or their joint offspring at the moment. More's the pity, he thought. Most of the time, he was pleased with how the children had turned out, at the adult dragons they had become and how they continued to grow, and he thought Varvara would be, too.

"Now," Irtysh said to his assembled brood, "you must listen to me carefully. This is not difficult. You can learn to do it if you practice it.

You already know the fundamentals. Pay attention and watch what I do closely. That includes you, Zhenya. You don't know everything yet." He reached out to touch the model he had made using the tiny claws at the middle join on the front of his wing. "This is wood. It is an organic material. This is how you will make it. We will start here, at the beginning. Do what I do, exactly, please."

Irtysh really didn't think this was a particularly difficult task. *Atoms*, as the smallest readily available bits of existence were called modernly by the English scientist Newton and his successors, and *molecules*, as currently explained by the Italian Count Amadeo Avogadro, were based on far older theories that the children knew full well. At least, he had taught them about these things when they were primary students so they should know them perfectly still.

Earth dragons in fact used these principles all the time as they grabbed these bits and pieces of matter, assembled them in the form of minerals and planted them in the depths of the planet's crust to grow as natural attrition and, now, humans, depleted them on the surface. That was the job of Western dragons, their role in the environment.

"Every one of you can make metals and minerals. Those are inorganic," Irtysh said. "This is exactly the same thing, but we'll be going in a slightly different direction to make the organic compounds that form wood. I showed you this before. Watch!"

Batya *has only just started learning how to make organics himself,* Vassilli thought. *It isn't fair of him to expect all of us to jump right into it.* His thoughts leaked into Valeria's mind.

We don't have to discover it, though, Valeria thought back. Batya *already did that. We just have to do what he tells us.*

***

A quarter of the world away, Ryuujin and Rizantona worked on learning each other's skills. Ryuujin had become adept at making flames and enjoyed his new-found ability immensely. Rizantona could build an excellent storm and practiced pin-point tornados in the form of waterspouts when she couldn't safely do so on land. Had she been able to make tornadoes when their Renko was a toddler, she would not have needed to snatch the child from humans who wanted to abduct her and remove her to safety with her father. Instead, she would have whirled those humans up into the stratosphere where she would let them fall and gone on with her peaceful life.

Rizantona knew she was not very nice. At least, not when anybody threatened anything of hers.

They were in Ryuujin's undersea palace. It was organic; in fact, most of it was alive, made of corals and shells that were actively growing as Ryuujin carefully and artistically directed. Plants rose from the sea floor: stands of kelp waving like trees, sea grasses, algae both small and large, none of them very much like their distant land-based relatives. Ryuujin did not make the sandy floor—it would take Rizantona to do that, though he could and would learn—but he did control it through the action of the water so it lay in patterns like a carefully raked Temple sand garden, floating back into position when disturbed.

He had set up a process whereby air was transferred from the surface automatically, whether he paid attention to it or not. He had first done this for his daughters' chambers, preferring to utilize individual bubbles for himself and such of his guests and staff as required air in the public rooms. Now, though, he had so many air-breathing guests it was easier to fill his entire enormous audience chamber with air and provide water enclosures for those requiring them.

"Ryuujin?" The Dragon King of the East swiveled his massive head to regard his consort, the Dragon Queen of the West. He found Rizantona endlessly fascinating. She was intelligent, capable, fiery in a very literal sense, intolerant of fools, short-tempered, fearless, and altogether a nearly perfect dragon. The very things that kept his interest made their relationship rocky. Despite that, they had managed to make it last long enough to have two children together. Now they were getting along better than they ever had before. Ryuujin didn't wince, even internally, when Rizantona demanded his attention.

"How do you do this?" She reached out with the very end of her wing to touch the growing edge of his long coral throne, which she tucked into a slender envelope of water Ryuujin kept continually fresh.

"What do you—oh, yes." Ryuujin had to think for a minute. "It just grows," he said at last. "It wants to grow. I keep water circulating around it to bring it the nourishment it needs, and give it suggestions, little pushes, now and then, to direct it in the directions I want it to go."

"I can't do that." Rizantona's neck ridges rose and fell, a sign she was thinking. "Then again, I've never tried. I wonder if I could learn."

"Do any Eastern dragons use living plants in their decor?" Ryuujin wanted to know.

"Irtysh is the one who would try it, of course," Rizantona said. This son of hers, who paid attention to aesthetics and to details, who loved making jewels and was as creative as any artist, would not have pleased her for those reasons alone. In fact, she largely disapproved of his artistic bent. But he was also a very good prince, governing his realm judiciously and diligently. It never occurred to her that he excelled at his job, among other reasons, to make sure she wouldn't interfere with the things he really wanted to do.

"His caverns are not above the foliage line?" Of Ryuujin's children, Otohime was the only one who did not live in water, and the caves that formed her residence were far above the altitude where any plant life could survive. He wasn't sure about Rizantona's. She had nothing in hers that he recalled but what she made of precious metals and some few gemstones.

"They are not. He might already be doing this."

"Shall we announce ourselves?" Ryuujin thought dropping in on Irtysh a splendid idea. But Ryuujin and Irtysh both experimented with human simulacrums in human societies in the hopes of attaining greater understanding. Humans, they had found, did not usually just show up.

"Ffft," Rizantona hissed. "I am his mother and his Queen. Come on."

6

"Sister, how are we going to do this?" Renko whispered to Otohime. Azuki sat beside Anko, smiling at the babies and trying her best to listen to what was going on while keeping her friend focused on her new children. Renko, she knew, was talented and resourceful. Otohime had centuries of experience. Anko could trust them. They both could.

Otohime shook her head. "I'm not sure. But it looks like getting Anko-*sama* and the babies out of here is the best alternative. I can take them so they arrive, say, four hours ago."

"All right," Renko said. "I can take Azuki-san and the boys back so they arrive—oh, that won't work. They'll arrive before they left. Brother says you can't cross yourself. You just bounce. But I don't know how that applies to others. Anyway, Azuki-san talked to *Sensei* just now!"

"We'll have to do something about that! But I have an idea. Tsuruko-san?" Otohime called the Crane-Woman silently.

"Yes?" Tsuruko looked up from helping Kiyo attend to Lady Satsuki, though she spoke silently.

"Where is Kichiro-chan?"

"With someone from our village who has a child his age. Why?"

"Can you go see Lady Noriko and *Sensei* earlier this morning and help Hanako-san get the house ready for Anko-*sama*?"

"I—yes. If I go get Kichiro right now, I can take him with me. I don't think that will cause any problems, will it?"

"I don't know," Renko said, also silently. They couldn't have Kiyo, much less Satsuki-*sama*, hear them. "But at least you weren't there. I think the worst that can happen is that we bounce. But we won't come in anywhere near where I was, so I don't think that's a problem. You'll have to walk a bit."

"I don't mind that. But what about the others?"

Otohime smiled. "They were going to see Prince Irtysh. Why don't they just do that, as they planned, only without you and Kichiro-chan?"

"That would work," Renko said and Tsuruko nodded.

"Azuki-san?" Renko silently asked, "Can you stay with Anko-*sama*, only hide out of sight, so you don't run into yourself? At least until you and I can sneak out and leave?"

Azuki nodded and smiled at Anko. She had already figured that part out. All she had to do was remember where she had been between the time they planned to arrive and the time she had left, and stay out of her own way. Or so she thought, anyway. Fortunately, she had found that with the things that dragons did that made no sense, there was a certain internal logic. If you assumed things would work in sensible ways, you would most likely be right.

Otohime clapped her hands together sharply to get everyone's attention and said aloud, "This is how we will do it. Renko-san and Tsuruko-san will leave now, to get Kichiro-chan and go to the Maeda residence to get the house ready for Anko-*sama* and the babies. Hanako-san will be most helpful there."

"I'll need to drop Tsuruko-san off and return," Renko whispered silently. She couldn't say this with others listening. This time manipulation was difficult, but they had to keep it straight. So was the switching between audible and silent speech, and remembering who could use what, when.

Otohime nodded, keeping to silent mode. "Our little brother and his friends were going to visit Prince Irtysh. They wanted Tsuruko-san to come with them, because Prince Irtysh wanted some information from her, things he wanted to show her, in person. Why don't you and Azuki-san go with them?"

"I can tell you anything I think His Royal Highness might need to know," Tsuruko said. "Anyway, Azuki-san knows almost everything that I do. You can always try to speak me, but I don't know if that would work. Under the circumstances."

This, Renko thought, was getting very confusing. She hoped her sister knew what she was doing. They would all have to, literally, wing it.

"The rest of you," Otohime said, one again audibly, looking at Lady Satsuki, though Lords Eitaro and Toshio were not too far outside the hut to hear, "will please immediately get on your way by more conventional means of transport. We will be there when you arrive. I will stay with Anko-*sama*, as will Noriko-*sama* and of course Hanako-san. Now, please, will those who are not going with my sister or me please step outside and shut the doors? We will be gone in just a few minutes."

"Wife?" Toshio called anxiously.

Helped by Kiyo and Anko's maid, Hira, who was reluctant to leave her mistress but did as Anko bid, Lady Satsuki limped to the door.

"Otohime?" Satsuki said, pausing at the entrance.

"I will take care of your daughter and grandchildren as if they were my own." Otohime's tone made it both a reassurance and a pledge. "You have no need to worry."

"It's all right, Husband," Anko answered Toshio, though she squeezed Azuki's hand tightly. "These are our friends. I may not be able to tell you all the details, but I know we are safe with them. You can have every confidence in that. This way, we will be safe and we will see you soon."

Lord Eitaro reached for his own wife to assist her down the last stairs as Renko closed the doors to the birthing hut.

"Satsuki?" he said. He had always relied on her judgment when his own judgment was not, he felt, adequate, and this was one of those times.

"I trust her, Husband," Satsuki told him. "All will be well. You know that. You already agreed to this. Why?"

"Because the Toki-girl trusted me," he said softly.

"I wondered if you remembered," Satsuki said with a little smile. She turned.

"Toshio-san, will you please see to getting our horses ready? I think I will need the oxcart. Kiyo and Hira will ride with me. The house should be ready, I think. I always keep it stocked. We will need to take very little. Kiyo, Hira, will you see to that?" Smiling at her husband, her demeanor nearly restored to normal since she had something to manage, she said, "You will want to get together any documents you might be working on in that area, since there are those *seikitan* deposits you and Toshio-kun could be looking at there."

Eitaro squeezed her shoulder and nodded. That was his Satsuki! She always thought of everything.

"What's happened is this." Renko told Akira and Shota the plan after she, Tsuruko, and Kichiro joined them outside Tsuruko's house.

"So the idea is that Anko-*sama* will supposedly have the babies at their house near our village?" Akira asked. "And all of us will be able to back her up, including Lady Noriko, *Sensei* and Hanako-san?"

"That's right," Tsuruko said. "With *Sensei's* prestige and the number of people who say that's how and where it happened, the authorities will think the midwife is making it all up to get more money."

"They'd be right," Shota said. "At least, I think so. Mifune-*Kannushi* can do all the Shinto rituals that need doing, and he'll be an impeccable witness."

"We're changing the time, Sister?" Susu asked. "So it will look like Anko-*sama* had the babies there before she actually had them here?

"That's exactly right, Susu-chan," Renko said. "We will go earlier to alert Lady Noriko so she can ask Hanako-san to rouse Lord Eitaro's staff to open the house. Then, later, Otohime will arrive with Anko-*sama*, the babies, and Azuki-san. In normal time, Lord Toshio and Lord Eitaro and Lady Satsuki, plus their staff, will show up. And then we'll have the time all fixed and normal again."

"I feel like we ought to hurry," Tsuruko said. "Even though I know we're going to change the time."

Renko laughed. "I know exactly what you mean." She gave her little brother a hard look. "Akira-san, Susu-chan and I can't stay around. I was there during those hours and I can't cross myself. We're all going to go visit our brother, just like you planned to do, only without Tsuruko-san." She fixed her little brother with a gimlet gaze. "Do you understand me, Susu-chan?"

"Are you going to show me how to make time properly then?" Susu interjected hopefully. "So we get where we're supposed to be when we're supposed to be there?"

Renko sighed. She really should ask their parents before she did this. Susu wasn't supposed to try this without their permission. She herself didn't feel like she had enough experience to teach him more than the most basic techniques. But this was an emergency.

"All right, Susu-chan," she said, "but you must follow me very carefully, and do exactly what I do. Do you promise?"

"Yes, Sister," Susu replied, using his humble voice, the one he used to stay out of trouble. But he thought he truly would do just as she told him, for once. He wanted to learn to make time!

7

R izantona and Ryuujin appeared simultaneously in Irtysh's audience chamber. Huge though it was, it seemed crowded with eight adult dragons milling about one very small loom perched on the edge of the Lake of Jewels.

There was no question of them asking if their arrival was convenient. When you were Queen of the West and King of the East, your arrival was always opportune.

Irtysh saw them first and swept elegantly into a deep bow with such flourishing of wings he hoped none of his children could miss it and would promptly see the importance of emulating it.

"Your Majesties," he said, letting the volume of his luxurious baritone amplify as it resonated off the rock walls. "Welcome!"

Vassilli and Adrik exchanged glances. Though Vassilli was supposed to be the least coordinated of the children, he wasn't slow at all. He just didn't learn detail work quite as quickly as his twin sister, usually because he was analyzing it. That was also why he sometimes seemed not to be paying attention to his physical surroundings. Girls usually matured faster, Vassilli had been told, but he thought he learned better. Adrik thought himself slower than Zhenya, too. It was so held among the sibs, at least, even though they weren't twins. Adrik thought he was just more logical and needed to learn all the steps to understand any process. Zhenya tended to jump around. Commiserating as they competed with their sisters, the dragon brothers had become close. Anyway, they were both faster than any of the girls when they took to the skies. Usually.

"Your Majesty," Irtysh continued, looking at Ryuujin, "May I present my children?"

Ryuujin nodded imperially, while glancing sidelong at Rizantona. He hadn't actually thought about it, but if he had, he would have realized a sophisticated and powerful dragon like Irtysh, especially since he wasn't a youngster, would be bound to have past consorts and certain to have had children with some of them. He wasn't sure how he felt about that yet, given that Irtysh was presently involved with Ryuujin's own daughter in a relationship that seemed to be deepening.

"My grandchildren," Rizantona amplified. "Some of them." She flicked the tip of a wing. "This is Irtysh's brood."

Irtysh bowed once more to his mother, then faced the Dragon King.

"Ryuujin, King of the Eastern Dragons, I am honored to present Prince Adrik of Gorunu Alfaysk"—Adrik bowed—"Princess Zhenya of Vostochnyy Sayan; Princess Valeria of Gora Ledyanaya; Prince Vassilli of Goro Pobeda and Princess Galina of Vulkan Ichinski." The rest of them bowed in turn, doing their best to match their picky father's level of formality and courtesy. Anyway, their grandmother might take it into her head to make this a diplomatic occasion. One simply never knew, and *Batya* had taught them it was better to be more formal than less if there was any doubt at all.

"A pleasure to meet you all," Ryuujin said, smiling at each of them in turn with his fierce and different squared off muzzle, surrounded by the long sensitive tendrils he used for detailed work, like the Western dragons used their little claws. This was yet more of Rizantona's family, and, through Renko and Susu, could be considered part of Ryuujin's own. He did not want to frighten them. He wanted to like them and for them to like as well as respect him. Irtysh was perfectly capable of frightening his children when he thought it warranted, Ryuujin thought. Rizantona certainly could. She could frighten him! He'd never tell her that, of course.

"Her Majesty and I want to talk to you about organic chemistry," Ryuujin got down to business.

"But, Grandmama," Galina burst out, unable to contain herself further, "We're making wood! That's what we're doing right now! Isn't that organic chemistry?"

"Come here, child," Rizantona said, extending her wing to the young dragon. She was not a child, but she was the youngest of Irtysh's children. Galina charmed them all and was indulged by everyone. She wasn't unintelligent exactly; her mind just worked a little differently than the others'. Rizantona shot Irtysh a stern glance. As Irtysh's "baby", Galina got away with nearly as much misbehavior as her little uncle, Susu. Rizantona wanted to make it clear to Irtysh that she countenanced Galina's interruption without saying so, and pulled her granddaughter close.

Ryuujin looked at Irtysh and winked. If the Dragon King was not angry or offended, Irtysh would let Galina's impetuous rudeness slide. Irtysh and Ryuujin had found themselves allied against the irresistible force that was Rizantona on more than one occasion. They both loved her in their very different ways, and as a result had become good friends.

"You've started on those looms?" Ryuujin asked Irtysh.

"We have. I had hoped my children would learn how to combine organic and inorganic chemistry faster, but it's slow. At the moment, we are studying the making of wood."

"Can you grow it here? Grow wood, I mean."

Irtysh had never thought about this. To create wood, the organic material, was one thing. To create wood, a living thing that grew on its own, was something entirely different.

"I can make it," Irtysh allowed carefully, "in that I can assemble its components from the materials at hand. That is what I am showing my children, with more and less success." He tilted his head with its pointed muzzle and expressive skull and neck features and breathed deeply, allowing a glimpse of the fire he carried within.

"I have never tried to fabricate a living plant that grows," he said, considering. "I am not sure it's possible. As far as I am aware, we dragons cannot create something from nothing, nor can we create life, if that's what you are asking for."

Vassilli surreptitiously poked Valeria. To see their father nonplussed was a rare occurrence, even when Grandmama was on a tear. *Batya's* imperturbability was one of his finer qualities, in his children's view, especially given their grandmother's well-known temper.

"Not that," Rizantona interjected crossly.

Adrik grinned at Zhenya and winked at Vassilli. It could be fun to see Grandmama go off, as long as she didn't go off on them. He was only just starting to realize, the only one of his siblings so far to do so, exactly how much *Batya* protected them from Grandmama's wrath so they could all live in peace.

"You know better than that, Irtysh," Rizantona went on. "What Ryuujin is asking is whether you can do with wood what he can do with coral or shell—take a living thing and guide its growth."

Irtysh nodded, showing no offense. "I haven't tried. My experiments in organic chemistry are new, as Your Majesties both know." He turned to his children. "Zhenya. Go get some trees. Alive. With all their roots. Adrik, go with her. Bring them back planted in pots."

They glanced at each other, communicating where they'd meet.

"Yes, *Batya*," they said together, and bowed to their father, then more deeply to their grandmother and the King. "Your Majesties," they said.

"Clean pots," Irtysh instructed as his eldest children vanished.

"Brother!" Susu crowed as he and Shota and Akira all appeared. "Look who I brought—Papa! Mama! What are you doing here?" He practically shook Akira and Shota off as he bounced to his parents. They flew to the ground, changing on the fly.

"Papa, did you know Brother has *children*? These are Vassilli, Valeria and Galina's over here with Mama. Where are Adrik and Zhenya?" Susu looked around.

"Your Majesties." Shota and Akira, in human form, bowed deeply. Akira thought they really had to get Prince Irtysh to show them how to do it with wings. They turned and repeated the bow with slightly less depth. "Your Royal Highness," they said together.

"Who are they?" Valeria whispered to Vassilli, who shrugged.

"I think they're my nephews and nieces, like Shota-san and Azuki-san are to *Sensei*," Susu said, confusing everybody, "but, Papa, that doesn't make sense because they're so old!"

Rizantona looked like she was going to speak, but Ryuujin forestalled her with a wave of a forehead tendril and for once she let him.

"Yes, Susu-chan, I have just met your brother's children," the Dragon King said with a smile. "They are your nephews and nieces because you and your brother are both children of your mother, and they are the children of your brother. Age has nothing to do with it. It's the way we're all related to each other." He tried to indicate generations with his whiskers, but wasn't sure he was getting the point across.

"Brother," Susu asked, "Aren't Vassilli and Valeria twins? Anko-*sama* is having twins and it sounds like that's a big problem among humans, so my sisters are moving everybody around so that the old *majo*—she's supposed to be good, but she really isn't—can't hurt them and so nobody will believe her."

Irtysh rolled his eyes at his mother and the Dragon King. Susu was their child. Let them deal with this.

"If we may," Akira inserted, with, he hoped, some of Prince Irtysh's social finesse, "perhaps we can clarify things."

"We are twins, though, little uncle," Valeria said. "Why would anybody want to hurt twins?"

"Some of them think twins are bad luck, Your Royal Highness," Shota inserted. He wasn't sure what titles or levels of respect Irtysh's children were entitled to, but he thought it better to err on the side of more respect rather than less.

"Princess Valeria is fine," she said. "And you are called?"

"Maeda Shota," he said with another bow. "Call me Shota. San for a title."

"San-Shota?" her twin spoke up.

"Shota-san," Akira said. "It's the Japanese way. And you are…"

"Vassilli." The prince sketched a bow.

"Oh, I'm sorry," Susu said. "This is Prince Vassilli and that's Princess Galina. It's Prince Adrik and Princess Zhenya who are gone. And this is Kaito Akira-san. He's an eagle. Call him Akira-san. Shota-san's a sparrow."

"I would be terribly confused if I were any of them," Irtysh shot a thought at his mother and the Dragon King.

"I am, myself," Ryuujin replied, but before Rizantona could enlighten him he thought, "It's interesting to see them all sort it out."

"Tell me about the human children," Rizantona said firmly and aloud. "And tell me what Renko and—would it be Otohime?—are doing about the situation."

"Let me tell you what's going on and where we are right now," Renko said, popping in, Azuki in tow. "I think I understand it a little better than Susu-chan. If it's all right? Mother? Father? Brother?"

8

"Noriko-*sama*?" Tsuruko tapped at the door leading to the *dojo* before sliding it open. Kichiro, human now, giggled and reached for the martial arts master's colorfully embroidered black belt, which he liked.

"Tsuruko-san!" Noriko rose, setting the ends of her belt swinging, to Kichiro's delight. "Do come in. You have Kichiro-chan with you? Are you here for instruction?"

Noriko was puzzled at the Crane-Woman's appearance this morning, especially since Otohime was not with her. Tsuruko could fly, of course, but flying on her own wings took much longer than coming with a dragon, and Kichiro-chan could not yet fly on his own. Noriko reached for the toddler and took him, smiling a greeting. He grabbed at her belt, but was less inclined to eat it than he had been when younger.

Usually Noriko held a class at this time, when she would teach Tsuruko, Otohime, Renko and

Azuki the necessary skills a human woman would need to move in polite society. Those had fallen by the wayside with Otohime's refugee project. They were all involved in that.

When they had visited Lady Satsuki and Lord Eitaro, their daughter, Lady Anko, and her husband, Lord Toshio, all her students had shown the efficacy of her instruction and got on very well. Noriko smiled at the memory. Tsuruko and Noriko had not gone on that trip, but Otohime had been a sensation, her title placing her far above everybody else present except her equally placed sister and the quite fabulous Russian prince who had appeared at her invitation. Those who had been there had of course told them all about it. Noriko was sure Tsuruko, too, could hold her own in any company.

In fact, Tsuruko knew Anko-*sama* and her family from when they had visited the Yamada house in the village here, and had come to know them better since the refugee project had begun.

"Not today, thank you, Noriko-*sama*."

Noriko gestured for her guest to sit at the table in the snug corner she had made into her office and sitting area. She returned Kichiro-chan to his mother, then turned to start a fire to make some tea.

"No, Noriko-*sama*. Don't bother, please. We have a situation. It's difficult and involves some concepts you may not be familiar with. I know I'm not. Will you bear with me while I explain?"

"Of course." Noriko sank to a cushion across from Tsuruko. But where was Otohime? Otohime routinely appeared after having fetched Tsuruko and her son from their home. Usually Susu, since Otohime often watched him, came along, so the two little boys, exactly the same age, could play. Kichiro, like his mother, was both human and crane.

"I should start by saying Anko-*sama* has had her babies, and she has had twins." Tsuruko raised her hand to forestall Noriko's questions. "Both are well, and she and Toshio-*sama* wish to keep and raise them both."

Noriko nodded sharply. Of course she knew how pregnancies were prevented and terminated, and that infants who could not survive, or some who were just unwanted, were often "sent back." That formed part of her training as a *kunoichi,* but she did not approve of sending back infants who were simply unwanted or inconvenient or who were held to violate some kind of foolish superstition.

"The problem?" she asked.

"The midwife," Tsuruko said. "She wanted to send one back and was trying to do so by force over Anko-*sama* and her mother's objections. She actually dared to strike Lady Satsuki and knocked her down. We saved both babies. Lady Satsuki's maid ejected the midwife. Lord Toshio and Lord Eitaro agree with their wives' decisions and actions and Lord Toshio has accepted both children."

"But the midwife assaulted Lady Satsuki and was ejected without payment."

Tsuruko nodded.

"So she is likely to cause trouble," Noriko said.

"Yes. I am not sure what she might do, but they were saying she could accuse them of cursing the entire area by failing to follow the superstition and keeping both children, calling the children cursed, and blaming them for anything that might go wrong."

Noriko nodded. "That can happen." She looked up at Tsuruko and bit her lower lip. "They do not believe paying her off alone will be effective."

"No. I am not sure why not, but they are all certain of it."

"The midwife needs to exonerate herself," Noriko said, thinking as she spoke. "She'd believe that was the way to do it: take the money and whisper evil. But you have an idea."

"It seemed to Otohime that sometimes nobles can simply make situations disappear." Tsuruko smiled. "You have told us of some historic instances. Otohime made a plan to do that more effectively than humans could even dream of. This is where it gets complicated."

"All right." Noriko would, of course, protect her friends, who also happened to be their most influential supporters. Among humans, anyway. "What is this plan?"

Tsuruko had expected Noriko to help, of course, once she understood the problem. She did not expect so much calm equanimity. Tsuruko didn't feel at all balanced herself. These events whirled around her, taking her into places she didn't even know existed, but Anko-*sama* was her friend, and Satsuki-*sama*, too. And then there were the babies! She could never abandon babies! She clutched Kichiro to her, so tightly that he squirmed resistance. Cranes mated for life and prized their families.

Noriko smiled. "You forget what I am. I accept what is and use the tools at hand to solve the problems that present themselves. Helping our friends is like an assignment, isn't it? Otohime's plan and our abilities are tools. How shall we use them?"

"This is where it gets…different. And complicated. I am not sure how to start."

"At the beginning," Noriko said with a smile. "Or wherever seems convenient. You can fill in as things occur to you and we will organize the story together. Right now, it looks like we have Anko-*sama* with two new babies, her mother with her, their husbands with them, and the midwife ejected. You are there. Who else is there?"

Tsuruko took a deep breath and began.

When she had finished, Noriko rocked back on her heels. She pursed her lips and gave the matter some thought.

"Let's see if I have things clear." She smiled at Tsuruko and shook her head as Kichiro, who had escaped his mother's vigilance, roamed the big *dojo*. "Let him be. There's nothing he can hurt out there. Nothing that can hurt him, either." This small corner of the large *dojo* was where the often hot Chinese stove was. The area was flanked by the cabinets housing various weapons Noriko taught her students to use. Those were secured against curious small children and other unauthorized entrants.

"Right now, we need to notify Hanako-san so she can get Satsuki-*sama's* staff readying the house. We have"—Noriko glanced at her Grandmother's clock, a Western timepiece that sat on a table by the entry—"just under two hours before Otohime will arrive with Azuki-san, Anko-*sama*, and the babies."

Tsuruko nodded. "Renko-san has gone to join Shota-san, Akira-san and Susu-chan at Prince Irtysh's palace. She's already here, so she can't be seen here again."

Noriko shook her head as if to clear it. "I see why this is so confusing. Azuki-san will arrive with Anko-*sama*, but Renko-san will return to take her to join the others. You and I will join Otohime and Anko-*sama*, and we will all conspire to have the babies 'born' here."

Tsuruko smiled. "I think you understand it very well. Kichiro! No!" The toddler had managed to release one of the climbing ropes depending from the roof beams and hung on it, beaming.

"It's all right," Noriko said. "That's what it's for. We should arrange for both Mifune-*Kannushi* and Sato-*Gosonshi* to be in place just after, both to perform the necessary rituals of Shinto and Buddhism and also to provide even more independent witnesses."

"Kichiro-chan!" Tsuruko leapt to her feet and raced to where her young son dangled, giggling happily, from the climbing rope. He'd ascended so quickly that by the time she got there, he was high over her head.

Then he changed.

To both women's shocked surprise, Kichiro spread his wings and smoothly glided into his mother's arms. She clutched him tightly.

"Did you see that?"

Noriko laughed. "He flew! He really flew!"

"He's never done that before." Tsuruko's voice shook as she looked at her child. "Don't do that again without telling me!"

"You'll want to take him flying right away, I think," Noriko said. "It's time to make sure he's doing it properly."

Tsuruko brought her son back to the table and sat them down again. "He's so jealous of Susu-chan. Susu-chan's been flying on his own practically since he was born."

"Soon they'll be flying together." Noriko wrinkled her brow. "We'd better get Hanako-san, and I will alert my husband. Maybe he can think of something I've missed."

"Oh, no," Tsuruko gasped. "I forgot, and this is important! *Sensei* can't know. Not yet."

"Why not?"

"Azuki-san spoke to him, using the Wishing Rocks. She remembered something he said about Temples taking in unwanted children and wanted to ask him about it, as an alternative."

"It is." So was giving such a child to an order like her own Mochizuki School, or something more sinister than that, if not as hidden. Or at least, it used to be.

"Yes, but the Yamadas don't want that for these children. That's why we're going to all these lengths to fabricate something else. I'm not sure how to express this, but *Sensei* can't know about this until after Azuki-san has spoken with him. That's what Otohime says."

Noriko worried her lower lip with her teeth. "I suppose it has to do with time and how the dragons can use it." She huffed a breath. "He's going to have to know, though. With Anko-*sama* and the babies showing up here, and the entire rest of the family to follow, he's going to have to know."

"But not until later. How can we tell him?" Tsuruko tried to work out the exact time, added a short period to make sure, and told Noriko her conclusions. Noriko nodded.

"Let's get Hanako-san started. We can just tell her Anko-*sama* will be here soon with Otohime, that the family's following and the house must be opened. She won't ask questions."

Tsuruko nodded. "She doesn't want to know."

"Kiyo will tell her, anyway, once she gets here," Noriko smiled. "Hanako-san hears quite a lot and knows just about everything. People think that because she can't speak she's somebody safe to talk to."

"Well, she never tells," Tsuruko said with a smile as the women rose.

In short order, Hanako was apprised of the situation, or as much of it as she needed to know to be helpful, and she and Tsuruko prepared to leave for Lord Eitaro and Lady Satsuki's house to rouse Reiko-san, their housekeeper, and help her prepare for Lady Anko's arrival.

"As soon as possible, I'll ask my husband to have Mifune-*Kannushi* and Sato-*Gosonshi* standing by," Noriko said, "so the rituals can commence as soon as the babies formally arrive."

Tsuruko looked alarmed.

"I don't think I will tell him all the details myself." Noriko smiled. "I think I will ask His Majesty to do that."

9

Renko's explanation of the entire situation surrounding Anko's infants was clear and concise, made easier because all the dragons were well versed in the intricacies of working with time.

Except Susu, who stood by Azuki, Akira and Shota, muttering as he tried to grasp what had been, would be and was still going on. Shota patted the young prince's shoulder much as he would a horse.

"You'll get it if you keep practicing, Susu-chan," he consoled his friend.

"It takes time," Azuki said with a small grin at Akira, who laughed.

"It's hard for us, too, Susu-chan," Akira said. "We're older, but we can't do time tricks like you dragons can."

"Oh!" Susu cried, remembering. "Mama! Papa! Renko-chan showed me how to make time! And I did it just fine, didn't I, Sister?"

Renko grimaced. She didn't want it coming out quite like this.

"It was important, Father, Mother," she said. "You can see we needed to move quite a few people around quickly, back and forth. We didn't have a chance to ask. Susu-chan needed to help, so I showed him. I apologize for not asking your permission first, but there really wasn't an opportunity. He did do an outstanding job."

She's your daughter, Rizantona thought at Ryuujin.

And he's your son, Ryuujin thought back before rumbling, "I accept there were exigent circumstances, as does your mother. But do not do it again, Susu-chan, without getting permission from one of us, so we can arrange proper instruction for you."

"Father!" Renko protested. She was fully competent! Of course she could teach her little brother how to manipulate time! She had mostly taught herself, hadn't she?

"We know you can do it, Renko, dear," her mother said in tones so gentle they surprised everyone. "However, everyone has individual talents. Irtysh, for example, is an excellent teacher, as you all know." Her steely gaze swept the room. "And dear Galina, here"—she squeezed her granddaughter with her wing—"is very talented with crystals."

"Yes," Ryuujin said moderately. "Let us all learn from each other. In fact, Renko-chan, your mother and I have been learning each other's skills, and when Adrik and Zhenya, is it?—get back from their errand, we hope to all learn together."

Renko swallowed her anger at being reprimanded, though in quite a different way than she had expected, fascinated by the notion of her parents learning each other's skills. What could *that* be about? And could they actually do it?

"Renko-san," Azuki whispered through their Wishing Rocks. "We have to deliver Aunt's message to your father!" Suddenly, something pulled at her leg. She looked down. The little *yosei* were back! That was all she needed. They were back in their original tool-head forms, smaller than knee high, brightly colored and with variable numbers of fingers and toes. She jerked her head at Akira and directed his gaze downward. He nodded.

"Lady Noriko has a request, please, Father," Renko said, anxious to get this last thing done and fade into the background, since she clearly had to stay for now.

"Yes?" Ryuujin liked Lady Noriko. She was eminently practical, a quality he valued, and didn't scare easily, if at all. He liked that, too. Too many beings were scared of him when he wanted them not to be. Scaring them was the easy part.

"*Sensei* found out about the twins' birth while we were searching for a way to handle the situation. But that means he can't find out about what we're doing until after that happens. You do see that, don't you, Father?"

"Yes." Ryuujin knew the ways of time.

"Lady Noriko wonders if you would tell him about it."

"Me? Why?"

"Lady Noriko will be busy with Anko-*sama*, as will Otohime," Renko temporized.

"She thinks he'll take it better from you," Rizantona interjected, quickly grasping the situation. Through her friendship with Otohime, she thought she had come to understand some of the intricacies of human relationships better than Ryuujin.

"Very well." Ryuujin glanced at Irtysh, whose expression was carefully neutral. Irtysh generally saw Ryuujin and his mother separately. He rarely saw them interact. They were being amazingly temperate, for them, and he wanted to think about that, too.

"I'll go now and return forthwith," Ryuujin said.

The Dragon King vanished just at Zhenya and Adrik returned with half a dozen trees in carefully cleaned pots.

"*Batya*? Will these do?" Adrik asked, arranging them in front of his father.

"His Majesty?" Zhenya inquired, looking around when they were done.

"He'll be right back," Rizantona told her granddaughter. "He had an urgent errand. There are things you've missed. Meet Renko and Sugaar's friends and catch up."

"Yes," Akira hissed at the little *yosei* who were now pulling at him. "I see you. I know you're here. I'll be right with you, truly."

"Mother?" Irtysh regarded the plants carefully. "Will you join me in having a look at these pending His Majesty's return?"

The little *yosei* seemed to give up, at least for the moment, and released Akira's leg.

Ryuujin's human simulacrum was still extremely tall by anybody's standards, but he was more bronze-beige in skin tone than he had been formerly, the green undertones having vanished. His hair was black and mostly concealed by the tall American-style hat in a material that was a brown so deep that it, too, was almost fully black. He understood it was some kind of animal's fur and it concealed the skull features he had occasional difficulty keeping hidden. He looked like a riverboat gambler, a fashion he liked and which amused him. He wore dark brown breeches, knee-high black boots and frock coat in a buff color. The moustache extending down beyond the edges of his wide mouth felt as natural to him as his whiskers. The coat was a modern and fashionable cutaway that divided smoothly in the front to expose the bronze buckle of his black leather belt, which had a slight patina and bore a sculpted relief of a dragon. Of course.

The school appeared to be closed, he found. Its doors were locked, on both the primary and secondary sides. Ryuujin wasn't sure if it was the day of the week or whether the school was in recess due to the *O-bon* holidays. These could be celebrated any time during the seventh month, now called July, or the eighth month, now called August, he vaguely recalled, though he might have them misnumbered. This depended on the denomination doing the celebrating. He supposed the national schools tried to impose some order on this religious chaos. He wished them joy of that.

Everybody, but particularly the deceased who were supposed to be returning to their earthly homes for the ceremonies, would be extremely busy. Given the human penchant for reincarnation, which Ryuujin understood to mean appearing through time in many different forms and having many different lives, the deceased, who might not be deceased at all presently, had a lot of places to go.

He pondered this as he walked from the school to the Maeda house. He didn't have to walk, but he enjoyed exercising this form. Two legs made walking interesting. Noriko spotted him and ran to meet him.

"Your Majesty," she called, then stopped to bow. "Good day."

"Noriko-*sama*!" He nodded to her and smiled. "I am pleased to see you. I have come to visit your husband, as you asked. Is there anything more I need to know? Where is he?"

"In his study at home, I believe. Anko-*sama* is here, closeted with Otohime and the babies, supposedly in labor. Hanako-san and Reiko-san, their housekeeper, are making sure the house is ready for everyone. Tsuruko-san is helping me oversee both. We plan that the babies will be born, officially, in about an hour, which is actually the time they were born in Hakata." She shook her head at the contradictory confusion. Ryuujin smiled. It made sense to him, but then, it would.

"The staff has no questions?"

Noriko smiled at that. "Between Otohime being a princess and Hanako-san being as all a-dither as she can possibly manage as a potential foster 'grandmother' no-one has any time to question anything! I'm going to need to get back. Until Kiyo and Lady Satsuki get here, I am the figure of stern authority."

Ryuujin laughed. Because of her background, Noriko was entirely at ease among the very highly placed while still knowing and keeping to her own.

"*Sensei* needs to know the current plan, and to alert both Shinto and Buddhist authorities for whatever rituals will be needed following the official births?"

"That's correct. It is gracious of Your Majesty to assist us. I think he will comprehend the information more quickly if it comes from you, and you can also explain the nuances of time manipulation. I do not understand them at all. I am simply taking Otohime at her word and looking at the clocks."

Ryuujin nodded. "Very practical of you. If you think it appropriate, wish Lady Anko and Lord Toshio and their children good fortune from Her Majesty and me. You might just want to say, 'Otohime's father,' now that I think about it. I am already known to them in that capacity. I am sure Prince Irtysh and his family also wish them all well, and I know they know him. That will naturally include Her Majesty."

"Minamoto Tatsu-*sama*," Noriko said, nodding. "That is you, Your Majesty. Prince Irtysh they will remember. If I can do so without raising more questions than I can answer, I will."

Ryuujin nodded. "Someone's staring at us."

Noriko turned and nodded at Reiko-san, who waved a towel vigorously as soon as she saw Noriko notice her.

She gestured up the hill. "You have been visiting Kaito Minoru-*Sencho-sama*. His house is beyond the school closer to the sea. He's Akira-san's adoptive father, but I don't think you'll need to know that. He's a sea captain, retired, and the person around here most likely to have a distinguished but unannounced foreign visitor. Up the hill, past our house, which you know, the trail leads to the road over the pass. That leads to a large town. I have been giving you directions. Thank you, Your Majesty." With a final gesture, she bowed again, then turned to hurry back to Lord Eitaro's compound.

She was nicely competent, Ryuujin thought as he proceeded up the hill. He ran over her instructions in his mind so he wouldn't forget.

"Your Majesty?" he heard through his own mental communication system. "Should you meet *Sencho-sama*," Noriko said, "just tell him you are Renko-san and Susu-chan's father." Abruptly, the connection broke. Ryuujin lifted a brow. He liked eyebrows. He couldn't use his usual expressive physical features in this form, but the eyebrows served well enough. This sea captain knew his dual-natured younger children? He wanted to know more about that!

"*Sensei*?" Ryuujin threw small rocks at the door to *Sensei's* study. He knew the human custom of taking shoes off in the house and did not wish to remove his tall, fitted, boots.

"Your Majesty?" Yuta slid the door to the gallery open and spotted the tall figure fingering gravel. He gestured at the stairs that led to the front door even as he bowed. "Please come in," Yuta said.

"No, thank you. Join me out here."

"Yes, Your Majesty." Whatever His Majesty wanted, of course. It took Yuta mere seconds to race through the house, jerk open the front door and hurry down the stairs, stepping into his shoes just as the Dragon King strolled around the corner of the house.

Yuta bowed again. "How may I serve Your Majesty today?"

"At least it's not raining," the Dragon King said, looking around. Pleasant house, pleasant courtyard, and out here he could keep his boots on. He'd have to come up with trousers and shoes like Irtysh usually wore as a human so it would be easier to go inside.

Yuta nodded warily.

"You are aware that Anko-*sama* is having her babies, I think?"

"Yes, Your Majesty."

"And you have spoken to your niece about options for the children?"

"I have."

"Good." Ryuujin became brisk. "It will not be necessary to place one of the children in a Temple.

My daughter has come up with an alternative." He draped a long arm around Yuta's shoulders and led the shorter man over to a bench by the pond in the center of the courtyard, gestured him to sit and started to talk.

"So," Yuta said, when the Dragon King had finished, "You are here to tell me that Anko-*sama* is now at her family home by the village, that the babies will shortly be born here, that her family will arrive tomorrow, and that I need to arrange all the necessary ceremonies."

"Yes. I knew you would understand immediately." Ryuujin was pleased. He liked *Sensei*. He was a sensible human.

"The point of this activity is to make sure that the midwife in Hakata cannot cause trouble because many reliable witnesses will certify that the children were in fact born here at the same time she says they were born there, under her supervision."

"Absolutely. You see how simple it is?"

"But this isn't actually the case?" Yuta desperately wanted to understand. "Otohime, Renko-san and even Susu-chan have manipulated time so that Anko-*sama* and her children are in two places at once."

"That's it!" Ryuujin smiled encouragingly. "All you need to do is get the Shinto and Buddhist priests alerted so they can see the babies and perform whatever human ceremonies are required.

Then you coo appropriately over the babies and congratulate Toshio-*sama* when they all appear tomorrow. Very straightforward."

"Ah, yes, Your Majesty." Yuta was not sure he liked this at all, but didn't think objection would be profitable or even possible.

"Since you were involved with a possible solution, you have to know about the one that will be implemented."

"I do see that. But what about everybody else?"

"Oh, they're at Irtysh's. He and his children are working on the looms. Rizantona and I are there working on something else on which we want Irtysh's expertise. It doesn't matter, of course, because I can get back whenever I wish, but I think you might want to go to Lord Eitaro's house and speak with your wife."

"Yes, yes, I think I should. She is involved in this?" Irtysh had children?

"Otohime felt they needed to start with the women because human birth is a largely female activity, as you may recall." Ryuujin grimaced. "Still, we do have Susu-chan and that episode reached a successful resolution."

"That is true," Yuta admitted. "I am very happy to be Susu-chan's First Friend."

"Good." Ryuujin slapped Yuta on the shoulder. "We can make this work out, too."

Then he vanished, leaving Yuta stupefied and wanting nothing more than to talk to his sensible, practical wife.

10

"Ryuujin, join us," Rizantona said the instant the Dragon King returned to Irtysh's audience chamber. Rizantona and Irtysh focused intently on a beech tree in full leaf. Irtysh was so consumed with his study that he nearly forgot to bow.

Zhenya poked Valeria. *Batya* was surely being put through his paces today. Galina had rejoined her sisters when Rizantona went to join their father to peer at the potted trees. Renko in her dragon form stood with her nieces and nephews to watch, but Susu stayed off to the side with Azuki, Akira and Shota.

"They're all so big," Susu whispered, though to the bird-humans, he was pretty big himself.

Shota laughed softly. "How do you think they look to us?"

Akira dropped to his haunches, leaning against Susu as he did. Susu rubbed affectionately against the Eagle-boy.

"Little ones?" Akira said. "I can talk to you now. How can we help you?"

Azuki had to smile. The *yosei* appeared, lined up, sprouted arms, and hauled a stick of burned wood towards Akira as though it were a log. It looked like they'd obtained it from Irtysh's Western Room, where he had a human scale fireplace. Azuki wondered what they would write on. Prince Irtysh liked things tidy!

The ceiling was covered in soot, she noticed, so somebody had been flaming. That meant either that somebody or somebody else had some serious cleaning to do. The prince might not even notice the tiny bit of dust the *yosei* could leave, in light of all the commotion going on, but it was better not to annoy any dragon. Not even Prince Irtysh, who seemed to consider them in a different and more friendly light than Their Majesties, who never, ever, forgot to respect their own positions, even if they were Renko and Susu's parents.

The *yosei* couldn't talk, not having heads, but they were learning to write, one slow *kanji* at a time. To Azuki's relief, Akira pulled a pencil out of the *inryo* pouch attached to his *obi* and some folded paper out of the pocket formed by his sleeve. He held it out to them.

"Clever," Azuki whispered.

"Will you write down what you want to tell us?" Akira said, placing the paper and the pencil on the ground in front of him.

The *yosei* scuttled around excitedly, bowing to each other as they grabbed for the pencil until one with a mallet head snatched it and grew taller.

"Renko-hime, what is going on over there?" Zhenya touched her aunt with her mid-wing claw.

Renko nearly sputtered with laughter. "Those are some kind of little *yosei*. Hmmm. I am not sure what you call them in the local human language. They are *yokai*, like us—beings humans would call preternatural or even supernatural—but a special kind of little one. *Sensei* tells us they are everywhere in the world. He has found that all the human societies he has studied have some form of them."

"I don't know of any around here," Zhenya said, with a dubious glance at where the *yosei* were scribbling busily.

"Our friend Akira-san is from the far north of Japan, in Hokkaido," Renko explained. "He made friends with this group up there, or they decided to make friends with him. I think they are the same group, anyway. They seem able to travel wherever they like. But they are shy."

"I think they're cute," Galina said, watching the *yosei* with interest. "I live in the far eastern part of *Batya's* domain, near where my mother lives," she explained to Renko. "I'll have to see if *Mamasha's* perhaps heard of them. We are fairly close to your Japan."

"Father's Japan," Renko said with a smile. "I don't have a place of my own yet. I'm not old enough. Anyway, Father's got much more than Japan to look after. My home is in Father's palace under the sea, which is near Japan, but I live with the Maeda family—that's Azuki-san and Shota-san's family—like Akira-san does, so I can go to school and learn how to be human, because I am dual-natured like all of them. You know my sister, Otohime, of course?"

"*Batya* has spoken of her in connection with this project," Adrik said. "It's her idea to help humans in Japan, he says, because she feels responsible for them. I don't see how. But he wants us to help."

"What he's asking us to do is interesting, though," Valeria added. "It's fun to do something together. I don't think any of us have actually met your sister yet."

"I think *Batya* likes her." Vassilli gave the word a very Japanese meaning.

"Yes," Renko laughed. "I think he does. She's my sister, just like he's my brother, so I know her fairly well, even though she's so much older. She's the one who is actually in charge of Japan. Give her a chance. You'll like her, too."

"You know our mother left even before the twins were hatched," Zhenya said. "*Batya* told us she was very tired after having two eggs at one time and must have gone somewhere to rest. He says dragons do that."

"Our grandfather did that," Adrik explained. "*Batya's* father. None of us have ever met him."

"Grandmama more than makes up for his absence, though." Rizantona's grandchildren sniggered.

"*Mamasha* does her best," Galina said, pouting.

"Galina's mother," Valeria explained. "Agniya. Yes, Galina, she does. She has always been very good to all of us. We appreciate it and we hope she knows it."

"*Batya* goes to see her, usually, when he comes to see me," Galina said.

"He's always flying around to check on things," Vassilli explained to Renko. "He's in charge of a very large area."

"My father does that, too. He's all over China and India and I don't know where all," Renko said absently. Prince Irtysh had a former consort present in his domain? The mother of one of his children? And he went to see her frequently? Renko did not know what that might mean for her sister's relationship with the Western prince. But Renko had to admit that she didn't know nearly as much about draconic relationships as perhaps she should. She'd been spending all her time studying humanity!

"Renko-san," Azuki called aloud. "Would you please join us?" Smaller, if you can, she thought at her friend.

"Excuse me," Renko said to her relatives and popped across the huge chamber to land in human form.

Irtysh's children watched her switch, bemused.

"He built that room for Otohime," Zhenya said, gesturing at the entrance of the Western Room.

"I wish we could go in," Galina said.

"How does *he* get in?" Vassilli wanted to know. Valeria nodded.

Adrik looked at his siblings. "I suspect *Batya* has figured out how to look like a human when he wants to."

"*Batya* can do *that?*" Galina looked aghast. Sometimes it seemed like their father could do anything! But he always said what he could do, any of them could.

"So it seems," her eldest brother told her. "Maybe. I popped in one day when Grandmama was giving him difficulties about it, so I left before they saw me."

"*Batya's* not dual-natured," Valeria said positively.

"No," Adrik agreed. "He isn't. But our aunt Renko is, just like Susu."

"And so is Renko's sister, Otohime." Vassilli followed the logic.

"So it seems, indeed," Zhenya concluded, "but there's nothing we can do about any of it right now. We can't even ask him; they're all busy." She nodded at Their Majesties and her father, her other relatives and their bird-human friends, looked at her siblings and smiled. "Why don't we go swimming?"

When five adult dragons dove into the Lake of Jewels, everybody took notice, even though they were careful not to splash.

"I want to swim!" Susu cried.

"I think you should," Renko told him. "I don't think you even need to ask, since everybody else just jumped right in."

"Will you come?"

"Not just yet." Renko looked down at what the little *yosei* had written. "I have something else to do first."

11

"Come," the kanji written on the paper Akira had placed on the floor of Irtysh's audience chamber said. "Now."

"Will you show us where?" Akira asked. All the little *yosei*, half a dozen of them, lined up and nodded.

"But why?" Azuki wanted to know.

Renko, Azuki, Shota and Akira watched as the little ones dragged the pencil around. Now they were cooperating with each other, though the one who had grown taller seemed to be directing. This was a much more efficient system.

"Help?" Shota said, catching the meaning even before they finished writing the *kanji*. "Somebody needs help?"

The *yosei* danced around happily, their usual response when others caught their meaning.

"Do you think we can help?" Akira asked. The dance became more vigorous. Then they ran to Azuki and pulled on her kimono.

"I can help?" Azuki asked. Dancing resumed.

Renko stared at her brother's fabulous Lake of Jewels where his children—her much older nieces and nephews—and her own little brother disported themselves among the large cabochon stones. She wanted to swim with them! The stones felt so good on her dragon hide. The light from prisms in the roof flashed rainbows off the multi-colored gems. Renko wanted to join in the play.

She glanced at her parents and her elder brother, all gazing intently at the beech trees planted in pots that Zhenya and Adrik had brought back at Irtysh's direction. If they were trying to make them grow in some specific way, she wanted to get in on that, too.

But if the little ones wanted Azuki to come help someone, Renko would be the one to take her. Take them all, since Akira was the one who got on with the *yosei* best, and Shota would never agree to be left behind.

"Father?" she whispered.

"What is it?" her mother answered as both her parents and her brother turned. "Those little pests? What do they want?" Her Majesty found the *yosei* annoying.

"They want us to go somewhere. May we please be excused?"

"Yes," said Her Majesty.

"Where's Susu-chan?" said the Dragon King.

"Swimming," Prince Irtysh said, nodding to the group now playing some organized game in the Lake of Jewels. He smiled. He was pleased his children, like so many other dragons and even the few others who had tried it, enjoyed his Lake of Jewels. The design and execution of that huge work of art had taken him many human years! It would be shame if nobody outside of himself understood or liked it. He was also pleased that his children got along with Susu and Renko, his young half-siblings, so well. That would make his future plans—he did not think of them as hopes or dreams—much easier to implement. Irtysh always thought about the long term.

"All right," said the Dragon King. "Don't be long, or if you will be, let your mother or me know."

"Thank you, Mother, Father, Brother." Renko swept into a pretty bow as did Azuki, Akira and Shota.

"Gather round, everyone," Renko said, first waving farewell at her siblings before extending her human arms. "Hang on."

Shota changed form to perch in Renko's blonde hair, leaving Azuki to take one of her arms and Akira the other, all of them except Shota in their human forms.

"We're ready, little ones," Akira said. "Will you please show Renko-san where to go?"

The *yosei* grabbed the skirts of her kimono and, suddenly, they were off.

The landscape was different where they found themselves. They were at the edge of a large plain covered with verdant rice crops, just starting to yellow, ripening before harvest. Orchards spread across rising hills, with some of the apples and pears nearly ready to pick while others, green, had some time to go. The hills became woodlands at the edge of the orchards and the woodlands climbed into foothills that turned into mountains.

"Taste the air," Akira said, with a huge smile and a very deep breath. "We're up north. Maybe not as far north as Hokkaido, but the air is different here!"

"We're north in Japan, you mean," Azuki said with a smile. She also took a deep breath. "Not like north in Russia or Siberia. Yes. Smell the rice! It's warmer here than where we were, but I can feel the difference. It's more like home than Prince Irtysh's mountains, but it's not home like home!"

"Do you know where we are, Renko-san?" Shota, back in human form, asked.

The dragon-girl shrugged. "We could all fly up and take a look from the air. I just followed the *yosei*." She gestured down to where they continued to pull at her skirts. "They want us to keep following them."

"Let's go, then," Akira said. The four of them trudged off in the direction the *yosei* led, towards the woods. A small trail wound between two trees, so narrow and so well-concealed by summer-dried yellow grasses they would not have known it was there if they hadn't been shown it. It twisted and turned as the air cooled in the shade of the trees and the path steepened as it led up a hill.

"Somebody's crying," Azuki said. "Is it a child?"

The *yosei* switched their attention to Azuki's skirts and tugged.

"I'm coming! I'm coming," she said, nearly stumbling as she followed their increasing pace up the hill. Suddenly, they burst into a glade, and there, on the ground, under a tree, sat an *oni*. It snuffled as it looked up, then smiled wanly.

"Azuki-Toki! You came!" The *oni* waved at the tiny *yokai*. "The egrets told the *yosei* and me you were a human girl some of the time, but I wasn't sure, even though they showed me. The *yosei* told them they knew you, but I only remember you as a toki!"

"What you see now is the *Azuki* part of Azuki-Toki. Yes, I remember you," Azuki said, both gratified and puzzled at the summons. "But I don't remember your name."

"I don't know if I ever told you. It's Kukanko."

"That's an *oni*!" Shota said, outraged.

"Hush," Azuki admonished. "This is Kukanko-san. She is an *oni*, but she let me go after she caught me, and told me how to get to Sado-ga-shima, where I found my toki-kin. I met Renko-san on the way, so it's because of Kukanko-san, at least in part, that we're all able to be here together today!"

"Not a demon?" Akira, arms akimbo, regarded the red-skinned *oni* skeptically. It had light brown hair sticking up at all angles and the long, bright teeth characteristic of *oni*. Typically, it was clothed in straw garments that looked rather like the foul-weather clothing people wore against rainstorms in the south, or even over furs in the north, but under that he caught glimpses of what looked like leather in the form of a skirt or perhaps a long loincloth and a vest or shirt laced across the front.

"We're not demons," Kukanko said. "Not like you mean."

"You guard the gates to the underworld at Noboribetsu and everywhere else the underworld opens to this one," Akira pointed out. "I've even been to Noboribetsu!"

"That doesn't make us demons any more than you, Eagle-boy," Kukanko shot back. "You didn't see us there, did you?"

Akira wondered how she knew, or had guessed, his eagle nature.

"Where are your horns?" Renko wanted to know. *Oni* were supposed to have horns.

"Same place as yours," the *oni* retorted. "Under your hair."

Renko wondered how the *oni* knew that! Anyway, her draconic skull features weren't hidden under hair, at least as far as she knew. When she was in her human form, she didn't think she had her skull features at all! Fleetingly, she wondered where they went.

"Come on, everybody, please," Azuki cried. "Kukanko-san was good to me when she didn't have to be. Now she's called me. I want to find out what she wants of me!" Azuki sank to her knees beside the *oni* as the other three withdrew into a huddle. Akira seemed ready to pounce at need, though Renko would be a far more efficient protector, if it came to that. Azuki didn't think protection would be needed. Like Renko, she really wanted to know how Kukanko came to find out so much about all of them.

"How did you know the little ones could find me?" Azuki asked.

"The egrets, Azuki-Toki. The egrets sing songs about you," Kukanko gulped. "About all your friends, too. They sing about Something-girl and Eagle-boy and your brother, the Sparrow, and more. I listen because I like music. They dance, too."

Akira shot a look at Renko and Shota. They both nodded.

Shota said through his Wishing Rock, "True. They do."

"They go everywhere," Renko added. "They have national contests!"

"So the egrets talked to the *yosei*?" Azuki asked.

"I talked to the egrets and to the *yosei*. That was easy, because I am *yokai*, just like you and just like them. The *yosei* said they might be able to find out where you were. I-I-I didn't know," the *oni* blubbered.

"But why me?" Azuki asked. "Kukanko-san, I will help you if I can, but what is the problem and why do you think I can help?"

"You came all this way to find the toki, your relatives, and you were brave and resourceful and hardly any older than me when you did it!" Kukanko's eyes, red within her red face, gazed pleadingly up at Azuki. "So the egrets asked the toki how to find you. But the toki said you'd left with your brother a long time ago. The egrets told the *yosei* about that, but the *yosei* said they could find you because of the eagle."

"That makes no sense," Renko objected.

"Yes, it does," Azuki answered, waving for her friend to be quiet, though she wasn't quite following herself, not all the way, not yet.

"Now," Azuki continued, "I know how you found me, but I don't know why! Kukanko-san, how can I help you?"

Tears started rolling down the *oni's* streaky face. "I just wanted to borrow it," she said. "I said I liked music. Since she's blind, sometimes I could sit and listen to her play her *shamisen* without scaring her. I thought I could learn how to play it. That's why I borrowed it."

She pulled a *shamisen* out from behind the tree against which she leaned and held it up.

"But my hands are too big," she wailed. "I broke it."

Shamisen (1877),Kano

12

"It's so nice of Anko-*sama* to choose to have her baby here," Sato-*Gosonshi* said to Maeda Yuta-*Sensei* as the two men walked from the tiny Buddhist Temple to find Mifune-*Kannushi* at the larger, but still small, Shinto Shrine.

"Babies come when they will," Yuta replied, "but it will be a cause for the community to rejoice."

This new addition to the Yamada clan, Yamada being the ancestral name of Anko's family, would be seen as a benefit to the community since Anko's father had held the fief, when there were still fiefs.

Anko's husband, Toshio, formerly Morimoto, had been adopted by Anko's father on his marriage to Anko to provide continuity of her family name and give Lord Eitaro a direct-line male heir. This was a fairly common practice, popular with younger sons who would not inherit from their biological fathers, or at least, not much.

Girls customarily married "out" and joined their husbands' families if there was a male heir in their own. Boys joined their wives' families by adoption. Since heirship was male-preference primogeniture, with the oldest son scooping the lot, these complicated adaptations made sense, and provided a way for a daughter and her children to inherit her family's wealth, land and position.

"I understand the rest of the family is on their way," Yuta continued with a smile. "Anko-*sama* rushed because she was concerned the birth might happen on the journey."

"We barely had time for Lord Eitaro to get to know the area before the fiefs were abolished and we became prefectures instead of domains and all the names of everything changed."

"As did the government." The two men turned into the Shrine gates, passing under the Torii on one side, as was proper, rather than directly under its center. They made their way to the fountain and performed the ritual of cleaning their hands and rinsing their mouths, even though both men were devout Buddhists and Sato-*Gosonshi* was actually the chief priest of their local Buddhist Temple. Buddhism and Shinto usually rubbed along together with mutual consideration and respect.

Mifune-*fujo*'s withered-apple face with its pointed, well-defined, features appeared at a window of the residence next to the Shrine. Quickly, her husband, the senior Mifune-*Kannushi*, now *emeritus*, and therefore mostly retired unless he wanted not to be, appeared at the door. His personal appearance signaled his respect for his visitors.

"Come in, come in," he called, "and welcome!" He beckoned them to come to the residence. "Please join me for some tea!"

"We are delighted to see you looking so well," Sato-*Gosonshi* replied. "We have a need for a Shinto priest!"

"You?" The Shinto priest guffawed. "I will be glad to assist you, but can't you come in?"

"For a moment only, perhaps," Yuta said. "We need a Shinto priest to attend a birth, but there are some extenuating circumstances."

"I will come, of course. My son has gone to market with our *Miko* and won't be back for a while. My wife can serve as the second priest if one is needed. Who is having a baby and when?"

The younger Mifune-*Kannushi* was now the serving Chief Priest of the Shrine. The Mifune's daughter, once a Shrine Maiden or *Miko*—a female junior priest in training—had been, quite illegally, initiated as a *shaman* and left home with a travelling band of what were now rogue women Shinto *shaman* and mediums. Now the Shrine housed only the two Mifune men; Aika, the young woman who had been their maid as well as a *Miko* in training; and Mifune-*fujo*, a full *shaman* in her own right.

It was the current rule that women Shinto priests leave the service of the *kami* on marriage. Some few, mostly those married to male priests, were allowed to stay in service as priests themselves, but women initiated as *shaman* or mediums had become illegal. The senior Mifune-*Kannushi* thought that ridiculous and now referred to his wife solely by one of the formal titles for a Shinto *shaman*. This was not something he had routinely done before her status had become illegal. Yuta thought he did it just because he found the whole situation absurd.

Surely they missed their daughter, but this also showed that Yuta's wife had been right. Both of Nobuko's parents were proud of her success in becoming a *shaman*, even if it meant she was now an outlaw. Mifune-*fujo* might be an outlaw herself as a practicing *shaman* but she could still serve as a priest.

"Yamada Anko-*sama*," Sato-*Gosonshi* replied. "She is here, in her father's house, with Noriko-*sama*, Otohime and Tsuruko-san in attendance." Like many people in the neighborhood, Sato-*Gosonshi* knew Otohime as Renko-san's sister and both she and Tsuruko-san as friends of the Maeda family, but he was not aware of any of their other identities. Or at least he didn't speak of them if he was.

"Her husband and her parents are on their way," Yuta added. He didn't mention any of the staff, either in residence or soon to arrive. They were assumed. "Anko-*sama* rushed to get here, I understand, because they wanted the baby born here, and she was afraid to wait. Tsuruko-san and Otohime were with her in Hakata and traveled with her."

"Very quickly," Sato-*Gosonshi* said with some approval.

"I will go now." Mifune-*fujo* appeared at the door with a basket and her customary shawl covering her official garb. "Husband, I think I have everything here." She whipped the cloth off the top of the basket and shoved it under her husband's nose for his approval.

"If you will please bring anything I may have forgotten or that you think we might need?" The little woman bowed to the three men and recovered the basket.

"You can go by the Temple and get anything Sato-*Gosonshi-sama* might require, and I will meet you at the Yamada compound. They would not," she said, aiming a ferocious gaze at the men, "be asking for priests to perform the rituals unless the birth was imminent!"

Upright and dignified, the elderly woman stalked away.

"She's right, you know," Yuta said.

"Just let me get dressed," Mifune-*Kannushi* said. "Please come in and sit down while I prepare myself."

He looked so distressed at the idea of leaving the others standing outside that they went in and found Mifune-*fujo* had left them cool barley tea and cups in an anteroom. Yuta and Sato-*Gosonshi* sat while Mifune-*Kannushi* hurried away.

"*Fujo-sama!*" Noriko bowed as Reiko-san, the Yamada housekeeper, showed the older woman to the building they were using as a birthing hut.

This was actually a Western-style house built by Lord Eitaro's predecessor, a man fascinated by all things Western who had spent some time stranded in the West before being able to return and take up his hereditary position as the local Sheriff, a semi-accurate translation of his official title as fief-holder.

Consumed by greed, this man had killed Yuta's older brother, Hachibei, while kidnapping Azuki to keep her enslaved in her bird form so he could have exclusive access to the beautiful feathers she shed. Those feathers brought a pretty price on the open market. When Chizuyo—Hachibei's wife, Azuki and Shota's adoptive mother, and the one who had taught her husband and her daughter the weaver's craft—freed Azuki, he had killed her, too.

Yuta knew the tales that followed, how new statues of Boddhisatva Jizo had mystically appeared and one that strangely resembled Hachibei had toppled to crush the late Sheriff Genmai, and how another, looking oddly like Chizuyo, had somehow fallen into a *rotenburo*, an outdoor bath, and caused the water to heat unmercifully until Genmai's western sponsor had to be hauled out by the staff and fled as soon as he was able, terrified by his encounter with something he characterized as supernatural.

The two new statues, along with six much older and more usual looking ones, now stood by the Temple of Mary, a building constructed to look like a Western-style Temple, which the Westerners called a "church." Genmai had built it at the top of the pass along the road that tracked above the Maeda house, leading to the next and larger village. Yuta privately thought the new statues did look very much like his late brother and his wife.

The building was presently being used as a community center of sorts and also as a shelter for passers-by who didn't want to descend into the village. Nobody was quite sure what to do with a Western Temple, so this seemed as good a use as any.

"Mother hates this place," Anko said with a smile, cradling her infants. "She'll be glad of a reason to demolish it."

Birthing structures, among those who could afford to construct separate ones, were usually dismantled after the birth took place. Tsuruko smiled back, reaching down to gently touch first one tiny hand, then another. The babies seemed fine, neither significantly weaker nor stronger than the other, though the first-born, the little girl, was larger.

"It's a big house, though." Tsuruko tried to be complimentary, though she found it lacking ventilation in the persistent stifling heat of summer.

"It is big, but inconvenient. The rooms all seem to have designated uses. You can't change them as you see fit. And now, in summer, you can feel how hot it is. Come winter, it is cold. There are no central fires, so it's difficult to heat."

"The only Western building I know isn't really a building. It's just a room. It belongs to Prince Irtysh," Otohime said, smiling at the little ones, feeling only a tiny pang of jealousy at seeing a mother enjoying her healthy babies. "That's in a cavern," she went on, "so the stone helps control the temperature. You are all right, Anko-*sama*?"

"I'll tell you if I'm not, truly," Anko said. She smiled as she shifted her children. "But I am. Just look at how beautiful they are!"

Mifune-*Fujo* followed Noriko into the Western house. "It's the usual ceremonies to cleanse the mother, the child and the premises that you'll be wanting?" she asked after formal greetings were exchanged.

"Yes," Noriko told the *shaman*, "but there are two babies. I don't know what is proper in that instance."

The two women entered Anko's room. Otohime and Tsuruko rose in deference to the older woman's religious position, but Anko, naturally, did not.

"Let me see your babies, child," Mifune-*fujo* said gently, bending over Anko.

"They are beautiful," she said with a smile. "What sex?"

"One of each," Anko said proudly. "One boy and one girl. She was born first, if that makes a difference in the rites."

"Twins." Mifune-*fujo* huffed. "Some people believe that's bad luck."

"We don't," Otohime said, standing tall, her gaze piercingly regal. "That is why we are here."

"These babies—never mind. Noriko-*sama*?" The *shaman* moved away. Noriko followed.

"*Fujo-sama?*" Noriko bowed.

"These babies are several hours old," the older woman said.

"I think the official records will show they have just been born," Noriko said, raising her eyebrows and looking firm.

"And twins." Mifune-*fujo* mulled this over.

"We could not hope to hide anything from you," Noriko capitulated. "But we can hope you understand. Because they are twins, there is the potential for trouble from someone in Hakata if the time of their birth here is questioned."

The *shaman* smiled. "There is no reason for any of the men to know exactly when they arrived, is there? And I have no reason to doubt the accounts you four have given me about the time and place of their birth."

"None whatsoever." Noriko smiled in relief. As she had hoped and trusted, they were in perfect agreement.

13

"Look," Irtysh said, poking mentally at the cells of the beech tree's leader tip at the end of a branch, the place where new growth emanated. "I think I can encourage it, right here." He agitated the cells.

"Ryuujin?" Rizantona asked. "When you get your coral to grow, is that what you do?"

"Not quite." The three enormous dragons crowded around the half dozen potted trees Irtysh's two eldest children had fetched for experimental purposes.

"The coral is animal. So are the shells," the Dragon King explained. "Both are very basic. There's a just the smallest bit of difference along in here." He sent a mental tendril flowing along a line he could not describe, but hoped the others could sense.

"Are you saying the coral and shell have more natural volition?" Rizantona inquired. Though she didn't entirely approve of Irtysh's artistic bent, finding his fascination with gems frivolous, she recognized her son's abilities. In one way, he was surprisingly humble about it. Irtysh thought that if he could do something, anybody could. Of course, that often had the opposite effect, given the extent of his talent, power and influence, and made him appear overweeningly arrogant.

Rizantona's own talents lay along the lines of organization, governance and executive ability. Somebody had to do those things. She was Queen and that made it her job. She was good at running an empire but she didn't think that took any special skill or talent, just dedication and hard work. Ryuujin, in her opinion, took those administrative necessities too much for granted. She found it amazing that his empire functioned as smoothly as it did. But, here, now, as always, it was left to her to ask the questions that pushed the others along in the exercise of their talents.

"That could mean plants are easier to direct," Irtysh said, giving the growing tip of the branch the tiniest molecular shove.

"I'm not sure if I could get something with any real intelligence to do anything," Ryuujin admitted, conveniently forgetting his ability to covertly "suggest" things to humans in such a way they thought the ideas their own. This was something quite different. "The shell and coral are animal, yes, but not intelligent, exactly. They're more centrally organized, and that makes them fixed in their ways. Inflexible."

"Watch." Rizantona couldn't keep her mental gaze off it. The cells at the tip of the branch's leader began to turn as they divided. "Are you directing them that way, Irtysh?"

"Yes." Irtysh's concentration showed in the sharp edge to his normally lush voice.

"I see it," Ryuujin said. "Do you have to keep your mind on it to keep it going?"

"I don't know"—

"*Batya!*"

His children's frantic call broke Irtysh's concentration. Infuriated by the interruption right when he felt he was on the edge of a breakthrough, his icy control shattered.

"What?" He whirled, whipping his tail around with such force that his mother had to step back to avoid getting slashed with the barb. She saw no threat but nothing except a threat to his children, as far as she knew, could make Irtysh break his usual polished discipline. She certainly couldn't do it, and she had tried.

"I've got this, Irtysh," Ryuujin said calmly. "I can hold it until you come back." He thought. He hoped. He had never seen the suave and diplomatic Irtysh angry. In anger, he very much resembled his mother.

Irtysh nodded. Their Majesties could see him regain his composure as he saw his children were in no immediate danger. He brought his tail under control, and wrapped it tightly around his feet.

"*Batya*, we're sorry!" Galina implored. "Please don't be angry. It's just"—

"Vassilli's done something truly remarkable, *Batya!*" Valeria interrupted as she waved a wing at her twin.

"It's nothing, really, *Batya*," Vassilli said. "I just did what you said, but more, somehow."

"He made this all at once." Adrik thought to clarify, stretching out a wing claw to touch a loom that was the twin of the one already resting on the cavern floor. "That's not nothing!"

"It just *happened*," Zhenya said. "*Bratan*, brother, you must tell *Batya* how you did it!"

"Tell us all," Irtysh said. "Ryuujin"— he stopped as he remembered his manners. He and the Dragon King were usually informally friendly when alone, at His Majesty's suggestion, but they were not alone and it wouldn't do to set a poor example for his children. His mother wouldn't like it. "Your Majesty, I think if you would prefer not to hold the plant right now, I can pick up where I left off once Vassilli has shown us how he did this. I suspect we will all want to see that. Vassilli, tell us what we are looking at."

Irtysh reached out with a terminal wing claw to stroke the loom. It seemed perfectly normal, exactly like the one he himself had fabricated, except right along there, where the wood and metal met—

"It's a loom, *Batya*." Vassilli scuffled his clawed feet on the floor and his tail swung to bump into his sister's. Zhenya hissed. "Pay attention," she thought crossly.

"You were having us try to join the wood and metal like you did on this other one you made," Vassilli went on, with a glare at Zhenya. "I was trying that, but it seemed more complicated than it needed to be. So I just kind of—well, I'm not sure what I did, exactly, but it came out all at once!"

"It feels like you made the wood and metal at the same time. Is that right?" Irtysh asked his younger son.

"Yes, I wanted to try to do that," Vassilli replied. "It was easier."

"Rather than make them discretely and join them the way humans do, you mingled the materials while you made them!" This was fascinating. Irtysh had simply never thought of trying that, but it seemed to work. Vassilli nodded. He couldn't tell if *Batya* was peeved or pleased at his accomplishment.

"Give me a minute," Irtysh said, and focused on a vortex he built. It was actually a little easier to meld the materials in their making, Irtysh found, than to make them separately the way the humans did and join them with bands and fasteners made of yet other materials. But what Vassilli had done here—probably because he had no idea how difficult and complex it became—was to continue to produce not just one piece of the loom but every piece all in one single unit. A third loom popped into place beside the other two as the vortex dissipated.

"You did it, *Batya*," Galina cried, with a little plume of congratulatory smoke.

Irtysh smiled at his youngest child. "And so will you. All of you. Vassilli, make another one. Do it slowly so you can show your siblings how you did it. All of you watch carefully. I want one from each of you." He turned to his second son. "This is very nice work, Vassilli." Vassilli dropped his head, embarrassed at the exceptionally lavish praise. His father took outstanding ability for granted. For Irtysh, this was downright fulsome.

Irtysh regarded all his children sternly. "Vassilli developed this advancement and is to be congratulated. It will make our work much easier, both with this project and with others we may undertake in the future. We have now discovered that I can do it just as he can. What that means is that you can all do it, too. Get to work!"

What Irtysh did not point out was something yet to be addressed. Assuming they could all do it, and he saw no reason why they couldn't, they'd produce as many looms as they needed in short order. But once the looms were in human hands, being used as they were intended to be used, they would, over time, inevitably break.

Could humans fix them? Or would they find these machines could only be fixed by dragons?

14

"His Majesty said that Azuki-san, Shota-san, Renko-san, Akira-san and Susu-chan have *all* gone to bother Prince Irtysh?" Noriko said to her husband as they walked companionably up the hill from the Yamada compound by the village towards their own home.

"I doubt if it's a bother," Yuta said judiciously, giving the prince his due. "He seems to like them all but I'm sure he could send them away easily if they weren't wanted."

"He is smooth, isn't he?"

"Very." Yuta kicked a fallen stone off the path. "Renko-san and Susu-chan are his siblings, anyway."

Anko's babies were now officially born and all the rites Shinto and Buddhism required pertaining to their arrival had been dutifully performed. Otohime had surprised Yuta by slipping him small bags of coins for the men. She gave the *Fujo-sama* a larger one for herself, since she was the one who knew the truth.

This gift would not be construed as a bribe or payment for silence. It was a mere expression of appreciation for the older woman's help in a tricky situation, nothing anyone could take exception to. It would be recorded as an offering to the Shrine.

Otohime's coins currently mimicked the most recent and now uniform Japanese coins perfectly, Yuta noted, only they were as sparkling new as if they had come fresh from the mint.

"They can come back any time now," Noriko said. "Or, in Susu-chan's case, go wherever he is supposed to be. Do you think we should let them know?"

Yuta shook his head. "Not yet. They are responsible young people. They will appear before we start to worry about them."

Noriko smiled. "Or we'll hear from them. Renko-san might communicate with her sister. There is something I would like to talk to you about. May I make you some tea?"

"In my study," Yuta said with a nod.

Noriko replenished the ewer, filled the kettle and fetched some *senbei* along with some of Hanako's special cookies from the kitchen before the kettle boiled. Her husband bent over a letter from his colleague, Professor Kawabata, while she made these arrangements. She had filled the pot and wet the tea before she realized she need to run up to her *dojo*. With a quick bow, she hurried to her own little nook to fetch Sachiko's letter.

They had first met in the Shogun's *O-oku*, where Noriko was a lady-chaperone and a very special kind of guard. Sachiko was a wardrobe mistress. She itched to get the self-contained security guard who studied martial arts with the Shogun's officers some nicer clothes. At least the *gi* she wore when she practiced or taught the ladies the fundamentals of self-defense was new. As it should be, Sachiko had thought, for even then Noriko's belt was black and embroidered with an impressive number of colored *dan* lines. Now there were many more of those.

When one of Noriko's charges had been attacked while on her way home from a moon-viewing party outside the confines of the *O-oku*, Noriko had been stabbed and slashed dangerously in the lower abdomen while neatly dispatching two of the attackers and summoning soldiers to take care of the rest. The young concubine she escorted was not injured, but seemed as frightened of Noriko's defense as of the attack itself.

Noriko's injuries were not neglected, of course. She had the best medical care that was available. But men other than the Shogun were not allowed in the *O-oku* and the female physicians who attended the women were much more familiar with pregnancy and childbirth than combat trauma.

Sachiko had a certain amount of freedom because of her position, and of course she was a worker as well as a resident. She met with textile artists, tailors and merchants in the area where men like them, with business in the *O-oku*, and artists, music instructors, dance teachers, jewelers, wigmakers and male relatives were allowed. This allowed her to speak to the male soldiers who guarded the *O-oku's* perimeter.

There were other women guards inside the *O-oku*, of course, and also staffing the entrances and gardens. Those women didn't train with the men the way Noriko did. In fact, it was Noriko who taught them. But that meant the men knew Noriko, so Sachiko was able, through them, to meet with doctors who knew about trauma and how to tend injuries sustained in combat. One guard even managed to bring her packets of Chinese medicine from their Chinese martial arts master, Master Peng. The men liked Noriko; they admired her skills and her heroism. They did not want her to die if it could be helped.

While Noriko's injury was bad, it was not like the abdominal injuries resulting from *seppuku*, which were not meant to be survived. She had been very lucky, everybody concluded. While her abdomen would be hideously scarred, and it became clear she would never have children, her intestines were not ruptured and she did not develop that kind of infection, from which there would be no coming back.

Mistress Feng, Master Peng's mother and a formidable martial arts master in her own right, came to call, tottering on her tiny Chinese bound feet, drawing astonished glances. As a woman, she could be admitted to visit Noriko personally. She stroked Noriko's forehead and palpated her abdomen. She left Sachiko with a large basket of medicines and specific instructions about how to help Noriko recover fully.

Eventually, Noriko was able to go to the *dojo* regularly to train. It was as Noriko recovered that she and Sachiko became friends. Sachiko guessed what Noriko must be, but respected her need to keep it secret.

When the Shogunate fell, Noriko accompanied the Shogun's women and children when they fled Edo. When she returned to the capital at the end of the Boshin war, having been dismissed from her post, Noriko was left with very little. She wrote her school as soon as she had a place to receive mail, as she had been instructed, but got no response. She needed to survive. Her savings were going too fast. She needed a job.

When she found her friend, Sachiko had just started immersing herself in women's causes. Far too many women had simply been tossed aside and abandoned during the Restoration and the war surrounding it. This happened to men, too, but men had more options within Japanese society.

Sachiko, when she found herself unemployed and out on the street, used her own savings to buy a house and started working as a dresser for *geisha* and their *hangoku* apprentices. She had hopes of starting an *ochaya*. That was the kind of tea house that served as an entertainment venue featuring *geisha*, a place for confidential meetings, and somewhere *geisha* might study and dress. Sometimes they even lived there.

Sachiko rightly concluded that women who operated on the borders of polite society would find it easier to survive social upheaval with their lives mostly intact. Easier, certainly, than either the women constrained by high social position or the women who fell completely below polite society's notice. It was women like the *geisha* entertainers, she thought, who could best use—and afford—her skills.

The friends had literally run into each other, as Sachiko made her way home from dressing one of her ladies for a late appointment and Noriko returned to the *dojo*. This night she had dressed as a man to take the place of a fellow senior student who had fallen ill and was unable to escort an *oiron* courtesan on a formal parade to a tea house where she had an assignation. The women recognized each other despite Noriko's disguise, and happily repaired to an *izakaya* tavern. A kind of partnership was born.

The first person they rescued was a *kamuro* assistant to an *oiron*, a child sold into prostitution. Though she was fortunate indeed to have a chance to become a top-level courtesan, neither of the women wanted her forced into that life, and the child did not want to stay. Noriko snatched her, Sachiko provided her with a place to stay and found her a role in domestic service.

The *dojo* could not provide Noriko with an actual job, only a place to sleep until she found real work. Sachiko could provide no more. Soon, though, Noriko found work as a night maid at the Inn of the Golden Phoenix, where she got room, board and a tiny salary. She advanced at the Inn. She continued teaching at the *dojo* to earn her own instruction, and she stayed in touch with Sachiko, helping in what became Sachiko's passionate avocation: the rescue of girls and women from the streets or indentured servitude in the pleasure quarters and the new industries that seemed determined to grind them into dust in the name of progress.

Indentured mill workers at a giant silk mill behind the Inn of the Golden Phoenix engineered a daring escape attempt while Sachiko and Noriko were still planning how to rescue them. Yuta, a guest staying at the Inn for the First Educational Conference, discovered the attempt before Noriko. During the brawl that ensued she discovered Yuta's secrets and he discovered hers. That formed the basis of their marriage—stronger than the basis of many others. After all, according to the dictates of her school, she should have killed him when he let her know he had discovered what she was.

More recently, they had learned that some of the girls they had rescued had been taken up by a troupe of puppeteers who were really human traffickers sending the girls overseas for jobs that would not be as represented, but, again, what amounted to slavery in brothels instead. They sent those girls back to Sachiko again, except for one. Junko had been accepted, on Noriko's recommendation, to the secret Mochizuki School where she, too, in time, might become a *kunoichi*, a woman *shinobi* or *ninja*.

"I have a letter from Sachiko-san," Noriko said breathlessly, as she sank to a cushion opposite her husband and poured him tea from the steaming pot.

Yuta looked up, interested. Absently, he picked up a *macha* flavored cookie and nibbled.

"How is she?" he asked. "How are our girls?"

This was one reason Noriko had come to love him. Neither of them had any obligation to these mill girls, but he would always feel that he did. She smiled.

"Sachiko-san is well. She has not heard from Junko-san since her first letter. That tells me all is well there. The girls we sent back to Sachiko-san were special cases, as you might recall."

"Except our brave Junko-san," Yuta smiled. He had a special fondness for the buck-toothed hunter-girl's courage and hoped she would do well.

"A mountain girl who grew up killing animals is always going to be a special case."

It took a special dispensation and amulet from a Shrine to hunt animals for medicine and occasionally meat, but there were groups of mountain dwellers who made it their livelihood. It was from one of these groups that Junko came.

"Well, she's all right, at least," Yuta said, quaffing his tea. He set down the cup and Noriko poured a refill. "What about the others? Little Hisa-san?"

"Hisa-san and Kotoe-san both are doing very well." Hisa was slow and Kotoe was crippled. "Sachiko-san placed them in a print-making workshop. They work together, Sachiko-san says. Hisa-san fetches and carries what Kotoe-san tells her, and rubs simple print layers out. Kotoe-san sets up the blocks, paper and inks. She is even doing some carving! They complement each other and are quite efficient. Sachiko-san is very proud of them."

"The others shouldn't be a problem." Yuta bit a *senbei* and sipped his tea.

"Rio-san and Takeko-san went north to become *tondenhei*." *Samurai* displaced by the replacement of domain armies with a national one not based on class alone needed jobs and missions.

Far-off Hokkaido needed *wa-jin* settlers to keep creeping foreigners at bay and assimilate the native Ainu people. They weren't exactly interested in assimilating, but didn't seem to have an option.

The unemployed *samurai* became *tondenhei* soldier-farmers, provided with small farms, uniforms, weapons and assigned to military groups. They trained together to form cohesive units and they were in place when and if they were needed. The soldier part was easily seen to. The farmer part was less simple: farms needed families to succeed and families needed men and women both to make a life together and raise children to follow them.

Neither the men nor the women knew what they were getting into, or with whom, but the formality of Japan's marriage system and social structure meant that it would work out for most of them. They didn't expect romance. They expected respect and cooperation, hard work, and plans extending down the generations. Liking and perhaps even love, if they were lucky, might follow.

"Those two were talking about being patriots," Yuta recalled. "This ought to suit them quite well. That leaves two more."

"Those two are the problem. Miyuki-san is the girl with all the smallpox scars. She refused to go north. She feels she is so ugly that no man could possibly want her except the dregs, who would probably abuse her, yet she does not want to be a nun. Yae-san looks perfectly ordinary, but she's the one Junko-san called a troublemaker. Sachiko-san has no fault to find with her behavior, but she is unwilling to undertake any opportunities Sachiko-san can put in her way."

"This is why you want to go to Tokyo, then," Yuta said. "To see what you can do for these girls."

"Yes. The *tondenhei* scheme is working very well for many of the girls Sachiko-san helps. I am not sure why it won't work for these two. Looks are not nearly as important as character."

Yuta smiled at his wife. "A face doesn't have to be beautiful to be pleasing."

Noriko blushed. She knew herself to be no beauty, not like Otohime or Tsuruko, but at least she was fit and healthy.

"I'd better see about getting dinner for everyone," she said. It did not occur to either of them to question that this was ultimately her responsibility as lady of the house. "I suppose I should ask Otohime what the situation with all our young people might be." She stood and placed their used cups and the snack plates on a trytray.

"You have good fortune," Yuta said, gesturing at the open sliding door. "Or I do." He smiled. Cooking was not one of Noriko's skills, though she could make a basic, simple meal.

Noriko's gaze followed his hand and she saw Hanako-san coming up the hill, accompanied by

Minoru-*sencho* bearing a large basket that no doubt held a fish meant for their meal.

"This is good fortune for both of us," Noriko said with a smile. With a quick bow, she picked up the tray. She'd take that to kitchen and see if Hanako knew how many they might expect for dinner.

15

"But who are you *oni*, anyway?" Renko wanted to know. "You say you aren't demons, but Akira-san says you guard the gates of the underworld. We chase you out by throwing roasted beans at *Setsubon* while we say '*oni* out.' People talk about that like we're repelling demons, and the word '*oni*' is used, but you're telling us that's not it?"

"We aren't demons!" Kukanko cried. "We aren't evil!"

"We say 'fortune in,' too," Azuki said. "Should we be saying 'evil out,' or 'bad luck out' rather than '*oni*'?"

"But where did you come from?" Shota wanted to know. He knew about the *oni* who had kidnapped his sister then released her on being told she wasn't allowed to eat Azuki or keep her captive. Kukanko had freed her nd sent her off with reasonably accurate directions to Sado-ga-shima, the main toki nesting grounds she sought.

"We've always thought *oni* were *yokai*," Akira said.

"You eagles?" Azuki said, interested.

"You really are an eagle? Akira-Eagle, like Azuki-Toki?" Kukanko was curious. She had called him "eagle," but wasn't quite sure how she knew that. It was like she could sometimes, but not always, see overlaying veils of identity and meaning.

"Yes," Shota said. "I'm Shota-Sparrow and Renko-san is Renko-Dragon. So we're all *yokai*. Just like you."

"But all of us can look like humans," Akira pointed out. "I was talking about the Ainu humans from Hokkaido, where I'm from. They're not Japanese. They aren't eagles, either."

"They are Japanese now," Renko pointed out. "Everybody's supposed to be Japanese and only Japanese, no matter how we started out."

"There were humans right here before the *wa-jin* Japanese people came, and some of them think we *oni* started out as foreign humans who couldn't get home. Regular humans were scared of us because we looked funny and couldn't talk to them in their language," Kukanko said. "The *wa-jin* are the humans that look like all of you except Renko-Dragon."

Kukanko suddenly realized what she had just said and scrabbled backwards. "You really turn into a dragon?" She stared at Renko.

Renko laughed. "I do, but you start out as a *oni* and that's scary to us. Try to take me as you see me here, the way I'm trying to take you."

Shota glanced at Azuki who nodded slightly. Renko-san had come a long way in accepting herself as well as in accepting others.

"Azuki-Toki?" Kukanko nearly shook with fear, though Renko simply looked like a European girl. Kukanko looked like a monster.

"She's our friend," Azuki said. "When you sent me off to Sado-ga-shima, it took longer than I thought it would. I was over the ocean when I got hit by a storm. Renko-san rescued me. We've been friends ever since! She looked a like a dragon and I looked like a toki, but we could be friends anyway."

"When I met Renko-san," Shota said, "she looked like this, like a girl, and I looked like I do now. Only younger."

"Renko-san and I met in our human forms," Akira added. "But I got hurt and she rescued me when I was an eagle and she was a dragon."

"Only after you helped rescue me!" Renko said.

"See?" Azuki said. "It doesn't matter what we look like or what else we can become, as long as we act with good will towards others and try to be friends. You did that. And now we can be friends."

"So you borrowed that *shamisen*?" Akira wanted to know. "Because you wanted to learn how to play it?" The *oni*-girl nodded. "But your hands are too big for it, so you broke it when you tried, right?"

Kukanko fixed the Eagle-boy with a wide-eyed gaze that seemed to wonder exactly how he became an eagle.

"Let me see." Shota reached over to pick up the instrument. It had a long narrow neck down which were strung three strings, held in place by pegs that could be tightened to tune it. The strings terminated at the far end of a resonance chamber that was hollow and covered with skin like a drum. It was the narrow wooden neck that had snapped. He gulped as Kukanko reluctantly released it. The *oni's* hands were extremely large and she didn't have enough fingers.

"Renko-san," he said as he held the instrument out to his friend, "can't you fix this?"

"I think so, maybe," the dragon-girl said. "This is all wood, and I can certainly make wood. You saw Brother fix the strut on that loom where it was broken, and if he can do it, I should be able to. Let me have a look." She took it.

"Don't hurt it!" Kukanko lunged upward.

"It's all right," Akira said, using his eagle strength to grip her shoulders as Azuki nodded and touched the *oni's* arm with her entirely human hands.

"She's just going to fix it," Azuki reassured Kukanko. "Dragons can do things like that."

"And if I can't," Renko said with a smile, "my brother can. He's older so he's more experienced. He's very talented, too. More than I am, I think." She held the *shamisen* with one broken half in each hand, held together by only its strings, and focused. A little vortex formed around the break and the edges seemed to melt together. Azuki remembered seeing Prince Irtysh do something similar when he fixed the loom Susu accidentally broke.

"Will this do?" Renko held out the *shamisen*. Shota took it.

"Ouch, that's hot!" Where it had been broken it had somehow heated when it was repaired. Shota moved his fingers away from the join.

"Well, don't take what isn't handed to you!"

Akira and Azuki grinned at each other.

"Let me have it," Akira said. "Will it just cool off?" He took it gingerly to examine it.

"I don't remember the strut that Brother fixed heating up." Renko shrugged. "He probably knows how to cool it off, but I think it will cool by itself in a minute."

Akira gently tapped the join with his fingers to test it. "It's fine now. You might want to ask Prince Irtysh, though, Renko-san. We're all doing fine now, but sometimes we might not be able to just forge ahead."

"That's why we met, Renko-san," Azuki said. "I should have asked Kukanko-san more about what she meant." She smiled at the European girl. "But I am glad I didn't, because that's how we became friends."

"May I see it?" Kukanko reached up.

"Of course," Akira said. He passed it to the *oni*.

"It's still too small for me," Kukanko said. "But if I am very careful"—

She turned the pegs and plucked. "Ow-w-w-w!" The strings screeched. "That's not right."

"Let me have a look." Shota settled down beside her. "My hands might be the smallest."

"You don't know how to play it," Azuki objected.

"None of us do," Shota replied. "At least Kukanko-san's seen it done." He turned to face the *oni*. "What I do is turn these pegs so the strings tighten and then I can pluck them? Is that it?"

"You're supposed to use a *bachi* for that. It's not like you do it with your fingers, not down there. Where you use your fingers is to hold down the strings along the neck to change the tone and pluck the strings from up there."

The strings squealed.

"That's awful!" Azuki cried, wincing.

"What's he doing wrong?" Renko asked the *oni*.

"Nothing," Kukanko said. "It shouldn't sound like that! Now it's worse than ever!" She began to cry again.

"Maybe," Akira said, taking the instrument from Shota, "we ought to go ask Prince Irtysh."

Renko pursed her lips. She didn't like thinking there was anything she couldn't do. But it was certainly true that her brother was a master at all things having to do with making things, inorganic and, now, organic.

"All right," she said at last. She dropped to her knees beside Shota, at the young *oni's* side. "May we take your *shamisen* to my brother?" she asked. "He really is an expert. I thought I could fix this for you, but it looks like I can't. If anybody can, though, it will be him."

"Azuki-Toki?" The *oni*-girl's welling eyes focused on Azuki. "Will you bring it back?"

"Oh, Kukanko-san! Of course we will bring it back! We'd never just take it from you!" Azuki looked at Renko. "Do you think we could bring it back by this time tomorrow?"

"I promise," Renko said to the *oni*, and reached out her hand. "We'll leave now, but we will be back tomorrow, with your *shamisen*."

With a heavy sigh, the *oni* handed the *shamisen* to the dragon-girl.

"You really will bring it back?"

"Of course she will," Akira said in a no-nonsense tone, as Shota echoed that, sounding slightly outraged, and Azuki softly and kindly joined in.

16

"I tried, Brother," Renko told Irtysh as they both regarded the *shamisen* Akira, in his human form, held.

"It's just not sounding like it ought." Shota sounded aggrieved. The three birds had assumed human form on appearing in Irtysh's palace.

"The tone's off," Azuki explained. "Kukanko-san would like to return it, but it really should be fixed first. She didn't mean to break it."

"I need to be human-size to fix this. If I can." The prince smiled his ferocious dragon smile. "Take it into the Russian room, please. I'll be with you directly."

Azuki had to admit it was a relief to be in human-scale room Prince Irtysh had carved from rock and furnished with painstaking care to identical to a room in a disused human palace in Yekaterinburg, the closest human settlement of any size. Nearly identical. For the most part. For one thing, Irtysh didn't like the silver *samovar* given the gold of almost all the other accessories and decor, so he'd made his *samovar* and tea service from gold.

"This is a nice room," Renko said as she sank into a chair. Since her human form was European, and she had amused herself by changing into a European dress–although without the heeled Western shoes she found so uncomfortable–she fit the room much better than the others. Nobody could see her *tabi*-clad feet under the voluminous skirts, anyway.

"We should have a fire," Shota decided. Even though it was still warm at home, fall not having fully arrived, the room's location in the cavern kept it at an even temperature year-around and a fire was always pleasant, even if not required.

"We can make tea," Renko said. She glanced at Azuki and Akira who weren't so sure about making themselves so much at home. "You know Brother will like it. He likes having guests enjoy what he's built."

Akira shrugged and joined Shota at the fireplace.

"I don't fit in here anymore." Susu's dragon head poked through the door.

"Change, then, Susu-chan," Azuki said with a smile from where she examined the *samovar*. "Join us."

"I don't like that," Susu complained. "I can't talk as well."

"You can, too," Shota said over his shoulder. "You just have to do it mentally."

"Oh, all right, then." The air shivered around Susu, and he became a very small human boy dressed in expensive and formal traditional Japanese wear, like the royal prince he was. Renko almost sputtered in laughter. Father had never dictated what she wore, but Mother certainly had, and when Rizantona was in charge, it was European girl-finery. Except Renko had gone to live with their father when she was just about the age Susu was now, and it was there Renko had discovered more comfortable clothes. Living with Father most of the time had been, for her, good in that respect as well as others.

Otohime, though, had spent centuries dressing like an Heian-Era Imperial Princess, with layers upon layers of gorgeous silks that were immensely heavy and would have restricted her movements, if she had been a regular human. She had done this more to annoy their father than to honor her dual nature, for she felt he had wronged her when her human consort had left her and then died. She had been unable to find him or their child anywhere in the universe. She now didn't believe her father could have done more than she did herself, but she still thought he could have helped her, if only out of sympathy for her and empathy for her grief.

"Otohime?" Irtysh silently called. His children were off at the opposite end of his immense audience chamber, on the far side of his Lake of Jewels, working on the production of looms. This left begging the question he had originally wanted to pose to Tsuruko-san. Yet, while he could speak directly to Tsuruko-san through her Wishing Rock, that might interrupt her when it was not convenient for her. Though they were not technically related, he could speak mentally directly to Otohime, and nobody else could hear.

"Irtysh!" Otohime had started to admit that her fondness for the prince had gone beyond a kind of cousinly sort of friendship, especially since they had started to dance together after Irtysh had taken her to the moon. "Good-day! Is everything all right?"

"Fine. I had a question for Madam Tsuruko, but I understand there is something complicated going on there because of the twin infants, and I didn't want to interrupt the human rituals. You, at least, can tell me to go away if it's inconvenient and nobody need know we spoke. Is it convenient?"

"Yes, certainly. Anko-*sama* and the babies are fine, all the rituals have been properly performed and there are plenty of reputable witnesses to certify that the babies were born here, no matter what that horrible woman in Hakata tries to say."

"You'll have to tell me about it. Twins are not common among dragons, but nobody is displeased when they occur. This is why I wanted to speak with you: my son Vassilli has come up with a most ingenious way of producing those looms you need.

I've got him showing the others how to do it. I should have eight for you very soon. What I want to know is how many would you like to start out with?"

"Your son?" Otohime wasn't immediately sure if she had never known he had children or if she had simply buried the knowledge under her own grief.

"Yes, I have two sons and three daughters. Surely I have told you this? Vassilli is one of my twins—Valeria is the other. I don't think you have met them. They're all adults, of course, and scattered all over my domain." He tried to stay informal and affable, but in fact, come to think of it, he was quite sure he had never mentioned his children individually to her because he didn't want to rub salt in the open wound the loss of her own child had left in her heart. Yet she had to know sometime. Perhaps keeping it casual was the best way to broach it.

"We knew we'd have to ask others to help make the tools for your refugee project," he continued, "and it seemed easiest for me to start with them. At least, they'll do as I say and I know they're smart."

"Of course." Otohime found herself a little breathless.

"With this discovery of Vassilli's we should be able to produce them much faster than I had hoped.

Since I can do what he did, the rest of them should have no difficulties. This should make the whole production process go very quickly, which should please you. And we won't have to involve more dragons. Explaining what we're doing and why we're doing it can get tedious, as can showing them what to do."

"You are proud of Vassilli." Otohime could hardly bring herself to say the younger dragon's name.

"I am," Irtysh admitted. "Zhenya, my oldest daughter, always seems the quickest, but Adrik, my elder son, is likely the smartest. Valeria is logical and diligent and Galina is simply charming, but Vassilli is proving to have an intuitive inventiveness I did not suspect."

Otohime wanted this conversation to end. The pain of her child's loss ripped at her heart yet again. To hear Irtysh, always so considerate, brag about his children, whom he obviously adored, was an additional burden. She was certain he'd never told her about them. Like her father, she chided herself on missing the obvious: a dragon like Irtysh—handsome, royal, courteous, creative, and not all that young—would be bound to have had consorts and almost certain to have children. Not everybody was as damaged as she, thought Otohime.

"Tsuruko-san is with Anko-*sama* right now," Otohime said. "The Yamada's housekeeper has sent for food from Hanako-san for Anko-*sama* and the staff here. Tsuruko-san will need to go home, and after I take her there, I will return to stay here. I don't want her alone with no-one but the servants. Only the housekeeper sleeps in. Noriko-*sama* would stay, I am sure, but she has her own family." And I do not, Otohime didn't say.

"I don't like to bother her right now," Otohime said, "but I think twenty-five would be enough to start with."

"That's all?" Irtysh sounded disappointed. "I suppose we can always make more as they are needed. I tell you what, though. Why don't we start with fifty?"

Otohime couldn't help but smile at the way his voice brightened as he doubled her number. There were certainly enough refugees, but there were difficulties she wasn't sure Irtysh saw.

"That would be very nice," Otohime said.

"Our young siblings and their friends are with me. Their Majesties have taken half my beech trees and gone off somewhere, I suspect to continue our experiments. I have yet to tell you about those, but I will. For now, enjoy the fruits of your labor and get some rest. Let me know when you want the younglings home, and I'll send them."

"Thank you, Irtysh," Otohime said. "Have a good evening."

"*Batya!*" Galina breathed as she saw her father stop talking to the air and disappear into a whirl of smoke that looked like a creative vortex.

"What?" Zhenya asked, following her sister's gaze.

"What is he doing?" Vassilli wanted to know.

"That's amazing." Adrik saw the vortex shrink and coalesce around a small form that resolved itself into a human man. "Grandmama spoke of it, but I didn't suspect it was more than theory."

"I would never have guessed even *Batya* could actually do that!" Valeria said.

"None of us did before right now," Zhenya said drily.

"He's handsome for a human, though," Galina said with a nervous giggle as the figure strode towards the door of the human-scale room.

"No-one would expect him to be anything else."

17

"Good," Irtysh said, looking around as he entered his Western room.

"You've started a fire and I see you are making tea."

"I told you he'd like it," Renko said to her friends. Susu had climbed into the chair beside her, but stretched out his arms to his elder brother and commanded, "Pick up!"

Irtysh smiled at the child. "Not just yet. I want to have a look at that instrument. You call it a *shamisen*?"

"Yes," Akira said. "It's kind of a like a *pararayki*, that the Ainu people use. I guess that's like a *balalaika*, or so they say."

"Indeed." Irtysh looked sharply at the Eagle-boy. He didn't talk much, Irtysh thought, but he soaked up any information that came his way. "This instrument is Japanese?" he asked Akira, who nodded.

"Prince Irtysh?" Azuki thought it time to get to the point. "Just before I met Renko-san, I met an *oni* called Kukanko-san. She likes music. Humans in her area play this instrument. It is Japanese. She wanted to learn to play it, so she borrowed it. Her hands are too big for it, and it broke. She asked us to help fix it so she can return it."

"Lots of people play them," Shota added. "They're small and light so musicians can carry them around. This one belongs to somebody who is blind, I think. Many of the traveling musicians are blind. Do you know what *oni* look like? Only a blind person wouldn't be scared."

"People think they are demons," Akira amplified. "I thought so, too, but now I'm not so sure."

"So you tried to fix it, Sister," Irtysh said, nodding, then transferring his attention to Renko, "but although it's back in one piece, it doesn't sound right. Do I understand this correctly?"

"Hmm." The prince ran his long, elegant hands over the instrument, his eyes losing focus and then gently closing as he reached into the wood to see what he could sense within its molecular structure. It looked right, he thought as he traced it from the fracture to the ends. But there was something wrong. He could tell where the fracture had been. His thoughts raced ahead. If he could perceive the fracture, it was not properly healed, even though it might be strong enough for ordinary work.

Irtysh began moving molecules, encouraging atoms, jiggling arrangements and adjusting connections. After a while, he shook his head and opened his eyes.

"There's something wrong here," he said to his young sister. "It isn't that you didn't make a good repair, but there's something different from the original structure of the wood I can't remedy." He set the instrument on the table and, with a nod, accepted a cup of tea from Azuki.

"Thank you," he said, placing the empty cup and saucer on the table. "This may have something to do with the experiment we were performing with beech trees. You know that your father directs the coral and shell that grows in his palace, yes?"

"Yes," Renko said. "We all know he does it, but I don't think any of us know how."

"He and Mother wanted to know if I could do the same thing with plants. That's what we were working on when Vassilli made his discovery about the looms. Susu, do you know where your parents took my trees?"

Susu giggled. "Papa's house," he said in his little human voice. He switched to mental speech. He was much better with that. "Mama's is up too high for the plants, they said. Al-ti-ti-ti-tude."

"That's right," Irtysh nodded approval. "Plants can only grow up to a certain distance above the sea. That is altitude. As you go up in the mountains, you can get too high and plants won't grow any more. Where Otohime lives is also too high for plants. Here, we are not absolutely too high, but the snows limit how tall the plants can get."

"The snow keeps them from freezing," Akira said, understanding this because he grew up in Hokkaido.

"Yes. Why don't I take this *shamisen*—and you, Susu—to your father's so I can talk to him about this. The rest of you, I think, will want to get home. Shouldn't you join your household for your evening meal?"

"Oh, yes," Azuki breathed. "And our Buddhist practice! Thank you for reminding us, Prince Irtysh. Are we terribly late? Uncle and Aunt will be so worried!" Shota rolled his eyes.

Irtysh smiled at that. "I think my young sister will make sure you get home in time. I did speak to Otohime earlier. Everything is well with Lady Anko and her infants. Otohime will take Madam Tsuruko home and return so that Lady Anko is not left alone before her family arrives."

"I can manage the time we arrive," Renko said. "Brother, will you tell us what you find out from Father?"

"I may call on you, with your permission." He thought he would like to see Otohime in person, not just talk to her.

Renko nodded. Irtysh was always welcome as far as she was concerned, and she thought Otohime felt likewise.

"At the least, I will let you know." He gripped the *shamisen* in his left hand and extended his right. "Come, Susu. You are old enough to take my hand while we travel so I can carry something that isn't you."

Susu clambered out of the chair and swaggered, or tried to, over to take his older brother's hand, excited at this proclamation of his maturity.

"Good-day," Irtysh said, and they vanished.

In Ryuujin's palace under the sea, the Dragon King and the Dragon Queen contemplated the potted beech trees. One was near Ryuujin's long, sculpted coral throne. Two were by flexible walls of shell that moved with currents, enclosing the chamber, now flooded with air.

"I think I see the difference," Ryuujin told Rizantona. "Do you?"

"Yes," she said, all her energy concentrated on the beech tree before her.

"Papa! Mama!" Susu cried as he released Irtysh's hand and ran through the sand towards his parents. The sand swirled around his feet as they changed from two to four when he assumed his dragon form. "Look what I did!"

"Your Majesties," Irtysh said, changing and bowing simultaneously. He clutched the *shamisen* in the middle wing claw of his left wing. "Is it convenient?"

"Of course, Irtysh," Ryuujin said. "Come in. We took your trees so we could keep the experiment going. We thought it better here so we could watch what I do with the coral and shell."

"Altitude!" Susu inserted, getting the new word right this time.

"Yes," Rizantona said, sweeping her youngest child into the curve of her tail. Sadly, he would soon be too big for that. "We also needed to think of the altitude. I suppose your brother told you about that."

"I did," Irtysh admitted. "Have you learned anything?"

"As we thought, it's much the same," the Dragon King said. "If you'll have a look here, you'll see we have been able to continue the pattern of growth that you started, but we can't quite isolate how it's different from the animal pattern in the coral."

"I think it's intrinsic," Rizantona said. "We are not without limits. Dragons can use what is, but we do not create."

"That's why I brought this." Irtysh extended the *shamisen*.

"There's an *oni* and *oni* are demons only she isn't really, but she took the *shamisen* and broke it instead of playing it. Sister tried to fix it so the *oni* can give it back but she can't and Brother can't either!"

Ryuujin looked at Rizantona. She winked so only he could see. Really, they were getting along famously, he thought. They needed more joint projects besides their children.

"That's a fairly good explanation," Irtysh said. "I think the reason neither Renko nor I can fix it is because there is something we are missing. When we spoke about the possibility of directing plant growth, as you direct this animal growth, Ryuujin, we ran into the question of truly creating rather than merely assembling or directing what already exists. I think that's what is going on here."

"There's a missing factor, you mean," Rizantona said.

"Let me see that," Ryuujin said. Irtysh extended the wing-claw holding the *shamisen* to Ryuujin's reaching whiskers.

The Dragon King turned the instrument over, examining it carefully. He put it down on his throne and began an internal examination. "Can you play this?"

"I can't," Irtysh said. "I can attempt to locate music made with this instrument and reproduce it, but I can't play the instrument myself. I don't think any of us can."

"That's what is missing," Rizantona said. Her consort and her son looked at her quizzically.

"The art," she explained. "The creativity. I am not sure where it comes in, whether it is missing in the molecules of the wood itself or the process you are using to repair it, but somewhere, I think we will find, what is missing is the art."

18

"Otohime? Little Sister? Is it convenient if I come by?" Irtysh wanted to talk to both of them because he had an entire list of things to discuss with them both. But he was not sure where they were. Dragons usually only spoke to one other individual at a time, but Irtysh saw no reason he couldn't speak to two or even more, whether they were together or not. It was worth the attempt, he decided. One never learned unless one tried, and dragons had restricted themselves to what they already knew for too long.

"I'm at home, Brother," Renko said. "I'm sure you are welcome here. Just let me ask Noriko-*sama*." The senior lady of the house was, at least nominally, in charge of all matters domestic.

"I am at the Yamada house with Anko-*sama*," Otohime replied in mental speech. "Sister, why don't you ask Noriko-*sama* if she will be good enough to come sit with Anko-*sama* for an hour? Then we can go to my residence."

"Everyone's going to want to come," Renko said. "You both know that. Did you find out something about the *shamisen*?"

Irtysh slowly blinked. He glanced at his mother, who looked dubious at the idea of his talking to two separate people at once, who might not even be in the same place. The Dragon King, who appeared amused, also caught his gaze. Irtysh breathed deeply. He needed to get back to his own residence, too, and see what his children were up to, if they were even still there. He could always make some time, though, and it looked like he'd have to. It had been a busy day.

"We can meet in your audience chamber Otohime," he said aloud. "When?"

"Give me an hour," she replied. "I need to make sure Anko-*sama*'s not alone."

"What do you propose to do?" the Dragon King asked.

"I don't know," Irtysh replied.

"I'm pleased you can admit it," his mother said, tartly.

* * *

Noriko settled beside Anko-*sama*. It was no trouble for her to come down to the Yamada residence by the village for an hour. The new mother slept, as did the two infants, side by side, in a large, lined basket right beside their mother's futon.

Noriko felt happy for them all. So far, the matter of the unconventional birth was resolving itself well. By this time tomorrow, Anko's parents and husband would have arrived with the ultra-competent Kiyo and Hira, Anko's own maid, who Kiyo was training to be as formidable as herself. The housekeeper, Reiko-san, with an able assist from Hanako-san and any local staff they needed to commandeer, would have the entire property comfortable and ready for occupancy long before their arrival.

Hanako had pressed on Noriko a basket full of foodstuffs from the Maeda stores so Reiko would have what she needed to prepare breakfast and get ready for everyone's arrival, in case they came before Reiko could stock up from the village market. The more exalted Yamada household boasted an actual cook when the family was in residence. Reiko had spoken to her and she would appear in the morning, though Reiko would handle tomorrow's breakfast herself. The Yamada gardener and groundskeeper could call on Endo, the Maeda gardener and farmhand, for any help he might need.

Noriko was grateful that Hanako had thought of providing interim supplies, even though the basket had been heavy. She certainly hadn't thought of it herself. Noriko knew the bare minimum of the domestic arts that women, regardless of birth or training, were expected to know as if they were instinctive, but no more than that. In her school, in her job in the *O-oku*, at the Inn of the Golden Phoenix, and now, as a *soke-sama* with a martial arts school and the redoubtable Hanako in charge of the household, her role had always been different.

Renko was supposed to be learning how to be a proper young human lady, just as Otohime was learning how to function in human society, something she'd never really learned, though she had often used her human form. Since they were dual-natured, this had become, on consideration, important. Unlike Irtysh, who did not have a truly human side but only a way to change his appearance, the dual-natured really did need a foot in each world.

While Irtysh had built a human-scale room specifically for an entertainment called a "tea-party" that Otohime had wanted to give, Otohime had done something different for her dual-natured siblings and guests.

Irtysh had helped her with much of the construction and decoration of the caverns in Mt. Fuji that she called her home. She'd never bothered until recently. Eastern Dragons normally lived in water, and she had quarters in her father's undersea palace. Ryuujin let all his children enjoy the oceans and seas freely, but most had their own residences in lakes, rivers, estuaries or inlets from which they managed the weather of their assigned territories.

Otohime had claimed the Japanese archipelago for herself because of her relationship with a human from those isles and their lost child. Humans called her the *O-kami* of Mt. Fuji, which she understood to mean a kind of an over-riding protective force or spirit, and she was also dubbed the Guardian of Japan. That was why she had chosen to spend most of her time in the immense volcano. She did, she thought, an excellent job overseeing the weather. Other dragons did most of the work in their specific areas, and, since she never complained when her father interfered with Japan's weather, Ryuujin was content to let her have the title and the job.

Now that she had a proper seat for herself, three guest caverns (one of which Rizantona had made her local residence), and was working on the design and construction of a variety of dragon-sized benches, platforms and basins for draconic guests, she had also given thought to her other, smaller, form and her dual-natured sister, their little brother, and their variety of friends.

Next to her own dragon-sized seat, away from the one she was still constructing for Irtysh, she had made an ovoid table of amethyst to a human scale. The base rose like a tree-trunk growing from its roots to fan out like branches on the underside, but with a perfectly smooth top. The chairs at either end—it amused her mightily to see that Irtysh promptly staked one of those out for himself—echoed that design. The seats around the rest of the table swooped down from the underside of the table top to finish in small, flat platforms supported by the arching branches. The colors ranged from the palest lavender to the deepest violet. Some areas were striped, some solid. This mineral was supposed to promote clarity, inspiration, honesty and serenity. Otohime thought all these qualities would be beneficial influences on any gatherings she might hold here.

While her quarters were ventilated through the volcano's caldera, some distance below the summit, she knew many humans found the air at the top inadequate. Some humans tried to summit the mountain every summer; of those, some had to turn back because of the thinning air. Otohime expected her guests would include bird-humans; some might even be entirely human. She had engineered a flow of denser air from lower elevations, and started it running. Dragons didn't need supplemental air, and not all members of other species would, but it was a courtesy to have it.

She brought a little fumarole to the surface to heat water. It smelled foul, so she fixed the draft to carry the odor away. She had done that using a series of rocky ledges, on which rested some quite nice *netsuke* in jade and ivory that she had taken from her quarters in her father's palace.

There was a water source, a nice spring, in one corner of the massive cavern she used as her audience chamber. She was still thinking about what to do with that. She did want a water feature of some kind, but wasn't sure what, yet.

Tsuruko had helped her select a very pretty white porcelain tea set, painted with a lotus pattern in shades of purple with touches of green. Otohime would like to add to this with a variety of the fabulous assortment of Japanese ceramics available, but so far, all she had managed to collect were an ewer in a shade matching the green on the tea set, trimmed with white, and the tea set itself. She had a nice ebony tea box and a small wooden cabinet to hold all of this tucked under the stone skirts of her own throne. She hoped to get a larger Chinese shelf someday. She had heard Noriko speak of an open display cabinet Mistress Feng had in her Tokyo *dojo*. Otohime wanted to see that!

The kettle Otohime used was simple black iron like the one Hanako used at the Maeda residence, or Noriko used in her *dojo*. She had a gorgeous ebony *chachuan* tray carved with a dragon to use for transporting the tea set to and from the fumarole and the kettle. Otohime was in no hurry. Now that she had started on this project, she wanted to do it right.

Renko popped in with Azuki, Shota and Akira.

"I didn't want to ask Tsuruko-san to join us," she explained. "It's night where she is, so we can tell her about it tomorrow."

"Yes, we will do that," Otohime said. "She has been away from her home and family quite enough for one day."

"She might know of something that would help Kukanko-san," Azuki said, "but that still can wait until tomorrow."

"Please sit down, everyone," Otohime said. "Sister, will you please see to the tea?"

"Of course." Renko went to the fumarole-stove.

Irtysh entered, largely, but switched to his human simulacrum immediately.

"I beg your pardon," he said to Otohime. "I didn't think." He placed the *shamisen* on the table.

"No harm done," Otohime said, smiling. "Do sit down. I think we have a few things to talk about."

"When are we going to the Exhibition?" Susu said as he popped in, exhibiting his new ability to land and change at the same time.

"That is one of the things we need to discuss," Irtysh said. "Do sit down, Susu."

"We're all going, I suppose," Otohime said.

"Aren't we?" Shota sounded aggrieved that there might be any question.

"Kichiro-chan can come, too, can't he?" That was Susu.

Irtysh looked at Otohime. "It would be useful to hear Madam Tsuruko's opinions. I understand there are several different machines on display you might find useful."

"Yes." Otohime looked at Susu. "If Tsuruko-san can manage the trip, she can bring Kichiro-chan. If she wants to."

"We'll be quite a crowd." Irtysh smiled. "Two Japanese women with two small children. Two young women, one Japanese and one European, two young Japanese men and me."

"Aunt will come with us as far as the city, anyway," Shota pointed out. "She wants to go to her *dojo* there and also to see her friend Sachiko-san."

"I want to go with her to the *dojo*," Otohime said. "Mistress Feng has some Chinese curio cabinets I'd like to see."

"Shota-san and I don't actually need to go," Akira pointed out. "We're not involved in building the spinning machines or teaching people to use them."

"No!" Shota cried. "We *have* to go!"

Irtysh shook his head. "You may not necessarily *have* to go." He looked at Akira and smiled. "In that you are right. But please consider my feelings. I would enjoy your company." He raised his expressive eyebrows. They were almost as good as the moveable spines on his head and neck in his normal form. "I will need allies."

Renko sputtered at that.

"It's nice of you to offer, Akira-san," Otohime said, "But it's no bother to have you accompany us and Prince Irtysh is right. You will save him from drowning in a sea of women and children. Your insights may well be useful. Please do join us."

19

Renko made a second pass with the tea pot. She liked being useful and she liked her sister's tea service. They'd selected a day to visit the Exhibition, pending Noriko-*sama*'s approval. This would allow time for her to write Sachiko-san and Mistress Feng to make sure the day would be convenient for them.

"It's really quite large," Azuki explained to the Prince. She found she had become very comfortable with him, when he was in his human form, anyway. "While there are exhibits of new machines to be used in industry, which is really why we are going, there are also art exhibits, science and nature exhibits, exhibits of export ware"—

"We'll want to see that one," Akira interrupted. "The cloth the refugee cooperative will produce will be for the export market."

"You're right," Azuki said, turning to the Eagle-boy. "What about the agricultural equipment? I read there will be a large exhibit of that, too."

"There's a windmill," Shota said. "It's right at the entrance of the park and it's really big."

"What does it do?" Renko asked.

"Pumps water out of the ground to irrigate crops," Shota told her.

"How?"

"I didn't understand that part," Shota admitted.

"I'll want to see that," Renko nodded decisively.

"Since the refugees will be growing the cotton before they make fabric out of it, we'll definitely want to have a look at anything to do with agriculture," Akira said. "Azuki-san, have you saved the information from the newspapers about the Exhibition?"

"Of course!" She shrugged. "There's a lot that is missing. I haven't seen a really good map of the grounds yet."

"I can take care of that," Renko said.

"We all can," Shota pointed out. Everybody present could fly, as could everyone who was going, with the exception of Noriko. And Kichiro, who was just learning. But that meant Kichiro could stay with Noriko while the others reconnoitered the area from above.

Irtysh rolled his eyes at Otohime. She laughed. He seemed to be taking all this nonsense calmly. She would be interested in seeing him with his children. She had already noticed he was very good with Susu-chan, who actually paid attention to his brother.

"Let us deal with all of that closer to the day," Irtysh said. "Or days. This program may take more than one." Without seeming to raise his beautiful baritone voice, Otohime noticed, he commanded attention from the group.

"Right now, we have something we must address immediately." He reached for the *shamisen*. "Your *oni* friend is upset. You want to help her. She wants to return this instrument, but to do so, it has to be fixed. You, Little Sister, could not fix it, not entirely. Neither could I. Neither could your father. There appears to be something missing. It looks like it is repaired, but when you examine it carefully–have a look, Otohime—you can detect where the repair begins and ends."

Otohime gestured to the others and they slid the *shamisen* down the table to her. She picked it up and looked at it and through it, outside and in. "Yes," she said. "I see what you mean."

Irtysh nodded. "Mother thinks that this is the reason why it does not work as a musical instrument now." He stopped and looked around the table.

"It may look to you as if we dragons do fantastic things, but we do not, not really. We can take what there is and use it or build with it, much as all of you can do, only we do it on a slightly different scale."

Akira nodded. What he could do as an eagle or as a human, what he had learned working on his adoptive father's—and his—new house, involved taking material that already existed and using it to build something new. Like the way he used the wind to sail or to fly, he took what was there and turned it to his own purposes.

"I see you understand," Irtysh said, tipping his bearded chin approvingly at Akira before sending his gaze around the table again. "What none of us can do is create. Mother suspects that since music is art, and art is creative, the disruption in the instrument through the fracture in this long part disrupts the creative flow, making it sound wrong. Or so I understand her."

"*Mother* thought of that?" Renko was shocked. That was a surprisingly creative thought from their utterly no-nonsense mother.

"Yes." He gave his sister a tiny, dry, smile showing her he took her point.

"I would like all of you to think about this," Irtysh said to the group. "If we are to help your friend the *oni* return a working instrument to whomever she borrowed it from, we have to find a way to solve this problem."

"We said we'd visit her again tomorrow," Azuki said, "but we thought we'd have a finished repair to show her."

"We have to visit her," Renko said, "even if all we can report is failure."

"Let us hope it won't come to that," Prince Irtysh said.

"It won't," Shota, irrepressible, asserted. "We'll figure out something."

"Now, I think we should all go home," Prince Irtysh said. "All of you may know what you will find when you get there. I have no idea what I will find when I do."

Otohime made herself an extra hour so Noriko barely realized she'd left before she returned.

"All is well," the *kunoichi* whispered to the dragon as they regarded their sleeping friend and charge. "Anko-*sama* is very tired, naturally. Having a companion she can trust allows her to rest deeply. Not that she can't trust Reiko-san, but..."

"It's not the same," Otohime silently replied. "I understand perfectly. Babies this age sleep all the time, anyway. They only get noisy later. As long as someone's here to keep watch, Anko-*sama* will be fine. It's been a long and complicated day. If you would like me to, I can take you home and only be gone a second, just long enough so I won't meet myself."

"And bounce, as Renko-san says."

"Yes, bounce." Otohime laughed like chiming bells. "It's not quite as dangerous as most people think."

"No, you stay here," Noriko said. "I will enjoy the walk. It isn't far, and it will clear my head. I think you have had a longer day than I. Get some rest."

"Thank you, Noriko-*sama*. You are a good friend for us to have."

"So are you. Shall I hear about your meeting in the morning?"

"That would be a good time. There is nothing urgent." The princess yawned discreetly behind her hand. "I could do with some sleep myself. Azuki-san and my sister will tell you anything you want to know."

"Good night, Otohime." Noriko bowed and slid out the door, closing it in its odd Western way behind her, careful not to make a sound.

It was a pretty night, with the heat of the day diminished and the humidity of summer dwindling, so Noriko did enjoy her brief walk. When she came to the house she saw the light in the room Azuki and Renko shared was burning and heard the murmur of their soft voices. There was a light in Shota's room, too. Since Minoru-*sencho*'s house had been completed, Akira had moved down there. Noriko heard laughter. Shota was in with the girls. It wasn't quite proper, Renko not being his sister, but their lives were so odd, Noriko decided she would simply not notice.

The light in her husband's study was out. That meant he had gone to bed. Usually, almost always, he slept with her, in her room, the room that used to be Renko's before Noriko married Yuta.

Yuta could sleep in his own room, of course, but the floor was generally covered with books, periodicals and papers that he'd have to move before spreading a futon. Her room was larger—husbands often made themselves free of their wives' rooms—and Noriko enjoyed his company. She kept her own books and papers in her *dojo*. Quickly, silently, she slipped through the house and only let the door to her own room scrape a little so as not to startle Yuta by manifesting practically on top of him.

"You're back sooner than I thought," he said, scooting over and moving the comforter so she could slide in beside him.

"Otohime came back directly." She draped her *obi* and *kimono* over the rack and adjusted the under-kimono she wore as nightwear. "I haven't done enough today to be as tired as I seem to be."

Yuta's gestures invited her approach and she took advantage of this when she slid into the bed to rest her head on his shoulder, a comfortable and familiar connection.

"There's been a lot to think about. Our minds are tired. What did they decide?"

"Otohime said there would be things to discuss and do in the morning but nothing urgent tonight. I think she is tired herself."

Yuta laughed softly. "I didn't think dragons ever got tired."

Noriko smiled. "Renko-san does. But they are in the girls' room chatting with Shota-san. They'll all fall asleep soon."

"Akira-san went home?"

"I think so. It's so nice that he finally has one. He and *Sencho-sama* are a good match."

"Aren't they, though?"

"I want to talk to you about what to do with those two girls Sachiko-san can't place."

"Now?"

"No," Noriko said with the tiniest of chuckles. "Tomorrow."

***

Minoru waited up for Akira, sitting on the gallery of their nice new house, looking out at the stars hanging over the sea, smoking his pipe and whittling, or pretending to.

"'*To-san*?" Akira used a diminutive of the more formal "*Oto-san*" or "Father" that pleased them both. "You didn't have to stay up."

"Come sit down. There's *saké* in that jug. I'd pour it for you but I have too many things going on already."

Akira complied and poured for both of them.

"*Kampai!*" Minoru found a way to put down his knife and the ship's whistle he was carving long enough to raise his cup.

"*Kampai!*" Akira echoed. He tossed back the cool *saké* and poured another round for both of them. "Nice night," he said.

"Aye," Minoru agreed. "Reminds me of night watches at sea. I like the nights. We're going to have to get you out on a long voyage pretty soon. We'll bring Shota-san. Maybe even his sister. I know she likes the boat. Maybe now she'll be able to come out more often."

"Renko-san will ferry us all back and forth to shore."

"Not you, though." Minoru grew serious. "You need to learn your human trade, and while you can always be an eagle, your crew won't be able to do that, and you won't always have a dragon at your beck and call."

"True enough."

Minoru filled both their cups again.

Akira looked out over the water and sipped his wine. "*To-san*, you make whistles and pipes, and I know you know more about woodworking than that. What can you tell me about making a *shamisen*?"

***

Irtysh appeared in his audience chamber to find his children disported on and in various platforms and basins, curled up in sleep. Adrik snored gently; a tendril of smoke rose above him. A tidy line of looms stood next to the Lake of Jewels. Irtysh heaved a sigh of relief as he looked up. The ceiling was clean. He hated flaming inside because of all the soot it left and the massive cleaning job that followed.

"*Batya?*"

"Galina!" His youngest had curled on the floor near the columnar basalt throne—it was impossible to call it anything else—that rose from floor to ceiling and served as his personal seat. "Are you comfortable there?"

He climbed into the obsidian basin that fit him so well and settled, wrapping his tail tidily around his feet. He knew she could adjust the surface on which she lay to any shape that suited her with very minimal effort, but it was still nice to ask. He thought he might make her a special place there, right next to him, a small, jewel-lined basin. It pleased him that she chose to be near him.

"I like it here. I'm glad you're home, *Batya*," Galina said.

"I am, too. Thank you all for cleaning up, and thank you all for staying."

"Zhenya said you'd want us all in the morning, so we might as well stay. It was Adrik who reminded us that we should clean."

"They were both right. It looks like you did a nice job, and that pleases me. Tomorrow, we have more looms to make. Good night, Galina."

"Good night, *Batya*."

20

So much needed doing before the day proposed for their excursion into the capital to visit the Exhibition, Noriko thought.

First, she quickly wrote Mistress Feng and Sachiko-san. She could confidently trust her missives to the relatively new postal service, which had replaced various courier networks, and which would also see she received prompt replies.

"Mother says they're amazingly efficient," Renko told Noriko when she picked up the letters to drop them in the post box on her way to school. "They have similar things in her part of the world, but she says ours is easily the best."

"Does she say that to your father?" Noriko wanted to know.

"What do you think?" Renko laughed.

The Ladies' Class followed breakfast as it usually did, only today the discussion was all about the refugee project and how it might be organized to give the refugees a social structure in addition to the business structure of the cooperative.

"This is something Satsuki-*sama* will know about," Otohime pointed out. "We will want to ask her."

"Don't you think the Hiratas will want to help with this?" Azuki wanted to know. "I know the refugees will be from all walks of life, but aren't they going to need to come—I don't know. Together in the middle somehow?"

"So they can all get along." Tsuruko nodded as she lifted a cup out of Kichiro's hands, and wiped up the spillage. "I know that merchants like the Hiratas were considered the least of the social classes, but I don't see how that can still be true."

"And the *samurai* have thought themselves on top, and we know that's no longer the case." Noriko reminded them all. They were silent for a moment. The Satsuma Rebellion, fueled by disaffected boys and men from the *samurai* class, was reaching an ignominious end. Last they'd heard, the rebels, horribly defeated and reduced to under a hundred in numbers, with most killed in battle, a few surrendering and some committing *seppuku*, had fled south, presumably for Kagoshima. There was nothing at all they could do about any of this except get into place to pick up the pieces for those they could help.

Noriko went on, "We need a huge social adjustment that will somehow allow us all to work together for the betterment of the whole in what is becoming an entirely new world."

"In some ways, a total societal reform is what the Restoration has become all about, isn't it?" Otohime sounded thoughtful.

"We'd be part of the aristocracy," Renko said, grabbing Susu as he tried to destroy a cushion, "if we were human."

"Yet I am human, and was able to move from the daughter of the lowliest of tenant farmers to be accepted as part of the aristocracy by Lady Satsuki." Noriko glanced at Azuki and rolled her eyes. Azuki chuckled.

"What *Sensei* is doing will make a difference. If everybody has the same education and we all pay attention to our manners as children learn them in the schools, it will be easier for people to get along no matter what their background or employment is. Here is Kichiro-chan"—Tsuruko bounced her son on her knee—"son of a fisherman, with his best friend a prince."

"A prince with terrible manners! Stop that, Susu-chan!" Susu had picked up the cup Tsuruko had taken from Kichiro and made as if to throw it. "Also a dragon," Renko added as a giggling Susu kept the cup just out of his sister's reach.

"Yes," Otohime said. "One whose parents would not be pleased to see him ignoring his manners no matter his form! Dragons have manners, too! Give me that, Susu-chan."

"Do you know Brother's children well, Sister?" Renko asked. She was intensely curious about Irtysh's relationship with Galina's mother, apparently his former consort. She wondered how much Otohime knew about the rest of Irtysh's life, outside of his relationship with her.

"I've yet to meet them. I never really thought about him having any, although it's only natural that he does. Do you know them?"

"Not well at all. Susu-chan knows them better, I think."

"I like Galina best," Susu announced. "She plays with me. We go swim in the Lake of Jewels."

"They're all adults?" Noriko inquired.

"Yes," Renko said. "With their own residences and sub-domains of their own to tend. It's funny to see how they jump to do what Brother says. I'm much younger, and I don't."

"You're always polite, though, because you are his sister and you aren't a small child" Otohime said with a pointed glance at Susu. "We know he's good with Susu-chan. Rizantona has yet to take Susu-chan in hand."

"Mama doesn't have hands," Susu objected, making them all laugh.

"Neither has Father," Renko said, answering her sister rather than her younger sibling. "Brother does, and so do you. Maybe that's what makes the difference with Brother's children."

Susu held up his own hands and looked at them carefully. Kichiro reached out his own and the children touched palms, starting a simple game. Suddenly Susu looked up at his full sister and spoke mentally, because this was a little complicated.

"Brother only has hands when he's human. Can our nieces and nephews be humans, too?"

***

The central police system was less than three years old. Before that, law enforcement had been rather like the military, managed by the *Daimyo* domains and more or less loaned to the Empire as needed. Different jurisdictions jostled and argued but mostly managed to dole out a fairly reasonable semblance of justice.

This mish-mash created problems forging a unified nation to deal with the Western countries with their national systems. The internal strife and conflict that led to things like the messy Satsuma Rebellion had to be, the Imperial Government felt, suppressed. While it might be possible for different domains to jockey for power and the nation to operate with an odd combination of consensus and dictation, when dealing with the West, that didn't work so well.

Western systems were subjected to careful study and analysis. The usual internal tug-of-war resulted in a new national system that was multilayered, interlocking and uniquely Japanese, though from the outside it looked very analogous to various Western systems. The system was staffed by individuals of wildly different backgrounds and divergent training, but it looked good, and mostly worked.

The two men who trotted over the pass from the larger town carried with them a letter from Hakata. That had come across the island via police couriers, who were faster even than the postal service. They proudly wore their new uniforms. One was a *Junsa-bucho*, a local field supervisor nominally in charge of this area. He was thrilled with his new rank. Before, he'd just been a local farmer with additional responsibilities as tax collector and record-keeper for several households. He was assisted by a *Junsa*, his nephew, who was new to the force, and was lucky to have a job at all.

"There's the Temple of Mary," the *Junsa* noted as the crossed the high meadow at the top of the pass. The former and late fief-holder didn't know what Western people did with what they called churches, but he had liked all things Western. During his sojourn in the West, stranded by laws prohibiting his return, he noticed that a women in blue called "Mary" was a prominent religious figure. She was the mother of their chief deity, which would make her very important indeed. When he was able to return to Japan, he had this edifice, with its odd single pointed bell tower and a statue of the woman in blue enshrined inside, built at the top of the pass. That eight carved stone Bodhisattva Jizo statues stood outside this strange structure bothered no one.

"The turn's got to be right over here," the *Junsa-bucho* said as they trotted past. "Ah. There it is." He indicated and the two men took the path that circled the Maeda compound to descend to the village and the tiny harbor.

Not even Noriko heard the police officers pass her *dojo* because of the singing and laughing going on within. The officers, in turn, paid no attention to what sounded like a mother's group teaching children to count while having a morning out. They knew about the *dojo*, of course, and it was clearly signed, but having had no training themselves, they had no idea what might go on there. Anyway, a Chinese-trained woman *soke* was an absolutely terrifying prospect.

When they reached the Yamada compound just beyond the little village, on one of the two streams that fed into the estuary harbor, they found themselves faced with something more terrifying still.

The gate stood hospitably open. The gardener looked up from his rake and nodded as they entered. The *Junsa* pulled on the entry bell rope and they heard it sound, but the response came from the

Western house off to the side. Reiko-san opened the door.

"Good morning," she said. "How may we help you?"

Puffed up with a sense of his own importance, the *Junsa-bucho* stepped forward and said, "We have been given to understand Yamada Anko-*sama* is here, having been brought to bed in childbirth. We need to see her."

A tiny woman with a wrinkled face, well-defined features, and a shawl wrapped around her bent and skinny frame despite the growing warmth of the morning appeared beside Reiko. The *Junsa-bucho* recognized her and was immediately deflated by what seemed a palpable wave of Shinto *shamanic* power.

"*Fujo-sama!*"

"Indeed." She waved Reiko back, gestured for her to return to Anko, and blocked the entry. "Anko-*sama* is here. She has in fact been delivered of not one, but two infants, here, as she hoped. That is why she rushed to get here, and why you cannot see her now. Her husband and parents will arrive any time now. Tell me, what concern is this of yours?"

"We have a complaint from Hakata," the older man blustered, waving the letter. "It says twin babies were born to Anko-*sama* there mid-day yesterday, with the services of a midwife, who was forcibly ejected and not paid what was due her."

"That can hardly be accurate," the Shinto *shaman* said. "My husband and the Chief Priest of the Temple were both here yesterday long before the sun was overhead to perform the necessary birth rituals."

"But...people saw the midwife being removed by Lady Yamada's maid and their guard."

"Otohime arrived with Anko-*sama* before this hour yesterday," Mifune-*fujo* said firmly, though she sounded just a bit puzzled. "*Sensei* came for Sato-*Gosonshi-sama* and they came for my husband and me immediately. Hamasaki Tsuruko-san and Maeda Noriko-*sama* were also with Anko-*sama* when I arrived. We cannot all be mistaken."

"What about the midwife?" the *Junsa* said. "What does she have to gain with this complaint?"

A new voice spoke up behind them. Yuta had seen them coming from the school where he prepared for his secondary school classes.

"Perhaps she hoped to have the job of assisting Lady Anko," Yuta said. "She would have hoped, even expected, to be paid. But since Lady Anko chose to come here instead and was brought in a rush by Her Royal Highness, no commission would be forthcoming. She's trying to get paid for work she never did, don't you think?"

"*Sensei!*" The *Junsa-bucho* bowed. The monk turned teacher had become an important figure locally. "Do you agree with what *Fujo-sama* has said?"

Yuta smiled. "I would never question *Fujo-sama's* wisdom." He bowed slightly in her direction.

"But—two babies! How could she have known?"

Yuta smiled again, broadly. "Even I could tell there was more than one when Anko-*sama* arrived. Presumably the midwife had attended Anko-*sama* during her pregnancy. She would surely have known."

"She's impudent and greedy," Mifune-*fujo* said. "If she withdraws her complaint and apologizes to Yamada Toshio-*sama* for the trouble she has caused, he might consider paying her something even though she had no work to do."

"Was there a midwife here, then?" The *Junsa-bucho* asked.

"I do not practice as a midwife exactly, but I have attended more than my share of births in my own professional capacity." Reproof colored the *shaman's* tone.

"Were you paid?" the *Junsa* asked. Yuta contrived to look shocked at the implication.

"Her Royal Highness made generous donations to the Shrine on behalf of her friend. Those have of course been properly recorded." Now the little woman radiated dignity.

"I do not wish to leave Anko-*sama* for too long," Mifune-*fujo* said. "Reiko-san naturally has her own work to do. Are we quite finished?"

"Otohime is at my house with my wife," Yuta pointed out. "If you care to speak with either of them. Otohime will return here soon, I believe, so *Fujo-sama* may go home. Sato-*Gosonshi-sama* is at the school with the smaller children. I will walk you over so I can take his class, if you would like to speak to him."

"If you stop at the Shrine on your way up the hill," Mifune-*fujo* said, "I am sure my husband would be delighted to see you. He enjoys visitors."

The two police officers looked at each other. They had no way of knowing what had happened in Hakata, but confronted with layer upon layer upon layer of highly respectable local witnesses, they knew the report they would have to make.

"I will walk you out," Yuta said, extending his arm to show them the way. "You may wish to suggest that the woman apologize to Toshio-*sama* in writing, since he will be here. I suspect that he will be so overjoyed at the birth of his children that he will accept the apology, and no doubt make her a small gift."

He turned and bowed to Mifune-*fujo*, giving her a small smile. She smiled in return as she bowed her farewell.

It seemed they had succeeded.

21

Irtysh stretched, overflowing the basin of his seat, careful not to knock into Galina, whom he'd last seen curled in a curve of rock beside his throne. Valeria and Vassilli didn't live together or even very close to one another. Physical distance meant little to dragons. The twins did prefer proximity when they were in the same physical space. He glanced over to the gigantic basin that would easily accommodate Rizantona or Ryuujin, and in which he had last seen the twins. Gone. He lifted his massive head and rolled it back on his long neck, causing his neck to form a sensuous S shape. Dropping his chin, he looked at the couch where the snoring Adrik had sprawled and next to that the ovoid platter where Zhenya had slept. Also gone. Finally he peered down so he could see under the edge of his obsidian seat and found Galina, too, had vanished. He must have slept very late.

He had certainly been tired. The way he felt reminded him a little of the time he'd drunk too much wine when he was using his human simulacrum. He hadn't known about "too much wine" then. He knew enough to avoid it now. It could only affect him when he used his human imitation, because adult dragons didn't eat or drink as humans or other more terrestrial beings did. They absorbed what they needed from what was around them. This was connected with their ability to take the smallest bits of existence and build or assemble anything they needed. That did mean his children had not gone out to get a meal together at a restaurant, a human custom Irtysh found charming.

Irtysh quickly counted the looms that had been completed. As he looked them over, he found that he approved. They were all well-made and would do the job. He smiled as he saw the personal signatures in the work of each of his children. Galina had made one small careless mistake that emphasized appearance over function, and seemed to have liked it since she repeated it. That was easily fixed. Adrik could make his transitions smoother. He could be easily distracted. Irtysh fixed that, too. Vassilli showed real talent in the fluidity of his construction. Valeria, he saw, picked up and imitated some of her twin's tricks, with clever twists here and there. Zhenya's work was simply flawless; nothing to criticize, but nothing to specially praise. On the whole, though, these were nicely done. They would definitely work. But they were only about half finished. Irtysh figured they'd be back soon. For now, he decided he'd go out and get some exercise. He tucked his wings in, hunkered down and sprang into the sky .

***

"It's like making a belaying pin, you see?" Minoru demonstrated the technique to Akira. "It's a solid shaft of wood, so start with that. Then shape it, getting finer and finer in your tools as you approach the final shape. Mind, I don't know how to craft any instrument more complicated than a ship's pipe, so I can't say this would work, but this one you've brought me is all of a piece in that area. These pins at the top for tuning the strings look very like belaying pins."

"I wish we knew why this doesn't play right," Akira said. He'd brought the *shamisen* to Minoru in the hope that the sailor could help him figure out what was wrong with it.

"It looks all right." Minoru turned the instrument over in sea-roughened hands. "I can't feel a difference." He plucked the strings. "I don't know what it's supposed to sound like, so I can't tell if it's off."

"It doesn't sound off to me." Akira shrugged. "It sounds off to some of the others, but then, I don't know music either."

"Well, take this roll of tools with you. You're bright." Minoru smiled at his adopted son with pride. "You'll figure it out."

Akira smiled back. He enjoyed learning, not just in school, but all the things Minoru could teach him, too. Speaking of learning, though, "I better get going," he said. "Can't be late for school. I'll see if Renko-san can go see the *oni* later."

"Don't be too late," Minoru said. He didn't like putting limits on the boy, who would be a full adult crew member if they were at sea.

"Are you going up for dinner?" Akira jerked his head in the direction of the Maeda compound. Since the adoption had been finalized, Akira wasn't nearly as worried as he had been about Minoru's budding relationship with Hanako. He could smile now as he thought of it.

The village boasted a new *izakaya* tavern that served noodles. It supplied the village *sento*, or bath house, with food and beer. Midori ordered wine separately from a brewery in the larger mountain village nearby, which took great pride in its snow-melt water. It was more expensive than what the *izakaya* bought from Oita.

"If I catch some fish," Minoru said with a grin. Minoru was well versed in survival skills, like any ocean sailor, and could put together a fairly tasty meal. The *izakaya* would, for a very small charge, cook any fish or shellfish he brought them, and supplement his catch with pickles, rice and miso soup. Midori, who ran the *sento*, would not charge for the extras as long as she and her son could share the main course. Minoru thought she made pretty good pickles. The *izakaya* bought theirs. Hanako, however, bought very little prepared food. Since her job as housekeeper for Yuta-*Sensei* and his family included cooking, she only bought things that she couldn't make, and everyone agreed she was a very good, even inspired, cook. Minoru liked that very much.

"Probably see you there, then," Akira said, picking up the bundle of tools and heading for the school. *Sensei*, Lady Noriko and Hanako herself had issued both Minoru and Akira standing invitations for dinner, whether Minoru brought provender or not. Minoru had visited often before, but when the adoption was finalized and the new house finished, Akira had moved down there. Everybody wanted to continue the close relationship between what had become two households.

Minoru took any chance he got to take the boat out, usually with Akira and often Shota, sometimes visiting larger ports nearby. Now, Azuki came on day sails when she could, since her workload had decreased, and even Renko showed up sometimes, though she wasn't as enamored of sailing as the others. She liked it, but her personal abilities exceeded those of any boat, and she didn't see a reason to learn the skill. She preferred to practice her calligraphy.

When the weather did not permit sailing, Minoru actively enjoyed doing boat maintenance, some of which could be performed under cover if it rained. Once the work was done, if it wasn't raining, he could fish.

While at sea, his boats would drag a trolling line when possible. This was for food, not fun. After losing his leg, he missed the sea and was afraid it was gone from his life for good. Once he learned to walk on his wooden prosthesis, Minoru would walk from his house to the docks just to gaze at the water and watch the tides come and go. There he discovered sport fishing. The Empress, someone told him, was an avid angler, though she preferred freshwater fishing. Minoru like the saltwater coast so he learned to fish from the shore. He turned his woodworking skills to various kinds of fishing lures, rods, floats and made himself a nice wooden tackle box. He was now making one for Akira, as a gift. The Eagle-boy didn't know about it yet.

Still, Minoru longed for the sea, for days and nights away from land when the stars spilled overhead and dolphins might rise to travel companionably with a boat under sail for hours, the only noise being the blows of their breath and the susurration of the sea.

He was collecting his fishing tackle for a trip to the docks when he heard people coming.

He went outside to watch them come down the hill. His new house was on the track that ran beside one of the two streams that enclosed the village and created the estuary that made the little harbor. There was a lot of noise. This was a fairly large group of people, and not just walkers, either. Minoru heard horses.

There they were! A small guard marched in front, followed by an oxcart. Several women rode in the cart, including Noriko-*sama* and Otohime! He recognized Satsuki-*sama* of course, and the fierce Kiyo, whom he knew, with a girl who must be Anko-*sama's* younger, gentler, Hira, of whom he had only heard.

The men, mounted, had split because of the narrow trail, with young Toshio-*sama*, unprepossessing in looks though proving himself to have character, riding all the way out in front. No doubt eager to get to his wife and children, Minoru thought with a grin. Yamada Eitaro-*sama* rode behind the cart, in front of another contingent of guards.

Pretty grand, the Yamadas, Minoru thought. Even with the loss of the fief and its tax revenue, they maintained a guard. Eitaro-*sama* peeled away from the group, jerking his head roughly to tell them to go on, and came to speak to Minoru.

Minoru had bought the property on which his house stood from Eitaro. The men exchanged greetings and Minoru once again thanked Eitaro for selling him the home site.

"Looks good," Eitaro said. He looked over the house critically. "Looks well built."

"I think it is. I know a fishing captain who used boat building techniques in his own house. We tried some of those here as being stronger."

"View's splendid. Thought you'd want this one." Eitaro smiled.

"You were right, and I thank you," Minoru said.

"Did you hear? I have grandchildren!" Eitaro waved expansively in the direction of his house.

"Congratulations. One of each, I heard. Born yesterday right at your house here. Toshio-*sama* looks like he can hardly wait."

"I better catch up with them," Eitaro said. "He'll have the oxherd running!"

"Come back and see the inside," Minoru invited, with a grin. "Got some pretty good *saké* in. If you have time."

"I'll do my best to make the time," Eitaro said with a nod. He turned his horse and trotted off.

22

"What's Noriko-*sama* doing down here?" Tall Akira had seen the riders and the oxcart. Nobody else was tall enough to see who rode in the cart without standing, except Yuta, who was at his desk on the other side of the room.

"You're supposed to be studying," Yuta admonished, but he heard the jangles, hoofbeats and squeaks of the passing group and so rose to go look out the window himself.

"That's all of them," Yuta said. "They've arrived." He gestured at the procession. "You met Toshio-*sama*, I think, Akira-san? My wife and Otohime are riding with Satsuki-*sama* and the maids, with Lord Eitaro behind. Toshio-*sama* must be thrilled." He turned to the room. He had few students at this level. Close to half of them came from his own household.

"Yamada Eitaro-*sama* used to hold the fief here, as some of you may recall. He maintains a house here still, of which his family is fond," he

209

explained to the rest of the group. "He adopted Morimoto Toshio-*sama* when Toshio-*sama* married Anko-*sama*. She arrived urgently yesterday and they now have twin babies. Toshio-*sama* is, of course, anxious to see them."

"What about Aunt's class?" Shota always seemed to blurt out impolite or inconvenient questions. If chided for it, he'd say he merely wanted to know and keep doing the same thing. Yuta would have despaired of his nephew, except everybody liked Shota despite his occasional impudent lack of manners, and that included Dragon Queen Rizantona, whom nobody ever dared gainsay.

"She would have left a senior student in charge with directions," Yuta replied absently. "Teaching junior students is how some senior students earn their own instruction."

"Aunt did that," Azuki recalled. "You must remember that, Shota-san. When she got her Chinese training."

"The path to martial arts mastery is long and difficult," Yuta said to the class. "My wife also worked at an inn during that time. Martial arts are a lifetime study if you want to be a master."

"Didn't you used to study, *Sensei*?" Yukio, a rather round boy who came from the neighboring village, asked. "But haven't you given it up?"

"I started as a *sohei*, yes," Yuta said. His history as a monk was no secret; his leaving religious life was seen as normal and responsible, since he did so because of family responsibility, and had official permission to do so. "I have not given it up, though. I practice every morning in the hopes that someday I may become a worthy sparring partner for my wife." Yuta smiled to show he was not offended by the question nor embarrassed by his answer. How could he not be proud of Noriko?

"Practice," he continued, "is the key to mastering many things. Yukio-kun, where were we?"

Toshio could hold back no longer. The gates were open, and he saw the staff waiting to welcome them with bows and smiles.

"Give over," he called to the guard before him, as pushed his horse through the dividing rank. Using his heels, he brought his mount to a gallop even though the distance was short. He pulled up in the court just as Tsuruko opened the door of the Western house.

A boy grabbed his horse's reins and Toshio unceremoniously dismounted and ran.

"Lord Toshio," Tsuruko called, "Welcome. Your family is ready to greet you!"

He kicked off his boots on the platform below the first step. "My babies? My wife?"

"All are well." Tsuruko was laughing but she didn't move. "Lord Toshio, have you forgotten? You must first be presented with the children and acknowledge them!"

"But"— Toshio had already accepted the children! Yesterday!

"Toshio!" Eitaro growled the interruption, his omission of a title underscoring Toshio's standing as his adopted son and his daughter's husband. "Wait! Come back down here!"

Toshio skidded to a halt halfway up, and backed slowly down the stairs. Eitaro had been his commander when Toshio had served in Eitaro's personal guard as well as kind of a private secretary. Disobeying Eitaro was just not possible.

"It's all right," Lady Satsuki said as she swiftly glided across the yard. She hadn't found the ride comfortable and she ached from the midwife's battering the day before, but Noriko had given her some secret "Chinese" medicine, though it actually came from the Mochizuki School pharmacopeia, and that was taking hold. Even if it hadn't, Satsuki was not about to let anything upset this particular basket.

"Stay here," she continued as she brushed past Toshio and up the few stairs to the porch of the Western house. "With Otohime and Noriko-*sama*. Tsuruko-san and I will bring the babies out right now." She shot Noriko a sharp glance to make sure Noriko knew she had Satsuki's permission to restrain her adopted son and son-in-law if he lost control.

But Tsuruko appeared at the door holding a swaddled infant that she swiftly passed to Satsuki. "It's the boy," she hissed.

"Toshio-*sama*," Satsuki said as she turned, "Here is your son." She smiled with a compassion worthy of Kannon herself as she seemed to float down the stairs and held out the child. "Do you acknowledge this child as yours?"

Toshio was smart even though he looked vague and rather dull. He only caught up slowly now because he was more than excited: he was awed at the sight of his infant son.

"I do," he said, taking the baby from Satsuki. "I acknowledge this child as my son!" He proclaimed. Then he looked down at Satsuki, befuddled.

"Yes," Satsuki said. "There is more."

Tsuruko brought the other infant down the stairs. "Here is your daughter, Lord Toshio," she said. "Do you likewise acknowledge this child as yours?"

Eitaro stepped around to relieve his son-in-law of his first-born son so he could reach for his first-born daughter.

"Oh, yes," Toshio said, looking down at the perfect little face in which he fancied he saw hints of his Anko. "I acknowledge her. She is my child." He looked at Eitaro and the group of women. "I want to— Can I— Go see my wife?"

"Of course you may," Otohime said. "Is that not how it is done here?"

"That is exactly how it is done everywhere I know of," Noriko replied.

"Perhaps if you would give your daughter to her grandmother," Satsuki said, extending her arms, "her grandfather and I will bring the children while you go ahead." Toshio wouldn't dream of contradicting Satsuki, either. He handed her the baby and rushed up the stairs.

Like Ryuujin, Irtysh had learned to eavesdrop on certain individuals when he pleased, using the Wishing Rock network. Whether Rizantona was aware that the mechanism she and Irtysh used to communicate through the rocks without having to have personal ones would allow Ryuujin's level of intrusiveness, Irtysh did not know. He did not plan to tell her.

He soared over Mount Beluka and circled until he spotted his children playing with Susu, riding the air currents created where the secluded Tien Shan Mountains ran into the virtually empty Talamakan Desert. At least they had the sense to pick some place where nobody would be likely to see them have their fun.

He flew toward them, gratified that they enjoyed each other's company enough to play together still, even though they were all grown and there were hints that Adrik, at least, had found someone to keep company with, perhaps a potential consort.

Irtysh tuned into Renko's rock, hoping to hear what Otohime was up to. If she was embroiled with humans, he wouldn't bother her. They could talk later. He thought his young sister would forgive his eavesdropping, if she ever found out.

Thus he heard *Sensei* tell his class, now all gathered around the window, "That's done, then. Toshio-*sama* has accepted the children and all is well. Here come Satsuki-*sama* and Eitaro-*sama*. They'll go to their own house and make sure everything's ready. Otohime and my wife—see? Here they come—will follow so Toshio-*sama* and Anko-*sama* can have some time alone with their new children. All of you, now, get back to your work."

Irtysh decided to try something new. His curiosity, not natural to most dragons, sometimes got him into trouble. He reached for Otohime's Rock and tried to expand his range. Perhaps with a little more altitude...yes, that did it.

Prince Irtysh circled as he shamelessly eavesdropped.

"You're sure you're all right?" Toshio asked his young wife.

"Of course!" Anko replied. "Except, I had a baby. Well, two babies. But Mother says that was no harder or different than it usually is. I had my friends, Otohime and Tsuruko-san, there, too and they agreed. You know that! You were right there, yourself!"

"But you got here so fast!"

"As the *Fujo-sama*, the *Kannushi-sama*, the *Gosonshi-sama*, Noriko-*sama* and *Sensei* can all testify, as well as Tsuruko-san and Otohime." Anko started laughing, but then she quieted.

"I don't want to tell you exactly how she managed it without her consent, but truly, thanks to Otohime, we had a quick and comfortable trip. Much more so than you!"

"I am afraid your mother wasn't comfortable at all, but there was nothing we could do about it that we weren't already doing. Wife, we should talk about this very soon. Have you any ideas for naming the babies?"

"There are so many choices! I would like to underline that they are twins, just to throw it in the face of that accursed midwife. I don't know what you might think of that!"

Irtysh smiled and banked. He liked that idea, himself. Fortunately, Toshio did, too.

"It would be very modern and unconventional of us, but I had thought of something."

"I like being modern and unconventional," Anko replied. "What were you thinking?"

"Sora for our son," Toshio began.

"Like this?" Anko answered. Irtysh presumed she was drawing a *kanji* in the air. He'd seen humans do that. "Wind? Sky?"

"Yes," Toshio went on. "And maybe Sara—I was thinking of this, blossom—for our daughter."

"Oh, Husband. I like those." Anko started laughing. "If Otohime says I can tell you, you'll see just how appropriate they are!"

Irtysh swooped higher in the sky and took aim at his own children. Folding his wings tightly and elongating his body, head and tail straight out from his torso, he dove, laughing. He'd give them a surprise before he rounded them up to go back to work.

He liked being a father.

23

"It looks fixed," Kukanko said. Her three-fingered red hands caressed the *shamisen* Akira had handed her.

"My brother tried to fix it and so did my father," Renko told her. "But we aren't sure if they did any better than I did. I'm not sure it sounds right. Can you tell us?"

"But I can't play," Kukanko said. "Not really."

"Perhaps not," Azuki told her, "but at least you can strum the strings and use the plectrum and see if the tone is"—

"Ow-w-w-w!" Kukanko responded to the twang of the string. "No, no, it's still not right. If I can tell, the human I borrowed it from will certainly be able to. She's really good."

"We'll think of something else, then." Azuki dropped to the grass next to the young *oni*. Renko and Akira stood nearby, but Shota had flown into the trees looking for seeds from which he could make a snack. As soon as school had ended, the four had headed north as they had promised Azuki's abductor turned admirer. Azuki had noticed that besides the *shamisen*, which had traveled carefully wrapped against further damage, Akira had a wrapped roll of something she didn't recognize.

"There is something else we can try," Akira said. He squatted on his heels beside the *oni* and untied the mysterious roll. It fell open to reveal woodworking tools.

"I asked my father," he explained to Kukanko and everyone else. "He's a sailor, a sea captain, and he does some woodworking. He makes whistles and pipes for people to use on ships. He even makes whistles that blow when a teakettle boils, like the whistle on a steamship or a train."

"What did he tell you?" Shota appeared as a boy beside Renko. Kukanko started a little at seeing Shota change before her eyes, but their dual natures were not new to her. She was much more unusual looking than any of them, except maybe Renko, but Kukanko was never normal-looking.

"You know how we helped with the house," Akira said. He turned to Kukanko. "My father built a new house and Shota-san and I both helped with it. Me, more, because I'm living there and I suppose someday it will be mine." He sounded a little surprised at that. "Shota-san and I learned something about working with wood during the building, though, more than we'd learned on the boat.

"Renko-san's mother thinks the problem with the repairs is that the wood gets, maybe, warped or something, somehow changed by the repair process they've been using and isn't exactly the same as it was, even though it looks it."

"Her Majesty came up with that?" Shota was surprised. Azuki thought it funny the way everybody reacted to the Dragon Queen coming up with something inventive like that. Rizantona was known more for raw power and hot temper than intellectual subtlety, but that did not mean she wasn't smart and clear-sighted. She'd have to be, to be Queen.

Kukanko recoiled. Any queen was a scary proposition.

"Don't worry about that part," Renko advised the *oni* firmly. "That's a good way of putting it, Akira-san. Warped, on a level so small we can't see it, much less fix it. And we *can't* fix it. I mean, I can't, and if my brother and father can't, either, there is definitely something wrong with how we're doing it. What did *Sencho-sama* say about it?"

"He was working on a ship's pipe," Akira told Renko. "He showed me how the grain of the wood as well as the way it's carved can affect the sound. It was really interesting, especially when he showed me how even small variations on the way something's carved can affect the sound."

The Eagle-boy shifted to look at the *oni*.

"Kukanko-san, my father loaned me some woodworking tools. He looked at the *shamisen* and examined how it's made. He doesn't know, and I don't, either, but maybe we could make a new neck for it? That might work. Shall we try?"

Shota examined the instrument. "It's got a head, up here with the pegs for the strings, and then the neck, the part that's broken, and the body. That's where you play and where the sound comes from. But, Renko-san," Shota said, "You could actually make a new neck, couldn't you? I mean, why would we have to go out into the forest to find the right wood and carve it? Can't you just make it?" Shota thought he would needle her a bit and spur her into action. "I am sure Prince Irtysh could."

Renko shook her head, Shota's needle not touching her through her concentration. "Brother would have tried that, I think. I'll try it again, though."

"There's something we haven't asked yet," Azuki said. "Kukanko-san, where do the musicians get their instruments?"

"I don't know," the *oni* said. "They live in the *Goze* house except when they travel. That's usually in the winter. That's how I first heard them!"

She sat up, cross-legged, her ugly face animated to the point where her coloring and fangs could almost be forgotten. "They go out in groups of three. Two have *shamisen*, but one's called a *tebiki*. She's not a musician, but she can see. Her job is to help the *goze* at the *Goze* house and also help them travel safely."

"So they have *shamisen* in the *Goze* house?" Shota slid to the ground, sitting on one hip with his top leg stretched out. Absently, he toyed with a small wildflower.

"Yes, I think so," Kukanko said. "I saw them singing to Bodhisattva Jizo at a crossroads after *Setsubon* last winter."

"What did they sing?" Akira asked just as Azuki asked, "Do they always sing to Jizo-*sama*?"

"I liked their music," Kukanko said with a nod. "So I followed them around. They always sang to Jizo-*sama* when they came across a statue. Because they travel, I guess." Jizo protected children, yes, but also travelers, and was frequently honored with statues so he could be easily petitioned to protect vulnerable groups whenever his statues were sighted.

"What they sang was just praise and thanks. Then they asked for Jizo-*sama's* protection. It was always the same. It's short, but Jizo-*sama* must like it."

"What do they do on their trips?" Shota wanted to know.

"I couldn't see much of it, because they go from village to village. They stay in somebody's house. They go door to door and sing a little to ask people to a real performance. In the evening. I could sneak up and listen sometimes. Other times they attended festivals! Those songs are really long! I like those, but I can't get too close, so I don't know much. I wanted to hear more."

"Is that why you went to the *Goze* house?" Azuki asked softly.

"Yes!" The *oni* nodded, her odd face seeming to plead for understanding. "Parents bring girls who can't see there, or older ones come on their own, and they stay to learn to play the *shamisen*! I wanted to stay and learn like they did. But I couldn't because of the *tebiki*!"

Azuki waved at Shota, who seemed about to speak, cautioning him to silence. Kukanko had come to trust them. If they were going to help her, they had to keep earning that trust.

"The *tebiki* could see you, and they would know you were an *oni*." Azuki nodded her understanding. "Is that when you decided to borrow a *shamisen* to learn by yourself?"

Kukanko nodded, but her eyes filled with tears and she started crying again. "But my hands are too big and I broke it and now I can never learn."

Renko and Shota rolled their eyes at each other. Kukanko's level of distress was getting tedious, since they were working on fixing things.

"They might have extra ones there," Azuki said. "Or maybe they have spare parts. I think we ought to go look."

"I can't go," Kukanko wailed. "They'll see me!"

"I can't go, either," Renko told her, fluffing her yellow hair. "Look at me! To them, I'm as strange as you are! We'll stay here and see if I can make a new neck for this instrument."

"We won't be very long," Azuki told her friend after she had got what she hoped were good directions from Kukanko. "Thank you for staying."

"We should fly," Akira said. "It'll be faster."

"Good idea," Shota answered, changing quickly. "We can get an overhead view."

"Fly fast, then," Azuki called as she sprang into the air, waggling her wings as she took off.

"Ride on me, if you want," Akira said. Shota's small size only bothered him at times like this, when his sister and his friends would be so much faster. Akira circled slowly, so Shota could come land on the Eagle's shoulders. There were compensations, Shota assured himself in firm tones. It was just that sometimes it didn't feel like it.

The dragon-girl and the *oni* started searching for trees that might match the neck of the broken *shamisen*.

"If you're going to make it, or try to," the *oni* asked, "why do we need the tree?"

"We did a poor job on the repair," Renko replied. "Since we couldn't match the original, I don't want to try making a new part without having a sample of the original to copy. If I just make a duplicate of this one, the same error might carry over. I did ask my brother." Renko had shot Prince Irtysh a quick question and received an equally quick answer. "He agrees." She stopped to pat an oak tree. "This is it, I think," Renko said. "*Karin?*" She reached out to touch the *shamisen's* resonance chamber. "The *dou* is *karin*."

"It's the same as the *sao*," Kukanko said with a shrug. "That's what they call the neck. This isn't a very fancy one. That's why I borrowed it. But the *goze* value all of them."

"You probably have to have talent and experience to tell the instruments apart by sound. I've neither," Renko said, "but I want to compare. Please wait a minute."

Kukanko thought Renko might be falling into a trance and wondered briefly if the dragon-girl was also some kind of *shaman* or medium. Both, or even women who were both at once, were plentiful around here. Often, they were found among the *goze*. Kukanko watched warily. Renko-san as she was, dragon and European girl, was frightening enough.

Renko opened her eyes and nodded. "It's different," she said to the *oni*. "Let's see what I can do if I try to duplicate some lumber, using the tree as a model. Shall we sit down?"

Kukanko was fascinated by the slender vortex that formed in front of the yellow-haired girl whose skin was colored like the inside of a white peach. Kukanko had never seen a human with coloring like this before. And one who made vortexes! The first vortex vanished, leaving a length of wood something over a meter in length and perhaps ten centimeters square. Then another vortex built and another, both disgorging similar pieces of lumber.

"Let's have a look," Renko said and reached for the *shamisen*. She ran her hands over the repaired neck and then over the tree, and then over the lumber she had pulled together from the elements surrounding them.

After a couple of minutes, she favored Kukanko with a cheerful smile. "I think I've got it. The broken one's different, anyway. I don't think I can actually fix it, though. It seems like it's mixed up. Not much. Just a very little bit, but it's too subtle for me to make it right."

"Can't you make one of these just like this, now?"

Renko suppressed a sigh. No matter how fantastic the trick she pulled off, people always wanted more. "I don't think so, Kukanko-san. For the same reasons I can't just fix this one. If I started trying to duplicate the original precisely, I think error would creep in."

Renko tried to exercise compassion. And patience. Although she had met Azuki at the same time Azuki had met Kukanko, she didn't think either of them had realized how very young the *oni* was. Anyway, at that time, she had thought herself a little older than Azuki. It was only since they had become friends that their ages had equalized. The relationship dragons had with time as others knew it was complicated. She wasn't sure even her father understood it. Even though they all worked with it, or it worked with them.

She heard the not-quite-a-screech call of the Eagle overhead, joined by the caw-like cry of the Toki. She smiled. Shota cheeped in much more musical tones, but they were too far away for her to hear him. But she saw him dive from the shoulders of the Eagle as the larger birds circled to come in for soft landings. Shota landed, as a boy, with a thump.

"Did you do it?" he asked. Renko and Kukanko both nodded.

"We did our part," Azuki said as she landed in her human form, Akira beside her.

"We found out what we needed to know, anyway," Shota added.

"They wouldn't let Akira-san or Shota-san come very close," Azuki said. "It's almost like a monastery. No males allowed. All women and girls, almost all of them blind or with badly damaged sight. Oh, I felt so sad for them. When I thought about losing my vision—but that's over now. They do very well, though. I had a hard time telling which ones were the *tebiki*. But they told me they didn't have any *shamisen* to sell, and no spare parts, either, except strings."

"They thought that was very funny!" Shota inserted. "The idea of anybody repairing a *shamisen* by replacing one of the three major parts, was new to them. You can restring them, and re-cover the resonance chamber, the *dou,* they called it, but they hadn't tried anything else."

"Where were you?" Azuki asked. "I thought you two were outside!"

"Sometimes I have an advantage. I came in a vent and took a quick tour while you were talking to the mistress."

"She's the teacher," Azuki explained, "and runs the house. She said they had recently lost a *shamisen*, but they wouldn't sell one even if they had one to spare. Girls are always coming. Sometimes going. I took that to mean that sometimes girls leave with boys, but she didn't say that."

"They're not supposed to, though," Akira said with a grin. "While I waited outside, some of the girls came back. The ones who could see, uh, looked. Then they talked and I listened. They didn't know I could hear. It's to keep them safe so they can travel around and earn their keep without men taking advantage of them."

"Or those *karayuki* people," Renko said grimly, remembering the human traffickers who tried to enlist the liberated mill girls into going overseas for jobs that were not what they said they'd be.

"The factory recruiters, too," Shota added. "The ones who talked those girls into the mills in the first place."

"Have a look at this, Akira-san." Renko picked up one of her timbers and passed it to him. "This is what we did. I think this might work. I don't dare try to get any closer to the final shape."

Akira hefted the rough length and grinned. "This is exactly what I was hoping for! Kukanko-san, look at this." He knelt beside the *oni*, who clutched her damaged *shamisen*.

"With the tools I showed you and this piece of wood, I think I can make you a new neck"—

"*Sao*," Kukanko interrupted.

"*Sao*, then," Akira continued. "One that will work. I'd like to take this and your *shamisen* home with me so I can have my father look at it. He can make sure I do it right."

"That's a good idea," Shota said. "Then I can learn, too. The woodcarving skills are the same as we use on boats, aren't they?"

"Kukanko-san," Renko warned as she saw tension build in the *oni's* arms and back. Though she was just a child, it was clear that she was stronger than any of them, except Renko in the dragon form she did not want to assume. They did not want to upset this child.

"Don't worry," Renko told her when she had Kukanko's attention. "*Sencho-sama* carves beautiful things. He can make it right if anybody can. We will bring your *shamisen* back, I promise. You know that part's up to me, and I will do it, because I have promised."

Reluctantly, Kukanko, never taking her gaze off Renko, passed the *shamisen* to Akira.

Renko smiled at her, nodded, then looked at Azuki.

"Well?" she said. "Did you manage to find out where they get their *shamisen*?"

"The *Goze-sama* said they are expensive."

Renko shrugged her disdain. "Expensive" was meaningless to her.

"*Geisha* play them as well as *tono* or *bosama*. You didn't hear this part, I don't think," she said to her brother. "*Tono* are men musicians who aren't necessarily blind or aren't itinerant. They have their own guild. Blind men musicians who are itinerant are called *bosama*—like the first wandering musicians who were actually monks."

"Like Jion-*ama*?" Shota recalled.

"We met an *uta-bikune*," Azuki explained to the *oni*. "That's a Buddhist nun who teaches by singing. I suppose that's like the first wandering musicians, only modern. Jion-*ama's* group has a Temple where they live."

"But where do they get their instruments?" Renko's patience was wearing thin.

"I didn't get an exact place, beyond the capital." Azuki grinned. "*Geisha* play *shamisen*."

"And our aunt's friend Sachiko-san dresses *geisha*." Shota said to the *oni*, and Renko nodded, understanding.

"If Sachiko-san doesn't already know where to get new *shamisen*, she can easily find out," Renko explained to Kukanko.

"And we're going to the capital next week!"

24

"The Exhibition is open every day," Otohime explained to Irtysh. "Businesses have started keeping a Western schedule, some of them, so they have a seven-day repeating schedule, and one of the days, most things are closed."

The two dragons rested on their respective custom seats in Irtysh's audience chamber. They planned to jump into the Lake of Jewels once they had discussed their trip to the Exhibition.

"They do that in Yekaterinburg," Irtysh nodded. "Many places also close on the day before that, the one they call Saturday, at least in the afternoons. It has something to do with their religion, I think."

"Yes," Otohime replied. "I don't understand it myself. We have festivals connected with the seasons—and we have lots of seasons to celebrate— or the phases of the moon, or sometimes historic events. It isn't done just by counting days. Although *Sensei* says the government and businesses are starting to do that, with the schools and the postal schedules."

"That means that more people can go to the Exhibition on those leisure days."

"Yes. So we will not."

"Will *Sensei* go with us?"

She twitched her whiskers and shook her head slightly. "He claims he cannot close the school. I think he'd like to go to the Exhibition, but I think he just doesn't want to go with all of us. He thinks we're going to get into trouble."

Irtysh shifted and rewrapped his tail. He didn't think that was *Sensei's* reasoning at all. He and Ryuujin had discussed it. *Sensei* was not happy at the extent to which dragons were meddling in human affairs, especially after Ryuujin and Rizantona had agreed they would not.

This dissatisfaction had been brought to a head by Irtysh's assumption of his human simulacrum and his public appearance in human society while using it. Ryuujin also had one, but he didn't use it to mix socially with humans, at least not so far. He just used it so he wouldn't scare everyone when he engaged in necessary business involving his children. Or friends, though *Sensei* tended to forget that part. *Sensei* had to admit, though, that Ryuujin's involvement in his children's lives showed proper parental feeling.

Irtysh, however, used his human guise to satisfy his own curiosity about humans and about the dual-natured. Humans were propagating and expanding at a breakneck speed and both Ryuujin and Rizantona thought dragons might need to take as yet undetermined steps in their role as planetary protectors and managers of various aspects of the planetary ecology.

As Prince of a large domain, Irtysh had an interest in that, of course, but his real interest was in Otohime, who was indeed truly dual-natured. Since she was entirely human in one of her natures, he decided he better learn as much as possible about humans. The only consort, as far as he knew, she had ever had was a human. She had been happy with him, Irtysh thought, even though he had left her and the ending had been tragic—for Otohime, at least. Irtysh was much sharper in his thoughts about her dead consort: his death had been his own fault and Irtysh would waste no sympathy on him, wherever he might have gone in the vast universe.

"We will do our best to avoid getting into trouble," Irtysh said, putting aside thoughts of repairing his relationship with *Sensei* for the moment. "We know the four older dual-natured youngsters have learned how to behave in human society. Madame Tsuruko is good at it, and, of course, you have a great deal of experience at it. I think I can manage to pass well enough, especially since I look Western and that will excuse some gaffes. Lady Noriko is not only human but our social expert. The problem is with the children, and since both Susu and Kichiro will have to remain human"—

Otohime laughed. "That's what would be the problem, wouldn't it? Tsuruko-san will have Kichiro-chan and I will keep a firm hold on Susu-chan. It will look perfectly natural for us to stay close to each other. Renko-san and Azuki-san will want to stay fairly close to us, so we can discuss the machines." She smiled. "The boys will want to stay close to you. They both quite admire you, Irtysh."

Irtysh raised what would have been eyebrows and twitched the tip of his tail. The corners of his mouth turned up with a hint of a smile.

"You will arrange their clothes, won't you?" Otohime said. "They both enjoy elegance. If they're in Western wear, like you, it will look quite natural for them to attend you. And behave as you do. That will keep them out of trouble."

He thought about it for a second. "The way you have us sorted, those who would have a difficult time leaving instantly on their own, if necessary, will be within easy reach of those of us who can."

"Yes. Lady Noriko is torn. She wants to see the Exhibition, but she also has her own errands to run. I thought I'd drop her off on my way. I would like to stop and see her martial arts mistress if I can. I understand she has beautiful wooden furnishings in the Chinese style. Tsuruko-san can go with Renko-san, or with me, as she prefers."

"I'd offer to do it, or at least go along, but I think this invitation would be better coming from you. Perhaps you might arrange to take *Sensei* and Lady Noriko on a separate visit?"

Otohime knew Irtysh was not one of *Sensei's* favorite people at the moment though she was not nearly as sure about why as Irtysh was. He seemed to want to remedy that, though.

"I'd be happy to do it," Otohime said, "but I have a better idea. I think Father would like to go, and they are all friends." She smiled as sweetly as a dragon could at Irtysh. Irtysh was not sure how *Sensei* would react to Ryuujin making this offer, but Ryuujin was not only an adult dragon, he was King of the East, and could presumably handle himself in any circumstances.

"Ask him, then," Irtysh suggested. "Are you ready to swim?"

"I'll race you!" Otohime, lissome in her Eastern Dragon form, captured a head start for herself. Irtysh rolled off his throne, eager to catch her.

***

Noriko's husband came to her *dojo* after she dismissed her afternoon class. Yuta liked things under control, tidy and orderly, without too many surprises. Unfortunately, since he first met his niece, his life had been full of surprises and difficulties. While many of those surprises, like his wife, were wonderful, others—not so much Renko-chan and

Susu-chan, of whom he was fond, but dragons in general—had become overwhelming in the ways they upset his life.

Noriko sat at her desk, making entries in her account book. A basket of *kaki*, persimmons, of an early variety they didn't grow in their garden, was beside her, a gift from a student's family, no doubt. She did have set rates, but people paid when they could and with what they had. This student's family would get ample credit for the persimmons.

"I brought your letters," he said, holding them out to her. The afternoon post had been left at the school and since the household young people were off somewhere or other, he brought the household mail up himself.

"Oh, good," Noriko said, taking the letters from her husband and gesturing for him to sit. "Thank you. Can you stay for tea? That way, I can read them and you will know what they say as soon as I do."

"By all means. Let me see to the tea. You open your mail." Yuta poked up the fire, made sure the kettle was full and moved the basket of persimmons to the door. He'd take them to Hanako when he went down to the house. She'd be glad of them as soon as she could get them, he thought. He started imagining the things she could do with them. The young people could assist her with stringing extras to dry for the winter, since there were plenty.

Things were working out well for his niece, he thought. She had much more free time, and she seemed to be enjoying it.

Everyone was busy with the refugee project, though, and Azuki was, too. She copied and cataloged her patterns assiduously for others to use, but still she had more free time than she had before. Yuta was glad of that. In the modern world, she was young to be as committed to her craft as she had been, he thought. Especially for a girl of her class, though that wasn't supposed to matter anymore, and one who was pursuing her education. Surely, though, normal apprentices following a classical pattern in learning a trade or craft were just as busy as Azuki had been, maybe more so. He wondered how those children—for some of them were very young indeed—were keeping up with their educations now that primary school was compulsory. He'd have to look into that.

"Husband?"

Yuta started. The whistle signaled the kettle was nearly boiling over. Quickly, he pulled it off the fire and poured water into the pot his laughing wife had prepared.

"I was distracted," he said, sitting down across from her.

"No matter. The tea will be ready in a moment. But I have good news!"

She placed cups and small plates on the table, looked for a persimmon to cut for them, saw Yuta had moved the basket and abandoned that idea in favor of the tin of cookies that Hanako kept filled. This she opened and set before her husband.

"Mistress Feng will be able to see me the day I requested, and Sachiko-san asked me to dine with her and stay the night!"

"How will you travel?"

"With Otohime," Noriko said, as if it were the most usual thing in the world. Yuta guessed that for them it was.

"Otohime would like to see Mistress Feng's Chinese cabinets, so I asked," Noriko continued. "Mistress Feng said I could bring any of my friends with me if I desired." Noriko patted the letter. "Otohime's title opens many doors." She smiled.

"After that?" Yuta smiled back.

"They'll join the others, and I'll walk to Sachiko-san's." Her face became animated. "Unless I can take one of the horse-drawn carriages! There are several routes in commercial service now, Sachiko-san says. One runs close to her house, but I don't know if there is one near the *dojo*."

Yuta laughed at her enthusiasm. He, too, liked the wonders of the modern world. "I hope you can find one. Now that it's cooler, we should ride our horses more often."

"I'd like that. The refugee project is overwhelming." Suddenly her face turned serious. "When it's over"—she did not have to elaborate on what; they both knew she meant the final bloody end of the Satsuma Rebellion—"do you think we'll have a further onslaught of refugees?"

"It's hard to say, but I don't think so. The Imperial forces will take care of their own, I suppose, and take them home."

"That's one of the advantages of a centralized military," Noriko said with a nod.

"There aren't going to be any of the rebels left," Yuta said.

"None?" Her face twisted.

"They'll fight to the last man."

They looked at each other, the sadness they felt unbearable and unspeakable.

"At least there won't be more refugees," Noriko said at last, her face drawn.

"Yes," Yuta said, rising to leave. "At least there is that."

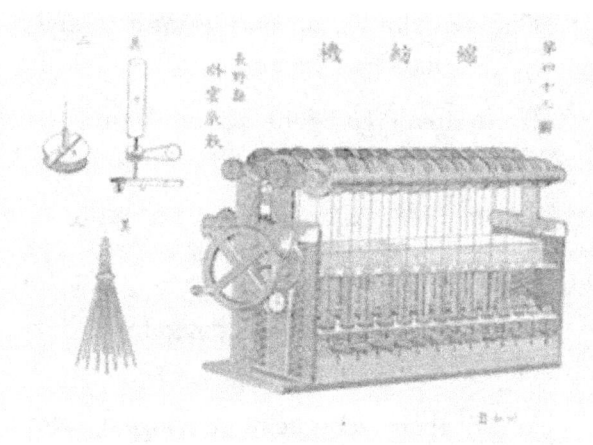

Tachi Gaun's Cotton Spinning Machine (1877),
Attr. Kano

25

Azuki and Renko sailed what was now Minoru's boat on a glorious late summer afternoon. The winds were light to moderate, out of the east, so they sailed roughly northeast, away from the shore. Eventually, they'd head southeast, then turn to head downwind, directly towards home. They had no destination, no goal, not even much of a plan. This was just for fun. Azuki rejoiced. It had been a while since she had much time for pure fun.

Akira sat on the deck, working on the new *sao* for Kukanko's *shamisen* under Minoru-*sencho*'s supervision and Shota's curious gaze. Shota was supposed to be watching the trolling line off the stern of the boat and helping Renko and Azuki as needed, but he was curious about everything, his help wasn't needed and the trolling line was quiet.

On the other hand, the making of a new part for the *shamisen* fascinated him. He'd heard Renko explain what was wrong with their repair. He kept scooting forward in the cockpit to get closer so he could see better. While he could understand what everybody had talked about, he also wanted to see if he could see it. So far, he was disappointed. Minoru pointed out the grain of the wood, but it looked to Shota like the flaws in the repair were too small to be seen with human eyes.

While sailing wasn't a passion of Renko's, it was clear to her it was one of Azuki's. Renko made her own air currents when she flew. Lacking all but vestigial wings, that was how Asian dragons managed flight. Masters of wind and water, Asian dragons bent both elements to their liking. Azuki, like Western dragons and birds, captured the wind and used her wings to ride it, playing with it, teasing it and using it to get where she wanted to go. Sailing was like that.

Renko could manipulate the air currents as she pleased, if there was a need to do so, but she understood that was not the point of what they were doing now. When they were younger, she'd tease Shota with pinpoint storms and focused gusts, challenging his sailing skills, until *Sencho-sama* made them stop. How could they both have missed that he'd known what she was and what the two of them were up to, all the time? She hoped they had grown up enough to learn caution. They'd been lucky *Sencho-sama* had an open mind and liked adventure. Another kind of person might have made trouble.

Sailing like this, simply helping Azuki run the boat when necessary, Renko started enjoying herself. She was beginning to see that there were other ways to enjoy the interplay of wind and water than through brute force.

Azuki found herself happy all the way through. She continued to make progress on everything she had to do, but she was no longer overwhelmed. She had time to enjoy the things she simply liked, sailing being one of them. She had missed this so much. Her partnership with Lily, her horse, was another. Lily's relationship with time was not a human one, Azuki had come to realize, any more than Renko's was. Lily was happy to see her when she saw her, but didn't really miss Azuki when she was gone. They had times together and times apart, and it was all fine with Lily. The whole subject of time was interesting, but it was far too complicated to think about on such a beautiful late summer day.

The small season had just changed from "Heat Starts to Die Down" to "Rice Ripens," marking the end of *Shosho*, the larger season of "Manageable Heat" that was part of summer. Next would come *Hakuro*, "White Dew," the very end of summer, the last fifteen days before the Equinox. Japan enjoyed its climate. In addition to the four main seasons divided by the solstices and the equinoxes, there were twenty-four small seasons of about fifteen days each. Those were divided into three periods, each about five days. Anyone who wished could look for the changes and revel in them. Azuki did so as she watched the wind ruffle the water and thought about their upcoming trip to the First International

Industrial Exhibition. Even the few days remaining before their departure would make the weather more pleasant and the trip more fun.

"I read today that there are several cotton spinning machines on exhibit," she said to Renko as she pulled the large tiller to follow a tiny wind shift. As they were simply sailing, well off shore and with no set goal, Azuki just steered to the wind and left the sails alone.

"How will we know which one we need?" Renko asked.

"That's one reason why we have to go," Azuki said. "We need to look at them to see which will work best for family operations working as part of a cooperative."

"The way Kojiro-san's fishing boats do." Renko nodded. Tsuruko-san's husband had been instrumental in starting a fish-canning enterprise at the harbor near their home where he moored his boat.

This new kind of cooperative business allowed individuals to join together to reach wider markets so they could all prosper. While large concerns, like the Yamada-Morimoto mining consortium, formed by Anko and Toshio's respective families, ran from the top down and the workers were employees, the cooperatives used a different model.

Renko was fuzzy on how the mineral rights had been allocated, because they had been part of

Eitaro's fief, but the *Daimyo* and the Emperor of course had interests, since Lord Eitaro had owed allegiance, and taxes, to them. Then everything had changed as *Daimyo* domains had turned into provinces, and at that point she simply gave up trying to follow it. The important thing was that Anko-*sama*, their friend; her family and now her children, were well provided for, and very able to help with the cotton cooperative Otohime had thought up as a way to benefit the refugees from the Satsuma Rebellion.

"You're the one who is good with machines," Azuki said. "I think you will be able to tell which one will work the best and be easiest to maintain."

"I'll certainly try. Shota-san's a good designer, too. He sees things from a large perspective. My brother's the one who's going to be making them, so his observations will be important."

"Prince Irtysh is good at everything," Shota interjected.

Akira looked up with a grin. "He's going to make our clothes, Otohime said."

"Not make them, exactly," Shota said.

"Not mine, anyway. He's going to have to make yours." Shota was the only one of them who could not make his own clothes every time he changed. This was a sore spot with him. He always showed up in the rough peasant wear he currently had on, unless he took fairly complicated steps to transport other clothing with him. Even then, he had to make arrangements or he ended up leaving his human clothing behind when he became a sparrow.

Fortunately, he'd become pretty good at this.

"Akira-san?" A new voice called from above. Shota spotted Susu hovering overhead and the water ruffled around the boat as the wind shifted with Susu's hover. "Brother said I should bring this to you!"

"I think you're fully accepted as a friend, as far as Susu-chan is concerned." Akira grinned at his adopted father. It was Susu who barged in and ended up taking them to and from Kokura, where Minoru was able to enter their new surname— Kaito—in the Shrine's official family register and make his adoption of Akira final.

"You can land, Susu-chan," Minoru called. "As a human!" He roared as the small dragon prepared to touch down. Susu was small only by dragon standards. He wasn't as big as the boat, but he was getting there.

"I can't, Sencho-*sama*," Susu called. "I've got to give this to Akira-san!"

"Can you hover without making a lot of wind?" Akira asked. His vocal tone was normal but he also spoke mentally.

"I don't know!" Susu sounded dubious but he floated gently down.

It wasn't gentle enough. The wind from his hover slammed into the sails. The boat yawed alarmingly.

"Release the sheets," Azuki cried, and Renko rushed to do so as Azuki pushed the big tiller over.

"Go up," Minoru, Akira and Shota yelled as one. Susu increased his altitude and though his wash roiled the water, at least the boat straightened and balanced.

"Let me come to you," Akira called. The air around him shivered and he became an eagle.

"Be right back," he said mentally and took off.

Minoru thought he'd never get over the thrill of seeing Akira change form. All of the wonders of the world he'd seen during his many years at sea he thought he'd never see again. Then he had the chance to sail with Shota, and enjoyed his own amusement at realizing what the boy and his sister really were. When they ran into the *Ume-boze*, and he'd thought he'd lost Shota, then found him again with the help of the dragon he soon realized was Renko, he knew he had a new lease on life.

He'd clutched his amazement and his enjoyment close until he had to reveal it when he wanted to adopt Akira, and now, it seemed to him, that his life was getting better—when he had thought it would settle into stultifying boredom at the bottom of a flask as he aged.

"Hold still, Susu-chan," Akira said mentally. "I'm going to come close and snatch that on the fly. Let it go when I say!"

Susu hovered. Akira swooped to grab what looked like a pole from Susu's outer wing claw. Akira found, to his relief, that it wasn't too big or too heavy for him to manage easily, but he didn't know what it was, either. He circled back to land, forcing both Minoru and Shota to duck under his wide wings, setting what he'd brought with him down before changing back. Minoru picked it up.

"You can come down now, Susu-chan," Akira called. "Do that thing you've learned about changing and moving at the same time, so you land as a boy. Can you?"

"I can!"

And there he was, Susu in his human form as a small Japanese boy. He was picking up some of his elder brother's fashion sense, for he was attired in work clothes exactly like Shota's. Akira and Minoru were slightly better dressed, but not by much, and neither were Renko and Azuki, because they were out, working, on the boat.

"What is it?" Akira asked.

Minoru had picked it up and looked it over carefully. "It's what you are trying to make—the *sao* of a *shamisen*." He looked sharply at Susu. "Did your brother make this?"

"Yes!" Susu nodded his enthusiasm. "Sister needs to look at it, too." Susu's physical human speech was improving quickly, but his mind, as usual, raced ahead of his physical development. He switched to mental speech as Minoru passed the *sao* to Renko.

"What do you think, Renko-san?" he asked. "Do we need to make more?"

"I think," she said slowly, turning it over in her hands as she probed it with her dragon mind, "this just might work. It's kind of big, though. We won't know until we try it."

"I made it bigger," Susu said. "So Akira-san could grab it easily."

Renko shot her little brother a sharp glance. Susu did things without thinking, but came up with ideas that never would have occurred to her when she was his age. She wondered what she might have done when younger if she hadn't been so afraid of their mother. But that was long ago. What she needed to do now, she told herself, was not worry about what might have been and go forward instead.

"Have Akira-san and I just wasted our time, then?" Minoru's tone was good humored enough so that they could tell he wasn't serious, but Akira took it seriously.

"I don't think we have." He ran his hands over the *sao* he had almost finished. "If it works, we have

251

two, only the one Susu-chan brought is bigger. That gives me an idea. Can we take these to Kukanko-san tomorrow?"

26

"Y ou're going when, exactly?" Yuta asked his wife at the breakfast table. He peered over his spectacles as he looked at her around a newspaper.

Noriko smiled. It was hard for her to conceal her excitement. While she was more than grateful for her life here, she had enjoyed her time in the capital. All the hustle and bustle, the art and fashion, the learning and ideas—she would enjoy seeing it again. She had missed Sachiko, too. Letters were good, but sometimes not quite enough.

"We're leaving the day after tomorrow, after breakfast," she said, "and I will return the following evening, or maybe even the next day."

Yuta's brow wrinkled. "You're closing the *dojo* for the latter part of the week, then?"

"I think so." Noriko smiled. "My older students can find some casual work easily at this time of year. I'll suggest they go help with the housing for the refugee project; Lord Toshio can tell them where to go and who to see. They'll be glad of the opportunity."

Noriko's older students not only had to pay *dojo* fees but also had to support themselves. A few were local, but many came great distances. A *soke* with Noriko's skills, some of them only rumored, was a rare find. Several students had found places with families who needed a spare pair of hands on their farm or in their business sporadically and were willing to exchange help for room and board. Other students lodged at Temples, again working for their keep, finding the monastic lifestyle harmonious with the discipline of martial arts. The few who had means rented lodgings, though usually inexpensive ones. Because of their training schedules, Noriko's students could not take regular jobs, but there was enough of a need for casual labor to keep her students going.

"What about the children?"

Noriko's afternoons were occupied by a class of children who came up after the primary school closed.

"I thought of talking to Sato-*sensei* about them." The local Buddhist priest taught at the primary school to supplement his Temple's income since Shinto was now ascendant. "This would be a good time of year for some nature study. Any children who couldn't simply go home right after school ended could stay with him, if he has time."

Yuta nodded. He pulled off his glasses and set them down. They made it easier to read, but disturbed his vision for anything further away. "That sounds like a good plan. He'll enjoy it."

"I'll compensate him for his time, of course," Noriko said.

"He'll probably want it as a donation to the Temple," Yuta said with a smile.

"And I'll probably have to insist on doing that much." Noriko smiled back. Sato-*sensei* was the kindest of men and truly enjoyed the children.

It was a shame he had been so old when the Emperor decreed Buddhist clergy could marry. He wasn't that much older than Yuta and Noriko, but he was too old to easily find a wife whose life would be compatible with his work as a Temple priest in such a rural area, though he might have found one had he lived in a city.

Yuta smiled at Noriko. They had met in Tokyo, after both of them had given up on the possibility of marriage, Noriko because of her work as a *kunoichi* and her continued training, and Yuta because he had been part of the clergy until his resignation to take care of his unusual niece and nephew.

Noriko returned his smile. As a *kunoichi*, she might have hoped for an arranged marriage to an older man someday, perhaps a widower, perhaps while she was still young enough to have children.

Intelligence gathering would be her school's prime objective in arranging such a marriage. The collapse of the Shogunate and the Meiji restoration had left Noriko jobless and unable to connect with her school. Her injuries left her unable to bear children. She had turned her attention to other parts of her life, until she had the fortune to meet Yuta—and the wisdom not to kill him. They were both pleased with the result.

"We'll only be gone a day, I think, Uncle," Azuki said.

"We can come home for the night, even if we need to go back the next day," Renko explained.

"What about Tsuruko-san and Otohime?" Noriko wanted to know. "They'll be with me to start with but they'll be meeting you later. They'll have Kichiro-chan and Susu-chan with them."

Azuki shrugged. Tsuruko-san would want to come home to her husband, surely, something that didn't need saying.

"Sister will take her home when she wants to go," Renko said. "Or I can. What my sister is going to do, I don't know."

"Go off with Prince Irtysh," Shota sniggered.

Yuta replied icily. "They will have much to discuss about the kind of machines they'll want for the project." He did not want to hear about Irtysh's and Otohime's personal relationship.

"Brother's children should meet my sister, too."

That sent Noriko's head spinning just a little. She dropped her gaze then let a glance slip sideways to her husband. Familial relationships among humans could be complicated, what with multiple wives and official concubines still existing among the highest classes. The Western disapproval of those arrangements had led to a precipitous decline in such relationships and changes in laws and customs. Social relationships were being allowed to evolve naturally for the most part. It was more of a question of not entering into new extraneous yet official relationships rather than dissolving existing ones.

Dragon affairs seemed slightly more convoluted, since dragons were all independent adults with responsibilities to fulfill and who provided for themselves. She wasn't quite sure how they provided for their children, but didn't feel she could ask. Perhaps her husband could inquire of Ryuujin. Men—males, rather—seemed to take such things much more lightly.

"Today we're going to take Kukanko-san the new *sao* from yesterday," Shota announced. "After school. We have two, and two blanks."

"Blanks?" Yuta frowned at the word.

"Yes, Uncle." Shota grinned. "Renko-san made some rough lumber to be carved. Sencho-*sama*

257

showed Akira-san how to make a *sao* from the lumber. It was almost done when Susu-chan showed up with one Prince Irtysh had made. Only Susu-chan made it a little bigger so Akira-san could grab it easily."

"He was an eagle," Renko explained.

"And Susu-chan was a dragon." Azuki thought that clarified things until she saw her aunt begin to giggle behind her hand.

"Susu-chan's wings were creating air currents that were knocking the boat around, so Akira-san told him to hover higher and then flew up to take it from him."

"My little brother couldn't figure out how to land as a human and still keep hold of the *sao*," Renko added. "Making the *sao* bigger was a good solution. Susu-chan is clever, and he never knows what he can't do."

"That gives us one regular-sized one, one larger one, and two of the uncarved ones Renko-san made. Akira-san said he has an idea of what to do with them."

Noriko could contain her laughter no longer. "I'm sorry for laughing, but listen to us, Husband! What we think of as normal conversation would utterly baffle anyone else!"

Yuta started laughing, too. "Or else they would think us mad." He looked at his niece. She could usually be counted on to be responsible. "Just be back for Buddhist practice and dinner."

After school, Akira fetched what he needed from home, told Minoru where he was going, and joined his three friends to walk up the hill to Renko's field.

"Why are you bringing tools?" Azuki asked, noticing he had not only the two *sao* and the two *sao* blanks but also the cloth bundle of tools. "Kukanko-san has a few."

Akira hefted them. "These are better. When I told *'To-san* what I wanted to do, he said I could take these and loan them to Kukanko-san if she needs them."

"What do you want to do?" Shota asked.

"Tell you when we get there," Akira said. Shota started to speak but Renko cut him off.

"Change and get into my hair, Shota-san," she said. "We'll all find out sooner if we hurry and hear it all at once."

Renko brought them in where they'd last met with the *oni*. All but Shota were in their human forms, because Azuki and Akira had linked their arms with Renko's. Shota had ridden in her hair as a sparrow. He could have ridden on her shoulder, he supposed, but he usually rode tucked in her crown when she was in dragon form. Riding in her hair meant that if she changed, that's where he'd find himself.

Azuki carried the blanks and Akira carried the finished *sao* and the tools.

"Kukanko-san," he called. "I have some *sao* for you to try."

"Akira-san?" The *oni* emerged from the woods. "One of the *tebiki* has gone off with a boy. We have to be careful. There are humans around."

"And we're not?" Shota snorted.

"Not all the time," Kukanko correctly pointed out. "Did you make those?"

Taller even than Akira, Kukanko nonetheless regarded him with awe.

"We all did," Akira told her. "Come on, let's go sit down and see if these fit."

"You were here when I made the wood," Renko said as they shuffled through the dry grass to avoid leaving a path. "Then Akira-san and his father worked on making this new *sao*. My elder brother made that one," she said, pointing to the heftier one, "but my little brother made it bigger when he brought it."

They all sat down and began reassembling the broken *shamisen*.

"Akira-san's is the one that fits, the one that's the right size," Kukanko strummed and plucked the strings when they were done. "Listen! Oh, listen! It works!"

"That's excellent!" Azuki said. "That means you can return this *shamisen* to its rightful place."

"Yes, but I wish I could play it." The *oni* sighed as she put the instrument down onto its wrappings.

"Hold this one in your hand," Akira told Kukanko, handing her the *sao* Susu had modified. "How does that fit?"

Kukanko held it and shifted it. She slid her odd hand up and down it. "I want to put it together with the rest of it." Quickly, with surprising dexterity, she disassembled the one instrument and reassembled it with the larger *sao* in place.

"This is better!" She strummed the instrument. "It's longer and bigger but it sounds fine! It's still not big enough for me."

"I thought that might be so," Akira said, taking the *shamisen* from her and reassembling it in its original form. He set it aside. Nobody noticed the child peering at them from behind another tree.

Susu giggled as quietly as he could manage. He was not happy that his sister and his friends had gone off without him. He'd already helped on their project and he really wanted to see the *oni!*

"I have a much better idea," Akira told the *oni.* "The first thing I want to do is make the other parts for this *sao*, this bigger one, so we'll have a second complete instrument. I think Renko-san can help us there."

"Now that I've seen what my brother can do," Renko affirmed, "all I have to do is ask him if I have any questions."

Susu almost burst out from the trees, but he couldn't really talk as a human, not as well as he wanted, and although the *oni* looked very strange, his sister was in her human form, so it would probably be rude to appear as a dragon.

"I asked Uncle about *shamisen* generally and we looked it up," Azuki said. "Aunt knows something about *shamisen*, too."

When had his sister managed that? Shota wondered.

"Aunt wrote some things down for us," Azuki continued. "There are different sizes for different uses, but there's no reason there can't be more, I don't think."

"When we get this larger one finished," Akira said, "we'll have a good idea how to make a *shamisen*. You can give back the one you borrowed and give the *Goze* house an extra one for any trouble you might have caused them and then"—he held up an admonishing hand as Kukanko seemed about to speak—"we can make one that's just the right size for you!"

27

O tohime thought it might amuse Irtysh to listen to the music he was helping to create through his work on Kukanko's *shamisen*. As he had, she used air vibration—a technique she had learned from her father—to produce music as though an ensemble of musicians were present. She enjoyed Edo-Nagauta music. In form, if not sound, it resembled the "symphonies" Irtysh sometimes played for her.

This one was in the *utaimono* style, focused on the music rather than on vocal parts telling a story.

Irtysh was not sure what to make of it. The sounds seemed harsher than the music he usually enjoyed, and were often discordant to his ears. He thought the scale that formed the foundation of the music was different from the one he was used to. Human music was always less round and deep in tone than that which came naturally to dragons. The harmonies were different—then he suddenly recoiled as his former consort, Galina's mother, perhaps the very last dragon he wanted to see right now, appeared before him.

Otohime, too, started as the Western dragon materialized in Irtysh's audience chamber. She was a beautiful snowy silver in color, shading to pale grey underneath, and she was staring at Otohime.

"Is it convenient?" she said. "Your Royal Highness."

"You don't have to call me that, Agniya"—

"I wasn't talking to you," the visitor said, twisting her long glistening neck to glare at Irtysh and treat him to a minor display of flame. "Is it convenient?"

"Of course," Irtysh said. "I will always welcome you."

Irtysh, though completely in possession of his manners, was definitely not happy at this intrusion. Though his words were warm and his voice liquid, his tone made of them a formality while he almost invisibly collected himself for explanations he did not care to make.

He huffed a little smoke and turned smoothly to Otohime, letting a polite introduction make clear who was who and their respective ranks. "Your Royal Highness, may I present the Lady Agniya. She lives closer to you than to me, governing a sub-domain near the home of our daughter, Galina. Agniya, Otohime—'hime' is princess in the language of her land—comes from the archipelago to the east of you. They call it Japan. She rules that under her father, Ryuujin, the King of the East, as I rule here under my mother."

"It is a pleasure to meet you," Otohime responded gently, herself relying on conventional courtesy to smooth what was shaping up to be an awkward situation. "I have yet to meet your daughter, but I would like to."

"Have you met any of Irtysh's children?" Agniya asked sweetly. "I know they are anxious to meet you."

Otohime shot an amused glance at Irtysh, who was practically squirming.

"Agniya, I don't think this is the time"—

"What is that caterwauling?" Agniya interrupted.

"I beg your pardon." The music had changed to a vocal duet that Otohime had to admit might sound discordant to someone unused to Japanese music. She extinguished the sound.

"We were listening to music from my country," Otohime continued. "I wanted His Royal Highness to hear some of the music from the East, just as we sometimes listen to music from the West."

"Galina told me her father is helping to repair a musical instrument from your land."

"He is, yes. While that is a kindness, it is not the most important thing he has been doing. He and his children have been assisting my sister and brother in a project of mine to help resettle humans in my lands uprooted by a civil war. He is, as you no doubt know, very gifted in fabricating material goods." She flicked her whiskers at the rows of looms standing by the Lake of Jewels. "I understand that His Royal Highness's children are almost as skilled as he is." It was Renko and Susu who had told her most of this, of course, not Irtysh, and she wondered why he hadn't.

She was glad to see Irtysh turn slightly gray. Did he think he could keep his family a secret?

"You have a sister and brother who are working on this project?"

Otohime was amused to note that Agniya, who might be expected to omit the titles and honors of the father of her child, also avoided her own. That was why Otohime underlined Irtysh's.

"It's a complicated situation," Irtysh interjected grouchily.

"Not so very," Otohime silenced him with a flick of the tendrils above her eyes. "It's quite simple, really. His Royal Highness's mother, Her Majesty, Queen Rizantona, and my father, His Majesty, King Ryuujin, have two children in common. They are, therefore, both His Royal Highness's and my young siblings, although he and are I quite unrelated. Surely Princess Galina mentioned Renko-hime and Prince Suoh-Sugaar?"

"Susu," Irtysh clarified. Otohime and Agniya glared at him. Wisely, he shut up.

"Oh." Agniya said to Otohime. "Susu. That child is a bundle of trouble." Then she smiled and became quite pretty, her crystalline fangs glinting brilliantly. "He is quite delightful trouble, though. I knew he was Her Majesty's youngest, but I didn't know his father. He likes to get Galina to come swim with him."

"He does enjoy the Lake of Jewels." Otohime had not known that Susu had relationships with his elder brother's children. And why should she? she chided herself. She still wasn't entirely sure about her relationship with Irtysh. Though he had not exactly hidden his children from her, he had not introduced them and did not speak of them. That distressed her. Especially since his children were working on her refugee project.

"I would like to meet all of them," Otohime continued. "From what I have seen here, their work is beautiful. Do you also practice the arts of chemistry?" That was what Irtysh called his feats with matter.

"I grow diamonds," Agniya said. Humans had first discovered the massive diamond reserves in her territory some fifty years previously, but had yet to start exploiting them on any scale. She was keeping a careful eye on the situation. She was not fond of humans. There were few of them in her Arctic domain and she wanted to keep it that way. "Do you like gemstones in your country?"

Otohime carefully kept her mental attention off her watermelon tourmaline pendant, the one that Irtysh had made her, the one she always wore. She hoped the set of her forelimbs hid it from Agniya's view.

"They are not traditional with us in Japan," she said, "but of course my father's empire includes China, Siam and India, and in Siam and India, particularly, gemstones are valued and often worn. My mother enjoys them." Her mother did enjoy them, in passing, but preferred imitating their forms and colors in the glaciers and blizzards she created. Her consort liked them more, bringing them to her so she could copy them in clouds and ice. Sometimes he even returned them to where he got them.

"We Eastern dragons work with air and water," Otohime said.

"If you would care to come visit my Diamond Fortress and see my work with minerals, I could make the occasion an opportunity to present my daughter and my step-children to you," Agniya said. "Galina is the youngest. I helped raise the older four after their mother left."

"That would be very generous of you, Agniya," Irtysh said. He was going to have to find a way out of this. He did not want Otohime to hear his familial history from his former consort! "They are all most fond of you."

"They're going to have more work to do here very soon," Otohime said. She liked the way Agniya was maneuvering around Irtysh. Sometimes he seemed just too powerful, and she didn't like him keeping secrets from her.

"Soon we will attend an International Industrial Exhibition in my country," Otohime explained. "There we will be examining new machines that will be used in conjunction with those"—she flicked a whisker at the looms—"to make a fabric the humans of my land can exchange with other humans, to provide themselves with a livelihood. Their lives have been badly disrupted by a local war. I want to help them rebuild."

"Why?" Agniya asked. It was a reasonable question from a Western dragon. Or any dragon, for that matter. Dragons normally paid little attention to other sentient or sapient beings. Their concerns lay elsewhere.

"I feel some responsibility for them," Otohime said. Surely, Agniya knew this much! "You may not be aware of it, but some of us, including Renko-hime, Prince Suoh-Sugaar and me, possess a dual nature. We are dragons, yes, but we are also human. We are truly dual-natured; it is not merely a guise we can put on when we wish. This means our relationship to humans is a bit different from yours. I did not realize this until recently"—

"Galina was right!" Agniya interrupted. She whirled and directed a flame at Irtysh, who ducked out of reach. "She said Renko and Susu could turn into humans, and that was bad enough, but she also said you, her *batya,* were playing at it. And there! I see that!" She shot a jet of flame at Irtysh's human scale Western room. "You want to turn your children into half-humans! Just like"—

She caught herself. She could be as furious as she wanted at the father of her daughter, but it would be a mistake to offend the daughter of the Dragon King, half-human or no.

She turned on her tail to face Otohime and bowed. Even if it was perfunctory, it was still a proper bow.

"Excuse me, Your Royal Highness," she said, and vanished.

28

"It's organic," Renko whispered mentally to Azuki. "It's animal, animal skin, I think. I'm not sure what to do about it. I don't know how to get it and I've never made it." Surprisingly, she found herself distressed by the feel of the skin when she went into it deeply. She did not want to examine that feeling too closely. It didn't seem like it would be hard to make, technically, she thought. Or would it?

"You do make it, though," Azuki hissed back. "Every time you wear Western clothes, you make the matching shoes. Those are leather, and leather is processed animal skin. We don't use it much, and the Eta people are the ones who process it, but it does exist here."

While Akira and Shota sorted wood pieces that Renko had made or they had found, Renko and Azuki examined the now-repaired *shamisen* so that Renko could figure out how to make the non-wood parts of the instrument. These included the strings. Those were silk of different sizes, and those Renko found simple to duplicate. She'd never had a problem with silk, even though it came from insects. The *bachi*—the pick or plectrum—was made of *bekkou*, tortoise shell. Renko had fabricated shells before, but there was something about this shell that bothered her, too.

"There's something different and strange about the *bachi*, too," she told Azuki. "I'm going to go ask Brother." Without further ado, Renko took the *shamisen* and vanished.

Irtysh was alone, in his Western room, working on his wardrobe for the visit to the Japanese capital city and the First International Industrial Exposition. He had made a foray to a tailor in Yekaterinburg where he borrowed some fashion broadsheets, news publications, and patterns. He planned to return them so quickly the tailor would never know they'd been gone.

Styles had not changed much since he last looked, he was gratified to discover. This outfit, he saw, looking at a drawing of an elegant diplomat, was called a morning suit, but was specifically for day wear, all day until evening. The coat came below the hip, though it was cut away over a waistcoat in the front, but was straight across the back without tails. Otherwise, it was essentially similar to the evening wear they had all worn for the musicale in Hakata.

Shota had wanted to keep his Western evening clothing, Irtysh had been pleased to learn, and said he certainly could. Irtysh had not made those from his own substance, like he did his own clothing, so that posed no obstacle. But this suit to wear to the Exhibition was subtly different in fabric and design. Akira could simply copy Irtysh's own, once he'd made it, but Irtysh would need to make Shota's. That the fashion was Russian did not trouble him; Irtysh himself passed as Russian. Why would his Japanese escorts dress any other way?

"Brother, is it convenient?" Renko swiftly switched to human when she saw his form.

"Yes, of course. Come in." He rose—a Western conceit, since she was, in his eyes, a young woman now and not a child anymore, and that was the courteous thing to do—and gestured her in with a small half-bow. Renko wrinkled her nose but dropped a shallow curtsey before sitting in the chair he indicated and placing the *shamisen* and *bachi* before him.

"I need to make the *dou* covering and this *bachi* plectrum, Brother. They call this a skin and I think it really is an animal's skin. Azuki-san says that's the same as the leather we make when we make Western shoes. I can make it, I think. But there is something different about it, and about the *bachi*, too. That's tortoise shell, as far as I can tell. I've made shells before, but there is something different about that, too. They don't feel right, somehow, and I don't know what to do about it."

Irtysh picked up first the *shamisen* and then the *bachi*. He examined them carefully, then grimaced.

"When you make your shoes, are you copying real shoes you can see and touch?"

"No," Renko said, puzzled. "I work from photographs and drawings, like you are doing here." She waved her hand at the papers on the table.

"When you have made shell, what have you used for a model?"

"Shells I found on the beach," Renko said. "I only did it once, for a game I made for Akira-san when he was learning *kanji*."

So she had never tried to duplicate something that had been taken from an unwilling sapient donor, Irtysh thought. Actually, neither had he, but he thought he was better equipped to do this than his young sister. It wasn't going to be easy, though. This was an aspect of organic chemistry to which he had not previously given thought.

He had made wool, and he had made silk, and he had even made Western food. Sheep actually needed shearing, he recalled, and were pleased with the result, if not the process. Silk came from pre-sensate cocoons that were boiled, or cocoons hatched moths had left behind. The "meats" he had tasted were heated and seasoned as they were prepared in a process called "cooking." Possibly it was the cooking that made the difference, or the fact that he synthesized the finished dishes, so they weren't exactly natural. He could examine those ideas later, but wasn't sure he wanted to.

"Make us some tea, please, Sister," Irtysh said. "I'm afraid you'll have to add to the charcoal and fill the *samovar* with water. Give me a few minutes, if you would."

He picked up the *shamisen* and went to work. It wasn't technically difficult, he decided, as he pushed his way through. The problem was sorting through the painful emotional components that were layered throughout the physical material. Those were what he wanted to spare his sister. He felt himself break into a sweat as he teased those out. Finally, he had the purely material elements isolated. Then he was able to block off the unsettling parts and assemble the rest in what, he carefully assured himself, was the correct molecular structure. This should work. If anything, it should be better than the original, giving whatever was played on the instrument a significantly more joyous tone. He held that thought as he carefully withdrew.

He pulled his handkerchief from his sleeve to wipe his brow. What he had produced was a large irregular trapezoid of material. That should be satisfactory for their purpose. He picked up the plectrum and repeated the process. This time, it was a little easier as he knew what he was looking for. He managed to make three complete *bachi* before sighing heavily and opening his eyes.

"Are you feeling well, Brother?" Renko had made them tea. She had also stoked the fire in the fireplace, filled the wood box and resumed her seat across from him.

"Yes," he said, quickly modulating his melodious voice to make sure it didn't quiver even a fraction of a tone. "Will you please pour?"

Renko nodded, and poured for them both, him first. He sipped from his Russian-style tea glass, first sparingly, then greedily as though he were very thirsty. As he replaced the glass on the table, she picked up the pot and refilled it for him. He looked better. He'd stopped sweating, anyway.

"Are you truly all right?" There was almost no color to his face. His human skin was usually as fair as hers, with the same kind of pinky-peach undertones.

"I am." He smiled at her. "Everything is fine. Will you please do me a favor and not ask why?"

"If I can."

Irtysh produced a biscuit tin from a shelf under a small table. She took it from him and opened it while he placed small plates and napkins on the dining table where they sat. The cookies his tin contained were not like Hanako's, but they were still very good. Renko thought she'd have to take some home one day so Hanako could figure out how to make them. She took two, then held out the tin to him. He placed two cookies on his own plate.

He placed his oversized human hands on the edge of the table and looked at her solemnly. "Have a look at these, please," he said. He pushed the items he had made toward her.

Renko touched them with her own hands and then with her dragon mind.

"It's gone," she pronounced. "Whatever I was detecting that I didn't like is gone!"

"Good. This is what I want you to do. When you need to duplicate more, use what I have made here as your models. Do not try to work with the originals."

"That's what hurt you!" Somehow, he'd removed whatever she hadn't liked about the originals, and doing that, she concluded, was what had made him pale and made sweat drip from his usually imperturbable brow.

"That is why I don't want you to do it." He managed to smile at her, and felt his color returning. "Promise me?"

"I promise."

He ate a cookie, and Renko smiled back and did as well. Dragons as dragons obtained their nourishment from the atmospheric elements around them. Those who could assume human form, whether naturally as Renko did, or through the use of a guise, as Irtysh did, found they enjoyed human foods. Except alcohol, Irtysh thought with another, wider smile, using the thought as a distraction. One had to be careful of whiskey and wine.

"You're all right now, Brother?" Renko asked.

"I am. I will see you tomorrow for the Exhibition, yes?"

"Yes," she said. "Will you want to see Shota-san and Akira-san before we go?"

"I will. This afternoon. Will you tell them, please? I can come get them when they're ready. I'd like Akira-san to at least see his wardrobe so he can learn to duplicate it, and Shota-san's will need to be fitted. This," he said, turning the picture to face her, "is what we will wear. It's called a 'morning suit,' but can be worn all day."

"Very nice. You'll all be very handsome humans. Azuki-san will have ideas for the two of us, I'm sure, but I have something that might surprise her. I'll bring Akira-san and Shota-san when it's time. I will let you know we're coming, or you can ask me to bring them when you want them." She smiled at him and thought he was very good to all of them. "Thank you, Brother." She picked up her things, including the new materials he'd made for her, and was off.

"You weren't gone long," Azuki said as Renko reappeared beside her. "What have you here?"

"It feels like I was. Brother helped. He made this"—she held out the skin for Azuki to touch—"and these." He had marked the *bachi* he had made with a three stroke mark he had started using as a monogram on various Western things he crafted. He said it was the first letter of his name in Cyrillic, the Russian writing system. Renko was glad he had thought to mark them. She could tell the difference between what Irtysh had made and the originals, but wasn't sure she wanted to have to.

"I'll make more of this," she said, retrieving the skin from Azuki. He had marked that, she saw, too. "We're going to want a few pieces of it."

Two Walking Suits (1878), Attr. Godey's Lady's Book

29

The humidity had dissipated, the sky was blue and it was a lovely end-of-summer day. Toshio walked over to the large pasture where the horses grazed. It was right beside the Yamada family compound and on Yamada family land, but it housed the Maeda mounts as well. This had come about when the new public school buildings were built on the rocky field formerly part of the Maeda Imperial land grant but largely useless for agriculture.

Lord Eitaro, Toshio's adoptive father and, as the father of his wife, also his father-in-law, had worked with *Sensei* to provide a place for the schools and everybody's horses in a complex juggling of private and public lands. Toshio smiled. All of this would sound very odd to his Western business associates, he knew, and was therefore better not mentioned, but it was very normal in Japan.

He'd better ask Eitaro exactly how the swap had worked. How ownership and usage rights were

281

actually structured might be something he'd need to know someday. They'd run into property problems in the course of their mining venture, usually stemming from people failing to write things down.

He leaned over the fence and clucked. The gray colt looked up and nickered. He came over for a scratch.

Toshio liked the colt. He often rode a pleasant and serviceable chestnut gelding, now grazing on the other side of the field, but that horse wasn't really his and they had no special bond. Eitaro's bay war stallion was not here, as Eitaro himself had gone back to the city for a couple of days. The babies would, by custom, not leave home for a full month after their births, so they wouldn't get sick from being out and about. After that, they'd be taken to the Shrine to be presented to the *kami* or the Temple to formally become Buddhists, whichever the family preferred. Often that was both.

Eitaro had told Toshio to stay here for the month, while he rode back and forth to tend to the family business. Toshio had objected but Eitaro had gruffly insisted. Anko reminded him that her father could be very kind, and Toshio had remembered that Anko was an only child not for her parents want of trying.

Thunder Cloud had become his formal name, Toshio had been told, though he was always called Cloudy, to go along with his attractive dapple-gray coat. He nibbled playfully at Toshio's sleeves while Toshio laughed and rubbed his ears. You could see his parentage in the proud and sturdy set of his head and the long legs that promised swift gaits.

"Cloudy likes you."

Toshio turned to see Yuta approaching him from the direction of the schools. The red roan mare called Red Wind came to join them at the fence. She shoved the colt aside. Yuta laughed. He reached into his sleeve pocket and came out with a sizeable bag of carrots.

"I brought enough for all of them," he said, giving a small piece to Red Wind. "Here's one for Cloudy. What do you think of him?"

Toshio broke off a piece of carrot and let the colt take it from the outstretched palm of his hand. "Beautiful colt. What is he? Rising three?"

"Yes." Yuta gave the mare another chunk. *What do you think, Red Wind?* he said silently to the horse who had claimed him.

Long Tail likes him, she replied, crunching. *He carries him often. They don't talk, but he communicates well.*

"I need to find him another home," Yuta said. "Either that or geld him, but his blood lines and conformation are good enough to breed. He can't stay in his dam's herd much longer."

"This is his dam?"

"Yes. Red Wind is my mount. She is fast and agile, a joy to ride. I feel like I learned to ride from her. You may recall I used to be a monk so I hadn't ridden since I was a child, and barely then."

"Has anybody been riding this colt yet?"

"My nephew's been on him bareback a few times," Yuta said, giving Red Wind the last of her carrot and pulling out another, which he broke in two, passing half to Toshio. "Cloudy hasn't seemed to mind. Our farm hand has trained him to halter and lead and started tacking him."

Red Wind snorted and tossed her head. *What about me?*

"I often pony him when I ride Red Wind," Yuta said with a smile. "So he's learning from her, too. I think he'll be easy to train to saddle. Nice temperament, and he hasn't minded Shota on him or the saddle so far."

Don't make a liar of me, Cloudy, Yuta said silently. *See if you can talk to him.*

"Do you have any apples?" Toshio said suddenly. "I think he'd like an apple."

Yuta laughed and reached into his bag. It seemed Toshio could listen, at least. "I do. Red Wind is extremely fond of apples. I almost always bring a couple for her if I have them. It's no surprise that Cloudy likes them, too. Try talking to him. Our horses are very expressive."

Blackie had watched the whole exchange with great interest. But he and the rest of the horses were tired of waiting for their share of the treats and started moving towards the source. Even the cooperative but dim cart ox, here housed with the horses, started to wander over.

"Have another carrot and talk to Cloudy while I give these to the rest."

"He'll stay with me?"

"I think so." *If you think you like him*, Yuta said silently to Cloudy.

You better like him, Red Wind thought, sticking right at Yuta's shoulder. *You could do a lot worse in a human.*

You won't have as many adventures, Blackie commented. He and Red Wind both had been through several changes of human ownership, served as war horses and been stolen by bandits before coming to the Maedas. They'd had plenty of adventures!

That may not be a bad thing, Long Tail commented. *It's a good life in my current herd, now that we aren't at war all the time. If you work on him, he might be able to hear you. He doesn't have a special mount right now, but I carry him a lot. It's nice to have your own human.*

This is a good place, the buckskin, Phlox, said. *But there are other good places.* Bay Lily reached over and nipped Phlox to move her out of the way as

285

Yuta approached the manger with his bag of treats. Palomino Kiku kicked as Lily bumped into her. *Plenty old enough to find his own herd,* the Palomino said, *and our old herd was a good one, too.* All three mares had been gifts from Lord Eitaro at the time the schools were built. It reduced Eitaro's herd, gave Yuta's family the additional mounts they sorely needed, and worked neatly, if unofficially, into the land swap for the building of the school, which was, strictly speaking, public and therefore owned by the Emperor.

"All right," Yuta said, "Here you go. Behave yourselves." He shoved his way between them and scattered the treats from the cloth sack atop the hay already in the manger, then ducked around Red Wind to get out of the way. She always thought she deserved more than any of the other horses.

Yuta shook the bag out, made sure the ox could reach some of the treats, dusted his robes and folded the bag neatly to tuck it into his sleeve pocket as he walked over to rejoin Toshio.

"I like this fellow," Toshio said. "You're really going to sell him?"

"I have to. He can't stay with his parents unless he's gelded."

"Why not sell him to me? I'd like my own horse."

Cloudy? Yuta thought.

I could go live with Long Tail and all his friends, Cloudy thought, *where Lily and Kiku and Phlox came from, but come back here pretty often.*

If that's how things work out, Blackie cautioned. *Nothing's guaranteed.*

"Why don't you work with him while you're here?" Yuta proposed. "If it goes well, maybe we can make it final when you return to Hakata."

Toshio scratched Cloudy's nose. "I'd like that very much."

***

At the same time, Otohime, Renko and Azuki burst into Noriko's *dojo*.

"Come with us, Aunt," Azuki said. "We have to get you ready to go."

Otohime and Renko burst into laughter, Noriko looked so taken aback by the prospect.

"All I need to do is pack my small travel bag," she protested.

"She's worse than Tsuruko-san," Otohime said.

"Tsuruko-san always looks elegant," Noriko said.

"And so must you," Renko said. She and Otohime stuck out their arms and Azuki opened the door, saying "Come along!"

So Noriko found herself hustled along to the workroom, where Azuki had laid out several lengths of fabric.

"We didn't know what you'd rather wear," Otohime explained. "For what we are doing, we will have Western dresses. So will Tsuruko-san. We just finished designing hers, but she and I will be going with you first, to your old *dojo*, and then joining everyone for the exhibit. She can change her clothes at will, like the rest of us can, but we don't know how to dress you or what Tsuruko-san will want to wear while she's with you!"

Noriko found herself entirely unable to keep track of who was doing what, when and how each of them should dress to do it!

"Aunt will want her pockets," Azuki said. Designing the pockets Noriko required into any garment was not easy.

"Of course I want my pockets!" Noriko said. "I need them for my tools!"

"Tools?"

"Yes," Noriko said, realizing the Otohime might not know. "My original school of martial arts relies to a certain extent on tools. Although we learn to use whatever is available to us in the environment, some things are useful to have with us at all times." She reached toward the sleeve of her *gi* and a *shurikan* throwing star suddenly appeared in her hand. "This is most useful." She smiled. "I always have several tools with me. Not all are edged weapons." She turned to face her niece. The throwing star vanished as quickly as it had appeared.

"You have made me several beautiful *kimono* already," she said plaintively. "Those are all appropriate for anything I might do in the city, and are already equipped. I planned to wear one of those."

"We had to learn to make her weapons," Renko explained to her sister, "so she'd have a set in every outfit."

"They're tools!"

"You will need a Western dress," Otohime pointed out. "If not for the next few days, in the future. Don't you want to see the exhibits?"

"I'd like to, certainly," Noriko admitted.

"Western clothing will be best for that."

Renko glanced and Azuki and they both threw up their hands to hide their giggles. Few people could bully Noriko, but Otohime managed it while using perfect courtesy. She had, they decided, been learning from Lady Satsuki, who was an expert at this.

"But I"—

"My brother has been making clothing for Shota-san," Renko explained. "Akira-san can make his own, like we do, once they decide on a design, but you know Shota-san can't. Brother showed us how he does it."

"It's really very simple," Otohime pointed out. "It's not like what Azuki-san and Tsuruko-san before her did, making clothing while they changed and then taking it off. That depleted their very substance. Irtysh just makes it like he makes anything else, and you know how good he is at that."

"He assembles it out of what's already there," Renko said. "He showed us about clothes. They have lots of fiddly little parts to them, like buttons, and different materials are used, especially in the Western ones, when you make them like he does. He likes all that."

"So which fabric do you like best?" Azuki asked.

"Are you going to use this fabric?" Noriko picked up a lovely indigo blue taffeta with waves of light running through it, flashing every time it moved.

"That would take too long for our purposes," Renko said. "Azuki-san made the lengths on the table. Otohime and I will just duplicate this one, or whatever one is your favorite."

"Here's the dress design we were thinking of." Azuki held out a colored illustration. "This is from the new *Godey's Lady's Book*. People get it to look at new fashion and use it to make patterns to sew it for themselves. It would look very nice in this dark blue."

"It has room for plenty of pockets," Otohime pointed out helpfully. The long-sleeved and high-necked dress was plain in style, though it had bands of decorative fabric at the neckline and hip, but it was topped by a matching jacket that fell below the hip. The jacket cuffs and collar had plenty of room in which to hide things and the back of the jacket had a looped layer that fell atop an identical one on the back of the skirt, one over the other. Those seemed entirely decorative.

The skirt, from the knee down, draped in folds over layers of ruffles that swept the floor. Noriko thought she could conceal entire suits of armor and her husband's samurai swords in those folds, not just her own slender blade. The hat was beyond description, purely for effect, with its brim high on one side and low on the other. The crown was far too small to fit over her head, and was cinched with a wide buckled belt. The whole thing would rest on top of what looked to Noriko's eye like an untidy eagle's nest of curls.

"This is not a joke?" Noriko asked, hoping that it might be.

"It's quite simple," Azuki assured her aunt. "This is a Lady's Walking Suit, the sort of thing a well-dressed woman would wear in the day time to visit a museum or a park or something very like this Exhibition!"

"If you like this blue fabric, I can make this for you in just a few minutes," Otohime proclaimed.

"Let me, Sister," Renko said. "I want to try! Remember, I know where the pockets should be and you don't."

"Come, Aunt," Azuki urged. "Please. Just stand here and let them do it. The blue will look very nice on you and see these lovely woven patterned bands for the embellishment? They'll make it look better than the picture."

They were having a wonderful time, Noriko thought. They were expanding their skills and nurturing their relationships, and in this they were including her. She had no idea where she'd wear this thing. In Tokyo, she'd wear her second-best *kimono*, as she had planned. It hung on a nearby rack right over there. She glanced at it longingly.

"Noriko-*sama*'s *kimono* is right here," Renko pointed it out to her sister. "It not only has the pockets for all her 'tools,' it's fully equipped."

"Oh, excellent! We can do both together, then. We'll not only build the pockets into this dress, we can fill them." Otohime rubbed her hands together in glee. "Now, Noriko-*sama*, if we may…."

Noriko's niece and her two friends looked at her with glowing expectation. They were so excited. They wanted to do this so badly. Suddenly it didn't matter if she never had a chance to wear it and whether or not she liked it was beside the point. What was important were her niece and her friends.

"By all means," Noriko said.

Taijitu (Yin/Yang symbol), Unknown

30

Tokyo, the Eastern capital, was both the same and startlingly different, Noriko found. It hadn't been that long since she had left it, but everywhere there was new construction. Areas where foreigners might congregate looked extremely Western to her. Plenty of Western style buildings were going up and plenty of existing buildings wore false façades. She hoped the Inn of the Golden Phoenix hadn't succumbed to the lure of "modernization" and retained its old-fashioned charm. She had a hunch there would be a market for that, and not only among the Japanese.

Here, though, in the quieter back streets where she guided Tsuruko-san, carrying Kichiro, who was almost too big for that, and Otohime, carrying Susu, who was indeed too big for anyone who wasn't a dragon, little had changed.

It was primarily a warehouse district, with carts to-ing and fro-ing, carters loading and unloading their cargoes, and the occasional ox lowing. Early in the morning or in the evenings, this area would be nearly silent, the only sound coming from the large building they could see straight ahead on the right.

The *dojo* could almost have been part of a Shrine or Temple, the main hall, perhaps, set up off the street so that breezes could run underneath it, cooling it in the hot, humid summers, and protecting it from flood waters, if any, and rainwater runoff, which occurred fairly often. A gallery ran around the perimeter of the first floor, and sliding doors of heavy wood kept people and their prying gazes out. The Chinese hip roof design also made the building look like a Temple or Shrine. This alone marked it as very different from the warehouses in this area that had steep, gabled roof designs, like most storehouses.

This building was better built than the rest, of polished, glowing, *hinoki* cypress. A garden encircled it, with neatly tended shrubs clustered among huge hunks of petrified wood. These were new, and placed not simply to provide beauty but to hinder traffic. For all its splendor, Noriko realized how cleverly the design protected the building from attack without seeming to. She smiled; of this she much approved. She noted one or two improvements here that she could make to the Maeda compound. She chided herself: she should have thought of doing so before. That she felt safe in her new life didn't mean she actually was.

A graveled path, the pebbles crunching under foot, wound through the little garden, leading to side stairs that went up to the gallery and what was obviously, to Noriko, anyway, the entrance, though the wooden doors didn't look any different from those forming the building's walls.

There was, however, a sign beside the door and a bell. These were new.

"What does that say?" Tsuruko wanted to know. She recognized the characters, yes, mostly, but wasn't sure how to read them; the way they were written was different. Reading was still relatively new to her, but she worked to improve at every opportunity.

"It's new since I studied here," Noriko told her. "It means East Mountain Temple in Chinese. That and the *taijitu* crest together mean this is a Shaolin Teaching Temple, but you'd have to have some training to know that." The *taijitu* was sometimes called the Yin-Yang symbol and had more uses than its symbolism in Shaolin martial arts.

"How do students find it, then?" Otohime was genuinely curious.

Noriko smiled. "If they are ready to come here, they will know. Come," she beckoned her friends up the steps and touched the bell.

A Chinese girl in a beautiful blue brocade tunic and complimentary solid blue trousers slid open the door and bowed in the Chinese fashion.

"*Soke-sama*," she said to Noriko, in Japanese. "Please come in. The mistress awaits."

All Noriko's guests had been to her *dojo*, but this one was easily quadruple the size and held much more equipment for climbing, balancing, and other Shaolin training activities.

"I want to get down and play!" Susu announced, wriggling out of Otohime's arms but not entirely out of her grip.

"Look! Ropes!" Kichiro said. "Let's swing!"

Tsuruko looked appalled and shushed them both.

Otohime was more direct. "Hold still and behave or I will send you both to Her Majesty!"

A woman's laugh, slightly rusty, sounded and they turned to see a tiny woman with a dandelion fluff of white hair totter through the entry to the *dojo* from a back room. Wrinkled like a pickled plum, she looked ancient.

"*Sifu*," Noriko said, her tone warmly affectionate, though she bowed deeply. "Mistress Feng, may I present"—

"You're one of them," Mistress Feng interrupted, her black birdlike eyes fixing Otohime with a sharp gaze. "*Long's* daughter. As is this child." She bent in a medium-deep bow. "Please forgive my failure to show proper respect. I had a small injury on the balance tower."

"Oh, no, please, do not trouble yourself on my account, or on that of my young brother," Otohime said, slightly shocked that such an elderly person continued to practice martial arts. "I would not have you risk injury. It is a great honor indeed to meet such a long-time friend of my father's." She returned the bow respectfully. "He sends his greetings and regards. He is grateful for your help in rescuing my sister and me, as am I, and we all thank you."

Somehow, Noriko was both surprised and not surprised at all to find that Mistress Feng, her *Sifu*, or Shaolin martial arts mistress, to use the Chinese term, not only knew His Majesty but recognized Otohime as his daughter without introduction. Mistress Feng had not only natural gifts but unnatural powers. Even if Noriko continued her own training diligently, as she did, and lived to Mistress Feng's great age, she was not sure she could ever approximate that level of skill.

Otohime turned to Tsuruko and beckoned her forward. "Thank you for extending your kind welcome to Noriko-*sama's* friends, Mistress Feng. I am pleased to introduce our dear friend, Hamasaki Tsuruko-san, and her son, Kichiro-chan. My young brother, who is called Susu-chan, will also demonstrate he can bow properly himself."

"You are all most welcome," Mistress Feng said, amused by the little bows of Kichiro, who had squirmed his way to the floor to join his friend, and of Susu. Tsuruko thought they both did very well.

The Chinese girl appeared behind her mistress, standing by the opened door.

"Do come in," Mistress Feng said as the young women bowed, gesturing her guests towards the entrance, "Noriko *Lao Shi*?"

Noriko started a bit. She had not seen Mistress Feng since she had been granted the status of *soke*, or master-teacher, on her marriage, by Mistress Feng and her son, Master Peng, also her Shaolin master. To have her own teacher address her as "teacher" surprised her, though it was certainly correct. She was a teacher now, but certainly not Mistress Feng's, who would remain her *Sifu* as long as she lived.

Noriko gestured her friends to precede her and she followed them. Both the little boys were wide-eyed with wonder at the ornate splendor of the colorful Chinese decor. Otohime and Tsuruko looked at each other and smiled. While they were fascinated at this glimpse into Noriko's prior life and the opportunity to meet her teacher, this was what they'd come to see.

"Please sit down. We will have tea."

The elderly woman tottered to one of two large armchairs. A small step was placed before it that she used to climb into the chair, for it was too high for her. She rested her tiny feet on the stepstool. There were three other Chinese chairs, very like Western chairs, and two more little stepstools for the boys.

Tsuruko shot Noriko a glance. She didn't dare try to communicate mentally. This unremarkable looking old woman alarmed her. It was as though she had access to powers Tsuruko could not even imagine, but, like the flow of a pipe that was turned off, she did not currently express.

How did she know about the children? Tsuruko barely thought. Noriko caught her gaze and glanced at the girl, who hustled out behind a tapestry to another part of the building. While she wouldn't put much of anything past Mistress Feng, she thought the young woman had quickly set up the room during the short time Mistress Feng spent greeting them.

"I understand your *dojo* is doing well," Madam Feng said to Noriko, starting a train of small talk that persisted until the girl returned with a tea tray. She placed it on the low-lying central table, and poured. After she had passed the cups and laid out treats, she knelt next to Mistress Feng's chair.

Mistress Feng saw the little boys staring at her miniscule slippers.

"I see you staring." She smiled. "Not all Chinese people have such tiny feet," she told them. Frightened of the woman's great age, foreign-ness and the power she could not entirely conceal, they shrank away.

"There was a time," she told them, "a very long time, when some Chinese women's feet were deformed by binding them with bandages to make them small. This still goes on in many places. It was, to some extent, a fashion."

"It hurt," Kichiro said. His growing wings coupled with his dual nature had sometimes hurt him as he grew. Thankfully, he was past that stage, but it had been bad enough at times to make him want to express his understanding.

Tsuruko patted his shoulder to hush him.

Mistress Feng shook her head almost imperceptibly at the Crane-Woman.

"Yes, young fellow," she said to Kichiro. "It does hurt when it's done. It can hurt throughout a woman's whole life. But my feet were not bound in the usual sense. They were surgically altered—that means shaped by a doctor while I was asleep—to look like they had been bound. This was so I could continue my training. Have you seen Noriko *Lao Shi's dojo* and all the things she can do?"

Susu, rapt, nodded eagerly. He slid off his stool onto the floor to try to scoot across his sister's feet to reach Kichiro.

"Now this alteration is not necessary. My student"—she smiled at the young woman kneeling beside her—"will soon return to China. She is Manchu, not Han, so it was never considered advantageous for her to have that done to her, but now it becomes less and less common. In any event, she will be going to the north and will train at our main Temple there. In time, she, too, will be Feng." Feng was used as a family name by the women who joined the Temple where Mistress Feng had trained and taught and where her son had been born. This was also where he had begun his own training, but Peng was the name of his father's house.

"Not so long ago she would have needed to be smuggled out," Tsuruko said.

"As she was smuggled in." The old woman nodded.

The curtain parted and an older man with a long white braid and beard came in.

"*Sifu*," he said bowing to the woman, then, "Mother?"

"My son," she said to the assembled women. "Master Peng. Join us. Noriko *Lao Shi* has come to visit us, as promised, with her friends."

Susu was nearly breathless with an excitement he could just barely contain. He inched over to Kichiro. The little lady's power was clear even to the children, but was very well contained. This man reminded Susu of his father. He radiated it.

Master Peng made as if to kowtow to Otohime, but she stopped him.

"We are not in China," she said with a smile, "and I am not my father."

Noriko and Tsuruko exchanged glances. They behaved respectfully to Otohime, yes, but that the woman they thought of as a friend should command this level of protocol nearly paralyzed them, though they were both always careful to give either of Their Majesties the respect their positions were due.

Mistress Feng's attendant hadn't left the room, yet Master Peng knew about Otohime.

Either there were observation portals looking into this reception room, or Master Peng had powers that would scare Tsuruko, if she permitted herself to think about that.

"We are always pleased to see Noriko *Lao Shi*," Master Peng said. "We are honored that she brings her friends."

Noriko smiled. She felt relaxed in the presence of her superiors and teachers today. Last time she had been here, she was introducing her new husband and was anxious. She even feared that she might have incurred their displeasure, not just by marrying without their permission, but by marrying a retired *sohei* warrior monk turned teacher—with a very strange family. But not only had they accepted Yuta, they had elevated her to *soke*, the master-teacher rank that meant she could teach independently—not under the supervision of her *sifu* or master—start her own *dojo*, and could further award rank herself.

She was about to speak when Master Peng looked at Tsuruko and said, "You are welcome here, of course. It is an honor and pleasure to have to visit us with your charming son, but am I wrong in thinking you are not a daughter of *Long*, and yet not a human, either?"

"I am the Crane-Woman," Tsuruko replied. "There are tales told of me before my marriage. Because of Maeda *Sensei*, Noriko-*sama's* husband, and his family, I am now, as I said, married, and this is my son, Kichiro. Though his father is fully human, our child, like me, is also crane." Kichiro wriggled and squirmed. "No, no, Kichiro-chan. You do not have to demonstrate," Tsuruko laughed. "Remember, we do not change in front of humans unless they are our friends, and even then not casually."

"We are certainly your friends," Master Peng bowed his reassurance. "We are privileged to know *Long* and his family. That is because my mother has the ability to speak to dragons. To know Noriko *Lao Shi's* extraordinary family and friends is also a privilege."

"We have wondered," Mistress Feng said, "whether there are more of you in the world now and if that might be due to all the changes going on or whether all the changes are simply making communication among you more possible."

"I have no real idea," Otohime said. "Do you?" She looked at Tsuruko, who shook her head. "But

I," Otohime continued, "though not as old as my father, am very old. While Susu-chan here is quite young, there have always been young among us. I am not sure our overall numbers have changed significantly."

"I would venture to suggest that it is communication," Tsuruko said. "*Sensei's* dual-natured niece became ill. His nephew asked among the birds, seeking me because of the old tales. I realized I could help, and this is how we all met."

"It is because we can communicate, and are willing to do so without prejudice, that we can accomplish things, I think," Noriko said. "We are in the capital to work towards a goal of Otohime's—to provide refugees from the Satsuma Rebellion with a path towards new industry and give them a future."

"We do that by working together," Tsuruko said, ruffling her young son's hair with one hand and stroking Susu's with her other.

"And yet we have accompanied Noriko-*sama* on her visit to you for a much simpler reason," Otohime said. "I have become interested in human design. My residence has all been oriented towards my alternate nature. I would like to recognize this one. That is a beautiful cabinet." Otohime gestured towards a rectangular chest inlaid with jade and enamel work. "I understand you have others of Chinese design."

Master Peng was pleased to display several cabinets and shelves that lined the room, some with elaborate carving and art works illustrated with lacquer and jade, and some whose beauty lay in the shape of the wood and the way it was carved.

"I like this one," Tsuruko said, gently stroking the mahogany pillar of a display unit with small cabinets beneath. It was much taller than she, and the shelves were set out in a geometric pattern that was primarily lines and rectangles, but with a large curved fan shape in the center that entranced her. "It would make a wonderful room divider in lieu of a screen."

"We have those, too," Master Peng said. "Some are painted panels in the Japanese style, but we also have ones that are carved wood." He led them into another, smaller, room.

Noriko moved to a small stool, the better to talk to Mistress Feng.

"My friends and my niece and nephew are going to the International Industrial Exhibition this afternoon," Noriko said, after explaining why she was not. "They hope to see a machine that will help with the refugee project. If it will help, they will acquire more."

"This project and others like it will soon be needed more than ever," Mistress Feng said. "I did not want to say so, but the news just came in. The Rebellion is over."

Noriko straightened and tilted her head to listen.

"The rebels are all dead," Mistress Feng said.

"Saigo-*sama*?" Noriko breathed.

"We understand he was severely wounded and to prevent further loss of life and especially of honor, he committed *seppuku*."

31

"A re you almost ready to leave?" Renko asked Akira. He'd asked her help in spending the morning with Kukanko working on their *shamisen*. Renko liked what he was doing for the *oni* girl. He was showing much more compassion than she personally felt. The *oni* was rather irritatingly child-like. But, Renko told herself, she really was a child.

Kukanko looked up and beamed at Renko, her fangs bared. She held up a *dou*. Part of the skin Irtysh had made was now trimmed to size, stretched over the sound-box and clamped down so the glue that would keep it there permanently could dry.

"We're almost done with Kukanko-san's own," Akira announced. "We have the *dou* almost completed. The *sao* we finished first. Now we just have the *tenjin* and the other small parts to finish and we'll be ready to attach the strings and try it out!"

"What are the *tenjin*?" Renko had not kept up on the *shamisen* construction as well as she might have. Akira was doing it. He was the clever one in this instance. She was just providing him with transportation.

"These." Akira held up three pegs. "These hold the strings at the top of the *sao* so the player can tune it. We have them carved; we just have to finish them. Kukanko-san is getting very good at carving things."

He sounded quite proud of his red-skinned, horned, pupil. That was nice of him—to act like he didn't notice, and like it didn't matter. As human and as eagle, he looked like something found in the normal world, even though he was himself a *yokai*. Renko shifted a bit as she realized, uncomfortably, that as a dragon she no doubt looked as odd to someone closer to the normal world spectrum as the *oni* did. Though she was no child.

"I can give us some extra time, but they'll be expecting us soon. We'll go to my brother's palace and we'll all go together."

"Yes. Shall I change now or later?" He wore regular working clothes, but those would not do for the First International Industrial Exhibition.

"Do you know what you're wearing?"

"Prince Irtysh showed us yesterday. He had to make Shota-san's clothes, but I just needed to memorize the pictures and see what the parts the pictures didn't show looked like, and then practice a couple of times. Shota-san likes clothes much more than I do. It's a shame he can't just make them when he changes."

"I want to see you change!" Kukanko said.

"Not much to see," Akira said as the air shimmered around him, his eagle form flashed into being for an instant, and he returned as a human in the natty Western suit Prince Irtysh had told him was called a "morning suit," though it could be worn at any time during the day.

"Here you go," he said. "Like my new suit?"

"Oh, yes," Kukanko breathed.

"Very modern," Renko said. "Brother does have excellent taste. Take my arm and I'll just come in wearing my Western dress."

"Can I take the *shamisen* we finished to the *Goze* house?" Kukanko asked.

Akira shrugged. "If you want to. Or we can do it together. I'll be back tomorrow to see how the glue's drying on yours, if Renko-san can bring me."

"Susu-chan will bring you if I can't." Susu would have fun doing that, Renko thought.

"That's a good idea. I think Susu-chan and Kukanko-san would enjoy each other's company."

"Let's be off, then. I'll see you again, Kukanko-san."

"Tomorrow! Thank you, Akira-san!"

Akira smiled as he took Renko's arm and they vanished.

Kukanko thought the Eagle-boy was very clever. And he was so kind to her! With his help, she was going to have her very own *shamisen* to play, and that made her feel so happy she couldn't find words to express it.

She settled down to give the *tenjin* a final planing, but looked up when she heard the music coming from the other side of the wood, and smiled. The boy was back.

He was the person she wanted to have the new *shamisen* she and Akira had made. The boy had big hands, not as big as hers, but she thought the wider neck of the one they'd made after they'd repaired the one she borrowed would suit him better.

Quickly, she applied a coat of camellia oil to the *tenjin*. That was the preferred finish for all the wooden parts of the *shamisen*, she had learned.

One of the *tebiki* had gone off with her lover, a man from the Matagi group of hunters who lived secretly up in the mountains not far away. She couldn't come back. Neither the *goze* nor the *tebiki* could marry or keep company with men. Supposedly this kept them safe from the unwanted attentions of any men and made respectable people comfortable opening their doors to the *goze*, giving them lodging and providing them with places to play.

Kukanko's people knew the Matagi, of course, because one of the places the *oni* lived was high in the mountains the Matagi hunted. They were careful to avoid them, even though they couldn't always help it. The Matagi were likely sources of some of the tales of the origins of the *oni*. The mountain hunters and the Yamabushi ascetics both often crossed paths with the *oni* without meaning to, so demons, foreigners, spirits and monsters all easily became part of the *oni* legend. The Matagi, specifically, were to be avoided. They'd hunt an *oni* as easily as a boar or deer, bear or wolf.

The boy she wanted to have this *shamisen* was a *bosama*, a blind musician like a *goze,* only a boy and an itinerant. Without her *tebiki*, the sighted women who helped the *goze*, the girl from whom she borrowed the *shamisen* was much freer in her movements as far as the boy was concerned, even though she would get in trouble if caught. This girl liked the boy and liked the music he played as much as Kukanko did. The girl couldn't really see, of course, but she could distinguish light and dark, sun and shadow. As long as Kukanko didn't get too close, if the girl came alone Kukanko would be safe.

She put her supplies carefully away in a hollow in the trunk of a large cedar tree. She wanted to be careful with Akira's tools. They didn't really even belong to him, but to his father. The *tenjin* she wrapped gently in paper and rolled in a reed mat. These would need to dry. She might be able to rub them with oil again later.

There was something else she wanted to give the boy, too. The last time she watched him play, he'd chipped the corner of his *bachi*. The ones the dragon prince—seriously, a dragon prince? Plus Azuki-Toki; her brother, Shota, the sparrow; Akira the eagle and this Renko-san? They were all plenty strange, yet they were concerned about her being an *oni?* The *bachi* the prince had made were a bit larger than the one the boy had been using, but there was enough of the shell and wood for the boy to shape it however he preferred if this wasn't just right. She picked one up and wrapped it in a soft cloth, enclosing it in the bag covering the larger *shamisen*.

Kukanko really wanted him to like them both. Maybe he'd play more of that music of his, the music that wasn't really like anybody else's.

She slipped through the woods, trying to move silently so the boy could not hear her footfalls. Kukanko was good at that.

The boy sat on a rock in the middle of a glade. A tiny brook ran through it. The leaves of the beech trees dappled the afternoon sun. They were mostly yellow now at the end of the Eighth Month—so confusing, these Western adjustments to the calendar, but she did think it was the Eighth Month, though she could not remember how they named it. Soon the leaves would fall and the floor of the wood would be covered in a golden carpet that would turn to tan and be covered with snow as the year turned to winter.

Kukanko took advantage of the gurgling brook and the boy's own music to slip up beside him and set down the covered *shamisen*.

"Nitaro-san?" a girl's voice called.

That was the *goze* girl! The boy's name must be Nitaro. Kukanko, happy to find out this secret, slipped back into the woods to listen.

"Wasn't that you?" Nitaro called. The girl used a staff to guide herself into the clearing. Her *shamisen* was bagged and slung over her shoulder to hang down her back.

"Wasn't me what?"

The boy reached out to feel around him. "This." He picked up the bag with the new *shamisen* and the wrapped *bachi*. "A bag."

"No," the girl answered. "I didn't leave that. I'm not even supposed to be here, not by myself. What is it?"

Nitaro set his own *shamisen* aside and unwrapped this new one.

"Somebody left me a *shamisen*. And here, here's a new *bachi*." He lifted the *shamisen* and started to tune it. A *shamisen* is fingered, plucked, strummed and chorded all at once to create immensely complicated music from a deceptively simple-looking instrument.

"This is bigger," Nitaro said. "Different. Come and feel it."

The girl came over to sit near him and take it from him.

"It *is* bigger. The *sao* is bigger and longer, too. Where did this *bachi* come from?"

"It came with the *shamisen*. Move over. Can you put away my *shamisen*, please? I want to play this one."

"Yes." As the boy experimented with the new one, the girl quickly disassembled Nitaro's original instrument and put it back in its bag.

"Get out your own," the boy said with a grin. "Let's play together!"

"Shall we try *Jiuta*?" The girl named a popular folk song as she began to tune her instrument. It had a vocal part, but could also be played as an instrumental. Everybody who played the *shamisen* knew it.

"Let's." Nitaro strummed a chord with the *bachi*, then struck the *dou* with it, producing an entirely new sound. "Will you play the regular instrumental the way we've always done?" he asked. "This *shamisen* is not the same as the others," he explained. "Neither is the *bachi*. It lends itself to innovation. I want to try something different."

The girl answered by plucking a chord.

Then they were off, and though Kukanko knew the old folk song well, the joyous way the boy played took the instrument and the music to new heights, and she thought that if she could ever learn to play like that, she would burst with the pure joy of the song.

She had never heard anything like it before, and she had a part in making it happen.

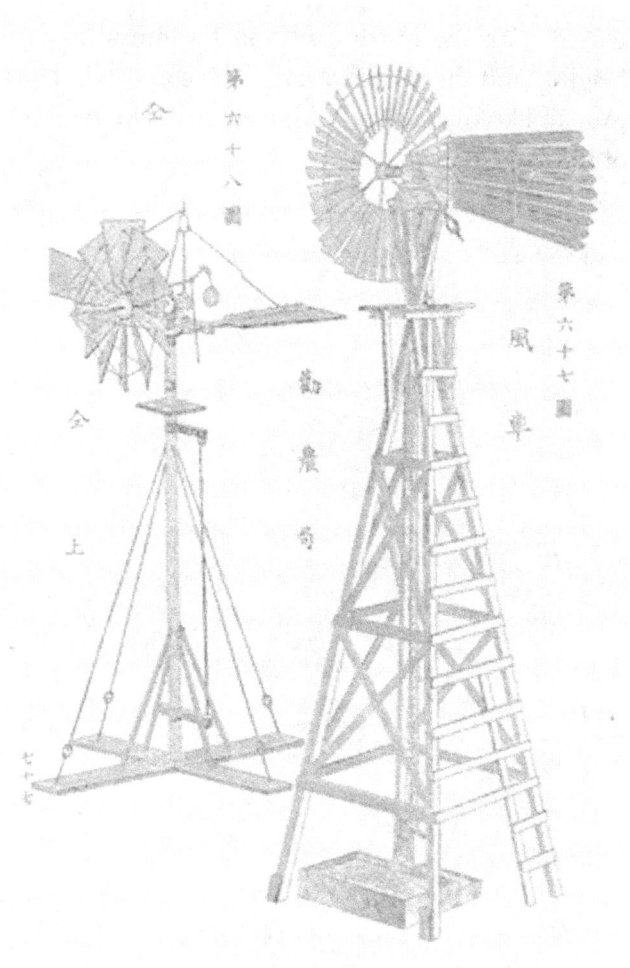

Windmill from 1877 Exhibition, Attr. Kano

32

A zuki bent over her reference book of patterns and fabric samples as she showed them to Prince Irtysh. She was dressed in the persimmon colored Western dress that she thought suited her well. It hadn't been quite as up to the minute as the ones in the newest *Godey's Lady's Book*, but the fabric was fabulous, naturally, and styles didn't change that quickly. She'd modified the back to gather and fall like it was now supposed to, and the little bonnet that perched atop her wig was the latest mode—adjusted, of course, to accommodate the Japanese style of her artificial hair.

"Each sample shows a finished weave," Azuki explained. "The patterns show how to set up the loom. These looms aren't as complex as mine, and neither are the fabrics. We hope just about anyone will be able to set them up and produce these fabrics with minimal difficulty."

"Your work is beautiful," Irtysh said.

"Thank you," Azuki replied. As a human, the prince was a pleasant-looking man with a full beard and distinguished, if Western, features. The hands reaching out from his perfectly proportioned layers of sleeves were large and strong, but beautifully groomed with long, elegant fingers. She could visualize him playing that pianoforte instrument she'd seen in pictures. The article had talked about "reach," which meant the ability to cover many keys without moving one's hand. He would have it.

"If I might," Azuki continued, shyly, "perhaps I could beg a favor."

"You may ask, of course." He looked at her quizzically.

"You've made us many looms," she said, "and so we will be able to give employment to many refugees. For that we are grateful. But they will need more than one pattern book. I could make them but…."

"You think it would be easier for me?" Irtysh smiled.

"Well…."

"I think it would be, too. It looks like each page took you a lot of time." He flipped through the pages of the book.

"I enjoy doing it," Azuki admitted, "but I am enjoying having some leisure so much. You don't have to. I shouldn't have asked. It's my job." She reached for the book.

"Not at all," Irtysh said, lifting it out of her reach. "Merely copying isn't such a great chore for me. And I won't even do it myself, if you don't mind. I will delegate the task to my children. Agniya—Galina's mother and the stepmother of the rest of them—is not particularly diligent outside of attending to her particular duties. I wouldn't call her lazy, but she doesn't extend herself either in learning or in helping others. Not"—Irtysh held up an admonitory finger—"that she did not and does not do very well by all my children. She is a conscientious parent. They just don't require her to exert herself. I think my children should learn to exert themselves on behalf of others even if it doesn't benefit them directly. It will make them better rulers and better dragons."

"Who will learn what?" Otohime appeared in the Western Room door. She held Susu and Tsuruko held Kichiro. All were dressed in the latest Western fashion. Azuki was impressed.

"What's this?" Shota came up behind her to make faces at the two toddlers, with Renko and Akira behind him.

Irtysh rose and beckoned the others to enter. He complimented Otohime, Tsuruko and Renko on their dresses and took a long moment checking the boys.

"Azuki-san," he said, "What do you think?"

She smiled at the way his language and hers changed as they spoke.

"I think the ladies are lovely," she said. "Otohime, Tsuruko-san, those are wonderful walking suits. The boys look like the children in the *Godey's Lady's Book*. Akira-san and Shota-san match you, Prince Irtysh, and you all look very well."

"What about me?" Renko asked.

"You know I think that dress looks splendid on you! And you've altered the back just like I did!" She turned to show off her own gown. Renko's, in green, complimented her coloring as much as Azuki's persimmon dress complimented hers.

"Who's going to learn what?" Renko asked as she moved off to start tea while the others took seats around the table. It probably wasn't necessary, since they were going to leave soon, but she thought it better that she do it than anyone else, except for Irtysh himself. In the West domestic chores usually fell to women, if any were present, and she as Irtysh's sister was the best candidate for hostess duty. Renko had been doing some reading herself. Since she was appearing more often as a Western human, she had decided she needed to learn how it was done. Noriko's training was having the intended effect.

"I was shy about asking," Azuki admitted, "but lately I have been having so much fun. I could do it myself, but Prince Irtysh seems to find these things so easy"—

"Finds what so easy?"

"Making things," Azuki said. "I asked him to make more of my pattern books. He assured me it was easy for him, but he said he won't do it at all! He'll have his children do it."

"Like he did the looms." Renko nodded.

"Leaving me all the time in the world."

Otohime kept her face in perfect order, unable not to hear what her sister and young friend were saying. She turned back to Tsuruko, who was letting Prince Irtysh show her the pattern book while Kichiro and Susu, far across Irtysh's principal chamber, threw cabochon gemstones into the Lake of Jewels under the watchful gazes of Shota and Akira.

"You could have asked me," Renko pointed out as she and Azuki placed tea glasses on a silver tray. She wasn't angry, exactly, but people had been passing her over in favor of others who were older when assigning duties she could easily handle.

"Don't you think you have enough to do?" Azuki asked. "I'd feel badly seeing you do my work while I laid about. I'd rather we had fun together! Prince Irtysh seems to enjoy this, and he could say no, whereas I don't think you'd feel like you could."

"Brother just likes doing things that will please Otohime," Renko said, a touch caustically.

Nobody really wanted tea. What they wanted was to get to the Exhibition. After some squabbling about who exactly would go, Shota and Susu took a rapid reconnaissance jaunt to the capital and soon enough, all the travelers linked arms in their small groups and were off.

"Renko-san, Akira-san, you've got to see this!" Shota pulled them off to examine the windmill. "Did you see the pictures? It pumps up water from a well!"

"Have a look, Renko-san." Akira stepped back to let the smaller Renko in front of him. "Thanks, Shota-san." He scooted the other way to let Shota get in front of him from the other side.

"I see it!" Renko's gazed swiveled between the actual pumping mechanism and the sign explaining it. "Here is the pump—see it? And it is the wind that provides the power!"

"I've seen water mills before," Akira said. "But not wind-powered ones. If you take the power of the wind and harness it"—

"Like we did with the steam engine"— Shota interrupted.

"We could power almost anything!" Renko was thrilled.

Susu was restive in Irtysh's iron grip. He wanted to get down and find out what Shota, Akira and Renko were doing. Instead, he was stuck here, listening to boring adult conversation about this stupid machine. And that stupid machine. And the other stupid machine over there. One of the cotton spinning machines had garnered its inventor, Tatchi Gaun, the highest award at the exhibit. But this other one ran by waterwheel, which was what his sister and Shota-san and Akira-san were talking about. In fact, there were easily half a dozen cotton spinning machines alone!

"There are disputes about the technology," Tsuruko-san said. Kichiro seemed to be examining the machines closely, although Susu couldn't imagine why. They all looked about the same to him.

"Gaun-san, it seems, made the first one, and everybody agrees it's the best one."

"It got the award, anyway," Prince Irtysh said aloud. Susu wiggled. "Don't do it," his elder brother said silently. And firmly.

"It hasn't stopped people from imitating it, even if they aren't trying to improve it," Tsuruko said. "They just want to make the money from selling their versions without giving Gaun-san credit for his original work or paying him for it."

"I'm sure they should do that, but just look at all the machines there are that purport to do the same thing!" Otohime did not sound pleased at this prospect. "How can we pick out what's best?"

"Renko-san is the one who is good at this," Tsuruko said. "Renko-san, please come over here," she called with both her voices.

"These are the machines we are looking for," Azuki said when her friends hurried over. "Some say they are for cotton, and others say they are for silk. A couple don't specify. Some look like they are foot or hand powered, but here's one powered by a water wheel, like you were thinking could be done with wind." She smiled at them. "Can you look at these and decide which is the best one for our purposes?"

Renko nearly climbed into the exhibit, trying to see all the details of the engineering. Shota wanted to change so he could fly in and help her do that, but he couldn't change here, and that annoyed him. Akira carefully examined all the machines.

"Prince Irtysh?" he said.

"Hmmm?" the prince handed Susu to Otohime, who set him on the ground, took his hand and walked him over to the exhibit of power generation machinery. The others would be interested in this, too. It included windmills, mostly, but several steam engines and a water turbine. She pointed out to her little brother that any of these could be used to power a cotton spinner, in the way Renko and Shota had set up a steam engine to power Azuki's loom.

"We aren't going to buy the spinning machines, are we?" Akira asked the prince.

"No," Irtysh replied. "We are going to make them, like we did the looms."

Azuki's eyes got wide when she saw where Akira was going with this idea.

"If we are going to make them," she said, "we can make them any way we want!"

Akira nodded. "Isn't Azuki-san right, Prince Irtysh? Can't we decide what parts of each kind are the best and put them all together to make the very best machine?"

Irtysh regarded the machines carefully. He strode over to Otohime and Susu, who were examining the power generation equipment. Quickly he returned to the spinning machines, shoved his hands in his pockets, rocked back on his heels, and said, "I think we can do better than that." He glanced around.

"Tsuruko-san? Azuki-san?" he said. "If you wanted us to, we could make more than one kind, I think. One could be powered by foot, one by water, one by wind, one by steam."

Renko skidded in, wanting to hear her brother and chime in. "Or we could set any one machine so it could draw power from several different sources."

"That's good, Renko-san," Shota said. "That would work really well." He hoped he could help. It seemed like Akira was much better at this than he was. Shota tried to be generous, but ended up being very much afraid he was jealous.

"Can you design it here, Irtysh?" Otohime approached with Susu trotting unsteadily beside her. Kichiro had fallen asleep.

"I don't need to," the prince said with a grin. "Susu, you will help me here. So will you, Renko, and, if you will, you, too, Otohime. Fix the image in your mind and transmit it. We will want images of all the spinning and weaving machines and all the power ones, too. Susu, do you think you can send the images to Galina?"

"I can do that!" He puffed out his little chest and swaggered in confidence.

"Otohime?" She nodded. "Will you reach for Zhenya?"

"I will do my best," she said. She'd never actually met Zhenya. What was he playing at? How could he be so caught up in his project of the moment that he forgot that?

"Renko, will you please try for Adrik and I'll take the twins."

"Little Sister," Otohime said, "will you walk with me? Perhaps the signal will be strongest if you and Susu and I work together. Then we can all try to reach everybody."

"Good idea!" Irtysh boomed so loudly that his exquisite voice overwhelmed all the people within twenty meters.

"This means everyone will have complete sets of images, I think," Azuki said.

"That's right," Renko said.

"Can you transfer them to paper?" Akira wanted to know. "I mean, if you have paper?"

"Yes," Irtysh sounded entirely confident of that, but Renko shrugged. They'd try. "Brother, do it with me," she said.

"If you can get them on paper," Shota said, "it will be easier to work on the design."

"Indeed it will," Irtysh said, nearly chortling with glee at the idea of industrial design. "Tsuruko-san, will you and Kichiro-chan give us just a moment, then accompany my sister and me?"

"What are we going to do?" Shota wondered as the others moved off.

"We can't all be telegraph machines," Azuki said, "but if the rest of us look, we might see things we can improve. You were looking at the windmill pump outside. Let's go look at the power-generating machines."

"I hope we can get this done soon," Akria said. Azuki looked askance. He shrugged. "I know we are here specifically about these machines, but there is the entire rest of the Exhibition to see, and I want to!"

Azuki smiled and Shota all but whooped mentally. There was a reason he liked Akira.

Inside the Art Pavilion, 1877 Exhibition,
Hiroshige III

33

"What are we doing here, Ryuujin?" Rizantona wanted to know. "And where exactly are we?"

"What did you think of our voyage?" Ryuujin said. He was cheered not only by the results of his experiment but by Rizantona's cooperation in it. "We got here easily enough, you'll have to admit."

"Yes," the Dragon Queen replied, but that was not the point. She wanted facts. "That's certainly true. There are materials everywhere. As long as we travel together, we can keep on going as long as we want to. We learned that today. It is likely we could form larger groups and travel much faster in concert, too. Simply finding that out justifies this experiment. There is obviously much more research to be done. But where are we now? And why do we want to be here?"

The two gigantic dragons, one Western and one Eastern, stood within the conjoined air enclosures that Ryuujin's daughters called "bubbles." They'd become so good at coordinating their air supplies they didn't even have to pay attention to the way the barrier filter had changed so they were now handing their atmospheric needs in an entirely different way than they had mere minutes ago. Rizantona did notice, though, and added another area of inquiry to what was becoming a long list.

They were on an orbiting body of some sort. She could see that. It was not Earth. Earth was over there, so far away it was hard to spot, a small blue speck floating in a sea of tiny lights. This was far too big to be Earth's moon. Rizantona checked but she did not perceive life forms, at least not on the surface, just endless reddish dust and rock horizon to horizon. Ryuujin looked around with the wonder of a child, inviting her to join his amazement at the spectacle before them.

"Ryuujin, why are we here?" She enunciated each word carefully. She was not going to let him distract her any longer.

"I wanted to see if we could get here. You know, Irtysh and Otohime went to the moon."

"They didn't!"

"They did. Irtysh didn't want to tell me, I gather, but Otohime did. She was trying to convince me of what an excellent dragon he is—yes, Rizantona, he is; I have no question about that—but I saw something that might help us with our most pressing problem."

"Overpopulation?" the Dragon Queen asked. "I thought we had that solved."

"Not of dragons," His Majesty responded. "Humans."

Rizantona certainly agreed that humans were a growing concern; in fact, she forbore to remind Ryuujin, she was the one who first recognized it. At least he was finally acknowledging the problem.

Rizantona now found herself enthralled with the vistas of scientific exploration opened up before her due to their children's experiment and her consort's expansion upon it and how that could be used to solve at least some of their current problems. Once she had time to think about all of the potential this held, she thought they'd both be shocked at the implications.

"Do you think we could make something of this place?" She kicked at the surface and swished her tail across it. "There isn't much here."

"All the basic elements are here," Ryuujin pointed out. "If we have the ingredients, we can make things just as we can on Earth. This is the Red Planet." He waved his whiskers at the ground. "It's clear why they call it that. Its formal human name is Mars."

"We can make more water without difficulty, it looks like." Rizantona wanted to keep to the point. "There's some below the surface. The problem I see is atmospheric oxygen concentration."

"Between us, we could certainly make water. If we can do that, we can make whatever else we want, don't you think?" Ryuujin grinned. "Learning each other's skills and how to use them in concert allows us to grow."

"Once we have water and are on our way to an overall breathable atmosphere, any forms of life that are hiding here could be persuaded to develop so they could live on the surface," Rizantona added. When the dimorphic species of dragon started acting as one, the limits of each group shattered and they could reach farther than either had dreamed.

"We have not gone so far we could not bring life here from Earth."

"We'd do better to guide the forms that are here in any direction that suits us, like you do with your coral," Rizantona said.

"Or like Irtysh started doing with the trees. We will have to experiment and see."

"I think we will need to travel farther before we start that sort of thing," Rizantona said, looking around. For once, Ryuujin was talking sense. Dragons and humans were no longer compatible. Humans were going to destroy the planet faster than dragons could rebuild. It was about time he realized it.

"If we are going to be safe while we build and with what we build, this is too close," she expanded. "The speed at which the humans are developing their technology is frightening. Soon, they will have machines that can take them to the moon and even here and perhaps beyond. That will make them all the more dangerous to us."

"We can go as far as we want to," Ryuujin said, using his new ability to huff a smoke plume to express his satisfaction. "We have just demonstrated that. The materials we need get thinner as we get away from planets, but they are there and we can use them. I think we will find they will get thicker as we get closer to orbiting bodies and systems everywhere, just like they did here."

"We need to explore this, yes. But I am not sure I like it. We have our obligations to the Earth."

Ryuujin turned and faced Rizantona, regarding his fearsome consort quizzically. She was the one who first broached the idea of dragons needing to leave the Earth to escape what she felt had become a plague of humans that was only going to get worse.

Rizantona, though, had an inkling of a problem Ryuujin didn't know about. She wasn't sure she wanted to tell him yet, especially since it was, to date, so amorphous.

When Rizantona didn't elaborate, Ryuujin continued his exploration of the planet around them, delighted and confounded by what he found. He couldn't help but explain it all to Rizantona, in detail, but she wasn't really listening.

Agniya had come to see Rizantona, her Queen, with a complaint about Irtysh. She had learned, Rizantona assumed from Galina, that Otohime, Renko and Sugaar were truly dual-natured and that Irtysh could adopt a human guise when he pleased. Rizantona shook her head, puffed a little smoke, and flicked the end of her wing at a rock formation currently captivating Ryuujin, who took this as a sign of her interest in the possibility of surface water it implied.

Rizantona thought Agniya didn't care what Irtysh did with himself, as long as it didn't affect his abilities as a prince or as a father. All the attention he devoted to his hobbies and pleasures had never done that, something even Rizantona had to admit. It did make him, as far as Agniya was concerned, an ineffective consort, so she had left him to it and concentrated on her own affairs, especially the massive diamond deposits of which she was rightly proud. Since this aligned with Rizantona's own beliefs on proper dragon behavior, she approved.

But now Agniya believed Irtysh was so fascinated with the dual-natured that he planned to teach his children how to adopt human guises, too. With what end in mind, Rizantona could not guess. He was certainly not thinking of the possible consequences, many of which could be disastrous for dragonkind. Irtysh was not normally a fool, but in this she was afraid he might be acting like one. If Agniya was right, and that Rizantona did not know.

She would not mention it to Ryuujin. Not, at least, until she knew more. After all, her data came from Agniya and a former consort was rarely a reliable source of accurate information. More like malicious gossip. She shook herself and paid attention to where Ryuujin was pointing.

"A potential river bed?" she asked. "Let's go look."

34

Noriko had parted from Otohime, Tsuruko and the children in an alley behind an empty building where nobody could see them vanish. Once they had gone, she reappeared in the street so quietly and inconspicuously that she was quite sure no one would have noticed her sudden appearance, if indeed they noticed her at all.

She made her way to a busy boulevard. Sachiko's home wasn't particularly close to the *dojo*, but neither was it far. Noriko was accustomed to walking between them. The Inn of the Golden Phoenix was not on the most direct route, but off to the side in an area rife with redevelopment.

Noriko thought she might indulge herself by hailing one of the many *jinrikisha* that had proliferated in the city almost as if they were breeding. She chuckled to herself. Her own humor amused her, but she rarely shared it—it seemed just a little too odd.

But then! She gasped as saw something that had not been operating in the capital before she left it. This was what she had hoped to see: a horse-drawn coach, almost like a carriage of the kind the Emperor and Empress rode in, but not nearly as fancy. It was mostly enclosed, though, and held eight to ten passengers, depending on where they sat.

"Where are you going?" she called as she waved to signal it to stop. This was the transportation she'd wanted to find!

"Hanzomon," the–what was he? Footman? Groom? He wasn't driving but he was part of the coach's staff.

"May I, please?" Noriko gestured. Hanzomon was right on her way. The West Gate of the Palace was named for Hattori Hanzo Masanari. This leader of the Iga Ryu *Shinobi* clan was an ally of Iyeasu, and though he died before the Tokugawa Shogunate was established, the family contribution was recognized with land near this gate and prestigious Shogunal guard assignments. Iga Ryu and Koga Ryu, the two major schools of *Shinobi*, had gone underground, presumably destroyed, by Oda Nobunaga. The remaining forces were subsumed into the official guard, as had happened here.

In times before Noriko's the Hanzomon was maintained as a Shogunal escape route, though of course she knew the history. Her own Mochizuki

School almost certainly continued to maintain relations with both Iga Ryu and Koga Ryu insofar as they still existed. While those *Shinobi* schools had been largely and publicly destroyed, her own, women-only, school simply vanished from the public eye and remained hidden. But the Hanzomon was close to Kagurazaka, the *Geisha* district where Sachiko's *Geisha* clients lived and worked. There was no reason she couldn't travel by carriage, like the Empress!

Noriko took advantage of a step the man pulled down to help her ascend into the carriage. A passenger moved over to let her sit right by the door, so she could see out the window. He smiled at her. She smiled back. He was enjoying the adventure, too!

Horses moved faster than oxen. Their movement bounced and their tack jingled. Noriko was grateful for Phlox and the time she spent riding. Someone only accustomed to oxcarts might have found the carriage jostling. As it was, though she clutched a hanging strap now and again when the carriage stopped suddenly or jerked around a corner, she smiled her delight with the fast pace and the changing view.

She decided she'd been away too long as the crowded streets and unfamiliar new buildings flowed past her window. Western-style stores with their glass display windows and narrow entrances jockeyed for position side by side with classic

Japanese shops, with covered walkways and front walls rolled up so customers could see the merchandise from the street and enter where they pleased. Old-fashioned sellers of dumplings carried hot steam baskets from shoulder poles. Pushcarts run by chefs advertised sushi vendors preparing the latest catch. Oh, there was the turn for the Inn of the Golden Phoenix, which had been her home for so long. It occupied a discreet, highly respectable, location on the west side of the palace.

At the Hanzomon, she hopped out of the carriage and stood for bit simply looking, so overwhelmed with the sights, sounds and smells of the rapidly growing city she was sure she would remember none of it.

Now she could hail a *jinrikishaw* and perhaps digest some of the enormous changes to the city that was at one time her home before arriving at Sachiko's tidy residence.

Though the little human-powered vehicles seemed to be everywhere, none were free and willing to respond to her, so she walked until she reached Tokyo Shokonsha Shrine. Built in 1869 to enshrine as *kami* the souls of those who died fighting on the Imperial side in the Boshin War, in which Noriko herself had fought, she felt a special connection to this place. The souls of those who opposed the Restoration were currently enshrined elsewhere. There was a movement afoot to change the name and dedication of the Shrine to honor all of Japan's war dead. Noriko, not being among them, did not have a strong view on this one way or another.

Noriko had fought on the Shogun's side during the Boshin War, as it happened, since she was employed by the Shogun at the time. A few of the souls enshrined here had entered their next lives at her hand. It seemed fit to her that she stop here whenever she passed to honor them, ask their forgiveness, and wish them well.

Sachiko did not live in Kagurazaka proper, but in a quiet residential neighborhood at its edge, on a back street, away from the businesses that lined the larger avenue, most with living quarters above the shop. This area was peopled by artisans who made things used by the very rich former *Daimyos* and other nobles who formed the new nobility and fiscal aristocracy. They continued to live in their former city estates that surrounded what used to be the Shogun's Castle and was now the Emperor's Palace. This area seemed to hold off the intense commercial renovation of the city, probably because it had always hosted those large *Daimyo* estates and the smaller houses of those who served and sold to them. Noriko liked the neighborhood; she hoped it would stay that way.

"Noriko-*sama!* Come in, come in!" Sachiko opened the door herself.

"It has been far too long since I have seen you." Noriko bowed formally, but her smile showed her pleasure. "Please excuse this rude interruption," she added courteously.

"Do, please, come in," Sachiko responded. "I have been looking forward to seeing you!" Sachiko led her friend into the small formal reception room in the front of the house. It overlooked an elegant garden with a little pond and a stone lantern, the bamboo fence separating it from the neighbors and the street lined with shrubs and trees of varying heights to give the mountains-to-sea landscape that was basic to Japanese garden design.

"Is the lamp new?" Noriko asked. She did not remember it sitting where it was now, next to the pond on a slab of granite.

"It is," Sachiko said. "They were tearing down a big house not far away. I got what I could, but I really didn't have room for much. I took some of the fish, too."

"You have koi in your pond now?" Noriko found that exciting! Koi were expensive and could be tricky to keep. They had a few, but it was Endo who took care of them. Noriko rarely spent time in that part of the garden, except with Yuta, who enjoyed it; it was outside his study. Not only did her room face the other way, she spent most of her waking hours in her *dojo*.

"I do. I am enjoying learning to care for them. Yae-san has shown some aptitude for managing a fish pond. Miyuki-san and Yae-san both should be here shortly with our tea. How is your family?"

"We are well," Noriko said. "The children mature, my husband's school prospers and he enjoys his contribution to the national educational system. They're talking about having national universities like the foreigners do very soon, one in our area."

"And you?" Sachiko seated her guest on a cushion overlooking the garden and settled herself, too.

Noriko shrugged. "My *dojo* attracts students, I continue my practice, and I enjoy everything very much. It all surprises me. I never thought to have so much. How is your life?"

A tap on the door interrupted them and two young women slightly older than Noriko's niece entered carrying trays. The tall Miyuki with the pockmarked face held a simple lacquerware tray with a lovely *Tokoname* black tea pot on it in the *Yokode Kyuusu* style, with the hollow handle protruding from the side. It was accompanied by *Banko-yaki* columnar cups in a matching black. The simplicity and the delicate care taken in their making soothed Noriko even as she admired it.

The second girl, Yae, bearing a similar tray holding snacks, looked utterly average in every way, though she'd probably be attractive enough if she changed her expression, which was at once servile and defiant.

"Good afternoon!" Noriko greeted them. "I am glad to see you brought cups for all of us. I am looking forward to speaking with you."

The girls sat down and served the tea before they passed the snacks to Sachiko's prominent guest. What they did not already know about Noriko, who was almost a legend among those who frequented Sachiko's home in its capacity as shelter and resource center for displaced women, they sought to find out through discreet questions.

"I hope that Noriko-*sama* can help us find places for you both in the world," Sachiko said. "I'd like to keep you here, of course, but there are just too many girls and women displaced by everything going on in the world! There are labor difficulties. That affected you two. Then we have had the Rebellion. Plus there are men going off to factories and mines, deserting their families. There are even women still suffering from the Restoration and the Boshin War, which is when Noriko-*sama* and I became displaced ourselves."

Noriko caught Miyuki's gaze and held it until the girl flushed an unlovely, blotchy, salmon color and dropped her head.

"When you know somebody," Noriko said, "they look like who they are inside and the outside doesn't matter. I apologize for staring, but I understand you don't like to be seen, Miyuki-san. I don't think you need to worry as much as you do."

"Nobody wants to look at me," Miyuki replied. "I'm ugly. That's why my parents sold me and why they don't want me back." She shrugged. "Who can blame them?"

"It's just not that bad," Sachiko urged.

"I know you mean well, Sachiko-san," Miyuki said. "I know Noriko-*sama* is right, and you probably don't even see my horrible face for what it is anymore, but I do. I'm not a bad person, but I hate having anybody see me. I wish...I wish I was dead!"

Tears ran down Miyuki's scarred face as she jumped to her feet and ran out of the small room.

"I am so sorry," Noriko said. "I did not mean to hurt her."

"It's not you, Noriko-*sama*," Yae said. "It's anybody. She carries her scars around like a weight. She dreads going out in public. She thinks she's a blight on the landscape. I try to stay with her. I'm afraid of what she might do."

"There you have it," Sachiko said to Noriko. "I have not been able to find a place for her. She is too self-conscious, and I can't seem to talk her out of it and get her to recognize her intrinsic value."

"You can hardly blame her." Yae, dubbed troublemaker by Junko, who was now in training with Noriko's hidden school, spoke out bravely, even among older women of significantly higher status.

"Everything you have for us, Sachiko-san," Yae said, "is somehow connected with attracting a man for marriage. *Tondenhei* farmers need wives, but Miyuki-san thinks she would be picked last and by the worst of the bunch, that she would likely be abused, or her children would be. Working in shops, or restaurants, or domestic service–it's all the same! Our advancement depends on pleasing a man. She knows she won't and neither will I, not once they know me."

"I understand Miyuki-san's fears," Noriko said. "Our housekeeper was an outcast for some time; she has facial scarring from an injury that is much worse than Miyuki's and she is also mute. Yet, she has overcome all of that and now has what I believe is a happy life. There is even a well-placed man in our community who holds her in some regard. I have hopes for their future, and I think she is old enough to be my mother." Noriko smiled at Sachiko as her hostess refreshed her cup with more strong and aromatic green tea.

"I see nothing wrong with you," Noriko said, directing her smile at Yae, "except an outspoken nature. I know a fabric merchant who is famous for hers. Her husband appreciates the way that shields him from having to engage in the parts of business he doesn't enjoy. He appreciates her good business sense too. You are certainly intelligent enough to learn commerce."

"I've just about decided that Miyuki-san needs an environment that's sheltered, but I don't know what that might be," Sachiko said. "She could do what I do, but there is simply no work to be had; the profession is in decline. My ladies are themselves finding life difficult now. Western entertainments are more fashionable except at the highest levels. Western men have absolutely no idea what a *geisha* is and what she does. They expect some kind of *yujo,* and then get offended when they learn *geisha* are nothing of the kind."

Sachiko used a common word that generally meant prostitute, a sex worker of any class or kind. Noriko watched Yae under hooded lids to see how she reacted to Sachiko's deliberate vulgarity. Interestingly, she did not react to that at all, any more than her expression had budged at Noriko's suggestion that she could be good at business.

"Sachiko-san has never married," Yae pointed out. "Noriko-*sama*, you only recently married, I understand. What is so odd about Miyuki-san and I wanting to avoid marriage?"

"Things change," Noriko said, "when we least expect it. I don't know if Sachiko-san told you how we became friends. She nursed me back to health when I was wounded defending the young woman I was guarding–she was about your age. I cannot have children. No man wants to marry a woman who cannot give him children, or so I thought. But you were there when my husband joined me in fighting to free you and Miyuki-san and the others. Our interests are parallel. We fight well together; we found we also talk well together. I had never thought to marry. Neither had he. Yet, we did and we are happy. Things change."

"They will not change for me," Yae shook her head, rose quickly and bobbed a bow. "Please excuse me." She picked up the depleted snack tray and left.

Sachiko shrugged. "And now you know. Most of the girls and women who come through here are relatively easily dealt with. They can return to their families, many of them. The *tondenhei* program has been a miraculous gift, giving these women new goals and patriotic aspirations." Sachiko made a moué of distaste. On the one hand she appreciated the program's opportunity for her women. On the other, she hated the political cynicism that made such manipulative use of citizens.

Many of the women she helped had skills that could be turned towards earning them a decent living: restaurants, hotels, private domestic service, tailoring, millinery, trades and crafts, business of all kinds. Many could learn new skills, as Kotoe and Hisa had as they worked in a print shop. New industries required new workers and these new industries were not always fussy about hiring women.

"The best positions are those in smaller business, though, aren't they?" Noriko said. "Yae-san is right about that. In those smaller concerns becoming a part of the family is a young worker's best hope for stability, security and advancement."

"Unfortunately, yes, she is right. Many of these businesses are actually looking for young people to try out as workers and marry into the family if they do a good job."

Noriko laughed softly. "Toyoda-san thought my husband was turning my head with talk of marriage so he could avoid hiring a bookkeeper and estate manager who would have to be paid wages, and that I'd be a subsidiary wife."

"As though marriage is all that women want! But marrying to get a cheap employee does happen often enough."

"Soon we won't have subsidiary wives or concubines. Men will have to pay wages. I doubt if they'll like that."

"Can you think of anything to do with these girls? Can you even guess what Yae-san's problem might be? I provide academic opportunities here— your husband has helped with that, did you know?—and bright girls can, if they wish, go on to study further in some of the several schools for women that have recently opened. I will give them an education if I possibly can. But that doesn't seem to suit these two, either!"

Noriko shook her head. "I do not know. I'll think about it, though." Then she smiled. "And I would like to ask my husband."

35

"I brought all the tools back, *'To-san*," Akira said as he stepped up onto the gallery of their house where Minoru sat smoking his pipe and watching the view. "Where shall I put them?"

"Where you got them, Akira-kun," Minoru said with a grin. "You don't have to ask to know that."

Akira shrugged. "Wasn't sure." He returned the tools to the tool shed and came back, carrying a carafe of cold barley tea and two cups. "Want some?"

"Yes, thanks." Minoru smiled. Akira was considerate and kind, skilled and strong, eager to learn. Just about everything Minoru could have asked for in a son. And more. He only hoped his long-dead wife was watching so she could see this new incarnation of the son who died with her.

"*Kampai*," they said as though they were drinking beer or wine, and tossed back the refreshing tea.

"Fleet's coming in," Minoru said, nodding at the ocean where fishing boats were sailing into the larger port to the north. "Flags are up. Can you tell what they caught?"

Tairyo-bata flags were flown to show when a boat had a big catch. Fishing was fairly consistent around Japan, so it wasn't usually necessary to show exactly what the boats caught. Everybody knew what was in season. Sometimes, though, a special catch was celebrated with a special flag.

"Blue mackerel, I'd guess. It's their season. Flounder are in season, too, but I'd expect those to be fished inshore."

"You're right. I got a few off the rocks earlier. Took them up to Hanako-san. We're invited there for dinner."

"Beats cooking."

"Beats my cooking any day of the week," Minoru said. "You can tell everybody about that Exhibition."

"Everyone will be talking about that!"

"You all will have seen different things!"

Akira poured more of the tea as Minoru tapped out his pipe and refilled it.

"Do you know where I could buy some tools?" Akira asked his adopted father. The two of them fit remarkably well, Akira thought, between his Sea

Eagle nature and Minoru's sea-going bent. It was like they really were related.

"Why do you need more?" Minoru asked. "We have plenty here and on the boat."

"Kukanko-chan," Akira explained. "She did a good job on that *shamisen.* If she had her own tools, with some of them fit to her hands, she could do more woodworking and make more *shamisen* or whatever she wanted. She doesn't have much to trade or a way to earn."

"She's an *oni*, you said." Minoru tried to keep disapproval out of his voice. Making friends with an *oni* was not exactly usual, *oni* being widely viewed as not merely *yokai* but demons and therefore hostile. But Akira was not usual, himself.

"They aren't demons," Akira said. "At least, Kukanko-chan isn't. She acts like she's pretty much alone in the world and she's just a child."

Minoru used a safety match to light his pipe, sat back and thought for a minute. Finally he made a decision.

"We've got extra tools. You could give her some of those. Endo-san might have some, too. We can ask him when we go up the hill for dinner. Don't tell him who they're for, though. Not everybody's ready for you, much less an *oni!*"

Akira grinned. He was discreet, more discreet than Shota had ever thought to be. Renko, too. Azuki was good at keeping herself to herself, but she had always been so busy–and she had suffered more than any of the rest of them at the hands of unwelcoming humans.

"Can we go look through the shed so you can help me pick out ones we don't need?"

Minoru grinned back. He found it hard to express how happy he was having Akira as his adopted son.

"Let's go," he said as he laid his pipe away. "We have time."

Akira and Minoru assembled a good basic toolkit for Kukanko from what they found in the shed. Endo-san gave them a few tools that had broken handles. Minoru said Akira could make new handles. That way, they'd better fit the intended recipient, who had deformed hands.

Akira started to protest at that, but backed off when Minoru winked. Kukanko's large, three fingered hands were not large or deformed for an *oni*, true enough, but they were not at all normal for a human.

He set the bag of tools down outside when they reached the entry to the Maeda house.

"What's that?" Renko wanted to know as she and Azuki came out to welcome them.

"Tools for Kukanko-chan," Akira said. "If she has her own tools, I can help her learn to use them and that'll give her a skill. I don't know how she survives up there. Could you give me a ride up there tomorrow morning, please?"

"I'm sorry, Akira-san, I can't. But what about Susu-chan? You know he'd love it. Just ask him."

Akira smiled and nodded. He liked Susu. He was an easy child to like. Azuki and Renko led their guests inside and settled them in the small reception room.

"Giving Kukanko-san tools is a good idea," Azuki said thoughtfully. "I'm sure the *oni* have ways of surviving; they've lived up there in the mountains long enough. But the world is changing faster than we can keep up, and everybody needs to adapt. *Oni*, too, I suppose."

Yuta, from his study, overheard the conversation. He smiled and went out to speak to the new arrivals.

He was happy at the way things were going for his niece. She was growing up quickly, and learning to be observant and analytical, too. He was glad to see how relaxed she looked now that her workload had eased. That left her time to think and learn, and she was taking advantage of it, whether she realized it or not.

After their Buddhist practice, they sat down to dinner.

"How are your fabric patterns coming along?" Yuta asked Azuki as he lifted the lid of his soup bowl.

"I've had great fortune with that, Uncle," she replied. "Prince Irtysh is duplicating the books for me so I don't have to make more than one myself."

"His abilities are extraordinary," Yuta said.

Noriko smiled. She admired her husband's generosity, even though she could also see he still didn't approve of the prince.

"He's having his children do it." Renko smiled. "What I think I like best about my brother is that he thinks that if he can do something, any of us can. Because he takes that attitude he helps us all learn more about what we can do."

"How about your machines?" Minoru asked.

"Did Akira-san tell you about all the machines we saw?" Azuki asked. "There were so many! Just for spinning and weaving!"

"There were really interesting pumps," Shota said. "And windmills."

"The new mining apparatus was exciting," Renko chimed in. "I really need to tell Anko-*sama*. I picked up some written information for her."

"She'll be ready to receive a few callers soon," Noriko said. Hanako circulated with serving dishes to give them refills of anything they might lack. This was not a Japanese custom: servings were normally separate and given out on special dishes suited to each offering. Except for some hot-pot dishes and stews, the only foods that might allow for extra servings were tea and rice. Leftovers were incorporated into the next day's meals. But Hanako had learned the foreign custom of offering additional portions when she lived in Nagasaki, and she liked it. She enjoyed seeing people enjoy her cooking. She urged another *chawanmushi* savory custard on Akira and gave Minoru another bundle of greens topped with sesame seeds before giving the last *chawanmushi* to Shota. Minoru shot her a disapproving look. He liked *chawanmushi*, though he had to admit both boys were still growing and the only way he was going to grow at his age was out.

Hanako didn't notice. She nodded at Noriko vigorously. Anko-*sama* would appreciate visitors. Even though new babies and their mothers usually stayed home, isolated against disease and given ample opportunities to rest and recover, during that first tricky month, she did know from both Kiyo and Reiko that Anko was restive.

The babies were growing healthily and Anko was young and fit, so she was recovering well and quickly from being brought to bed of twins. Toshio worked with Cloudy every day, and it sounded like the two were developing a strong bond. Yuta knew more about that than Hanako did, and she listened as he spoke about it to Minoru.

While Anko was delighted her husband had pleasurable things to do in addition to enjoying his new infants, she wanted adult company besides his.

That was clear to the women she saw daily. Her mother and father both were traveling back and forth to their principle home, since the season permitted it. Lady Satsuki was working hard on the refugee project with Otohime, while Eitaro managed the mines alone in Toshio's absence. Soon, though, it would be time to present the babies at the Shrine and the Temple, and then they could all go home, where Anko could resume her own work with the refugee project.

"Perhaps we can go see her after school tomorrow, Renko-san," Azuki said. "I'm sure she'd like it."

"I could take her all the brochures from the Exhibition, too, not just the mining information. She'll enjoy looking at those. Shota-san can come, too. He's good at explaining the machines. Let's do it. Maybe Otohime can join us."

Shota liked that idea; explaining was one thing he knew he was good at.

"How are your looms coming along?" Minoru asked Azuki.

"We have a lot of them now," Azuki said. "We're going to have more machines as Prince Irtysh and his children make the spinning machines the way Renko-san redesigned them."

"I didn't redesign them," Renko objected. "I just saw a few things that could be improved."

"So you did it."

"I've been wondering something," Shota said. "We have all those looms and we'll have double that when the spinning machines are finished. Prince Irtysh lives far away from here. We've got to get the machines to the people who will use them."

"Brother will just…." Renko's voice trailed off.

"I see your point," Akria said. "That's a lot of machinery to transport."

"He can't just set them all down in the middle of a handy field like His Majesty did when Aunt came home," Shota said.

They all fell silent for a second, pondering this new difficulty when Minoru spoke up.

"What you need," he said, "is a ship."

"That's a good idea," Yuta said, awakening to the possibility.

"Is it possible to transport cargo to a ship?" Noriko wanted to know.

"You'll have to ask this Prince Irtysh," Minoru said, "but I don't know why not. If he could just set it down in some field somewhere, why not onto a ship? It would have to go in the cargo hold, though. Renko-san?"

"That would work," she said. "We usually bring things in outside, but I see no reason why things couldn't be moved from an interior—my brother has them stored inside, of course—to another interior. If I can do it, and I think I could, he can do it easily."

"Where would we get a ship?" Yuta asked. "*Sencho-sama*, is that something you could arrange?"

Minoru smiled. "Yes. Ships are often chartered for specific voyages to deliver cargo or even passengers. We'd have to work out the details, like where it's supposed to be coming from and where it's going to land to discharge the cargo, and the size of ship we'd need, but I haven't lost all my connections."

"Let's go talk about the specifics of it," Yuta said. "I want to know more." He rose and Minoru followed. "Wife?" Yuta said. Noriko had all the financial and logistical details of the refugee project at her fingertips; that has become her role.

"I'll be along in a few minutes. If that's all right with you," Noriko said. Yuta nodded and the two men left for Yuta's study and a jug of chilled wine.

"Let's clear the table for Hanako-san," Noriko said, "and then we can talk. I have something I want to ask you all." She was pleased to see both boys hop up and start picking up plates. The girls reached for trays to slide under them. While it might not be usual in a formal environment, or even in many homes, where cooking and clearing up fell to the women of the household, their situation here was different, Noriko felt, and was glad Yuta agreed. Hanako was their employee and this did fall under her duties, but she was also a valued member of the household and went beyond the official scope of her job in many delicious ways. Helping her was a way to express their gratitude.

It only took them a few minutes and they even managed to wash many of the dishes before Hanako shooed them out of the kitchen with a plate of cookies and a fresh pot of tea. Noriko finished wiping the table and took the small towel, which she carefully folded even though it would go right into the laundry basket, back to Hanako.

"You are all being so kind to Kukanko-san," Noriko said when she returned to the dining room. "Your ideas and solutions are ingenious. I need clever solutions to two more pressing problems."

"Yes, Noriko-*sama*?" Renko asked as she set out cups.

"We'll help if we can," Akira said. Shota shoved more cookie into his mouth and nodded. Azuki put a cookie on a tissue square and laid it in front of Noriko.

"Everyone but Akira will remember the mill girls." She turned to the Eagle-boy. "That was when my husband and I met, helping some indentured laborers escape from a burning mill and then get away entirely. We all helped, as did Tsuruko-san."

"Aunt's friend Sachiko-san helps girls and women like that, and she was able to place most of them," Azuki said.

"But some of them she sent home and that turned into a bad idea. They got involved with some *karayuki* people who wanted to send them overseas," Shota said. He took another cookie and then passed the plate to Akira.

"They said there would be jobs but none of it was what they said it would be," he elaborated. "Junko-san figured it out and got someone to write Sachiko-san. When we came, hoping to find them, Junko-san ran away to us."

"Aunt used some of her tricks to get them all away," Shota concluded as Noriko grimaced and shook her head.

"We did it together," she said.

"But now Junko-san is at your school, and the rest of them went back to Tokyo and Sachiko-san." Shota looked pleased at his tidy recap.

Noriko was taken aback. It was bad enough her husband knew about her school and her training, but now it seemed like they all did. Akira was one them, certainly, but that same training told her it was all a deadly secret.

"I no longer know where my school is," Noriko said repressively, "And I am not in good standing with my order. The consequence for outsiders who learn about us is death." She looked around. "I am still expected to enforce that."

Akira was clearly shocked.

"That I will not do so as far as all of you are concerned does not mean the penalty does not exist, and I am not the only member of my order. You must all be very cautious. My *dojo* here talks only of my Shaolin and normal Japanese training; my other training is not mentioned."

"It's rumored though, Noriko-*sama*," Renko said. "You cannot deny that."

"I know it is rumored, and I consistently deny the rumors and point out the similarities with Shaolin. I will not put my sisters in greater peril."

"Your secrets are as safe with us as ours are with you," Azuki said. "We trust you. Please know you can trust us."

Noriko nodded. She smiled gently. They were her family, all of them, and she did trust them.

"The problem now," she began, "is that two of the girls who returned to Tokyo are proving hard to place. One is Miyuki-san."

"The girl with the smallpox scars?"

"Yes, Renko-san, that's Miyuki-san. The other is Yae-san. Miyuki-san's scarring makes her reluctant to go among people who might see it and find her appearance offensive," Noriko said. "Yae-san looks perfectly normal and she seems quite bright, but she thinks there is something inherently wrong with her. She is adamant about not wanting to marry, and for her, that includes going to work for any kind of family business."

"Is it being around anybody, or is it just around men?" Shota wanted to know. "With Miyuki-san, I mean."

"That's a good point. She seems all right with Sachiko-san and around her women. She doesn't like it, but she can do it. Being around men troubles her too much."

"But Yae-san," Renko said. "There's nothing wrong with her looks. She says it is something within her?"

"She seems to want to isolate herself from everyone, like nobody anywhere ever can accept her."

"I may have an idea," Azuki said. She didn't like to say it, but she'd been turning the notion over in her mind. It seemed consistent with everything she knew of the girl. "Is it possible she is Eta?"

"Unless they have tattoos like the Ainu women do, or those they give to criminals, I don't think there's any way to tell that," Akira said. "I've never heard that Eta are anything but regular *wa-jin* Japanese."

"They are regular Japanese," Noriko said. "Now, they're called 'new commoners' or '*burakumin*'—people of the village—and are supposed to be integrated into the larger community. You don't know unless you know their families or their jobs or have seen their family registers."

"Or where they live," Azuki pointed out. "They have often lived in separate communities located near their work." She looked at her aunt. "Their traditional work is connected with killing and meat and death, as far as I know."

"That is true."

"Junko-san comes from hunters. She doesn't feel badly about it at all," Shota pointed out.

"Yes," Renko said. "But you heard Junko-san talk about her background. Her people do something both they and society think is necessary and they get permission from their Shrine to do it. They take pride in what they do."

"And they do not mix," Noriko pointed out. "What the Eta do is necessary, too, but they inevitably come in contact with the rest of society. Rather than get permission and respect for what they do, they have been vilified for it. This means they stay in their own communities and can never leave, no matter what the government decrees."

"But Yae-san is on her own. Who is to know any of that unless she tells people? I mean, you don't know I'm an eagle unless I say so. I look normal, I act normal. Why does she need to bring it up? Why can't she just go forward?" Akira sounded puzzled.

"What Azuki-san has deduced is correct, I think," Noriko said. "It makes sense. Yae-san made it clear that it was something inside her, not on the outside. This is a way she perceives herself and she views it like a fungus spot on fruit. To feel lesser like that must be a terrible thing. Junko-san feels she is equal, maybe even better, than others. Yae-san feels like she is below other people. It's not how other people might feel about her now, especially since Akira-san is right: she needn't say anything at all about her background. A girl rescued from the mills could have come from anywhere. It's about how she feels about herself.

"Let us assume Azuki-san is correct. And then," Noriko spread her hands to all of them as she looked from one much-loved face to another, "let us see if we can find places for them where they have a chance at happiness."

36

"Kukanko-san?" Akira called from edge of the wood where the *oni* seemed to live. "Come meet my friend, Susu-chan!"

The *oni's* red face with its fangs and horned head peeked around a tree.

"He's a human," she said.

"Wait for it," Akira said with a grin. "Both of you look around and check. Is there anybody else here?"

"I don't see anybody," Susu said. "Let me change!"

"There's nobody here but us," Kukanko said. "That's why I like to be here. Change into what?"

"I'm kind of big," Susu said. "Don't be scared. I won't hurt you!"

"You won't hurt *me?*" the *oni* replied. "People always think I'm going to hurt *them!*"

"I don't see anybody around, either," Akira said. "Let me go have a look." Swiftly he adopted his eagle form and leapt into the sky. He circled, looking for signs of humans—or *oni*, for that matter—who might see what they were up to. He saw nothing and gave Susu a mental all clear.

"You saw how Akira-san became an eagle. I do that, too, but I don't look like him. I look like this!" Susu proudly switched to his dragon form. The *oni* was the size of a very large human, tall and broad, but still within the realm of possibility.

Susu was not. "See? I have wings like Akira-san and I can fly, too." He stretched his large bat-like wings.

Kukanko dodged behind the tree.

Akria smiled to see Susu show off his wings. He even spat a little fire. Fortunately, Akira did not see humans, *oni*, or anybody else who might see or call attention to the two youngsters in the forest clearing.

"I can't make fire," Kukanko said, venturing out from behind the tree. "But heat and fire don't hurt me."

"You're kind of different looking," Susu said. "You have horns like my sisters and my Papa do, only theirs aren't shaped like yours. Theirs look sort of like the antlers deer have. I haven't seen any humans with horns. Do you change into something else?"

"I stay like this," Kukanko said. "We *oni* live high in the mountains and mostly we protect the humans in our areas. We can chase away evil humans who want to interfere with ours. Sometimes we can even eat them." The *oni* giggled disconcertingly. "At least, some of them think we will. Some of us live in the far north or down south near hot springs and volcanos that humans call the Gates of Hell. They say we guard them. I guess we do, but I'm not sure what Hell is."

Susu shook his head. He wasn't sure, either. Maybe Akira would know.

"Every winter we come down from the mountains and scare bad humans so they'll act like they're supposed to," Kukanko continued. "They run and hide and scream! We laugh when they do that! It's fun! Then they give us special treats and we go away again. What do you do?"

Susu settled his wings. "It depends. I'm not sure yet. Mama's a Western dragon. She makes minerals and things like that. I look like her. I mean now, as a dragon. Papa's an Eastern dragon. He makes the weather. He lives here in Japan, and when I am human, I look like humans from here, except Papa isn't human at all. Neither is Mama. So it's all kind of confusing. I don't know what I'm going to do when I get older. You've met my sister, haven't you?"

"Who is your sister? I have sisters and some brothers, too, but my Nanna took them further north, where the Gates of Hell are. There are starting to be too many humans around here. I didn't want to go because of the music."

Susu wasn't sure what she was talking about, but he supposed he'd find out.

"Renko-san is easier to describe than anything," he said. "She's an Asian dragon, all green and blue. She doesn't have wings like mine. She's really pretty. When she's human, she looks like a human girl from the West, with pinky-beige skin and yellow hair."

"Oh, her! I've seen her here. Some *oni* are blue and some are red, like me, and some are green or even yellow. I didn't know your sister was from far away; I just thought she was a different color!"

Akira circled, watching the interplay below him. The two youngsters seemed to be getting along just fine. Kukanko had looked scared of the larger Susu at first, but now both had settled down—

There was a human, coming this way. Akira dived in for a closer look. This was a boy or young man, about his own human age, swinging a staff back and forth in front of him and carrying a *shamisen* on his back. Akira suddenly realized the boy was blind. Beyond the boy, over a rise, was a big house. Pairs of women of all ages sat on the wide gallery porch holding *shamisen*. They were playing, too. Akira could just barely hear it. He didn't think the blind boy could. Eagle ears were better than human. Other women, he saw as he swooped overhead, did various outdoor chores. A couple harvested vegetables from a large garden. One swept the path. Another hung laundry from a drying line. This must be what Kukanko had called the *Goze* house.

The blind boy reached a small clearing in the wood. He struck his staff around until he found a stump he could use as a stool. Gingerly, though with more dexterity and assurance than Akira thought he could possibly have, the boy sat and began assembling his *shamisen*. Eagles can't smile externally the way humans can, but if he had been able to, he would have. The *shamisen* he was assembling was the one Kukanko had fashioned with the larger, thicker *sao*.

Akira swept in to land between Susu and Kukanko and changed.

"The fellow you fixed the *sao* for is back. I think he's going to play. Susu-chan, why don't you change into a human. You can be my little brother. Kukanko-san, can you stay back in the woods a little bit so if somebody comes who can see, they won't be able to see you? I think this fellow is blind."

"Why should I change?" Susu always had questions.

"I want to talk to him," Akira said, with all his best patience. "I have to get close to him to do that. You can come with me because you can look human. Kukanko-san can't. We don't know how much or how little he can see yet. You told me a girl has come to play with him before. I want to find out more about her, too."

"All right," Susu grumbled as he changed. "I don't know why I can't just fly."

Suddenly, Akira realized that Susu and Kukanko had been speaking mentally.

"Kukanko-san, see if you can talk to me without speaking out loud, will you?" he asked. "I know you can talk that way to Susu-chan."

"You mean, like this?" Akira heard the *oni's* voice sound in his mind.

"That's it. Good for you! Let's all talk that way." Akira took Susu's hand. "Come on, let's go over here. You're my little brother and we are just out for a walk. You talk like you are older than you look, so try to leave that part to me. Kukanko-san, tell me what you know about this boy. He looks about my age."

"His name is Nitaro-san," the *oni* said. "He makes the best music! He really likes the *shamisen* the way it is now. And he doesn't play like anybody else! Just listen!"

Akira was careful not to be too quiet as he approached the clearing where Nitaro tuned his instrument.

"Hey, hello there, good afternoon," he called. "Are you going to play?"

If nothing else had told him that Nitaro was blind, the way he responded to Akira's greeting would have. He turned his ear to the sound of Akira's voice, rather than his eyes.

"I'm just practicing," Nitaro said. "I'm hoping a friend can come play with me."

"That's all right, then, isn't it?" Akira asked. "My little brother and I are just out for a walk. We heard you tuning up—I guess that's what you call it—and we'd like to hear you play. We'll stay quiet and not bother you. I know that's a *shamisen* and that's about all I know. My little brother knows less than that."

"Hey!" an outraged Susu interrupted.

"Well, it's true," Akira said with a grin. "But we'd like to learn. We'll be quiet now and let you get to it." He sat down in the soft dried grass, pulled Susu onto his knee, and winked at Kukanko, taking her place in the woods behind the boy.

Akira and Susu both were fascinated at the way Nitaro first tuned the *shamisen*, then started to play by crying out and hitting the *dou* with the *bachi* before he started to finger the strings and pluck with the *bachi* while at the same time strumming— Akira couldn't figure out how he was doing that! The music was loud and sometimes raucous, fast and exciting. There was a twang to the tone Nitaro coaxed out of the strings that reminded Akira a little of the music of the Ainu people from Hokkaido.

There were so many notes; the music was so complicated. Akira found it hard to believe there were only three strings, two hands, and one *bachi!* The occasional cry was something that he'd also heard at home—he still thought of Hokkaido as home—but Nitaro coupled it with the clap of the *bachi* on the *dou.* Each type of music had its own strengths, Akira thought, but there was something about what Nitaro was doing—

"I told you it was wonderful," Kukanko whispered silently to them both. "I want to learn to play like that!"

"Now you can," Akira replied. "You have your own *shamisen*, made just for you. All you have to do is practice."

"Everything takes practice," Susu said. "I don't think there's anything that's easy. I wish there was something I liked enough to practice it the way you're going to have to."

"You do, Susu-chan. It's doing the things you like so much you don't even realize you're practicing. The way Prince Irtysh shows you how to make things!"

"But that's fun!"

"There you have it!"

Suddenly, Nitaro slapped the *dou* with the *bachi*, gave a final cry and ended the piece.

"That was fantastic," Akira said. "Thank you so much for letting us listen."

Nitaro smiled. Akira realized he knew exactly how good he was, but was too polite to let it show.

"I'm glad you enjoyed it. I was hoping my friend would come. We're starting to play this style together. But I guess she can't come today."

"Ask him why," Kukanko told Akira silently. "She's from the *Goze* house just over there. They're not supposed to have relationships with men."

"Your friend must be a musician, too. I hear there's a *Goze* house nearby. We thought we might find some music there, but we found you instead and this has been superb!"

"She's one of the *goze*, yes," Nitaro said. "The players aren't supposed to come out alone. They can't get married or keep company with men or they get expelled. I don't quite count because I'm a *bosama* musician myself, but she's not really allowed to come play with me if she's alone. She's supposed to have a *tebiki* with her."

"What's a *tebiki*?" Susu couldn't keep silent an instant longer.

"There's your little brother," Nitaro said with a bright smile. "He's been so quiet. Did you like the music, little brother?"

"A lot," Susu said. "What's a *bosama*? Could I do that?"

At that Nitaro laughed. "You don't want to do it. You have to be blind and then learn to play an instrument and sing. I got sick and became blind when I was little like you. If that happens to you, you can learn how to earn your living by being a *bosama*. We travel around and play for people. They make donations so we can eat.

"The *goze* are women, also blind, and also musicians. They travel in groups and have regular routes they take during the winter season, when the farmers have leisure time. The *tebiki* are sighted women who travel with them to help them out. '*Tebiki*' actually means 'guide' but they do more than that. The *goze* have to be very respectable so that farmers will let them stay in their houses. We *bosama* don't have to be respectable at all." He shrugged. "But mostly we are. What girl wants to marry a blind man who's hardly more than a beggar? They say we're not *hinin* outcasts any more, but that's not how they treat us. The girls have it a little easier. And they can play with us. As long as there's a proper chaperone."

"Today, that was to be me," a woman's voice called from the wood. "Good afternoon, Nitaro-san. I am sorry, but I cannot stay; I have to get back to my work. I heard you playing. There's no one to come out with Etsuko-san today. We're short a *tebiki!* Kura-san seems to have left us."

"With a man, most likely," Nitaro said. Akira could hear the disappointment in his voice.

"I think you are probably right," the woman said, stepping out from the trees. Akira saw a second women beside her. "I don't know how we'll be able to replace her. Few women want to live such an isolated life and agree to the stringency of our rules, unless they can be *goze*. But I cannot have my house's reputation sullied by having *goze* come out alone. You know very well that our security and our livelihood depends on our respectability. If they think we're less like nuns and more like those *hinin yujo* who follow the festivals, we'll lose our winter farming route, and that simply cannot happen."

"Can I come back and check again?" Nitaro said. "If we can learn to play together"—

"I understand," the woman said, smiling. "That's truly remarkable music, something entirely new. We will find a way for you to play together and develop it. But not today."

"Yes, *Goze-sama*," the *bosama* said. The woman turned and faded back into the trees, where her companion took her hand and placed it on her own shoulder.

"Hey, Nitaro-san," Akira said, "Don't worry too much about it. This problem might be something we can solve. I'll hope to meet you later. Susu-chan, stay here. I'll be right back." He ran after the women, his long legs making it easy to catch them.

"Excuse me, *Goze-sama*," he said, bowing. "I couldn't help but hear you. My brother and I were listening to Nitaro-san play. I understand you need a new *tebiki?*"

The woman tilted her head in the characteristic listening posture of someone with limited sight. The woman she followed regarded Akira rather fiercely.

"We do, but they are not easy to come by. A sighted woman who wants to live out here and live by our rules is rare."

"Are there any special qualifications?"

"Not really," the woman who Akira had guessed was a *tebiki* herself spoke. "Willingness and ability to work, mostly. We *tebiki* live here, with the *goze*. We do the chores that are difficult for them—just normal household and small farm chores—and help with records and guide when they travel. We free the *goze* to make their music. In return, they support us through their performances. We must be willing to make a life here, far away from others, to refrain from having relationships with men or marrying."

Akira nodded.

"Are you thinking of a specific girl?" the *goze* asked.

"Not one you're fond of," the *tebiki* said sharply.

Akira shook his head. Then remembered the *goze* was blind and said, "No, not really. I barely know her. I really only know of her." That was only half a fib.

"I do know she is badly scarred from smallpox and finds it hard to be where people she doesn't know well can see her. I understand she has no wish to marry or even meet men at all. I know she can do, oh, normal things, and has been learning to read and write. She was a mill girl, but no longer, so she does know how to work. I think she might like it here."

The *goze* tilted her head to the *tebiki*.

"She sounds suitable. Is she a biddable sort of girl? Can she learn? Will she?"

"She has been living in the house of a woman who helps displaced mill workers," Akira said. "There are no complaints I have heard about her behavior or abilities. She is just hard to place elsewhere."

The *tebiki* said, "Winter is coming. That's the touring season. We really need to get someone new in time to train her before the snow falls."

"Let's give her a chance, then," the *goze* said. "Is she very far away?"

"If she wants to come, and I can't speak for her, she can come very quickly," Akira said, grateful for the instantaneous speed of dragons. "Either way, she'll either be here or I can let you know she won't be in just a few days."

"Who are you, young man?"

"Nobody," Akira said. "I only came here to help out a friend with some tools. Maybe I can help somebody else, too. My good fortune. I will look forward to meeting you again," he said as he turned to run back to Susu.

Susu stood as Akira approached. "Nitaro-san had to head back. He was worried if I'd be all right." Susu sputtered a giggle. Of course Susu would be all right. "I said I'd be fine; you wouldn't leave me."

Akira held out his hand to Susu. "You know I wouldn't leave you; I was more worried you'd leave me! We'll come back and let Nitaro-san know you are safe."

"We'll be back soon, Kukanko-san," he said mentally to the *oni*. "You start practicing with your *shamisen* and your tools, stay hidden so nobody suspects you're around and we'll be back. I hope we'll have a solution to another problem then."

"Are we going?" Susu said aloud as he grasped Akira's hand and got to his feet as the Eagle-boy hoisted him up. "Where are we going?"

"We're going to see Aunt Noriko."

37

With Susu in charge of transportation, Akira and Susu arrived outside Noriko's *dojo* instantly. They were on the public side, the one reached from the track to the village and the harbor.

"I want to go see *Sensei*," Susu said.

"Do you know where he is?"

"He's coming up from the school."

"Go meet him then, but be careful not to let anybody else see you," Akira told the child, as he knocked. "And make sure you come in as a human!"

"Akira-san?" Noriko opened the outside door to the *dojo*. "Susu-chan?" She looked down. "What are you two doing here? Come in."

"Akira-san called you Aunt Noriko," Susu announced.

"And so he may," Noriko said. "So may you, if you like. I heard you say you wanted to see my husband." She, like all of them, was aware of the

383

special "First Friend" relationship between the dragon child and the human teacher. "I think he's on his way. Do you want us to walk you there?"

"No, thank you, Aunt Noriko," Susu said with an impish grin, and vanished

"I apologize for the presumption, Noriko-*sama*," Akira said with a bow. "I didn't want to try to explain things to Kukanko-san."

"It's quite all right, Akira-san," Noriko told him and beckoned him in. "You may call me 'Aunt' if you wish. I am honored that you would want to. Come in and sit down."

She settled the Eagle-boy in the cozy corner near the entry from the house. This was warmed by a Chinese stove that vented outside, had a table and cushions for comfortable lounging, her bookcases and files, and the desk where she worked on the books for the *dojo* and maintained all the family financial records.

Everybody carefully maintained the fiction that *Sensei* actually kept all the accounts except for those of the *dojo* and Noriko only reviewed them. *Sensei* did not like to be seen as shirking his duty, even though Noriko was much better at accounting than he was. He was willing to work harder, because he thought he should be able to understand it all. It wasn't like he wasn't smart, but it took Noriko much less time because she really did understand it. She was pleased to indulge him in a foible he thought was a failing.

She checked the kettle to make sure it was full and built up the fire in the stove.

"How did it go this morning, Akira-san?" Noriko set out cups and filled the strainer of her favorite pot with new tea leaves. "Did you get Kukanko-san her tools?"

"We did," he affirmed. "I even made some suggestions for things she could do with them. But what was wonderful was the music!"

"I didn't know you liked music!"

"The Ainu people have a whole culture of musical instruments, storytelling, music and song that's only sort of related to the Japanese music I've heard around here. Then there's the Western music like we heard in Hakata at that 'musicale'. I know Prince Irtysh and Otohime like it." He shrugged. "That's different from both the others. So that's three kinds. But what I heard today is like nothing else! I don't know if I can even explain it. But this fellow Nitaro-san has come up with something fun, exciting, unique—and it has to do with the *shamisen* Kukanko made him making it possible. The way the *sao* is carved makes it different."

"You made it," Noriko said. She liked the way he was willing to share credit, keeping little for himself.

"Say we all did, then." That part wasn't important. "Nitaro-san is what they call a *bosama*, a kind of musician who is blind and travels around to

385

festivals, markets and fairs. He didn't tell me the details. He told me more about his friend Etsuko-san. She's a *goze*. They're blind musicians, too, but they're women and live in what are called *Goze*-houses. Each winter they take kind of a tour around villages in their areas. The farmers let them stay in their homes and they give regular performances. People enjoy them and everybody has fun. It's like they bring a kind of festival with them. What's important here is that they don't go out alone."

"What do you mean?" They both smiled as the whistle signal Minoru had carved let them know the kettle had boiled. Noriko took it off and poured the boiling water over the tea leaves so they could steep.

"You or *Sensei* might know better than I do, but I guess there are women performers who follow the festivals and markets like the *bosama* do, but they, uh, aren't just musicians or dancers. They aren't always blind and they aren't always...respectable."

Noriko poured tea for them both, Akira first. She thought it innocent and rather sweet that he might think a woman of her age, with her training and her background might not know exactly what kind of extra services those women "performers" offered.

Noriko reached for her cookie tin. Hanako had refilled it, Noriko was pleased to see. This was one of the reasons she was happy to give Hanako whatever assistance she could without overstepping the bounds of the niche the housekeeper had carved for herself. She pulled out a couple of little tissue paper squares and set one before Akira, placing a couple of the cookies—these had nuts in them—on it. She liked these so she took one for herself, too.

"Do I understand that it is important for the *goze* to ensure their respectability? So the farmers will welcome them and they won't have to travel all the time?"

"That's it," Akira said gratefully. He liked the way Noriko-*sama* could cut to the heart of the matter, every time. "They live in *Goze* houses run by a woman who serves as the leader and teacher. They aren't allowed to mix with men at all. That Nitaro-san is allowed to play with his friend Etsuko-san is only because he's a *bosama*, and they're still not supposed to be alone." He bit off a chunk of cookie and followed it with a swallow of tea. He thought it would be really delicious if he could dunk the cookie into the tea, but he knew that was impolite, so he didn't. This was almost as good, though. He swallowed and went on.

"They travel in groups, usually of three. Two of those will be blind musicians. The other will be a *tebiki*, a woman who isn't blind, but who helps those who are with practical things. I saw some of those women at the *Goze* house, doing chores that would be hard for somebody blind to do."

He took another bite of cookie and let Noriko refill his cup.

"I thought of your Miyuki-san." He smiled and sipped the tea. "The head woman, I think she was, the *Goze-sama*, came out to talk to Nitaro-san. She was older and I think partially sighted. She had an escort, but her escort stayed off to the side. She said Etsuko-san couldn't come out because they were short a *tebiki* so there was nobody to chaperone her while they played. Doesn't that sound like something Miyuki-san would like to do?"

"I have seen *goze* musicians," Noriko said slowly, "though I didn't actually notice them particularly. They wear big round basket hats like the ones mendicant monks and nuns wear to protect them from the elements. If I remember correctly, those are tied on. We'll have to ask Azuki-san, but I see no reason why the ties couldn't also work as a veil. If she had to go out in public at all. Helping blind women in a *Goze* house would mean few people would see her."

"And none of them would be men! It sounded to me like being around men is what bothers her the most! Anyway, I ran after the *Goze-sama* and told her about Miyuki-san. They are willing to at least give her a try."

"It doesn't sound like all the *tebiki* travel," Noriko mused. "Some of them must stay at the *Goze* house to take care of the gardens and the building. Being a *tebiki* might just suit."

Akira looked shy again, Noriko noticed. He always looked shy after he'd put forth an idea that others thought good, like he didn't think he deserved to take credit, but he should.

"That is an excellent idea," Noriko said with a smile. "It's good of you to think of it. Drink your tea, and let's walk down to visit Anko-*sama* for me and Toshio-*sama* for you. Shota-san and Toshio-*sama* are out with the horses. I think Cloudy has a new home, and that's wonderful news."

"Of course, Noriko-*sama*." Akira finished his tea and helped her clear up, even though she tried to brush him away. Noriko banked the fire.

"I can't be gone long," Noriko said, "because my children will be coming soon, but I need to talk to Azuki-san and Renko-san, and they are with Anko-*sama* and I think Otohime. We, or the two of them, at least, need to visit the capital. We need to talk to Miyuki-san!"

38

"I do apologize for the rude interruption," Noriko said. "I am afraid I cannot stay. My class..."

"I am always happy to see you, Noriko-*sama*," Anko said. "The babies grow while I watch them and I can't wait to show them off."

"You'll be able to do that soon," Otohime said.

"And get back home!" Anko shook her head. "I don't mean that the way it sounds. I love it here, to be right by the sea and in these beautiful mountains, and to have my friends near me. But I am tired of being confined to our house and I want to keep working on the refugee project. Mother will be back tonight and I am sure she will have her own news and news from Tsuruko-san, too."

"Kojiro-san got some local people interested in helping the refugees." Otohime shrugged and smiled. "They are fishing families, but have relatives who work at other things, like building and farming. They are all interested in getting the refugees well settled so that they do not turn to crime or simply starve, so they are willing to help."

"Does this mean they are building houses already?" Azuki wanted to know.

"It does. Lady Satsuki will doubtless have more information on that. The plans *Sencho-sama* and Akira-san adapted from their own house are proving useful, Tsuruko-san tells me. Some of the farmers are already organizing workers. Lord Eitaro has assigned one of his foremen to help with that."

"I'm sure Mother had something to do with that arrangement!"

"Some of them might prefer to work in the mines," Noriko said. "It's a steady income, starting immediately. Lady Satsuki and Lord Eitaro both would want to make that opportunity available to the refugees, if they need workers."

"My husband tells me they always need workers," Anko said. "I am so pleased we can help these people!"

"It will help the whole community," Renko said. "At least local people are seeing the wisdom of helping the displaced people rather than just moving them on or letting them starve."

"They wouldn't all starve," Anko objected.

"Maybe not all of them," Azuki replied. "But some would—more than will this way."

"I need to ask Azuki-san and Renko-san if they can give me some counsel about more displaced people," Noriko said. "You, too, Anko-*sama*. You might have ideas, too."

"Who?" Azuki wanted to know.

"The last of our mill girls, Miyuki-san and Yae-san."

"What happened?" Otohime wanted to know.

Briefly, Noriko recapped the saga of the mill girls for Otohime and Anko. Otohime and Anko both smiled when they learned that freeing the girls from their indentured servitude was how Yuta-*sensei* and Noriko had met.

Fighting a common enemy as a basis for courtship was something Otohime had never heard of even among dragons, although something like it would not surprise her about Rizantona and her father. When she heard the sequel to the story, she frowned. That women were being shipped out of the country under false pretences for non-existent jobs was another form of indentured servitude, if not outright slavery, that she did not like at all. Neither did Anko. The refugees they were helping could at the very least be educated about that.

"These last two girls are problematic. I think Akira-san might have found a solution for Miyuki-san," Noriko said. She explained about *tebiki* and the opportunity Akira had found for her in the north. "I don't know what might work for Yae-san, but I think my niece is right about what her problem might be."

She turned to Azuki and Renko. "I hope you can explain this option to Miyuki-san, and find a way to talk to Yae-san. You both know what it's like to be different in this society. Maybe they will be able to open up more to you as young women their own age who have overcome similar problems. I want to check into something possible and I will let you know, but I don't think it will take long for me to find out."

Azuki and Renko looked at each other. They were neither of them sure about the "overcome" part. At least, not yet.

"I must go see to my students," Noriko said, and politely took her leave with many felicitations and a promise to call on Anko and her mother on the morrow, when Lady Satsuki had returned. "Otohime, will you please be kind enough to call on me before you leave the area?"

"I don't want to interrupt your class," Otohime said.

"That doesn't matter, if you would be so kind. I need a small favor."

Anko raised one slender hand from where her arm was wrapped around a baby—Noriko couldn't tell if it was Sora or Sara—and said, "Do come back tomorrow. I know Mother will be anxious to see you, and then we can talk."

"I will do that, thank you." Noriko spotted children spilling out of the school and starting up the hill, so she hurried to catch them.

"Hadn't you better go see those girls?" Anko asked Renko and Azuki, her expression and tone both artless. She wanted them to admit that they were going to use Renko's draconic transport ability and actually go see them without specifically asking, but Azuki knew what she was about and dodged.

"When Aunt tells us what else she wants us to know. She'd better hurry, though," Azuki laughed. "All this will make for a long letter."

"We'll need to make sure we're ready for school tomorrow before we start," Renko said, also smiling. "We can't be sure when Noriko-*sama* will have the information we'll need."

Anko laughed, too. She loved knowing things, especially secret things, and was becoming nearly as expert as her mother in ferreting them out and using them profitably. She'd missed this time, but she wouldn't always, not if she kept on trying.

Otohime smiled and shook her head as the girls left. "Then come and tell us both about it, when you can," she said. "I want to know, too."

Anko and Otohime spent a productive hour talking about the refugee project and reviewing Tsuruko's reports on how the building of houses and workshops was going. The rice harvest was almost past; it was time to think about how much land could be devoted to cotton farming for the coming year.

"They'll have to clear the land and make sure it's ready for crops," Anko said. "That will allow those who will become farmhands to start earning over the winter. It is very good to hear there will be housing soon. The little camps they've managed to put together really are not adequate. But, Otohime, forgive me for asking. This is very rude of me. But it is something that needs to be addressed. All of this will take a great deal of money. We have some, but I don't think we have enough. Father could apply to the Emperor if necessary, I think. I'm not sure how, but Mother could figure that out, and Father would be the person to do it. He's unstoppable when he thinks something is right."

Otohime waved that away. "Your family is making significant contributions already. Everyone involved is contributing. *Sensei*, Noriko-*sama*, Kojiro-san, Tsuruko-san, your parents, you, Toshio-*sama*, Sencho-*sama*—everyone! But what we are really doing is helping the refugees help themselves. I think I have adequate funds to support this endeavor." She smiled, knowing how simple it would be for her to make them. "But just in case I don't, my father is also interested. So is Prince Irtysh. These are not his people, but there are or will be refugees among his people at some time, no doubt. Learning how we handle things here will be useful to him when that occurs. Either of them will help if necessary."

Anko smiled. She thought she knew perfectly well why the handsome Russian Prince would happily help with any project of Otohime's. She knew what they were, of course, though it wasn't spoken of openly, but Anko wanted them to admit it and draw her into their inner circle. This was just another piece of the puzzle. She had even come here with her babies in Otohime's instantaneous embrace, though she was pledged to never speak of it and in truth barely remembered it. One second she was there, the next here, as if nothing had happened at all, only earlier. It created a combination of confusion and disbelief mixed with astonished wonder. Someday, she vowed, she would fly with her friends when her eyes were wide open instead of clenched shut for that briefest of instants at Otohime's insistence.

"Did I tell you Prince Irtysh is arranging for the manufacture of the machines we're going to need?"

"Manufacture? You are not purchasing them, then?"

"I don't think Prince Irtysh even thought of it. He's making them. Or having them made. He is interested in exploring new technology. His younger son is very inventive, it seems." That was a direction in which she could not go further. Instead, she glanced at the window. "And now you must excuse me. I need to meet with Lady Noriko."

Otohime reached down to touch the babies tenderly before she smiled at Anko and said her goodbyes. As she walked up the hill, enjoying the way her human form fit in so well with the human scale track and the trees and the shrubs, she thought again of her own lost child, and tried very hard to be entirely happy for Anko.

Noriko saw Otohime coming up the track as she sent her young students home, some racing down the hill to envelope the dragon princess in a flurry of laughter and others running up to take the wider road across the pass to the larger nearby town. They were fortunate, Noriko thought, that her husband's involvement with the national education system and the previous existence of his school here had resulted in the National Schools being built here, conveniently near their home. Someday, they would need more schools for more children, but first, she thought as she waved to Otohime, they would need to develop a way to train teachers—a topic for another day.

"Thank you for coming," Noriko said. "Please come in and let me serve you some tea."

"I'll be glad to come in, but I need no tea, thank you. Anko-*sama's* maid kept refilling the pot!" Otohime liked the clean smell of the *dojo*'s wooden interior, with just the smallest hint of the charcoal fire burning in the Chinese stove. Susu had told both her and Prince Irtysh that her father was producing fire and his mother was making storms, though he'd been sworn to secrecy about it, so they couldn't tell anybody. She hadn't tried making fire herself, not yet, and thought perhaps she should.

"What's funny?" Noriko asked as she showed Otohime to her little sitting area and built up the fire, just in case.

"Susu-chan," Otohime said. "He does not know the meaning of discretion and tells every secret he comes across to any friend he meets, abjuring them to not tell because it's a secret!"

"He'll grow out of it. I hope. Are you sure I can't make you some tea?"

"Not for me, thank you, but if you'd like some, please go ahead. How can I help you? You said you needed a favor?"

"Yes." Noriko put on the kettle, then clasped her hands on the tabletop and looked down. "I hate to ask it of you. It seems like such an imposition. I need to talk to Mistress Feng. It's an imposition on her, too, because I haven't time to write and ask first. However, I think it's important. Would you please take me?"

"I will always take you, of course," Otohime said. "I enjoy your company and it is truly no trouble for me." She smiled. "I learn things from you I can learn from no-one else. But do you really need to go?"

"How else can I speak to her?" Noriko asked sensibly.

"Mistress Feng can talk to my father," Otohime said. "She calls him *Long*, in the Chinese fashion. She knew I was my father's daughter right off. Didn't you hear her?"

"I did, yes. That whole trip was so surprising. And my *Sifu* really is amazing."

"It is rare that pure humans can speak to dragons who are in dragon form—and that is of course virtually all of us, all of the time. Father always looks and listens for such people. You probably don't realize how unusual this ability is because you have it, I think, even without the Wishing Rock my father gave you, and because you are surrounded by people who can do so. Whether this is through your training or simply an ability you have, I do not know. Mistress Feng was a graduate of her school, no longer a student, when she met my father, so I cannot say about her, either."

Noriko found this unnerving, and wasn't sure why, so she set the thought aside. Without thought, she moved the kettle to the warmest place on the stove and took out her finest tea pot.

"Did you know that when Renko-san and I were trapped, it was Mistress Feng who was able to hear Prince Irtysh and tell Father so he could rescue Irtysh and find the two of us?"

"None of you ever said."

"No, I suppose we did not. My point is this: I would like to attempt to speak to Mistress Feng from here. If I can do so, we can speak to her without going there, or we can arrange a time that is convenient for us all.

"Can you say what it is you would like to speak with her about?"

39

Otohime found she could easily speak with Mistress Feng, who sounded a bit disconcerted at communicating at a distance with the older *Lóngwáng de nǚ'ér*—a Chinese phrase that Noriko heard as "daughter of the Dragon King." Translation was slightly complicated by the fact that both Otohime and Mistress Feng spoke Japanese as well as Chinese and often mixed the two.

But Noriko, despite knowing some Chinese, mostly martial-arts related, was not fast enough to keep up with the few sentences that were exchanged before Otohime broke off, smiled at her and said, "Let's go."

"Now?"

"Yes. It will be much easier that way. It is not an imposition."

"She probably wants to meet you again in person."

Otohime stood and gestured. Noriko started, then saw what she was pointing out and moved the kettle. Otohime cocked her elbow so Noriko could take her arm.

"I think," Otohime said, "you are probably right."

And they were there.

"Age," Otohime said, "does not dampen curiosity or intelligence. Shall we go in?"

"Could you have appeared inside?"

"Yes. But that would have been impolite."

Noriko stifled a laugh and touched the bell.

This time it was a young man who opened the door. He bowed exquisitely in the Chinese manner and Noriko was amused to see the tiny gesture that indicated they were to enter, in case they were unsure. Here, in the Shaolin *dojo*, Noriko felt her Chinese manners settle on her like a cloak. She hadn't realized how much she had attributed to Shaolin what was really Chinese, until she was here with a Japanese Princess.

Both women stepped out of their *geta* and onto the *dojo* floor. Today, Mistress Feng and Master Peng both sat in their elaborate Chinese chairs on the dais, with two other equally elaborate chairs facing theirs across the lowered Chinese table. They made to rise, but Otohime waved the formality aside.

"Do not get up," she said. "Formality is not necessary when it is I who am disturbing you and interrupting your day."

Noriko, however, bowed correctly, and greeted her two *Sifu*, mother and son, with the formality she deemed suitable and correct.

"Please come and join us, then, Your Royal Highness, if it pleases you," Master Peng said. "We understand you have questions for us?"

"Noriko-*soke* does," Otohime said. "My immediate question is answered. It is not only my father you can speak to."

Mistress Feng smiled. She knew she could hear other dragons since she had heard the injured Irtysh calling for Rizantona, but now she knew she could speak to them, too, and that pleased her.

"What could Noriko *Lao Shi* wish to learn from us?"

When Otohime chose to, Noriko thought, she could be as regal as anyone could wish for in any court in Japan—or China, too, she supposed—old or new. This naturally made her want to giggle, something she of course suppressed with firm discipline as she followed her friend across the wide wood practice hall, caught between two sets of highly stylized formal manners seasoned with a dash of martial arts.

They stepped up the dais and took their seats, Noriko naturally waiting until Otohime had seated herself before settling into the tall Chinese chair. She glanced at Otohime and they both smiled minutely. What were they to do about their *obi*, with the drum knots suitable for their ages and stations bulging out from the back? Independently, they solved this by sitting well forward on the chairs. As these were Chinese chairs, they were not too high and they were able to rest their feet comfortably flat on the ground. The tiny Mistress Feng's "bound" lotus feet were, as usual for her, tucked to her side in her large armchair.

The boy entered with a large silver tea tray. Noriko knew and followed the nearly imperceptible signals Master Peng used to direct him in serving. The usual order of precedence was altered in recognition of Otohime, who outranked, Noriko thought, just about everybody, everywhere.

Otohime had learned her human manners well, and Noriko was proud of her. She let her student take charge as was proper for her position, and it wasn't until the tea was served and complimented that Otohime tilted her perfect chin and said, "Noriko-*sama*, would you please explain the situation?"

Noriko realized she hadn't really told Otohime what she was up to, either.

"It is complicated. *Sifu*, I do not see your young attendant. You said she was returning to China. Has she done so?"

"She is preparing to do so," Mistress Feng said. "She is arranging her passage to Nagasaki today. From there, she will sail to Tianjin Gang. That is the port from which she can journey home to our Temple in the Songshan mountains in Henan. It will not be easy for her, but one might call it a quest." The tiny woman with the dandelion puff of white hair turned to Otohime. "I don't suppose your father ever mentioned how we met."

"He has not," Otohime said with a smile, "but I know he has high regard for you."

"He rescued me, or perhaps one could say he helped me rescue myself. There are not so many humans who can speak to *Long* or the children of *Long*. That journey was my test, my quest, and part of that is how I got my son."

Master Peng bowed to his mother, who smiled.

"I am grateful," Mistress Feng said to Otohime. "I will always serve your family as best I can."

"I know of a girl," Noriko said. "I wondered if she might be suitable to serve you."

"What are her particulars?" Master Peng wanted to know.

Otohime stared at Noriko but so subtly Noriko thought nobody but Lady Satsuki would have recognized it as an expression of utter disbelief. What or who could Noriko be talking about?

"You know how I met my husband," Noriko began.

"You fought together," Master Peng said. Otohime thought he was amused, but it didn't really show behind his obvious fondness for Noriko. She wondered if Noriko had seen it.

"We freed girls who were indentured laborers in a textile mill," Noriko said. "My friend Sachiko-san, whom you have met, took them in and found places for most of them. Some had families they could return to. That is generally considered safe; the recruiters won't try to reclaim a runaway if she has made it home. They think she is too much trouble and they are right.

"But some of the girls either had no family left or none that would take them back. They were taken up by *karayuki* recruiters, who planned to sell them to brothels overseas. It is extremely unlikely that they could ever escape those direst of circumstances and it would be nearly impossible for them to return home to Japan. We freed them again and brought them back here, to Sachiko-san. All but two have now been placed. I think we might have an opportunity for one of them. Only one remains."

"You sent one girl to the Japanese school where you initially trained," Mistress Feng said. "Why not this last one?"

Noriko shrugged and shook her head as she grimaced just a little, but smiled as she spoke.

"Junko-san is the one I sent to my old school. She comes from a hunting background. She is courageous and disciplined and has the internal toughness that a woman from that background would need—as would a woman trained as I was. She has fine qualities and a keen intelligence, but is also, though I don't think I mentioned it, not pretty or even ordinary. She has teeth that rival those of Master Kung-fu-tsu." She used the Chinese pronunciation of the name Confucius, who was so often depicted with pronounced buck teeth that he must have sported them in life.

"And this other girl?" Master Peng asked.

"She is normal enough to look at, but she also comes from a poor background. Her family sold her"—

"You understand that well enough!" Mistress Feng's tone was sharp, as if she accused Noriko of acting from emotion, not reason.

"I do understand that, yes." Noriko glanced at Otohime, who sat placidly as though nothing could shock or even affect her. "I suspect her family sold her the way mine did. They were starving and the child was the only thing they had of any value to sell to keep the rest of the family alive through another winter. But Yae-san was older than I, I think. I was told I was going off to a special school with the nice ladies who picked me out specially. I did not question that especially as I found my training suited me." She barked a harsh laugh.

"My brother thought they sold me to a brothel. I suppose they could have. I do believe they were starving; when I finally remembered her, my mother's face was gaunt. My husband thinks they sold me to give me opportunity that I would not have otherwise had. I think he is too kind. When I found my brother, I remembered their anger and I thought they were angry at me. I still think they were; I think they had to be because otherwise how could they justify selling their child?"

Otohime's hand stirred. She very nearly reached out to touch her friend, she was so moved at the pain still affecting Noriko.

"But I knew we were farmers. I remembered the farm, the crops, the trees. I am not Yae-san. I do not know what she thinks or what she remembers, but I never found anything to be ashamed of about my background or who I was. I was a peasant child. Peasants are supposedly a respected class."

Mistress Feng snorted. "To be exploited and paid off with lip service and pride. You are too intelligent to take that seriously."

Noriko smiled softly. "I am now, yes, and now it doesn't matter, anyway. But I think Yae-san came from another class entirely. I think that she is likely Eta."

"*Hinin?*" Master Peng used the Japanese word meaning "outcast," or "non-person."

"Not merely outcast, but part of the group now to be known as *burakumin*, 'people of the village', or 'new commoners', supposed to be regular citizens, but that is lip service if you will. That class was hereditary; they have towns and neighborhoods of their own just as they have trades and jobs reserved for them. Someone outcast for other reasons, like our housekeeper was, can return to society fairly seamlessly."

"That is what she meant." Otohime said, her reserve cracking. "Not something on the outside, but something on the inside, something she could never overcome."

"Yes," Noriko said. "As long as she is in Japan, she will always feel separate from other Japanese people. We can tell her it means nothing; we can welcome her, make up a tale for her—I've certainly made up enough stories for myself—but unless she can believe in her own worth, she will always be at a disadvantage."

"She looks normal enough?" Master Peng asked.

"Perfectly normal. She's even pleasant looking. These people don't look different from anybody else. She was called a 'troublemaker' but my niece thinks—and I agree—that she is merely blunt and outspoken."

"She has nothing to lose," Mistress Feng said. "because she has no sense of self-worth. She is a perpetual outsider, worth so little to her family that they sold her to rid themselves of her, and her family is worth so little to society that they are hereditary outcasts. What do you think we could do for her?"

Noriko smiled. "Here, with you, she would merely be Japanese. What do Chinese people know about Japanese people and our society? She is merely another *xiao Riben guizi*"—

"Little Japanese Ghost?" Otohime sounded shocked. That was insulting, and very Chinese.

Master Peng laughed. "So we could teach her how to take pride in being Japanese while we teach her to be Chinese as she learns the arts of Shaolin?"

"Something like that, yes, *Sifu*." Noriko dropped her gaze. "I suppose it is not a very good idea."

"I think it is a very clever one," Mistress Feng said. "If the girl wants to come, I will give her a trial."

She leaned forward in her chair and looked closely at Otohime.

"You are surprised at this, I think, Daughter of *Long*."

"You may call me Otohime, as I was previously introduced," Otohime said coldly. The Chinese view of Japan was often scathing. Japan's view of China could be equally harsh. Ryuujin ruled everywhere in the East, but Japan was hers. No one could speak against Japan in her presence without feeling her displeasure.

"His Majesty would understand, I think," Mistress Feng continued, "because of the way he and I met. The three of us"—she gestured to include herself, her son and Noriko—"were raised and trained to be tools of the most powerful among humans. We have taken pride in learning to be cold as steel, hard as granite and to have no more concern for those we harm than would a blade. You are one of the powerful who would use us."

Otohime shook her head violently. She was not like that. She was not human.

"But we are also people like any other," Mistress Feng said. "When we get the chance, we can act for ourselves. Just as Noriko *Lao Shi* rescued this girl not once but twice, using her formidable skills to do something she personally wanted for the good of those for whom she felt sympathy, I will use what skills I have to help rescue this girl again. As will my son."

Master Peng nodded. He smiled reassuringly at Noriko.

"If she will come," he said, "bring her. I think you are right. I think we can help."

This time it was Noriko who reached out to Otohime. The dragon princess, the dual-natured Daughter of *Long*, was shaken. She had wanted to learn how to be human. Now all she wanted was to be a dragon.

40

They hadn't really talked about it, even though it was the next afternoon before they were able to get there, but it turned out to be Renko who asked Miyuki to show her the persimmon tree in the back service yard of Sachiko's sprawling Tokyo house. It was Azuki who asked Yae to tell her about the fish in the pond in the front garden.

"These will be ripe soon," Renko said. "Will you dry them for the winter?"

"I am sure we will," Miyuki said. "That big gallery by the laundry there will serve nicely to keep them out of any autumn rain."

"Or even a typhoon, if we get another one." Renko turned to face the other girl. "Miyuki-san, do you know where I am from?"

Miyuki shrugged. "You're foreign. I can see that. But from where I do not know. Your Japanese is quite fluent."

"It ought to be," Renko said with a twisted smile. "My father's Japanese. I grew up with him until I moved in with Azuki-san's family to go to school. He wanted me to learn how to be Japanese. Azuki-san's uncle has a school, you might recall, and she and I were already acquainted. But I look funny, don't I?"

"I am sure you are considered lovely wherever you are from," Miyuki said primly.

"I'm not so sure about that," Renko said, sitting down on a rustic bench and gesturing Miyuki to join her. "I've never lived in my mother's lands, not that I remember, really. I started out living with her, but there were problems with the local people and she brought me here to live with my father when I was still very young. So I grew up as Japanese, but I look strange."

"You can't help being a foreigner."

"I'm not a foreigner, not really. At least I don't feel like one, since I grew up here and my father is from here, but people see this pink skin and yellow hair and don't know what to make of me. I can cover my hair with a scarf like a nun or a farmworker, and I do fairly often, when I go out in public, but my face is still different."

"My face clearly shows I had the pox." Miyuki shook her head to dash away incipient tears. "My older sister died and I wish I had, too. No matter where I go, people stare at me like I am part of some show that travels around to fairs and markets and people pay to look at how ugly I am."

"Oh, Miyuki-san, it's not that bad! The shape of your face is pretty and your features are nice"—

"My skin is red and blotchy and pitted and marked! Renko-san, you are trying to be kind but my face stands out worse than your yellow hair! And it's not just my face!"

Miyuki grabbed the neck of her kimono and pulled it aside. "The scars are everywhere! All over my body. Look!" She released the neck of her kimono and shoved up her sleeve. "Here, too. And my legs, and"—she burst into tears and buried her face in her hands.

"But you don't mind being here?" Renko asked, offering a handkerchief, a European affectation she found quite useful. "With Sachiko-san?"

Miyuki lifted her head and stared at Renko through reddened eyes as she took the handkerchief. "Women aren't as bad. It's almost like they really do stop seeing me after a while. Sachiko-san says all people would as they came to know me, but men never seem to stop staring, even leering like I might be easy because I'm so ugly I'm desperate for their attention.

"Anyway, few people live here in this house, and not many come here except displaced women like me. Mostly, I stay away from people but I couldn't refuse to see you. You rescued me in the first place. And then you did it again, because I was stupid enough to be fooled at the thought of a job I might be able to do comfortably."

Renko turned away and looked at the persimmon tree and beyond it to the apple trees espaliered along the property line fence. "So you must have gone to festivals and fairs when you were young? Seen people perform at markets?"

"Oh, yes," Miyuki said, sounding wistful. "Before the smallpox came. That's how I know about the poor deformed souls people paid to laugh at. I am ashamed because I laughed, too. Now I am paying my karmic debt. Or so I tell myself. Maybe next time"—she shrugged before continuing.

"My family lived not far from a Temple town," she went on. "People would come for pilgrimages during the big festivals. We lived right on Lake Biwa and my parents fished. They sold fresh fish to vendors who cooked them and sold them at booths set up for travelers, or salted and dried them, and sold them that way in the markets by the Temple."

"Did you ever hear music? Did you ever see *goze*? Or *bosama*?"

"The wandering blind musicians? Of course! They always come to festivals. We'd see *uta bikune*, too, and not just during the festivals. But then there would be dancers, puppet shows, even plays sometimes. That's why working with the *Ningyo Joruri* troupe sounded so good to me. I could go to the fairs and make people smile, but nobody would ever have to see me!"

Renko nodded. She could see the attraction for Miyuki. But she had something better for the girl. She hoped.

"There is a *Goze* house up north that my friend Akira-san knows of. We go to the same school," she explained. "Up there, where it's cold and it snows a lot, the women musicians live in the same place all year. In the winter, though, they travel around the district and stay with farmers to give concerts in barns and granaries, Temples, Shrines and even people's houses."

"I'm not blind," Miyuki said. "Aren't they all blind? And I'm not talented, either. I can't play an instrument."

"Maybe you could learn," Renko said, thinking of Kukanko. "But what I was thinking was this. The *goze* are blind, or at least visually impaired, that's true. But they need sighted women to help them with the house and the garden and to travel with them. They usually go in groups of three, two *goze* and one *tebiki*, a sighted woman who serves as a guide and a kind of business manager, I think."

Miyuki started shaking her head.

Renko raised her hand. "Hear me out! Probably not all the *tebiki* travel. I don't know for sure. There must be some who just stay at the *Goze* house. But when they travel, I understand they all wear big round hats, kind of like flat, round baskets. Not quite like the ones mendicant monks and nuns wear, but similar. They tie them on against the wind. There is no reason I can think of why they couldn't be tied on with a veil. Azuki-san is talented with fabrics. She could figure out a way to tie a hat on to hide your face, if you wanted.

"You would have the privacy you crave there, Miyuki-san. Men don't come around because the *goze* cannot marry or associate with men, except maybe the occasional *bosama*, but if there is one, he'll be blind, too. Even most of the women will be blind or have very limited vision. How would you like to work in a place like that? Be a *tebiki*? Help the *goze*. Sachiko-san says you can read and write and do some mathematics now. Why not?"

Miyuki's face brightened until, Renko thought, she was almost pretty with happiness at the thought. Then she slumped.

"That sounds like a dream to me. Music, all the time, music everywhere. I could listen and maybe even learn. There would be nobody to see me. Nobody to stare. It would almost be like I was never scarred, but I could still be useful. Surely there cannot be places like that around here! How would I ever find a job like that?"

"Here is where I can help you, I think. You said it sounds like a dream. But what if you could go there? To the one we know about up north? Could you trust my Aunt Noriko to help you sleep for a little while? Like she did when we got you away from the false *Ningyo Joruri* people? You only noticed it then when you woke up! Then we could get you there, to an area where Akira-san says there are many *Goze* houses.

"If we could get you there, we already know of one opening, from him. That's when we thought of you. If not that one, he says there are many *Goze* houses in the district; there must be many openings for *tebiki*. There will be a place for you! The right place! I hope you will agree to at least try it. Because you and I are the same. We have to live here, we want to live here, this is our home, but we each stand out like a beggar at a banquet. Me more than you, if you think about it."

"Noriko-*sama* is your aunt? The one Junko-san calls the 'warrior woman', the one who arranged for that scary-looking woman to come and take Junko-san away?"

"The very same. I am allowed to call Noriko-*sama* 'aunt,' though she really isn't mine. You know Azuki-san and Shota-san. You met them when you met me. She actually is their aunt, married to their uncle, the *sohei*—at least he used to be—who runs the school where my father sent me."

"That would be—if it were real, it would be better than a dream," Miyuki whispered.

Azuki and Yae burst into the back garden together, Yae nearly dragging Azuki with her.

"Miyuki-san!" Yae cried. "Is it true? They really have places for both of us?"

Miyuki shoved her hair back and her face twisted as she looked at Yae. "They have a place for you?"

"I think so! Azuki-san said their friend Akira-san had found something that might suit you, too."

"Do you really think so? Renko-san, Azuki-san, do you really think so?"

Renko nodded. "That's what I've been telling you!"

Azuki said, "Yes, I really do."

Yae looked at Azuki seriously. "Will you show her your hair?"

"We can all see her hair!" Miyuki said.

"That's not what she means," Renko said. "I can't hide my hair. Azuki-san can't show hers. She's always had to hide it. She still does."

"But I'll show you, Miyuki-san. I showed Yae-san." She reached up and gently dislodged her wig. Renko stood and stepped forward to take it. Azuki raised her hands to run her fingers through her feathers. Yae and Miyuki both stared, trying to figure out exactly what it was that was growing out of Azuki's head. It looked like feathers, but of course that couldn't be.

"You see?" Azuki said. "Each of us has something that sets us apart from regular people.

But with the help of our families and friends, Renko-san and I have been able to do something about it. We live relatively normal lives with people who accept us. We offer that to you."

She took her wig from Renko and replaced it on her head. She was so practiced at this maneuver that she barely had to tuck in the edges. She was a little concerned about dislodging the adhesive she used, but was confident that when she changed or when she and Renko traveled together, her wig would behave as it always had and simply stick with her.

"When Aunt Noriko married my Uncle," Azuki said, "she knew a wig would help me. I used to have to cover my head all the time as if I was doing heavy labor. She asked Sachiko-san to see about getting a *geisha's* wig and one of Sachiko-san's clients, one of the women she dresses, actually gave her this one, and the man who makes and tends their wigs restyled it for me. It was all a gift."

"My parents," Renko said, understanding at last that she spoke the truth, "only want the best for me, but I'm so strange they don't know what to do with me. Yet, Azuki-san and Shota-san, *Sensei* and Lady Noriko and some few others have always accepted me. They've been willing to look beyond the outside. We hope we have found places where that can happen for you two like it has for us."

"At least, please know that we're your friends, anyway," Azuki said. "So are Akira-san. Shota-san.

My uncle. Aunt Noriko. Sachiko-san. There are more people out there who will accept you as you are, just like they have accepted us. Will you let us be your friends?"

"Will you give it a try?" Renko asked softly.

41

N oriko sighed contentedly as she cleaned her brush and set it to dry. Her inkstone and ink stick were ready to put away. She slid the beads of the abacus over to the start position and blotted the writing on the last of the account books again.

This was a chore she enjoyed. It was so satisfying to click the beads and enter the totals, verify the entries, and see all of the family's financial affairs tidily organized. The last ledger dry, she closed this final book, added it to the stack, and went down the stairs to show all of them to her husband.

She tapped, and when she heard him respond, she knelt to open the door and scooted in, onto the *tatami*. Placing the ledgers on the floor, she turned to shut the door.

Yuta didn't understand why her smile was so happy. He did not like this ritual at all. He took off his spectacles and cleaned them on a handkerchief he'd started tucking in his sleeve for exactly this purpose. She took such pleasure in it, he thought. He would not deny her that, so he smiled at her as he pushed the papers he was working on off to the side and made room for her to show him the ledgers.

Noriko thought of this as one of "their" times, a time when the two of them together could intimately discuss the details of their lives. They were always so busy, both of them, their separate interests and work taking them away from each other, and even the duties and pleasures they shared they often did not do together.

When they sparred in the morning, giving her the training exercises she held dear and helping Yuta advance in his own training—that was another time together that she enjoyed. Probably more than he did. He was good—the only person available who was even close to providing her with a workout— but she was still much better. His favorite time was probably when they snuggled under the comforters on the futons in her room, most likely with the window cracked open for a view of the garden and either a cool breeze to fight the heat or the chill of winter contrasting with a brazier's warmth.

She liked those times, too. But she also liked this one. She would start off easy. She started with the ledger for the *dojo*. She was making a small but steady profit and her income continued to grow. The actual cash she kept hidden in safety, locked in a chest tucked under a floorboard in a secret compartment.

"That's a very good result," Yuta said. "You really ought to consider making deposits with a bank. It's the coming thing, and you're building up quite a substantial amount of savings."

"Thank you. I'm not sure I trust banks. I understand they're the same as money-changers, only more complicated and Western, but I still like having silver and gold at my fingertips."

"Renko-san has told us many times that as long as precious metals and gems are worth anything, and as long as she can make them, we will never want."

"That's good of her. It gives me confidence. We need to make sure she truly understands money and how it works, though. She takes it a touch too casually. She has never done without anything she wanted. You are teaching them economics, aren't you?"

Yuta smiled. Noriko of course knew the upper school curriculum and it did naturally include economics.

"It's an interesting area," he said. "At least, I find it so. As we interact with the rest of the world, we must understand global markets and how those affect us as well as our domestic markets and affairs. I am afraid we are already starting to see inflation due to the Satsuma Rebellion and I think it's going to get worse."

"I read something about that in connection with the refugee project. Lady Satsuki brought the article. So many men from all over Japan were conscripted for the war that there were labor shortages. Working-aged women, the elderly and children could not make it all up. That means labor costs increased and the prices of essential goods and services went up, too. Hanako-san has already noticed the higher cost of food."

"That's to be expected. Fortunately, we can grow much of what we need, and we are not, at least not now, short of money."

"It's going to affect our refugees and the cost of producing cotton," Noriko pointed out.

"Also the cost of selling it overseas. We can't price our fabrics out of the market."

Noriko smiled tenderly. This was the sort of thing she liked, the way they agreed so smoothly on so many things, and the way they each could bring in new information that enriched their lives. She doubted if most marriages had such an intellectual basis, but other people's marriages were not her problem.

"I have advanced *Sencho-sama* funds for chartering a ship," Yuta continued. "You will recall that he did tell us that if he has a ship he can collect the looms and spinning machines from anywhere and deliver them right into Fukuoka port or anywhere else they might be wanted."

"I remember. What about documentation and customs tariffs? Don't those machines usually come from China?"

Yuta raised his eyebrows. "I asked about that, too. *Sencho-sama* merely winked at me and said to let him worry about that."

"What account did those funds come from," Noriko asked sensibly, "and how much?"

"My personal funds," Yuta said. "I left the final amount open. He quoted me a figure I found on the low side. He said not to worry about that, either. He'd let me know how much but it shouldn't exceed what he said." Yuta grimaced. "I suspect I should have checked his antecedents more carefully before I hired him to teach Shota-san."

Noriko's eyes widened. "He has an excellent reputation as a mariner."

"He does that, yes. He also has quite a lot of money, as we are only just finding out. Now that I seriously consider what he's spent on the boat and his new house. It's more than can be reasonably explained by an owner-captain who lost a ship— although he rarely mentions that part—as well as his leg. The cost of all that must have been enormous."

"And made a substantial dent in his savings. Unless he had far more savings than one might suppose. Do you think he—I hesitate to even think it—got it by some nefarious means?"

Yuta laughed. "For someone of your experience, you sound terribly proper. I don't think it was nefarious. You know him; you don't either, not really. I do think it was illegal, at least in part. There has always been a brisk smuggling industry around Kyushu. Some of it was quasi-legal, sponsored by the *Daimyos*. Satsuma and Choshu, mostly."

"You're right. He wouldn't have gone in for piracy," Noriko said. That, at least, she could be fairly sure of.

"Not when there was excellent money to be made in smuggling. Those would be the connections he's tapping to charter a ship to bring in an undocumented cargo, I think."

"He'll know how to get the permits for it and customs clearances if he needs them, then," Noriko concluded with relief. "Without spending a *sen*."

Yuta smiled. "We're lucky to have him."

"I'll make a note of the upcoming expenditure," Noriko said drily, using one of those handy new pencils to make a note in Yuta's personal ledger.

"There's something new for Shota-san's estate ledger, too," Yuta said, "other than what I already entered."

Noriko reached for the book in question and flipped it open. "You've done a nice job with this one," she pointed out. "There was only one small mistake and I've fixed that. You see here?"

She started explaining and Yuta felt his head start to spin. Like his nephew, he didn't really grasp accounting very well. People always told him how easy it was, how very simple, you just put this here and that there—and then it didn't add up and he couldn't see why!

"And that's all there is to it," Noriko smiled, pleased with her simple and clear explanation.

"I'll do my best to remember it," Yuta said, unwilling to admit that he was as confused as ever. This was what he didn't like about going over the accounts. It was his responsibility, yes, but he found it much easier to let his wife handle it, which made him vaguely ashamed of his lack.

"So what is the new event?" Noriko asked, pencil poised.

"Toshio-*sama* is going to buy Cloudy," he told her. "Shota-san already knows about it. In fact, it was Shota-san who actually negotiated the transaction. With Blackie's help, naturally. Blackie says he has a very good idea of Cloudy's worth to a human, since he himself is a very valuable sire."

Noriko laughed. Blackie's pride was so obvious it was almost a joke. "What did Red Wind have to say about that?" She had grasped the fact that colts

431

leaving their natal herd was simply the equine way. Blackie had set the terms of his own sale to a *samurai* in need of a mount in far north Niigata, paving the way for Shota to find Azuki and giving Shota both his boat and the infusion of gold necessary to restore the family fortunes. Later, when Blackie and Red Wind had traveled south and were stolen by bandits, they were recovered by the family and helped them escape the Tengu. Noriko shook her head. She barely believed her own history, but the history of the family she had married into was even more incredible than that.

"Red Wind pointed out that Cloudy gets his speed and agility from her, and that his value at least in part depends on how well he behaves himself, so he needs to practice talking to Toshio-*sama* so they will understand each other."

"How is that going?" Noriko had learned the basics of riding many years previously. It was something *kunoichi* were expected to learn as much as they learned to drive an oxcart or use a sword. It was also infinitely easier now, with her mount, Phlox, because they could actually talk.

"Nicely, I think. Toshio-*sama* says he's amazed at how well Cloudy understands him—that he acts like a fully trained horse, not a raw colt."

"I sometimes wonder if the abilities those of us who are merely human show in dealing with the dual-natured and other…unusual…beings are abilities all humans might have. If they would only use them."

"If they would only use them," Yuta echoed. He turned the book and wrote down an amount that made Noriko's eyebrows go up. "He'll pay that into the estate's accounts in Hakata and send us the receipt. He wants to ride Cloudy home when Anko-*sama* and the babies leave."

"I will be sad to see them go," Noriko said. "It's been pleasant having them so close."

Yuta looked at his wife. He thought that the injuries that prevented her having children affected her far more than they affected him. In his view, they had quite enough responsibility, and a surfeit of children in their lives. "We can visit often," he said mildly. "The refugee project will require it."

Noriko shook herself. Some things couldn't be helped.

"Here is the ledger for the refugee project," she said. "I would like you to review it with me."

42

rtysh and Otohime stood between his throne in his principle audience chamber and the seat he had made for her. The beautiful mineral striations on the rock walls had inspired Otohime when she had finally decided to make her chambers off the caldera of Mt. Fuji not merely a place she stayed but a home. Irtysh inspired her in many things, she thought.

Rows of looms that could be threaded according to Azuki's patterns and then operated by almost anybody lined the cavern floor near the edge of Irtysh's Lake of Jewels. The new cotton spinning machines, the design of which was copied from the best of the new machines shown at the First International Industrial Exposition they had visited in Tokyo, modified and improved by Renko with the aid of Shota, stood in tidy rows next to them.

Irtysh smiled. Their young sister was a gifted engineer. But it was his younger son, Vassilli, who had resurrected the ability to manufacture things of a piece, rather than making wood parts here and metal parts there and assembling them later. This made the production of the machines incredibly quick. Once Vassilli had discovered—or recovered—the process, Irtysh found he could duplicate it and so could the rest of his children. With all of them working at it, producing these human scale machines went quickly indeed.

Beyond, in the Lake of Jewels itself, a gigantic basin filled with huge cabochon gemstones that Irtysh had made for the sheer aesthetic pleasure of it, his children sported with Susu, their youngest uncle.

The multicolored brilliance of the younger dragons sparkled in the light cast by prisms worked into the roof of the chamber and various shining surfaces reflecting what was outside and in as they played. Irtysh hoped that he and Otohime would join them once they had finished their discussion of her refugee project.

He participated in that mostly for her sake, even though he told himself his eagerness to expand the collective knowledge of dragonkind and join the dimorphic branches together by increasing all of their skills was vital. But while he was enjoying the spectacle and looking forward to joining it, Otohime had other things on her mind.

"Irtysh?"

"Yes?" He turned his massive head to look at her. He loved her colors, blue and green shading into sand tones beneath. Her distinctive skull features looked rather like deer antlers; though Shota had, amusingly, dubbed them the Eastern Dragons' "crowns." The tendrils reaching out around them and above her changing multicolored eyes were so expressive. She used the prehensile whiskers around her blunt muzzle as he used the tiny claws at the ends of his wings and on the joints where his wings folded, something he found entrancing. The tiny vestigial wings, so light and almost translucent, folded neatly into her almost invisible shoulders. Her form was long and sinuous, with no real differentiation between her neck and torso, torso and tail, her limbs simply appearing from her body but folding up nearly out of sight when she flew—oh, he found her beautiful.

Among Western dragons, he knew was considered good-looking, with his deep earthen browns studded with the tones of the minerals in his lands, mostly black and yellow, though there were others here and there. He gave that little credence, because he was a prince and a powerful one. Those attributes might improve anybody's looks. His muzzle was pointed and his upper fangs slightly overlapped his lower lip. When he opened his mouth, it was possible to glimpse the fire within, which he could direct in anything from a focused jet to a wide blast or use to emit a finger or a pillar or a cloud of smoke. His lower jaw was graced with spines that ran down his chest. He could control these if he needed to look any fiercer than he already did, though sometimes they acted on their own, if he was truly angry or upset. Above his brow ridge, longer spiney features rose to top his head, forming what his sister Renko called *his* crown, though it looked nothing like hers. Those ran down his neck gradually flattening out into the smooth scales that formed his hide. His mood could be judged by their behavior, though he was very good at keeping them under control.

His long neck joined the muscular shoulders where his huge functional wings began defining his back, and his shoulders also supported his massive forelimbs. Where his wings ended, his hips supported his strong rear legs. The join of his lengthy and expressive tail could be easily distinguished, running all the way to the pointed barb at its end.

He was, Otohime thought, a very handsome dragon.

"I beg your pardon," he said. "I was distracted."

She flicked her whiskers as if to say it didn't matter before she spoke.

"Irtysh, why didn't you tell me about your children?"

"But I did!" He stared at her, his brow wrinkling. "When Susu was born. You were concerned he might be cursed somehow because your father was present. I remember quite clearly telling you I had been present at the births of all my children. I would not have done that had I thought there was any possibility of harming them!"

"Yes," she said slowly. "I hadn't remembered, but now that you remind me, I suppose you did, but that was all you told me. Yet you clearly not only love them but enjoy their company. You spend time with them. You're proud of them. And you never mentioned them again. You never introduced them. It was like you didn't want me know they existed, or was it that you didn't want them to know I existed?"

"Otohime." He didn't know what to say. Her words stung him as deeply as if she had flamed. "I didn't want to hurt you," he said at last.

"What do you mean?"

"Your own child"—

"The loss of my child hurts me, yes, and it will always hurt me. You are not naive and you are not a fool. You have to know that. But you also know Susu-chan brings me joy! Why wouldn't your children bring me joy, especially since they bring you joy?"

"There's more to it..."

"Like what?"

"Varvara left." At least that was out.

"Who is Varvara? You never mentioned Varvara, either!"

Otohime didn't notice his distress, but if she had she would not have cared. She had thought they were getting somewhere, developing a real relationship that might lead to—somewhere. Where she didn't know. But she had told him so much about her life and who she was, and he was concealing so much from her—was he toying with her? For what? Power? Power was a strong motivator; he had much, but someone who valued it could always use more.

"Varvara is Adrik and Zhenya's mother," he finally said in crisp tones. "She is also the mother of Valeria and Vassilli." He sighed heavily then and exhaled a narrow plume of smoke. "You know they are twins. You said your human friend Lady Anko had twin children. But she lived."

"Did Varvara die? You told me dragons did not die! I certainly never thought dragons died! Not from something as natural and normal as childbirth!"

Irtysh smiled sadly. "I do not think we die, unless we are killed. I'm not even sure what that means. I hope I did not kill Varvara." The spines on his neck rose and fell. "I loved her. I still love her—you must surely understand that! We share children and that is a bond that can't be broken, at least not for me. Even Agniya—we only became consorts because we were going to have a child, but we both did our best and I credit her for trying, no matter how angry she is at me now. I simply couldn't live up to whatever she wanted me to do or be. But she stepped in and did her best as a parent for Adrik and Zhenya and the twins, and I think she loves them and they will always love her. But Varvara..." his voice drifted off.

A flash of flame erupted from the Lake of Jewels, and Galina rolled over and dove.

"Hey," Susu squeaked and he flamed back at where she had vanished. "I can do that too!"

"Stop that, all of you," Irtysh roared. "No flaming indoors!"

He settled where he stood, wrapping his tail around his feet with great care, not whipping it elegantly like he usually did. He kept his focus on the Lake of Jewels, and did not look at Otohime.

"Varvara left," Irtysh said at last. "When she knew the eggs were coming, when she learned that there would be two of them, she said she was frightened. Even one egg is hard. Two is more than twice as hard, or so she told me. She would already, she said, be injured by the first one."

"Injured." Otohime did not follow.

"I understand it can be painful to lay an egg," Irtysh explained, remembering that Otohime had never done so.

"Like giving birth to a human child, I suppose." Otohime remembered that, but she also remembered what Anko had told her. "It is painful,

441

yes, even one child is painful, but it is natural. Normally the second of two comes fast, and there is no lasting injury. One heals in relatively short order. I did. Anko-*sama* has. The month mother and infant keep to their home and do as little as possible gives the mother a chance to heal as well as for the baby to settle in to being alive, you could say, and for the baby and the parents to become a family. I remember that as a good and happy time in my life."

"I do not know about human children," Irtysh pointed out. "Varvara recovered well after the first two. The time when the egg is nurtured before hatching may function much the same way. She was out and flying as usual long before Adrik and Zhenya were born. But the idea of having two at once weighed on her. Terrified her. Once the eggs started coming she called for me, and when the second was laid, and she knew I was there to take charge, she simply vanished. And she never returned."

"But where could she have gone?"

"No one knows where dragons who vanish like that go. Do they travel in space? Do they travel in time? Do they do both? Sometimes dragons vanish when they tire of life in the here and now. We think. But unless they say something, we do not know. My own father simply vanished one day in the same way."

"Rizantona never said."

"No. She is tough, my mother, and prefers to live in the present. He chose to leave; she took that as fact and dismissed him from her thoughts. If he returns, and we do not know if that is even possible, we can ask him where he has been and what he did there."

"So you were the only parent to nurture the twin eggs?"

"Yes." He shook himself. "I had naturally shared the care of the first two with Varvara, as dragons usually do. You may recall that Ryuujin and Rizantona both cared for Susu while he was in the egg."

"Rizantona was rather possessive, but, yes, she did let Father participate."

Irtysh grimaced. "She would be." He stretched his long neck. "But I enjoyed it, and so of course I was present when the twins were born, just as I had been there for the births of the older two, only Varvara was also there for them.

"My sister, Calliope, helped now and then, so I could get out, but the majority of the pre-birth parenting was mine. The two older ones were helpful, too. So excited and happy, eager to get to know their new siblings-to-be. Though they kept asking when their mother was coming back, and all I could say was that I did not know. I think Mother finally told them something because suddenly they stopped asking.

"Mother did help when she had time, but of course she is very busy and I was rather caught up, so some of my usual responsibilities fell on her. They are all my children and I do love them very much. I would be very pleased if you wanted to know them. But I hope you might now understand why I didn't tell you this before."

"I'm sorry, Irtysh," Otohime said softly.

"Come, then," he said, rising and shaking from one end to the other, extending and refolding his wings. "Shall we go swimming?"

43

The Sea of Japan couldn't have been more beautiful on this glorious autumn day. The sky was blue, there were a few high clouds, the wind blew from two points abaft the beam, and there was just enough of it to ruffle the water and keep the ship on course.

Kaito Minoru-*sencho* was content. He'd picked up the ship two days before and he and his young crew had sailed to a hidden cove he knew to anchor and wait out the time of their supposed passage. The entrance was dangerous without specialized local knowledge. Minoru, of course, knew all about that, and now Akira, Shota and Azuki did, too. Minoru was pleased that Azuki, now that she had time, had started sailing regularly again.

She remembered things she'd learned before, he had found, and, serious and studious, she listened and paid attention. Girls didn't ordinarily go to sea, but there was so little about any of their lives that was ordinary Minoru couldn't see how it would hurt to teach her everything he knew or have her along whenever she wanted to come.

There were some superstitions attached to women at sea among the foreign sailors, but in Minoru's view those were all bilgewater, anyway. He grinned and chewed the stem of his pipe. Just excuses for men who didn't want them along to leave their wives at home.

Akira and Shota were only two of Minoru's crew for this voyage. Azuki and the blonde dragon-girl, Renko, both dressed as boys and with their hair tied up in scarves, were two more. With Minoru, the five of them could handle this very simple "voyage." It was really a glorified day sail, though taking place over a couple of days, despite the larger size of what was in truth a cargo ship. That little dragon-boy, Susu, had shown up, too. He brought with him a girl with dark brown hair and perfect, pale, porcelain skin he called Karina, who looked about the age of the other girls. She was also dressed as a boy with her hair tucked up, though her clothes were as foreign as she was. When she was a human, that is. Minoru grinned.

Renko explained this Karina was a cousin of hers and her brother, Susu. The girl started at that, but Renko said, "It's easier that way," and Karina acquiesced in it. Minoru wondered what the relationships really were, but it was definitely easier not to worry about it.

He relit his pipe and watched the sea roll by. It had been a while since he'd had command of anything this big. It felt good.

Overhead, Azuki soared. She looped and corkscrewed and dove only to catch a thermal to rise upward again. She was having so much *fun!* It had been so long since she had not been bound to duty, even if it was duty she enjoyed, or to responsibilities, even if they were of her own making, that she thought she had nearly forgotten how to have real fun. It wasn't that she had no fun at all, but it felt like that, when she had only been able to snatch it in moments.

It was good of Captain Minoru to let them all come, especially Susu and that new girl, Karina. Is that how Susu had said it when he introduced them? She supposed it didn't matter. She was some kind of cousin of theirs, apparently. She was Western in form and looked kind of familiar. Her name was hard for Japanese speakers to pronounce, but as long as Karina knew what it sounded like when a Japanese speaker said it and was willing to answer to it, it was not a problem.

In fact, there were no problems at all today, Azuki decided. Oh, there were big problems, like the refugees, but they had a plan to resettle them. There was what Uncle called "inflation," and she wasn't sure how that worked, though she was supposed to. But not today!

Shota rode in Renko's crown like he almost always did when they flew in a group. He was simply too small to fly on his own when the next biggest bird, usually Tsuruko-san or his sister, was already far too large to fly evenly with him.

He'd go off and fly by himself or with the sparrow friends he found everywhere when he wanted to stretch his own wings. He was usually grateful for the small size that let him become almost invisible when he needed to be and let him get in and out of places inaccessible to everybody else. Especially Renko.

Tsuruko was making arrangements on the ground to move their anticipated shipment—when they got it—to where they wanted it. She and Kojiro were supposed to meet them at the docks. Kojiro's role was to work with Minoru to smooth the way at the port and organize the off-loading.

Everything in Susu's world was absolutely brilliant today, he thought. He could fly with his sister and with Karina and all his bird friends, too. He wasn't too young and he wasn't too small. Of course, when Shota was around, Susu was never the smallest. Bringing Karina was brilliant, too, he thought. She and Renko-san were becoming friends and that meant Azuki-san would become her friend, too. He thought Karina could use friends. He was certainly thankful for his!

He wanted to go back to Goshogawara where Kukanko-san lived. She was really big but it felt like they were nearly the same age. Maybe he could bring Kichiro—

"Look!" Azuki called. They all looked down. The ship settled in the water and rolled. Their cargo had arrived.

Minoru noticed it before anyone else as the weight of the ship increased. It sank lower in the water, pitched a little and rolled a touch although there was no change in the wind or sea. He thought he better go below and check to make sure the cargo was loaded properly.

He grinned and nodded when he saw it. Whoever had brought the cargo, no matter how they'd done it, had placed the machines for the spinning and weaving of cotton in exactly the right locations. He took a quick rough count to make sure the actual numbers would match his manifest, then turned and started humming a little sea chanty he'd learned from a sailor from the Ryukyus. Soon, he had heard, those were going to become finally and fully a part of Japan. He hoped there wouldn't be another—

Through the companionway hatch he saw something he should not see. Not today. Not on his ship.

Legs.

He reached for the axe he kept handy as a both a tool and a weapon and hopped to appear suddenly in the companionway.

"Captain!" A very tall foreigner with a drooping moustache lounged on one side of the cockpit, grinning. "We have brought your cargo."

"Is this convenient?" Another tall, though not quite as tall, foreigner, this one with a nearly black beard, sat on the other side, his long legs braced against the folded cockpit table.

Minoru was nearly certain who these two must be but he would not cede a single millimeter of control on what was, at the moment, his ship, to anyone else, no matter who.

"It's usual," he replied crisply, "that you announce yourselves and ask permission before you come on board a ship. Otherwise"—his grin was feral and he tilted his hand so that Moustache could see the axe—"you might be mistaken for pirates."

"We do beg your pardon," Beard said in exceedingly high-level diplomatic tones and suitably formal language, adjusting his posture to fit with a perfectly executed bow. "We are unaware of the protocols surrounding ships, and we sincerely apologize for that. We should have ascertained in advance. Please forgive us. We have brought your cargo."

"I didn't know you were coming with it." Both these men would tower over Minoru, but the sailor's command presence, learned and practiced, knocked them right down to size with blows from his steely gaze.

"I'm sorry for the intrusion," Moustache said, with somewhat less formality. "We truly did not know. I am Susu-chan's father. Renko-chan's, too. Call me Ryuujin," he suggested. "Neither of us have ever ridden on a human vessel and we thought we'd like to."

"Susu and Renko are my young siblings on their mother's side," Beard explained, matching Ryuujin's level of formality, but adding a sprinkle of humility. At least it appeared they were making progress and the axe was unlikely to be wielded in their direction. "I am called Irtysh. May we please stay? We will not board your ship without asking leave again."

Ryuujin looked at Irtysh with some admiration as the wiry Captain with the nasty-looking axe perceptibly thawed at the prince's lush tone as well as his words. Diplomacy had its uses, Ryuujin knew, and Irtysh was very good at it. Ryuujin supposed that helped a lot with Rizantona.

Minoru set the axe back in its brackets and came out on deck. He dodged Ryuujin's ridiculously long legs to reach the helm and quickly checked the wind, the sails, the sea and the loop holding the helm in position. They'd fallen off course a bit with all the added weight, so he corrected. He looked over at his guests, feeling just a touch weak in the knees since it looked like he had just faced down both the Dragon King and a powerful Dragon Prince.

"Never been on a boat before?" he asked. "Suppose you don't need to sail when you can fly."

"We both enjoy swimming," Ryuujin said. "But you are right. We haven't used vehicles in the water before."

"I think I like it," Irtysh said. "It's like using a carriage instead of walking on land." Irtysh leaned back as the small ship rolled. He moved lithely forward with its return. "Renko and Susu have told me about it. They enjoy it," he said. "I wanted to try it. This is done with purpose, not just for pleasure?"

This was the Prince Irtysh they all talked about, the one who actually made the machines, but he didn't know why people used boats? Minoru decided he would think about that later. Right now, he would explain.

"Sometimes people go out in boats for pleasure," he said, "but mostly we use them to travel across water, or carry cargo between ports when water is the fastest route. We also use them to go out and catch fish to eat. Today, we chartered this ship to carry the machines you brought to the refugee settlements. People are used to seeing cargo arrive at the port by ship and go from there by cart or wagon. We are doing this so people won't question where the machines came from."

"What's 'chartered'?" Ryuujin asked.

Minoru's mouth twisted around his pipe stem as he tried to figure out how to say it. "I don't own this ship," he said at last, setting the pipe in its rack, "but I gave the owner some gold and he's letting me use it, which makes me the captain. He doesn't need to know where my cargo comes from or where it's going. He only needs to know that he gets his gold and gets his ship back in good order."

"Why would people question where the machines came from?" Irtysh asked. He had asked Otohime, but had not found her explanation very clear. "Why do they care? I thought we could just take them where they'd be used."

Minoru raised his eyebrows. These two were a fascinating combination of skill, power, arrogance and ignorance. However was he going to explain customs, duties and taxes?

Azuki saw them first. She thought she was relaxing but found it hard to get over the habits of responsibility. Since she had noticed the cargo arrive, she'd kept an eye on the ship just in case anything went wrong.

"Who is that?" she whispered mentally. "Those—oh, no!"

"His Majesty," Shota said, just at the instant Renko said "Father," and Galina—only Karina when said with a Japanese accent—joyfully cried "*Batya!*"

Susu happily called out, "Papa!" and he began to dive.

"Human, Susu-chan, human," Akira called.

"You, too, Karina-san," Azuki echoed as they both started to follow, but then she pulled up short. "Maybe we better not," she said to Akira. "It's going to get crowded down there."

The eagle circled the toki. "I want to find out what's going on!" he said with a mental grin.

"Brother will tell us," Azuki assured him.

"I'll try to keep connected with you both, Sister. But you're right, I think you should—OOF! Watch it, Renko-san."

"Can you stay a sparrow?" Renko asked.

"I plan to."

"Galina?" Irtysh's beautiful baritone sounded harsh and loud even to Azuki and Akira as he spoke to his youngest daughter, sending circles through the water as though a boulder had dropped in it. "Is that you?"

"Yes, *Batya*," she said sweetly. "Do you like it?"

"Did you teach her this, Irtysh?" His Majesty's bass shook every timber on the ship. Clouds began to build on the horizon.

"Of course not," Irtysh snapped. "But who did?"

As one, they turned to the little boy perched on his father's knee.

"Me!" Susu was clearly proud of himself.

"How did you"—his father started just as his brother said, "Ryuujin, did you"—

"I watched you! I saw you both do it! Galina thought you'd like it, Brother, since you can do it and Otohime can do it and I can do it and Papa can do it! She can't do it like me," the child explained. "But she can do it like you. So I told her how you do it, and we practiced until it worked!"

Minoru wasn't sure whether to be terrified or amused at this interchange, so he held still and quietly managed the boat.

Prince Irtysh looked suddenly exhausted and dropped his head into his hands.

Susu looked appalled. "Papa? Wasn't I supposed to learn it? Weren't we supposed to do this? Am I bad?"

Tears ran down Galina's porcelain face. "*Batya!* I thought you'd like it if I could look human like you do! I wanted to surprise you! I think *Mamasha* guessed I wanted to try it, but we were careful to keep it secret until I could really do it so we could show you!"

"Mother will flame me from my nose to my tail," Irtysh said.

"No!" Susu cried. "Papa! Don't let Mama flame my brother! Mama's flames *hurt!*"

"If she's going to flame anybody, she's going to flame me," Ryuujin said. Thunder rumbled.

Irtysh sat up straight. He hadn't been this angry in centuries. This was a disaster in the making, a chaotic muddle he had no idea how to sort, but he better do it quickly, preferably before Rizantona found out.

Renko, with Shota hidden in the scarf covering her hair, scooted forward towards the mast, both to hide before anybody noticed her and so they could help Minoru if he needed extra hands. None of the others who were actually on board were going to be any help at all.

"I did not do this," Irtysh declaimed, his voice reverberating through the surrounding sea. "I did not want this. You and I, Ryuujin, have reasons to want to explore the human experience."

Ryuujin held his tongue, though thunder clapped overhead and chain lightning flashed. Irtysh was furious, and he was his mother's son.

"My children have absolutely no reason to need or want to assume a human form, ever." Irtysh glared at his daughter. "They need to do their proper jobs as dragons and let me decide if we will mix with humans and how. Susu is a child. You are not. Actions have consequences. You did not *think!*"

"*Batya!* Don't be mad!" Galina wailed.

"Papa! Is Mama going to flame you?" Then Susu realized that he, too, might be in the literal line of fire and he started to cry, too. "Will Mama flame me? Or Galina? But Brother flames, too. Brother, don't flame Galina! We're *sorry!*"

Galina's wails increased. "I...I thought...." She nearly choked. "*Batya*, I thought you'd like it!"

"No one's flaming anyone," Ryuujin said. "Stop that, both of you! Susu, go home at once. Take Galina with you. Irtysh and I will be there directly."

"Galina," Renko had never heard her brother sound so...princely when issuing a command. "Go with Susu. Wait for me there."

They vanished. The silence was deafening.

"I'll deal with it," Irtysh said after a moment. "She is my daughter."

"But he is my son," Ryuujin replied. "You and I need to talk."

"Yes." Irtysh turned to Minoru, who watched the handsome Western face melt from frozen fury to what was apparently its normal pleasant countenance.

"We must apologize again," Irtysh said in normal yet diplomatic tones, "for the actions of our errant children, and in my case for my own intemperance. We will take our leave and will not disturb your voyage again."

457

"I, too, apologize for my temper. I recognize that you enjoy sailing. I think," Ryuujin looked around, "that I would probably enjoy it, too, given time to learn it. But this is not the day for that. I would like to speed you on your way. Would it be a problem for you to make your harbor earlier rather than later?"

"Not a problem," Minoru said. He glanced up to see Azuki and Akira circling above. He flagged them to come in. Renko, and therefore presumably Shota, huddled by the mast. "If you can do it without being seen."

"We can," Irtysh said.

"All right then. Do you know where we're going?"

"Renko-chan," the Dragon King said, "do you know the harbor entrance?"

She nodded.

"Send us the image."

She nodded again.

"We have it," Irtysh said. "You will not notice the speed of passage, Captain, but you will be there forthwith."

"May I ask why?" Minoru asked mildly.

"I do not want Susu-chan's mother and Galina's grandmother to find you," the Dragon King said.

"I do not want my mother," Prince Irtysh said, with just a hint of humor, "to find me."

Azuki and Akira landed on the foredeck near Renko and changed immediately.

"I apologize for spoiling your voyage," Irtysh said with a bow, and suddenly, in a move Shota and Azuki both recalled from the time Renko had first speeded them home, surrounded by a whoosh of water, they were entering Hakata Bay.

Minoru barked terse orders at his youthful crew and guided the ship where the harbormaster's launch, which came alongside, directed. He went below to get the necessary documents as soon as they docked.

"Let Kojiro-san know we're in and where we're docked," he said to Akira. "We're a little early. We need him to put forward the off-loading." He jumped onto the dock, landing on his natural foot so easily that it was possible not to notice his wooden one, and started up to the appropriate office.

Minoru knew he looked the rough old sea-dog he was, and that was exactly how he meant to look, with his rolling sailor's gait hardly affected by his wooden leg. Inside he was laughing. They were large, they were fierce, they were royal. They had terrifying and wonderous powers. But in the end, dragon fathers were very much like human ones. He couldn't wait to tell Hanako-san!

Woman in Hat Digs Bamboo Shoots (1765),
Suzuki Harunobu

44

"I thought I'd give Yae-san a *gi*," Noriko said to Yuta. She caught him coming out of his study, where he had dressed in his Western suit. He looked very well, she thought: modern and sophisticated.

"You brought that from the *dojo*?"

"Yes, with a white beginner's belt. I think it will fit her properly. I hope she will wear it and think of me. She needs to remember that she has friends."

Yuta retreated back into the doorway so his wife could pass.

"You're not wearing a Western dress?" he asked.

Noriko looked over her shoulder in surprise. "I will if you want me to," she said. "It will only take me a minute to change. But I thought I would wear my good daytime *kimono*." She laughed. "I suppose it's just a matter of habit and practice, but I agree with Renko-san. I would rather not walk as much as we will have to in Western shoes."

"The women's shoes aren't the same as the men's, are they?" Yuta examined the bottoms of his own Western shoes. He carried them to take them to the *genkan* so he could put them on when they were ready to leave.

"They are not," Noriko said. "They have a higher heel that I find puts me off balance. I just need to practice in them, I suppose."

"You look nice in Western dresses," Yuta said. "But I always think you look nice, so wear what makes you comfortable."

She blushed and tucked her chin in her neck as she hustled to the kitchen to get wrappings for the *gi*.

"Wife?" he called, but she didn't answer so he guessed she hadn't heard. He wondered if she would prefer it if he wore Japanese clothing himself. But it was too late for that. Azuki burst through the workroom door with Renko and Shota on her heels. She carried a large hat, rather like a round but nearly flat basket—something like a classic *sandogasa*, or traveler's weather-resistant straw hat. More like that, he thought nostalgically, than the *takuhatsugasa* he had worn when he was a mendicant monk. Although there really was little difference between the two. It had, Yuta saw, a classic *amatadai* inside it, for the specific purpose of fastening the strings or ribbons that would tie the hat under the traveler's chin to the crown of the hat. But this one was subtly different.

"Look at what I made for Miyuki-san, Uncle!" Azuki cried. "It's like an old-fashioned noblewoman's outdoor hat! Otohime gave us the idea! Oh, Aunt, there you are! I wanted you to see this."

"Come in here, everyone, why don't you?" Noriko said, gathering the group into the spacious kitchen so Hanako-san could see what Azuki had done as well.

Hanako put the kettle on, of course, and also sliced a persimmon and prepared a plate of her cookies while Azuki lay the hat out on the kitchen table.

"Otohime told me that the veil used to go around the outside edge of the hat and might have ribbons on it to tie the panels of it together or tie them back from her face if they were bothering the wearer."

"This was so the woman couldn't be seen if there were people around, or to protect her from bugs," Renko explained. "She'd have ribbons attached to the *amatadai* to fasten it on her head. *Uchikatsugi*, Sister called it."

"Look," Azuki upended the hat. Hanako slid in with a tray of teacups to better examine the hat. She was good at all kinds of clothing construction and design and wanted to see what her clever Azuki-chan come up with now.

"See, Hanako-san," Azuki said, turning the hat so the woman could see the details of the interior. "This is the classic tie, like they all have. But in the front here, the two veil panels cross so that Miyuki-san can tie them to obscure her face."

Hanako fingered the material and held it up to the light. She nodded and smiled her crooked, scarred smiled. She approved. In fact, she wouldn't mind something like that herself.

"She'll be able to see, though," Renko said, "because the material's so light."

"Good thing, too," Shota inserted, unable to entirely relinquish all the attention, "since she'll be guiding blind women."

"She's going to be a *tebiki*," Azuki explained. "She had smallpox and doesn't like anybody seeing her."

"This looks like a good solution," Yuta said.

Hanako, she of the acid-scarred face and muted voice, had a brief pang as she wondered why nobody had thought of her when making accommodation for a woman who didn't want to show her face in public. But Minoru said he liked her looks because she looked like her, and the way she looked now was the way she had looked when all of her new household and community had met her. It wasn't easy, but she found herself able to wish this young Miyuki the confidence to believe that she was much more than her face.

"And Uncle, look at this!" Shota took Hanako's attention away from herself as he brandished a man's hat. "It's from Prince Irtysh. He says it's called a Homburg."

"Brother thought you'd like it, *Sensei*," Renko said. "He would have given it to you himself, but he said you were busy. It's supposedly the latest men's fashion and it's from someplace called Bad Homburg, in Hesse. That's in Germany, he says: it's an *onsen* resort."

"It's an informal style," Shota added. "For daytime wear. He thought this one would go with your suit. I think he's right."

Hanako nodded vigorously. She took the hat from Shota and brushed it lightly, while showing Noriko that the color of the hat went perfectly with the colors of *Sensei's* suit. Otohime's whatever-he-was, Prince Irtysh, certainly had fine fashion sense. Hanako was glad he was teaching it to Shota. Shota, however clever and inventive, tended to take things too far. Hanako knew how easily that could be applied to all these new clothes! A little restraint was definitely in order.

"Try it on, Husband," Noriko said. "I think it's a perfect match!"

Since Renko and Azuki were wearing Japanese clothes, and since her husband seemed to approve of her attire, Noriko felt no compulsion to change into a Western dress, even though the two of them planned to go to the Exhibition. Hanako helped Azuki wrap the hat, which made a large and cumbersome package.

Akira came to the back door, since he heard all their voices there.

"Where's Susu-chan?" he whispered silently to Renko as Shota explained *Sensei's* new hat.

"I don't know," Renko whispered silently back. "I haven't seen him since Father sent them away. Brother just popped in and out with the hat. He's still fuming, so I didn't want to ask him. I think he's hiding out. I don't think Mother's found him. Yet."

"You have a really scary family," Akira told her.

"They are, aren't they?"

"Are we ready to go?" *Sensei* asked, looking around.

Noriko had a brief last-minute conference with Hanako and hurried to join them outside the front door. Hanako, and Endo, who had been in the garden, courteously waved them off until they left the compound and Shota closed the gate behind them. They all linked arms with Renko in the middle, Shota as a sparrow tactfully concealed in the scarf hiding Renko's blonde hair, and in an instant, they found themselves outside Sachiko-san's house in Tokyo.

Sachiko welcomed them and thanked Noriko and her family profusely.

"I wish you all the best," she said at last to Miyuki and Yae. "Remember I am always a resource for you and others who have suffered as you have." She gripped their hands, too moved to say more. She turned to leave, and then turned towards them.

"Remember, you can always come back."

Then Sachiko left them alone in the front courtyard. Noriko wondered exactly how much she knew since this was both very rude and very tactful under the circumstances. She decided it didn't matter. This was Sachiko, the friend who had saved her life, someone she truly could trust with her family.

"Miyuki-san," she said. "Please take Renko-san's arm. Hang on to your new hat with your other hand. Azuki-san will hold onto the package and to you. Akira-san will take Renko-san's other arm and carry your bag." They quickly moved into position. "When you wake up," Noriko continued, "you will be far away from here, but you will be with your friends and they know what to do."

Quickly, she reached up and before Miyuki could even react, she used a *kunoichi* technique to render the girl unconscious.

"Farewell," she said to Miyuki, and nodded at Renko.

"Off you go," she said. "Let us know when you'll be back."

Yuta had taken Yae off to the side of the garden so she didn't see them leave.

"They've gone?" she said when they turned around. "But I didn't even get to say good-bye!"

"Leave it at that," Yuta said. "You may meet again."

"I hope in happy circumstances for both of you," Noriko told her. "Here, I have something for you." She presented the girl with her package. "Please open it."

"What is this?" Yae looked up, not recognizing the heavy cotton garments that both were and were not like a normal *samue*.

"This is a *gi*," Noriko said. "It's worn for martial arts practice and also often worn casually around the *dojo*."

"I thought I was going to be a servant!"

"Did you?" Noriko smiled. "There is much more to it than that." She didn't even see Yuta slip outside the gate.

"I have two *jinrikishaw* waiting for us," he said on his return. "Why don't the two of you take one and I will follow in the other?" The little vehicles held only one or two passengers.

Yae clutched the *gi*, still in its wrappings, as though it were as talisman, as Noriko assisted the girl into the *jinrikishaw* and handed up her small bag. Yuta gave the driver directions.

"You're going to be all right, Yae-san," Noriko told her. "Though this is not going to be easy," she warned. "You will be working hard and you will be learning all the time. There will be much effort and practice at things it will take you courage and determination to master."

"This is supposed to be an improvement?" Yae said.

Noriko laughed. "Yes. It is and it will be. You will earn the respect of my *Sifu*—that's Master in Chinese—through your efforts and you will also learn to respect yourself. I did. I have confidence in you. If I did it, so can you."

The little vehicle came to a stop outside the *dojo*.

"This is the place?" the driver said.

"It is," Noriko assured him. Noriko disembarked and helped Yae, with her package and her little bag, get down.

The second *jinrikishaw* pulled up behind and Yuta got out. He paid them both off and dismissed them. They'd find another when they were ready to go.

"Come," Noriko said. "You have a new life waiting for you."

The girl trembled as she started on the path, but then she took a breath, squared her shoulders and Noriko could feel her resolve firm. Noriko smiled. Yae would be all right.

The door slid open and Noriko was surprised to see Master Peng himself.

"Noriko *Lao Shi*," he smiled.

"That means *Sensei*," she hissed to Yae, and was rewarded with just a hint of a smile.

Noriko bowed. "*Sifu*, I have brought Yae-san. She is the one I have proposed as your new student."

"Welcome, Yae-san," he said with a tiny incline of his bearded chin. "I see Noriko *Lao Shi* has provided you with a *gi*. We will soon exchange that white belt for something else."

"As soon as you earn it," Noriko said.

Master Peng nodded to Noriko but he looked at Yae. "You will. Come in, child. You are home."

Noriko watched as Yae ascended the steps, realizing that she was not meant to follow.

45

"We're here, Miyuki-san," Azuki said softly. "Everything's all right," Renko said. "We're all safe. Do you want to put on your new hat?"

Miyuki opened her eyes. They were certainly someplace else. This was not a city. It wasn't even a village. There were plenty of trees. She spotted apple trees in neat rows about a hundred meters off. From that direction came two women, walking one behind the other, the one behind resting her hand on the shoulder of the one in front.

"The one in front," Akira whispered mentally to Azuki and Renko, "Is the *tebiki*. She can see. The woman behind her is the *Goze-sama*. She is the teacher and in charge of the whole house."

"Where are you?" Azuki asked. Akira and Shota had vanished the instant they landed, hurrying to the *Goze* house.

"Overhead," Akira said. "Shota-san and I are flying around. The *goze* don't mix with men, remember. I just told them the girl I mentioned had arrived with her friends, but they didn't know where to go. And then I left with my little brother."

"You have a lot of little brothers." Shota snickered. "They thought it was funny he has so many to take care of. He had Susu-chan with him before."

"We're going to look for Kukanko-san," Akira told them.

"Let us know when you want us back," Shota said.

The two women approached.

"You're the girls who want the *Goze* House?" the *tebiki* asked, and then, aside, "There are three of them, *Goze-sama*."

"Yes, ma'am," they said, together.

"Do you all want to stay?" the *Goze-sama* asked. "That boy said there would only be one. I can see shapes, but nothing else. Is it the one in the middle with the hat on who wants to stay?"

Miyuki stepped forward and bowed. "My name is Miyuki, *Goze-sama*. I am the one who would like to stay."

"What's wrong with your face?" the *tebiki* wanted to know. "Do you always keep it hidden?"

"Smallpox scars," Miyuki said. "Everywhere. All over. My friend found out you wear hats like this when you go on tour and she made me this one so I could go out without showing my face. In private, I manage without it."

"Where have you been living?" the *Goze-sama* asked.

"With a woman who helps find places for women and girls like me, girls who were sold for whatever reason, got away, and have no place else to go. But I can't stay there forever. There are too many of us."

"Our aunt helps this woman," Azuki interjected quietly. "Aunt was also sold as a child, but has been able to make a good life for herself despite that. She wants to help others do the same. She is now married to our uncle, who teaches school. Aunt told us about Miyuki-san's situation. Our friend from school, Akira-san, found out you might have an opening for a new *tebiki* here."

"What is that boy to you, girl?" the *tebiki* said.

"I don't even know him! I don't go to their school. They've told me about him but I don't know him. I wouldn't want him to see me!"

The *tebiki* nodded. Miyuki's sincerity was palpable. "What can you do?"

"She can read and write and knows numbers, so she can easily keep accounts as needed," Renko said pragmatically, putting the most valuable and least common skills first. Sachiko-san was right to make sure her charges learned them.

"Miyuki-san likes music but she's not a musician," Renko continued. "At Sachiko-san's—what did you do at Sachiko-san's?"

"I know how do all the usual housework and laundry and I can sew a little," Miyuki said. "I come from a fishing family near Lake Biwa, so I know how to cook and preserve freshwater fish. Not well—I was young when the smallpox came, but I do remember how. I remember the gardens and the orchards best. That's what I was doing at Sachiko-san's—working in the gardens and taking care of the fruit trees. We were just about to start drying the persimmons. You probably dry apples here, too."

"You don't mind being outside without your hat?" the *Goze-sama* said.

"Not as long as there aren't a lot of strange men around," Miyuki said honestly. "Men...men...especially in groups..." her voice broke.

Renko glanced at Azuki. Both of them wondered what had happened to Miyuki, but they could not ask. They were surprised she even hinted at it. Women who were assaulted were considered dishonored, even by themselves, even though what happened was no fault of their own. Sometimes women would run away from their homes and anyone who knew them, usually ending up in prostitution or dead of disease. Sometimes, especially if they were of high rank, they would kill themselves.

"This is why Aunt and Sachiko-san, as well as us here, thought that this would be a very good home for Miyuki-san." Azuki's voice was soft but strong. She hoped her hope that Miyuki would find favor with these women, that this might indeed be something that would work for her, would reach into these women's hearts and make them want to accept her despite the hint of possible dishonor.

"Once you come here," the *tebiki* said, looking directly at Miyuki, "you cannot just leave like you might a regular job. We have to train you beyond basic house and farm work in all the ways the *goze* need special help to live and work independently. You have to learn to support their work, because it is their work that supports us all."

"In some ways, it's like joining a monastery," the *Goze-sama* herself said. "To survive, we must be very respectable. You won't meet young men. You can't look for a husband or even think of marrying. You won't have a family. We of the *Goze* house will be your only family for the rest of your life. Do you understand that?"

"I do," Miyuki said firmly. "It sounds like a good place for someone like me," she continued. "A husband, a family—I would never have those anyway. But in a *Goze* house, I could have friends. I could have a home."

"You can come on trial," the *Goze-sama* said, making up her mind. "If in the spring you and we decide this is not the life for you, you may leave."

"You will be able to reach us, if you need to, at any time," Azuki said. "And if you need us, we hope you will." She had the foresight to put some small change, writing supplies, stamps and both Sachiko-san's address and her own in a small pocket she sewed into the hat. Renko, with her easy access to larger sums, had tucked more money into a compartment in Miyuki's bag, her own idea, and had also done the same for Yae.

"We know you must make your own way," Renko said, "but we really are your friends."

"Thank you," Miyuki said, smiling for the first time since they had arrived. "Thank you all, more than I can say. But I don't think I am going to want to leave."

Azuki squeezed her hand. Renko smiled and nodded. Miyuki picked up her satchel.

"Let me show you," the *tebiki* said, reaching for Miyuki's bag, "how to guide a *goze*."

***

In Tokyo, Noriko turned to join her husband. He was standing next to a horse carriage watching a very tall foreign man emerge from it. Yuta greeted this man with a deep and formal bow. Noriko hurried forward as they started speaking.

"Your Majesty," she said when she reached them, using her own deepest, most proper, bow.

"Good afternoon, Lady Noriko," Ryuujin said. He had learned from Irtysh that since he was dressed in a Western fashion, Western courtesy required that he properly acknowledge a lady despite his own far more exalted rank. He executed a small bow of which he thought Irtysh would approve.

"Have you come to visit the *dojo*?" Noriko asked. "I am sure they will be honored."

"No," the Dragon King said, looking from one to the other. "I have come to ask both of you to accompany me to the Exhibition. I have a carriage that can take us. If you would be so good as to join me?"

"Thank you, Your Majesty," Noriko said, glancing at her husband.

"We are honored," Yuta said with a bow.

"Do get in." The Dragon King nodded at the footman who opened the carriage door once more. "I'm not sure how we do this." He looked puzzled. Carriages were as new to him as ships. "Perhaps you first, *Sensei*, in the far corner, then me. We are wearing Western trousers and can perhaps mount easier. Then Lady Noriko can have the assistance of the footman if she wishes, and also my own."

Since neither Yuta nor Noriko had any idea of the procedure for riding in such a carriage with royalty, or, indeed, at all, they were more than happy to follow the Dragon King's directives.

"Did anyone tell you what happened?" Ryuujin said once they were settled and the carriage was under way.

"No," Noriko said warily. "They have all said very little."

"Only that the machines were safely delivered and Minoru-*sencho* was able to return the ship as planned," Yuta added. "Even Shota-san's been quiet about the rest."

"I'm glad that part all worked out. Something...happened. After Irtysh and I delivered the cargo to the ship, we decided to stay so we could experience sailing. Then—it was a catastrophe. I don't know what else to call it. Susu-chan figured out how Irtysh and I assume these human forms and he and Irtysh's youngest daughter, Princess Galina, worked at it until she learned how to do it, too. She asked for his help because she wanted to surprise her father."

Yuta and Noriko looked at each other across the carriage, wide-eyed.

"You might well look like that," Ryuujin said. "It was a total shock to both of us. Apparently, Lady Agniya, Princess Galina's mother, had already complained to Rizantona that Irtysh was going to teach his children how to become human at will!"

Now Yuta was completely horrified. This was exactly the kind of thing he had feared—

"Irtysh hadn't, of course," Ryuujin said with a dismissive flick of his hand. "And he wouldn't. It was all something Susu-chan and Princess Galina cooked up between themselves! Susu-chan didn't think about anything other than figuring it out, and Princess Galina actually thought her father would like it!

"In fact, I have never seen Irtysh so angry! Mostly at himself, I think, for not anticipating it. Once his children knew he could do it, naturally at least one of them would want to try it. I should have seen it coming, too. Susu-chan is capable of anything and the concepts of discretion or asking permission are far beyond him."

"I don't see how either of you could have guessed!" Noriko said. Yuta shook his head and winced, thinking silence the most prudent course.

"I wish Rizantona agreed with you. We sent both the children to my palace. Irtysh and I rushed the ship to the harbor so Rizantona wouldn't show up looking for it. Susu-chan had been crying at the thought of her flaming Irtysh, flaming me, flaming him, or Irtysh flaming his daughter or Susu-chan himself. Rizantona would naturally hear her child crying and come find him. We wanted the rest of them out of her way."

The Dragon King smiled, showing teeth. "Irtysh wanted to get out of her way, too, and I can't blame him. So did I. When we got home, we told the children in no uncertain terms that they were never to do anything like this again without specific permission in advance, nor were they to tell anybody else what they'd done. For anyone non-dual-natured to adopt a human form without specific advance permission of the Queen or King is absolutely forbidden! Even Irtysh had obtained permission from me!" Ryuujin shrugged. "More or less. He asked me how I did it and I showed him. But that was Irtysh, not some reckless youngster, and I did not elaborate further. That's about where we were when Rizantona showed up."

Yuta drew in a sharp breath as the carriage clattered around a corner and bounced onto a cobblestone street. They had passed the north side of what had been Edo Castle and was now the Imperial Palace, but none of them had noticed the moat, the wall or the glimpses of garden.

"She was flaming, of course. She went right after Irtysh and he gave as good as he got. They were both spewing fire and flapping those enormous wings, knocking things over, dodging each other's flames and wielding those magnificent voices like whips of molten sugar. The children were crying and wailing and trying to hide in my tail. I wish I could have joined them, but it was all I could do to keep up with repairing the damage

Rizantona and Irtysh were doing. I don't think either of them remembered they were under water!"

"But Your Majesty, your palace"—

"The least of my worries, Lady Noriko. I kept up with the damage and Irtysh—he does have nice manners—offered to make all the repairs and clean it up himself as soon as he could, but it wasn't necessary. That was after Rizantona banished both Susu-chan and Princess Galina off to Lady Agniya's Diamond Fortress. She went immediately after them and told Irtysh she'd deal with him later. I understand Susu-chan and Princess Galina are both grounded and under house arrest awaiting Her Majesty's pleasure."

"Both of them?" Yuta wanted to know.

"Rizantona is Susu-chan's mother so she has as much authority with him as I do. She is also Princess Galina's grandmother, and Lady Agniya is Princess Galina's mother. Irtysh won't interfere. I know I won't. I haven't any idea where Irtysh has gotten off to."

"Europe," Yuta said, extending his new hat. "He sent me this. It's from an *onsen* resort in Hesse, which is in Germany, I gather. It's called a Homburg and I am told it is the latest thing."

"That's like Irtysh. He'll stay safely out of the way amusing himself with fashion and culture until his temper cools, as well as his mother's, and they can start to talk sense rather than flaming everything in sight."

"And you, Your Majesty, would like to attend the First International Industrial Exhibition with us?" Noriko couldn't help but sound amused.

"I would, Lady Noriko. The future comes at us unpredictably sometimes. We are in for some surprises, I think."

"We can only do our best to prepare ourselves as much as we can," Yuta said.

Ryuujin responded with a nod. "And then go forward to meet it."

The carriage stopped at the entrance to the Exhibition grounds.

"Shall we?" the Dragon King said.

THE END

Author's Note

Nitaro Akimoto (known professionally as Nitabo) is considered the founder of Tsugaru *shamisen* music. A real person, he is credited with the invention of the "beat play" method (known as *tataki soho*) and eight-character narrative music (*hachiningei*), forming the prototype of present-day Tsugaru *shamisen* music. It is played on a slightly different instrument with a larger neck than was standard at that time. The style is dated to 1877, when **The Oni's Shamisen** takes place.

Tsugaru *shamisen* music is wild, free, happy, fun, filled with joy and has been popular from its inception to this day. There are festivals, contests and regular concerts in the Tsugaru district of Aomori prefecture, and venues in Tokyo (and elsewhere) that specialize in the style. Modern musicians often take off into other musical genres, specifically jazz. Ki&Ki and the Yoshida Brothers are among well-known modern musicians. Go listen! It's wonderful!

Nitabo and his followers get all the credit for this music. I hope his spirit enjoys the way I have used him as a fictitious character in this work. As far as I have been able to determine, historically there were no *Oni* involved.

As always, this book is dedicated to everyone who has had a hand in its creation, and especially, always, Adair Van Sant New (1948-2021), whose contributions to my work and to my life cannot be overstated. It is also dedicated to all the readers who enjoy the Toki-girl and the Sparrow-boy's continuing flights of fact and fancy through Meiji-era Japan.

Claire Youmans
Tokyo, Japan
April 28, 2022

Table of Illustrations

The art in this book was found in collections located around the world. Notable collections include the Museum of Modern Art, New York; the US Library of Congress, Washington D.C.; the Victoria and Albert Museum, London; Wikimedia Commons and the National Diet Library, Tokyo. All images used are public domain as far as it is possible to ascertain and the versions used are properly used and credited. The reader's attention is directed to the specific collections cited where many more wonderful works of art from this period may be found.

485

Man Playing Shamisen, Unknown

CPSIA information can be obtained
at www.ICGtesting.com
Printed in the USA
BVHW031843290422
635756BV00013B/305

9 781733 902076